Teacher Resource System

Multisyllabic Decoding

Using Six Basic Syllable Spelling Patterns & Introduction to Word Study

Benchmark Education Company

145 Huguenot Street • New Rochelle, NY 10801

Printed in Guangzhou, China. 4401/0516/CA21600916

ISBN: 978-1-4509-3302-5
For ordering information, call **Toll-Free 1-877-236-2465** or visit our Web site at **www.benchmarkeducation.com.**

Table of Contents

Introduction

Introduction

SpiralUp™ Phonics is a complete kit designed for use in the phonics block within Benchmark Literacy balanced core reading program. It presents a research-based, explicit, and systematic approach to teaching the phonics skills students need when learning to read.

Welcome to PHONETIC CONNECTIONS *SpiralUp Phonics*!

Thank you for selecting *SpiralUp Phonics* from Benchmark Education Company. *SpiralUp Phonics* extends the instruction begun in *StartUp Phonics* and continued in *BuildUp Phonics.* The kit provides all the lesson resources and tools needed to provide small group instruction, guided practice, and independent practice opportunities in an intervention setting. Teachers and students alike will find the lessons and materials engaging, hands-on, and motivating.

Why teach explicit phonics?

A good reader is like a builder who is able to reach into a box of familiar tools and pull out the right one at the right moment. Like tools, each reading skill or strategy has an important use in the complex cognitive process of decoding and comprehending text.

A student who is learning to read meets a large number of unfamiliar words in his environment. His brain keeps busy trying to categorize, integrate, compare, and analyze graphophonic information. Without the keys to this decoding process, the student cannot move quickly to reading for meaning.

What are the goals of *SpiralUp Phonics*?

In order to shape the development of phonemic knowledge, *SpiralUp Phonics* creates opportunities to provide students at different stages of literacy growth with varied experiences that promote automatic and flexible control of letters and words. The systematic lessons will:

- **Build a foundation for successful phonics instruction**
  SpiralUp Phonics provides carefully monitored daily review opportunities for previously taught phonics elements to ensure student mastery before new skills are introduced.

- **Explicitly teach new phonetic elements**
  SpiralUp Phonics teaches syllable spelling patterns, advanced phonetic elements using multisyllabic word-solving strategies, and word study elements to strengthen vocabulary development. Each of the 32 units follows an explicit, structured routine in phonics and spelling instruction. Each week, students:

  1. Learn a new phonetic or word study element through teacher modeling and guided practice
  2. Apply it utilizing blending, word sorts, spelling activities, and decodable passages
  3. Monitor their mastery through a spelling assessment, Quick-Check, and Reading Rate Assessment.

- **Support and motivate all learners**
  Some students grasp phonics skills quickly and easily. Others need more time to practice each new skill. Every *SpiralUp Phonics* unit helps teachers tailor instruction to their students' needs with hands-on activities, partner and independent extension opportunities, support tips for English-Language Learners, and take-home activities for additional practice.

- **Help all students achieve their full potential**
  SpiralUp Phonics are designed to be used flexibly according to each student's individual need. Each Skill Bag contains all of the resources needed to explicitly teach each skill. After identifying student needs, the teacher can easily select the skill bag or bags that will target an identified area of need.

What are the features and benefits of *SpiralUp Phonics*?

Like *StartUp Phonics* and *BuildUp Phonics*, the *SpiralUp Phonics* program reflects the most current research on how to teach phonics effectively, summarized in the bibliography on page xlv. *StartUp Phonics* focuses on phonological awareness and consonant and short vowel sound/symbol relationships. *BuildUp Phonics* extends instruction to long vowels, blends, digraphs, and basic irregular sound/symbol relationships with predominantly one-syllable words. *SpiralUp Phonics* helps students build the necessary foundation for reading longer and more complex text. Following is a list of the program's benefits to students:

Features	Benefits to Students
Direct, explicit instruction in basic syllable patterns	Students learn advanced multisyllabic word-solving strategies.
Direct, explicit blending instruction	Students learn to blend using larger units of information.
Direct, explicit word study instruction	Students learn to utilize structural analysis components such as prefixes, suffixes, and root words.
Direct, explicit spelling instruction	Students master irregular words to facilitate reading connected text.
Direct, explicit sight word instruction	Students develop their vocabularies utilizing synonyms, antonyms, homophones, and multiple meanings.
Word sorts	Students learn to sort and make generalizations about words according to their phonetic elements.
Decodable text passages	Students build decoding fluency and automaticity and increase reading rate.
Hands-on, multisensory tools	All types of learners are supported by instruction that is concrete, motivating, and multimodal.

The program also offers many benefits to the implementation site, such as:

Features	Benefits to Site
Systematic and research-based	Teachers implement best practices as they sequentially introduce skills designed for advanced phonics and word-study development.
Organized, consistently formatted units and materials	Teachers at all experience levels can confidently manage the classroom and teach advanced phonics and word study with a minimum of advance preparation.
Whole-group, small-group, partner, and independent activities for every skill	Teachers have reteaching strategies and extension opportunities at their fingertips.
English-Language Learner support	Teachers can offer additional assistance in each skill to students who are learning English as a second language.
Spiraled curriculum	Teachers continuously review prior units and build instruction on previously taught skills.
Overview & Assessment Handbook	Teachers get ongoing support, answers to important questions, and assessments to inform instruction.
Family participation	Parents can support their children's phonics acquisition utilizing the Home Connection activities.

Components at a Glance

Lesson Resources

- 5 Review Lesson Teacher's Guides
- 32 New-Skill Unit Teacher's Guides
- 1 Digital Blackline Master

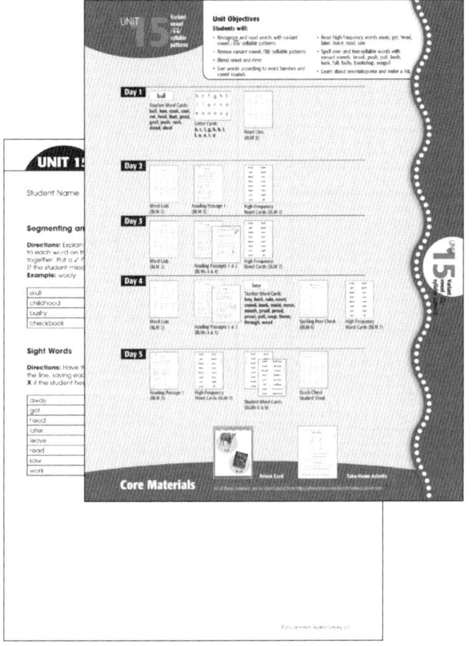

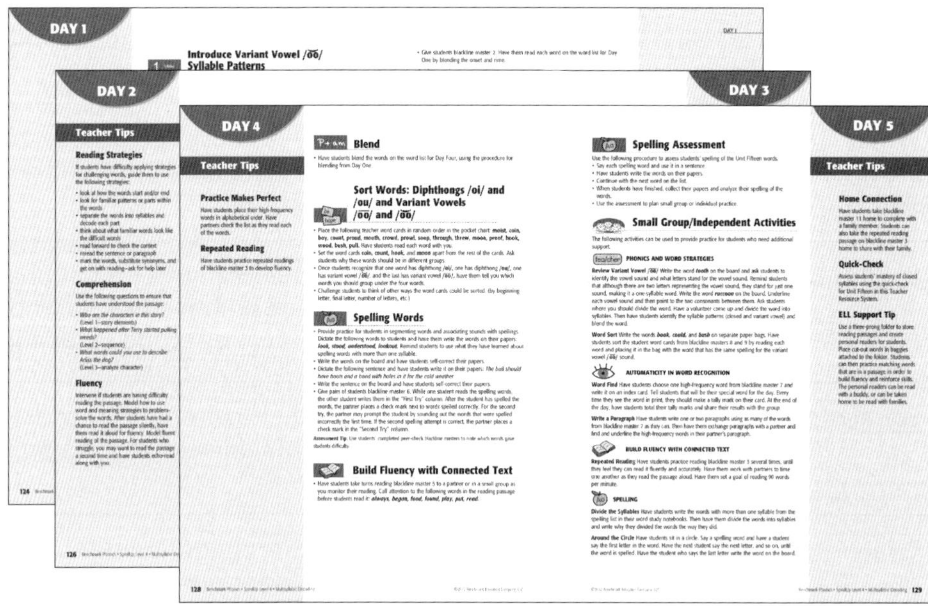

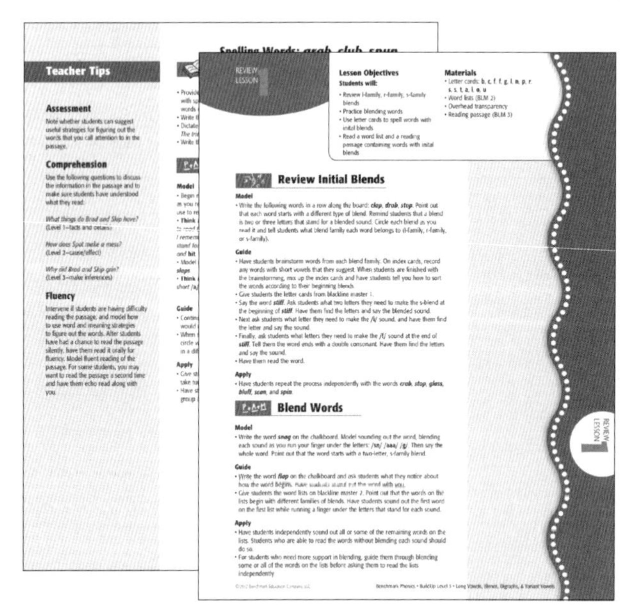

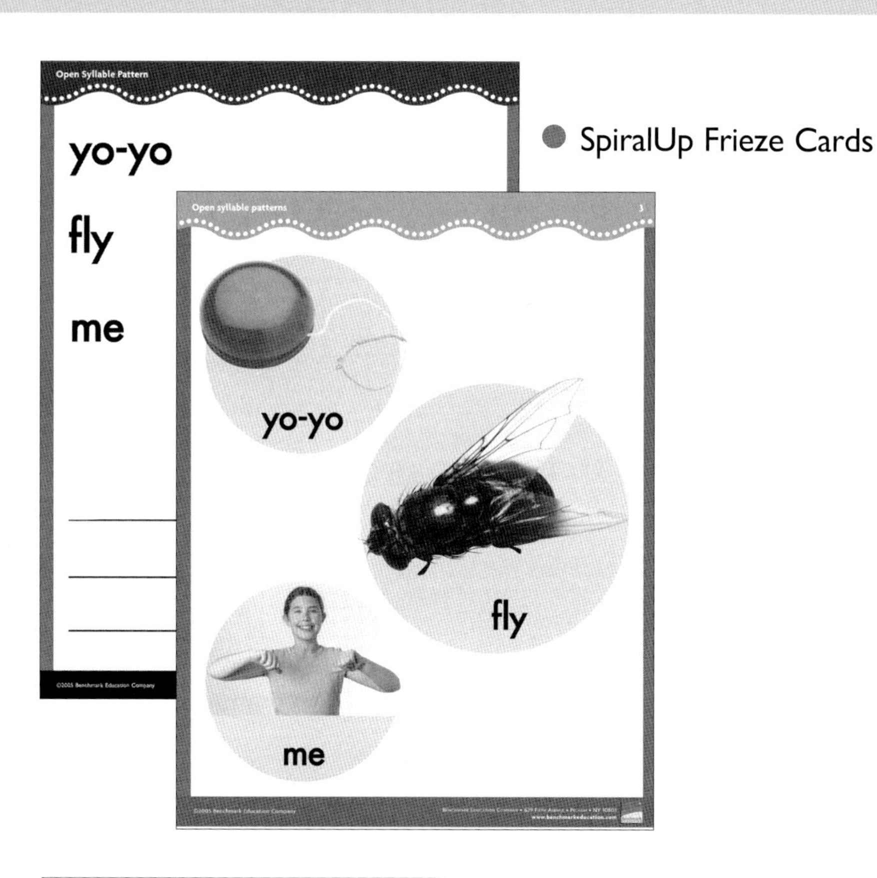

- SpiralUp Frieze Cards

A Day for Play

Tess and Ben play together at day camp. Tess unzips her backpack and unpacks it. She takes out a magnet, some string, and a lunchbox. She did not forget her sunblock. Ben has a lunchbox and three plastic insects in his backpack.

First, they play tennis. They stretch before they play. Tess likes to dash to the net and use her backhand.

After tennis, they play tag. They zigzag around the rocks and then sprint uphill to the swings. They have a contest to see how high they can swing.

Soon, it's time for a picnic lunch. Ben finds a sandwich, pretzels, and other good things to eat in his lunchbox. Tess eats a plum. She catches the drips on her chin with a napkin.

After lunch and a rest, they play hopscotch until it's time to go.

- 37 Decodable Reading Passages (available digitally to be printed as transparencies)

- Letter Card Sheets

shaky	label
shady	hazy
robot	crazy
total	bacon
program	raven
siren	focus
silent	open
iris	lilac

- SpiralUp Teacher Word Cards

Getting Started

Use the following checklist to help you get ready to use *SpiralUp™ Phonics*.

- ☐ **Unpack your program components.** Use the *SpiralUp Phonics* Components at a Glance on pages viii–ix to make sure you have everything.
- ☐ **Organize your classroom.**
- ☐ **Familiarize yourself with how to use the program.** Read Using the Components on pages xii –xxi and review the *SpiralUp* skills on pages xxiv–xxvii. Visit http://phonicsresources.benchmarkeducation.com to familiarize yourself with the digital tools available.
- ☐ **Study the teacher's guides.** Examine the decodable passages, support tools, and assessments.
- ☐ **Prepare for assessment.**
  - Download and print one copy of each student assessment page (laminate, if desired).
  - Make one copy per student of the teacher record forms.
- ☐ **Prepare for instruction.**
  - Make copies of the parent letter (on pages xlii–xliii) if you wish to establish a home connection at the beginning of the year.
  - Make student copies of lesson activities for upcoming lessons (using the downloadable blackline masters on the resource site).
  - Download the decodable passages, and create transparency versions as needed.
- ☐ **Administer the pre-assessment** and analyze the results to determine your students' starting point in the *SpiralUp Phonics* skill sequence and how to group students for small-group instruction.

Setting Up Your Classroom

SpiralUp Phonics includes whole-group and small-group instruction, as well as partner and independent activities. Use the model below to prepare your classroom.

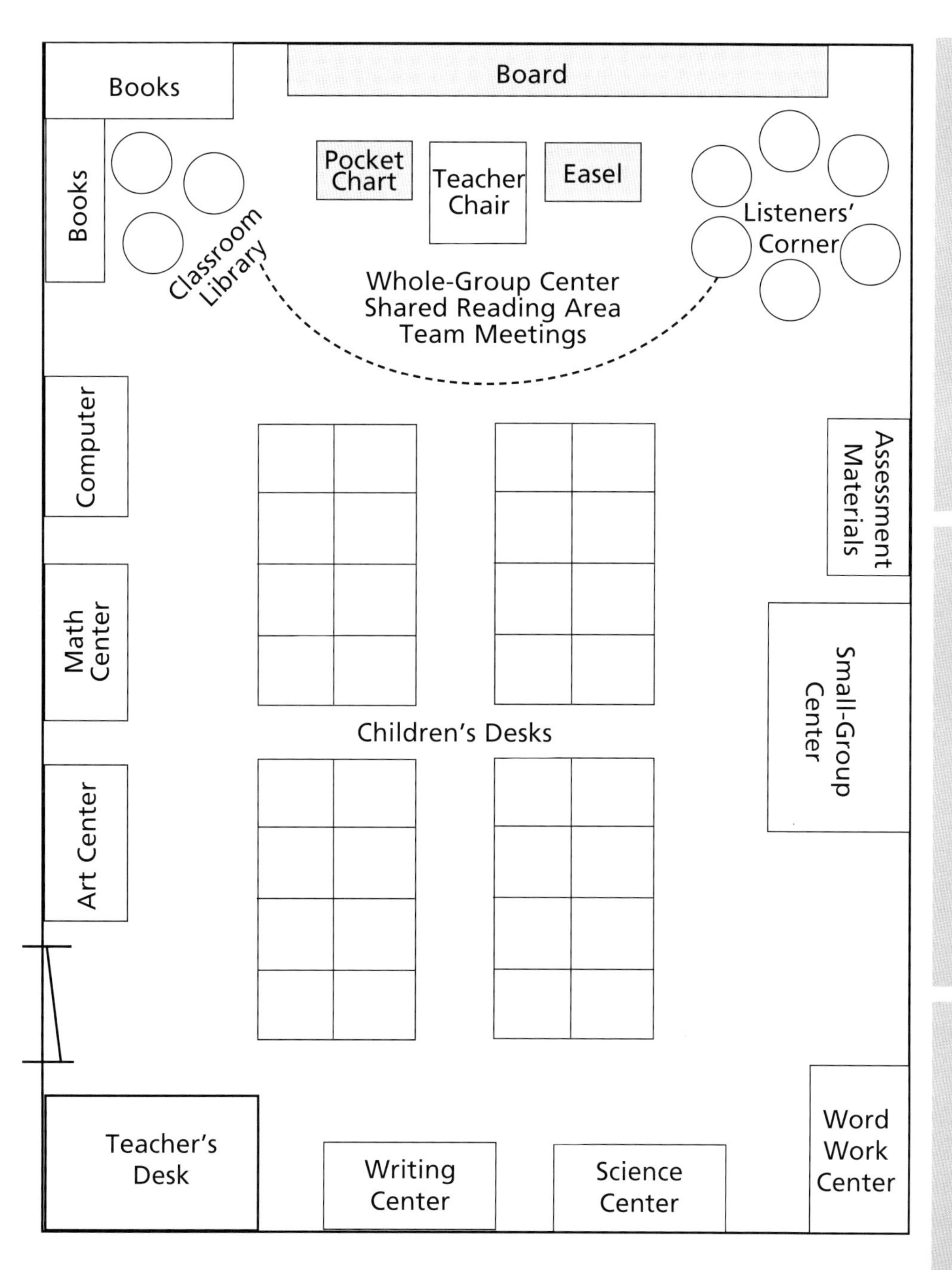

Whole-Group Instruction

Classroom Resources

- Overhead projector
- Pocket chart
- Chalkboard or chart paper

SpiralUp Phonics Resources

- Current lesson materials and needed support tools

Small-Group Instruction

Classroom Resources

- Pocket chart
- Chart paper

SpiralUp Phonics Resources

- Current lesson materials and needed support tools
- Decodable passage transparencies

Partner and Independent Activities

Classroom Resources

- Pencils

SpiralUp Phonics Resources

- Current lesson materials and needed support tools

Teacher's Guides for Review Lessons

Five review lessons begin the instructional sequence in *SpiralUp Phonics*. These explicit lessons are intended for students who need beginning-of-the-year instruction or review in blends and digraphs before they move to more advanced phonics instruction.

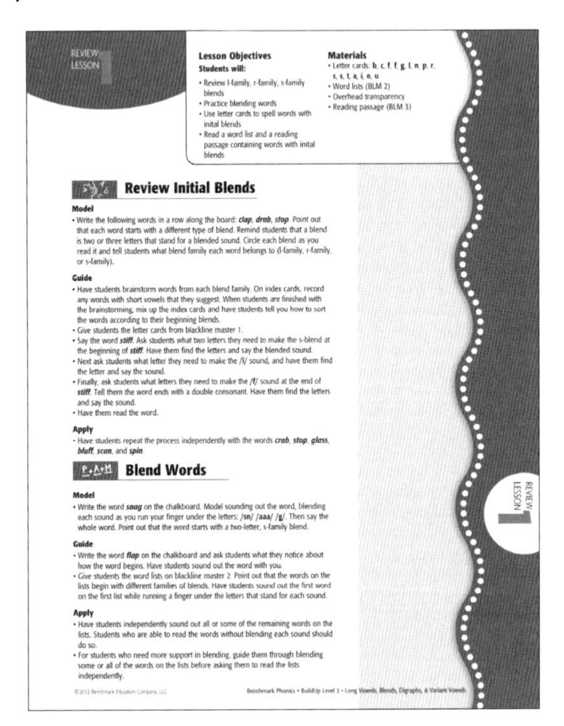

REVIEW LESSON 1

Lesson Objectives
Students will:
- Review l-family, r-family, s-family blends
- Practice blending words
- Use letter cards to spell words with inital blends
- Read a word list and a reading passage containing words with inital blends

Materials
- Letter cards: **b, c, f, f, g, l, n, p, r, s, s, t, a, i, o, u**
- Word lists (BLM 2)
- Overhead transparency
- Reading passage (BLM 3)

Review Initial Blends

Model
- Write the following words in a row along the board: ***clap***, ***drab***, ***stop***. Point out that each word starts with a different type of blend. Remind students that a blend is two or three letters that stand for a blended sound. Circle each blend as you read it and tell students what blend family each word belongs to (l-family, r-family, or s-family).

Guide
- Have students brainstorm words from each blend family. On index cards, record any words with short vowels that they suggest. When students are finished with the brainstorming, mix up the index cards and have students tell you how to sort the words according to their beginning blends.
- Give students the letter cards from blackline master 1.
- Say the word ***stiff***. Ask students what two letters they need to make the s-blend at the beginning of ***stiff***. Have them find the letters and say the blended sound.
- Next ask students what letter they need to make the /i/ sound, and have them find the letter and say the sound.
- Finally, ask students what letters they need to make the /f/ sound at the end of ***stiff***. Tell them the word ends with a double consonant. Have them find the letters and say the sound.
- Have them read the word.

Apply
- Have students repeat the process independently with the words ***crab***, ***stop***, ***glass***, ***bluff***, ***scan***, and ***spin***.

Blend Words

Model
- Write the word ***snag*** on the chalkboard. Model sounding out the word, blending each sound as you run your finger under the letters: **/sn/ /aaa/ /g/**. Then say the whole word. Point out that the word starts with a two-letter, s-family blend.

Guide
- Write the word ***flap*** on the chalkboard and ask students what they notice about how the word begins. Have students sound out the word with you.
- Give students the word lists on blackline master 2. Point out that the words on the lists begin with different families of blends. Have students sound out the first word on the first list while running a finger under the letters that stand for each sound.

Apply
- Have students independently sound out all or some of the remaining words on the lists. Students who are able to read the words without blending each sound should do so.
- For students who need more support in blending, guide them through blending some or all of the words on the lists before asking them to read the lists independently.

© 2012 Benchmark Education Company, LLC   Benchmark Phonics • BuildUp Level 3 • Long Vowels, Blends, Digraphs, & Variant Vowels

REVIEW LESSON 1

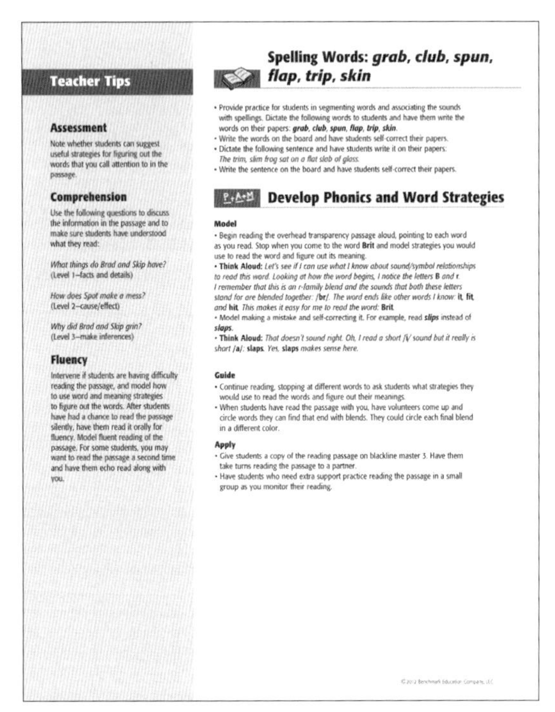

Teacher Tips

Assessment
Note whether students can suggest useful strategies for figuring out the words that you call attention to in the passage.

Comprehension
Use the following questions to discuss the information in the passage and to make sure students have understood what they read:

What things do Brad and Skip have?
(Level 1–facts and details)

How does Spot make a mess?
(Level 2–cause/effect)

Why did Brad and Skip grin?
(Level 3–make inferences)

Fluency
Intervene if students are having difficulty reading the passage, and model how to use word and meaning strategies to figure out the words. After students have had a chance to read the passage silently, have them read it orally for fluency. Model fluent reading of the passage. For some students, you may want to read the passage a second time and have them echo read along with you.

Spelling Words: *grab, club, spun, flap, trip, skin*
- Provide practice for students in segmenting words and associating the sounds with spellings. Dictate the following words to students and have them write the words on their papers: ***grab***, ***club***, ***spun***, ***flap***, ***trip***, ***skin***.
- Write the words on the board and have students self-correct their papers.
- Dictate the following sentence and have students write it on their papers: *The trim, slim frog sat on a flat slab of glass.*
- Write the sentence on the board and have students self-correct their papers.

Develop Phonics and Word Strategies

Model
- Begin reading the overhead transparency passage aloud, pointing to each word as you read. Stop when you come to the word **Brit** and model strategies you would use to read the word and figure out its meaning.
- **Think Aloud:** *Let's see if I can use what I know about sound/symbol relationships to read this word. Looking at how the word begins, I notice the letters* **B** *and* **r**. *I remember that this is an r-family blend and the sounds that both these letters stand for are blended together:* **/br/**. *The word ends like other words I know:* **it**, **fit**, *and* **hit**. *This makes it easy for me to read the word:* **Brit**.
- Model making a mistake and self-correcting it. For example, read ***slips*** instead of ***slaps***.
- **Think Aloud:** *That doesn't sound right. Oh, I read a short /i/ sound but it really is short* **/a/**: **slaps**. *Yes,* **slaps** *makes sense here.*

Guide
- Continue reading, stopping at different words to ask students what strategies they would use to read the words and figure out their meanings.
- When students have read the passage with you, have volunteers come up and circle words they can find that end with blends. They could circle each final blend in a different color.

Apply
- Give students a copy of the reading passage on blackline master 3. Have them take turns reading the passage to a partner.
- Have students who need extra support practice reading the passage in a small group as you monitor their reading.

© 2012 Benchmark Education Company, LLC

Review blends and digraphs through explicit whole-group activities using blending, word sorts, and reading decodable passages.

Assessment Tip:
While working with students in a small-group setting, assign partner or independent activities for the rest of the class.

To provide students with a quick beginning-of-the-year review of previously taught skills, complete each lesson in one day. To provide more intensive instruction and practice, spread the lessons over more than one day by slowing the pace, repeating some of the activities, and incorporating the small-group, partner, and independent activities.

Teacher's Guides for New-Skill Phonics Units

The 32 new-skill units in *SpiralUp Phonics* teach syllable patterns, structural analysis, and vocabulary in a systematic sequence that supports current research on best practices. All teacher's guides follow a consistent sequence that provides five days of instruction targeting one phonetic element.

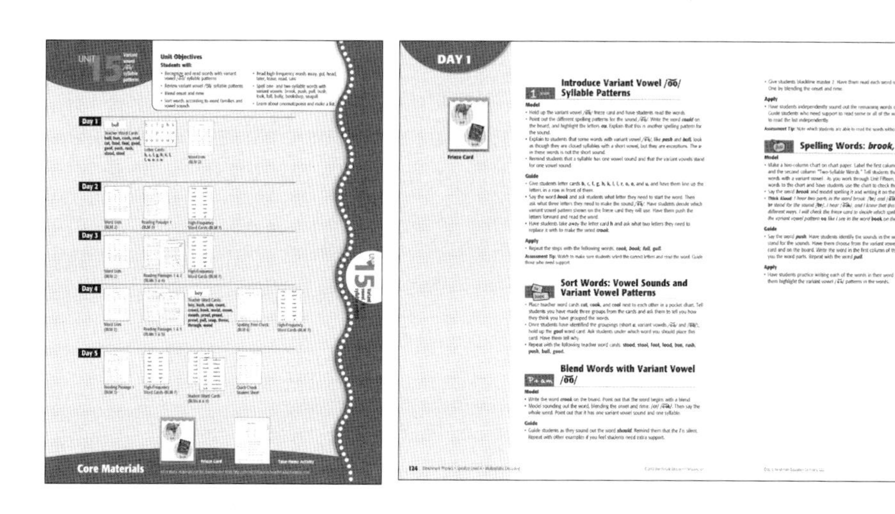

Units include objectives, a materials list, explicit instructions for five days of instruction, think-alouds, and teacher and assessment tips.

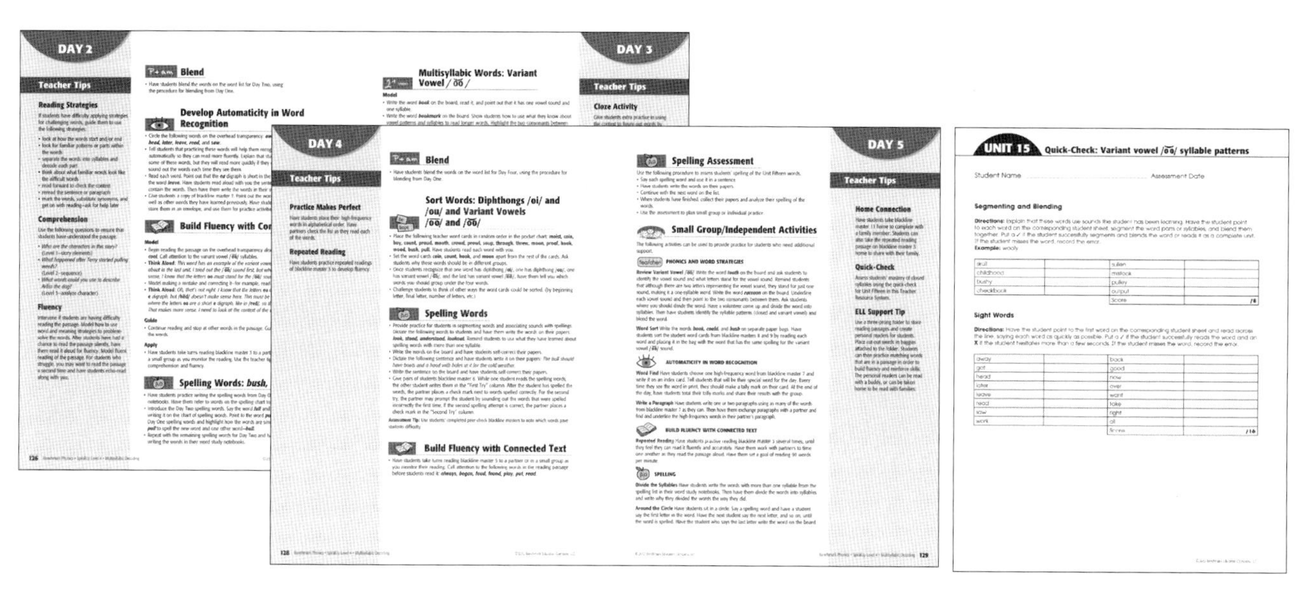

Teachers follow the research-based Model—Guide—Apply instructional pattern as students review, sort, blend, spell, read, write, develop automaticity in word recognition, and learn a variety of word-study strategies.

Support Tools

High-quality, durable, and motivating manipulatives are provided to support the instruction throughout *SpiralUp Phonics*.

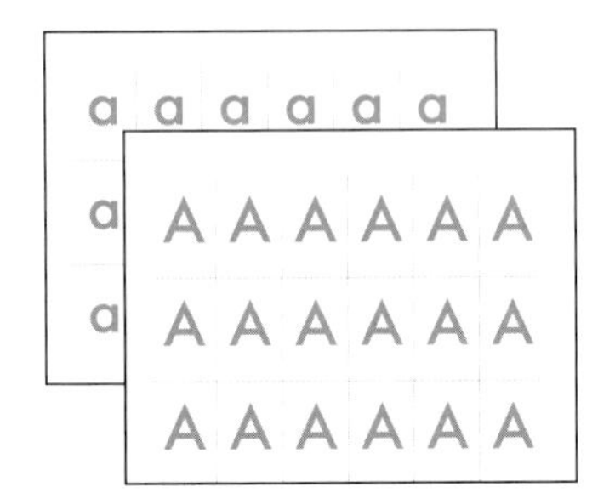

Phonetic Letter Card Set

Multiple copies of each letter of the alphabet are provided on cardstock for use in pocket chart, small-group, partner, and independent activities. Blackline master versions of these cards are also included in the new-skill unit reproducible blackline master booklets.

Frieze Cards

One laminated frieze card is provided for each new-skill unit. Use the words and photos on the front to introduce the target phonics skill.

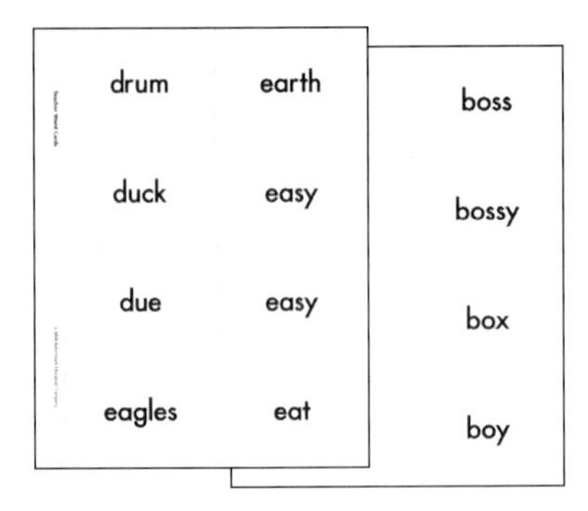

Teacher Word Cards

All word cards used in the new-skill units are provided alphabetically indexed. Because you will use these cards in different lessons, it is recommended that you continue to store them alphabetically for easy retrieval.

My Pet Hens

I have three pet hens.
At first, they were small chicks
with a lot of fluff. They could run
as soon as they came out of their
shells. Now, they are big and plump,
and they strut and flap their wings.
Each day, I go into their pen and find eggs
in their nest. Some days, I let them out to peck
on a patch of grass. I like to watch them.
They scratch in the dust to find bugs to eat.
Sometimes, they kick up the dust to take a bath.
When I send them back to their pen,
I check their food and water.
I like my pet hens.

Transparencies

A decodable reading passage is available for each review lesson and new-skill unit. Download them to create transparencies or to project them on a whiteboard.

Reproducible Tools, Activities, and Home Connections Resources

Every review lesson and new-skill unit has corresponding reproducibles needed for instruction which can be downloaded and printed at http://phonicsresources.benchmarkeducation.com.

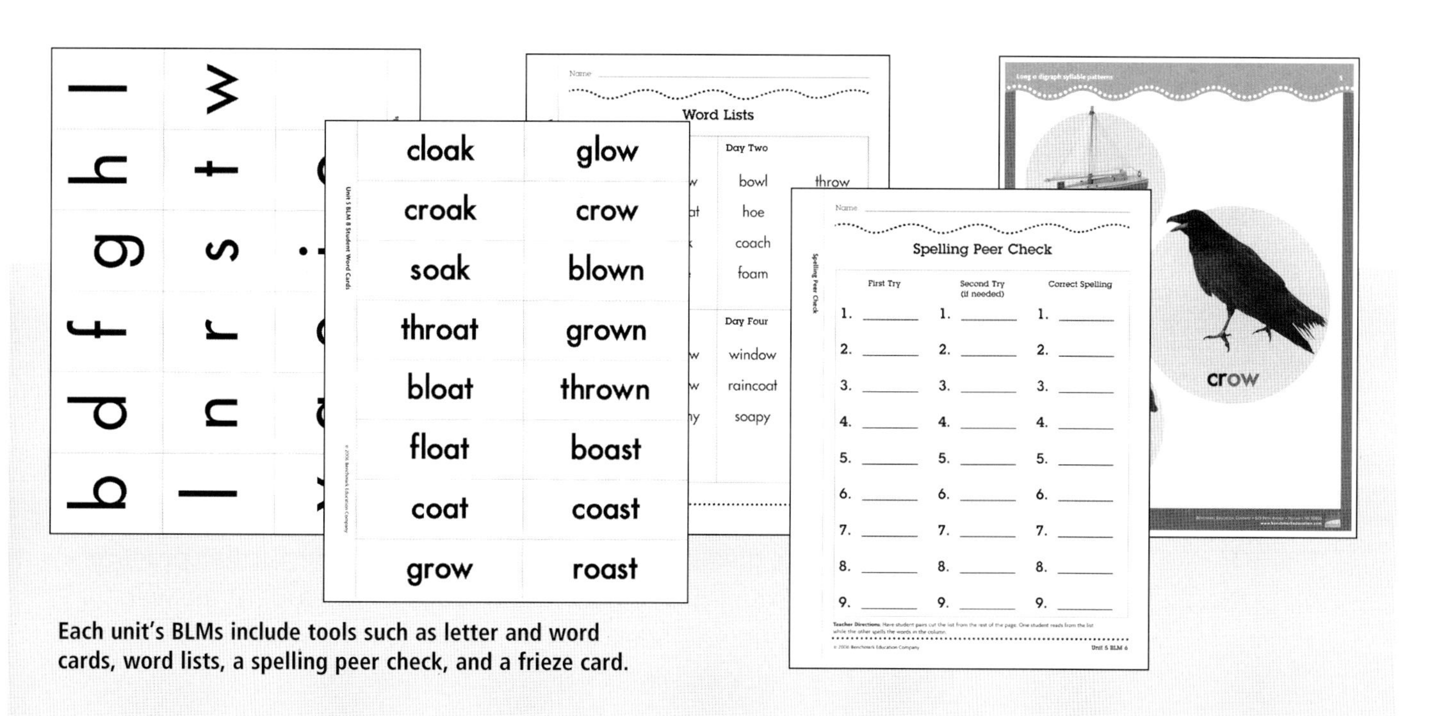

Each unit's BLMs include tools such as letter and word cards, word lists, a spelling peer check, and a frieze card.

Each unit also has a corresponding Home Connection activity for students to do with their families.

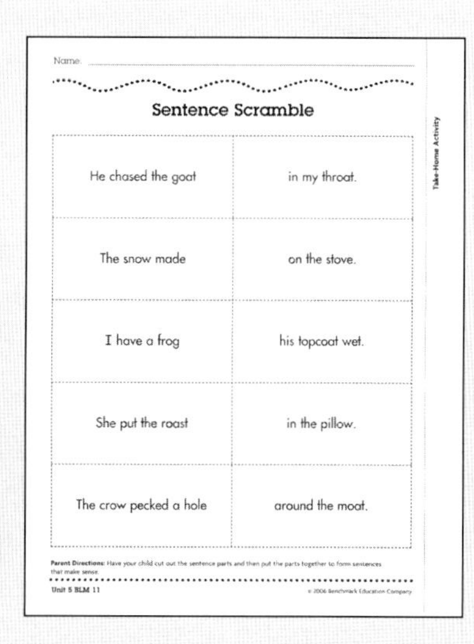

Name

Sentence Scramble

He chased the goat	in my throat.
The snow made	on the stove.
I have a frog	his topcoat wet.
She put the roast	in the pillow.
The crow pecked a hole	around the moat.

Take-Home Activity

Unit 5 BLM 11

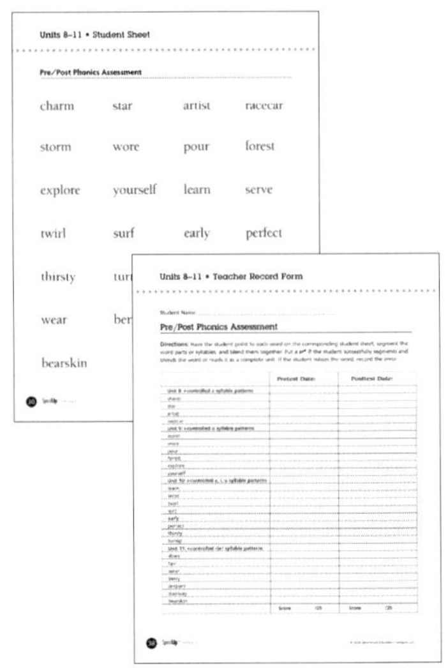
Units 8–11 • Student Sheet

Pre/Post Phonics Assessment

charm star artist racecar
storm wore pour forest
explore yourself learn serve
twirl surf early perfect
thirsty
wear
bearskin

Units 8–11 • Teacher Record Form

Pre/Post Phonics Assessment

Assessment

The *SpiralUp Phonics* Teacher Resource System provides a variety of methods for you to gather, record, and evaluate information about your students' phonics knowledge, sight word acquisition, and reading rate. Based on this information, you can decide what skill instruction your students need and whether they would benefit from additional small-group or individual instruction.

Pre/Post Assessments

The eight phonics assessments located behind the Assessments tab are used to determine students' starting point in the *SpiralUp Phonics* program and their mastery of the unit skills and words. Each includes a student copy and teacher record form and is accompanied by explicit directions for administering, scoring, and analysis.

Unit 15 Quick Check: Variant vowel /ŏŏ/ syllable patterns

Segmenting and Blending

skull childhood bushy checkbook
sullen mistook pulley output

Sight Words

away got
leave read
back good
want take

UNIT 15 Quick-Check: Variant vowel /ŏŏ/ syllable patterns

Quick-Checks

Quick-Check Assessments are provided for every unit after the last day of instruction and include words to segment and blend and sight words to read. As you analyze students' responses, note which skills or words give students difficulty and provide further practice by using the small-group activities in each unit. Student answer sheets can be downloaded and printed from the resource site. Review the Quick-Check instructions on page xxi.

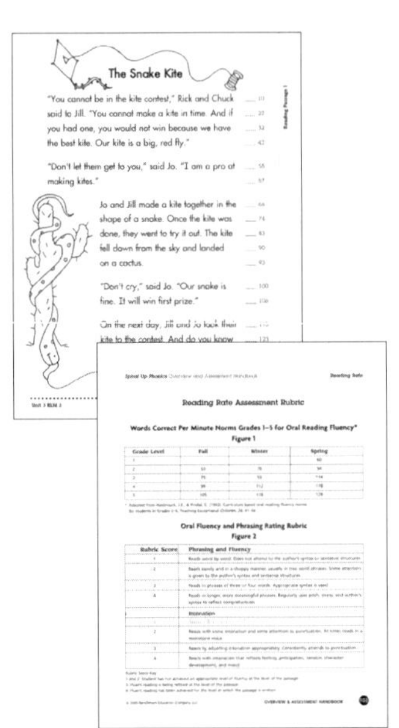
The Snake Kite

"You cannot be in the kite contest," Rick and Chuck said to Jill. "You cannot make a kite in time. And if you had one, you would not win because we have the best kite. Our kite is a big, red fly."

"Don't let them get to you," said Jo. "I am a pro at making kites."

Jo and Jill made a kite together in the shape of a snake. Once the kite was done, they went to try it out. The kite fell down from the sky and landed on a cactus.

"Don't cry," said Jo. "Our snake is fine. It will win first prize."

On the next day, Jill and Jo took their kite to the contest. And do you know

Reading Rate Assessment Rubric

Words Correct Per Minute Norms Grades 1–5 for Oral Reading Fluency

Figure 1

Oral Fluency and Phrasing Rating Rubric

Figure 2

Reading Rate Assessment

After students practice a selected decodable passage throughout the week, you can listen to them read one-on-one and assess their fluency with the provided rubric.

Informal Observation

In addition to the Quick-Check and Reading Rate Assessments, utilize informal observation to note whether students are mastering the skills. If you are uncertain about a student's confidence with a particular skill, call on that student to perform the task during the lesson and observe what he or she does. If you feel the student requires more practice, use the small-group mini-lessons provided within each unit. Throughout the unit, teacher assessment tips are provided to help you make observations about student progress.

Managing Instruction in the Phonics Block

Grouping Students

Use the Pre/Post Assessments to determine where in the kit you will begin instruction. These assessments will also help you determine whether you need to do all sections of the unit lessons and identify students who need more support in learning the phonics elements. The partner and independent activities for each unit allow you to provide meaningful learning for the larger group while you work with a small group or individual students who have not mastered the skills.

Most of the review lesson or new-skill unit teaching can be done with the whole class using a pocket chart, chart paper, chalkboard, or overhead for demonstration purposes. Assessment tips throughout the Teacher's Guides help you determine whether students need further support in a small group. It is recommended that decodable texts be read with small groups of students so you can more easily monitor students' reading.

Pacing the Instruction

SpiralUp Phonics is designed to be used during the daily 20- to 30-minute phonics block of your comprehensive literacy program. Students will practice sounding out words in a controlled, decodable format and then apply these skills, along with other reading strategies, during the small-group reading block.

You can choose to use some or all of the activities, depending on the needs of your students. Each new-skill unit spans a five-day period. However, you may find that you want students to work more quickly and learn a new phonetic element every three days. If this is the case, carefully select activities that will most benefit your students.

Skills

Lesson	Review Skill
Lesson 1	Initial blends
Lesson 2	Final blends
Lesson 3	Consonant digraphs ch, sh
Lesson 4	Consonant digraphs th, wh, ng, ck
Lesson 5	Initial three-letter blends

Unit	Review Skill	New Skill
Unit 1	Short vowels	Closed-syllable patterns
Unit 2	Long vowels	CVCe syllable patterns
Unit 3	Long vowels	Open-syllable patterns
Unit 4	Consonant digraphs th, wh, ck, nd	Long a digraph syllable patterns
Unit 5	Long vowels	Long o digraph syllable patterns
Unit 6	Long o digraph syllable patterns	Long e digraph syllable patterns
Unit 7	Long e digraph syllable patterns	Long i digraph syllable patterns
Unit 8	Long i digraph syllable patterns	r-controlled a syllable patterns
Unit 9	r-controlled a syllable patterns	r-controlled o syllable patterns
Unit 10	r-controlled o syllable patterns	r-controlled e, i, u syllable patterns
Unit 11	r-controlled e, i, u syllable patterns	r-controlled /âr/ syllable patterns
Unit 12	r-controlled /âr/ syllable patterns	Vowel diphthong /oi/ syllable patterns
Unit 13	Vowel diphthong /oi/ syllable patterns	Vowel diphthong /ou/ syllable patterns
Unit 14	Vowel diphthong /ou/ syllable patterns	Variant vowel /o͞o/ syllable patterns
Unit 15	Variant vowel /o͞o/ syllable patterns	Variant vowel /o͝o/ syllable patterns
Unit 16	Variant vowel /o͝o/ syllable patterns	Variant vowel /ô/ syllable patterns
Unit 17	Variant vowel /ô/ ; soft c and g	Consonant + le syllable patterns
Unit 18	Silent letters	Compound words and silent letters
Unit 19	Closed-syllable patterns	Contractions
Unit 20	CVCe syllable patterns	Regular plurals

Unit	Review Skill	New Skill
Unit 21	Open-syllable patterns	Irregular plurals
Unit 22	Vowel digraph syllable patterns	-ed, -ing endings
Unit 23	r-controlled syllable patterns	-er, -or endings
Unit 24	Consonant + le, al, el syllable patterns	Comparatives
Unit 25	Contractions	-y endings
Unit 26	Plurals	-ly ending
Unit 27	Review -ed, -ing, -er, -or endings	Prefix un-
Unit 28	Comparatives	Prefix re-
Unit 29	-y, -ly endings	Prefix dis-
Unit 30	Review prefixes un-, re-, dis-	Suffix -less
Unit 31	Review suffix -less	Suffixes -sion, -tion, -ion
Unit 32	Review suffixes -sion, -tion, -ion, -ation, -ition	Greek roots

Lesson Objectives

Students will:

- Review l-family, r-family, s-family blends
- Practice blending words
- Use letter cards to spell words with inital blends
- Read a word list and a reading passage containing words with inital blends

Materials Needed

- Letter cards: **b**, **c**, **f**, **f**, **g**, **l**, **n**, **p**, **r**, **s**, **s**, **t**, **a**, **i**, **o**, **u**
- Word lists (BLM 2)
- Overhead transparency
- Reading passage (BLM 3)

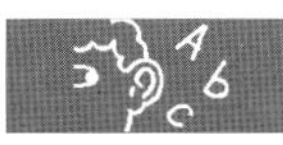

Review Initial Blends

Model

- Write the following words in a row along the board: ***clap***, ***drab***, ***stop***. Point out that each word starts with a different type of blend. Remind students that a blend is two or three letters that stand for a blended sound. Circle each blend as you read it and tell students what blend family each word belongs to (l-family, r-family, or s-family).

Guide

- Have students brainstorm words from each blend family. On index cards, record any words with short vowels that they suggest. When students are finished with the brainstorming, mix up the index cards and have students tell you how to sort the words according to their beginning blends.
- Give students the letter cards from blackline master 1.
- Say the word ***stiff***. Ask students what two letters they need to make the s-blend at the beginning of ***stiff***. Have them find the letters and say the blended sound.
- Next ask students what letter they need to make the **/i/** sound, and have them find the letter and say the sound.
- Finally, ask students what letters they need to make the **/f/** sound at the end of ***stiff***. Tell them the word ends with a double consonant. Have them find the letters and say the sound.
- Have them read the word.

Apply

- Have students repeat the process independently with the words ***crab***, ***stop***, ***glass***, ***bluff***, ***scan***, and ***spin***.

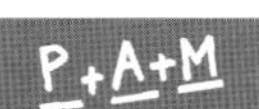

Blend Words

Model

- Write the word ***snag*** on the board. Model sounding out the word, blending each sound as you run your finger under the letters: **/sn/ /aaa/ /g/**. Then say the whole word. Point out that the word starts with a two-letter, s-family blend.

Guide

- Write the word ***flap*** on the board and ask students what they notice about how the word begins. Have students sound out the word with you.
- Give students the word lists on blackline master 2. Point out that the words on the lists begin with different families of blends. Have students sound out the first word on the first list while running a finger under the letters that stand for each sound.

Apply

- Have students independently sound out all or some of the remaining words on the lists. Students who are able to read the words without blending each sound should do so.
- For students who need more support in blending, guide them through blending some or all of the words on the lists before asking them to read the lists independently.

Teacher Tips

Assessment

Note whether students can suggest useful strategies for figuring out the words that you call attention to in the passage.

Comprehension

Use the following questions to discuss the information in the passage and to make sure students have understood what they read:

What things do Brad and Skip have?
(Level 1–facts and details)

How does Spot make a mess?
(Level 2–cause/effect)

Why did Brad and Skip grin?
(Level 3–make inferences)

Fluency

Intervene if students are having difficulty reading the passage, and model how to use word and meaning strategies to figure out the words. After students have had a chance to read the passage silently, have them read it orally for fluency. Model fluent reading of the passage. For some students, you may want to read the passage a second time and have them echo read along with you.

Spelling Words: *grab, club, spun, flap, trip, skin*

- Provide practice for students in segmenting words and associating the sounds with spellings. Dictate the following words to students and have them write the words on their papers: ***grab***, ***club***, ***spun***, ***flap***, ***trip***, ***skin***.
- Write the words on the board and have students self-correct their papers.
- Dictate the following sentence and have students write it on their papers: *The trim, slim frog sat on a flat slab of glass.*
- Write the sentence on the board and have students self-correct their papers.

P+A+M Develop Phonics and Word Strategies

Model

- Begin reading the overhead transparency passage aloud, pointing to each word as you read. Stop when you come to the word **Brit** and model strategies you would use to read the word and figure out its meaning.
- **Think Aloud:** *Let's see if I can use what I know about sound/symbol relationships to read this word. Looking at how the word begins, I notice the letters* **B** *and* **r**. *I remember that this is an r-family blend and the sounds that both these letters stand for are blended together: /***br***/. The word ends like other words I know:* **it**, **fit**, *and* **hit**. *This makes it easy for me to read the word:* **Brit**.
- Model making a mistake and self-correcting it. For example, read ***slips*** instead of ***slaps***.
- **Think Aloud:** *That doesn't sound right. Oh, I read a short /***i***/ sound but it really is short /***a***/:* **slaps**. *Yes,* **slaps** *makes sense here.*

Guide

- Continue reading, stopping at different words to ask students what strategies they would use to read the words and figure out their meanings.
- When students have read the passage with you, have volunteers come up and circle words they can find that end with blends. They could circle each final blend in a different color.

Apply

- Give students a copy of the reading passage on blackline master 3. Have them take turns reading the passage to a partner.
- Have students who need extra support practice reading the passage in a small group as you monitor their reading.

Lesson Objectives

Students will:

- Review final blends *ft*, *lp*, *lt*, *mp*, *nd*, *nk*, *nt*, *st*
- Practice blending words
- Use letter cards to spell words with final blends
- Read a word list and a reading passage containing words with final blends

Materials Needed

- Letter cards: **d, f, k, l, m, n, p, r, s, t, y, a, e, i, o, u**
- Word lists (BLM 2)
- Overhead transparency
- Reading passage (BLM 3)

Review Final Blends

Model

- Write the following words in a row along the chalkboard: ***bent***, ***clunk***, ***fond***, ***jump***, ***lift***, ***belt***, ***help***, ***past***. Point out that each word ends with a different type of blend. Remind students that a blend is two or three letters that stand for a blended sound. Circle each blend as you read it and tell students what blend family each word belongs to (***nt***, ***nk***, ***nd***, ***mp***, ***ft***, ***lt***, ***lp***, or ***st***).

Guide

- Have students brainstorm words from each blend family. On index cards, record any words with short vowels that they suggest. When students are finished with the brainstorming, mix up the index cards and have students tell you how to sort the words according to their final blends.
- Give students the letter cards from blackline master 1.
- Say the word ***stand***. Ask students what two letters they need to make the blend at the beginning of ***stand***. Have them find the letters and say the blended sound.
- Next, ask students what letter they need to make the /a/ sound, and have them find the letter and say the sound.
- Finally, ask students what two letters they need to make the blend at the end of ***stand***. Have them find the letters and say the sound.
- Have them read the word.

Apply

- Have students repeat the process independently with the words ***tank***, ***fond***, ***left***, ***frost***, ***limp***, ***runt***, ***yelp***.

P+A+M

Blend Words

Model

- Write the word ***fund*** on the board. Model sounding out the word, blending each sound as you run your finger under the letters: /**fff**/ /**uuu**/ /**nnn**/ /**d**/. Then say the whole word. Point out that the word ends with a two-letter blend.

Guide

- Write the word ***draft*** on the board and ask students what they notice about how the word ends. Have students sound out the word with you.
- Give students the word lists on blackline master 2. Point out that the words on the lists end with different blends. Have students sound out the first word on the first list while running a finger under the letters that stand for each sound.

Apply

- Have students independently sound out all or some of the remaining words on the lists. Students who are able to read the words without blending each sound should do so.
- For students who need more support in blending, guide them through blending some or all of the words on the lists before asking them to read the lists independently.

Teacher Tips

Assessment

Note whether students can suggest useful strategies for figuring out the words that you call attention to in the passage.

Comprehension

Use the following questions to discuss the information in the passage and to make sure students have understood what they read:

What things did Brent do on his trip?
(Level 1–facts and details)

Why does Brent send Hank over to the other ants?
(Level 2–cause/effect)

Why isn't Brent best pals with the ants and Hank at the end?
(Level 3–make inferences)

Fluency

Intervene if students are having difficulty reading the passage, and model how to use word and meaning strategies to figure out the words. After students have had a chance to read the passage silently, have them read it orally for fluency. Model fluent reading of the passage. For some students, you may want to read the passage a second time and have them echo read along with you.

Spelling Words: *spent, sunk, grand, lamp, rift, blend, west, help*

- Provide practice for students in segmenting words and associating the sounds with spellings. Dictate the following words to students and have them write the words on their papers: ***spent***, ***sunk***, ***grand***, ***lamp***, ***rift***, ***blend***, ***west***, ***help***.
- Write the words on the board and have students self-correct their papers.
- Dictate the following sentence and have students write it on their papers: *The pink mink left the camp in a vest of felt, kelp, and fronds.*
- Write the sentence on the board and have students self-correct their papers.

P+A+M Develop Phonics and Word Strategies

Model

- Begin reading the overhead transparency passage aloud. Stop when you come to the word ***fronds***. Model strategies you would use to read the word and figure out its meaning.
- **Think Aloud:** *Let's see if I can use what I know about sound/symbol relationships to read this word. Looking at how the word begins, I notice it starts with a blend: /***fr***/. The rest of the word looks like the end of the word* **pond** *with an* **s** *added, so the word must be* **fronds**. *Hmmm, I wonder what a frond is. I think it must be some kind of big leaf that would make a nice shelter for an ant.*
- Model making a mistake and self-correcting it. For example, read ***my*** instead of ***may***.
- **Think Aloud:** *Wait a minute. This word can't be* **my** *because I see that this sentence is a question, so I need a question word that starts with /***m***/. I think the word is* **may**. *This is a high-frequency word that I have practiced reading before.*

Guide

- Continue reading, stopping at different words to ask students what strategies they would use to read the words and figure out their meanings.
- When students have read the passage with you, have volunteers come up and circle words they can find that end with blends. They could circle each final blend in a different color.

Apply

- Give students a copy of the reading passage on blackline master 3. Have them take turns reading the passage to a partner.
- Have students who need extra support practice reading the passage in a small group as you monitor their reading.

Lesson Objectives

Students will:

- Review consonant digraphs *ch*, *sh*
- Practice blending words
- Use letter cards to spell words with consonant digraphs *ch*, *sh*
- Read a word list and a reading passage containing words with consonant digraphs

Materials Needed

- Letter cards: **c**, **c**, **f**, **h**, **l**, **l**, **n**, **p**, **r**, **s**, **t**, **a**, **e**, **i**, **o**, **u**
- Word lists (BLM 2)
- Overhead transparency
- Reading passage (BLM 3)

Review Consonant Digraphs *ch, sh*

Model

Write the following words in a row along the board: ***chip***, ***lunch***, ***dash***, ***ship***. Point out that each word either begins or ends with a consonant digraph. Remind students that a digraph is two letters combined to make one sound. Circle each digraph as you read it (***ch***, ***sh***).

Guide

- Have students brainstorm words containing a ***ch*** or ***sh*** digraph. On index cards, record any words with short vowels that they suggest. When students are finished with the brainstorming, mix up the index cards and have students tell you how to sort the words according to whether they contain a ***ch*** or ***sh*** digraph.
- Give students the letter cards from blackline master 1.
- Say the word ***crunch***. Ask students what two letters they need to make the blend at the beginning of ***crunch***. Have them find the letters and say the blended sound.
- Next, ask students what letters they need to make the /**un**/ sound, and have them find the letters and say the sound.
- Finally, ask students what two letters they need to make the digraph at the end of ***crunch***. Have them find the letters and say the sound.
- Have them read the word.

Apply

- Have students repeat the process independently with the words ***clash***, ***fresh***, ***fish***, ***shift***, ***shell***, ***such***, ***punch***, ***chill***, ***chop***.

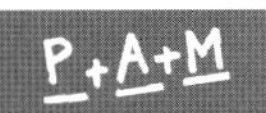

Blend Words

Model

- Write the word ***flash*** on the chalkboard. Model sounding out the word, blending each sound as you run your finger under the letters: /**fff**/ /**lll**/ /**aaa**/ /**sh**/. Then say the whole word. Point out that the word begins with a two-letter blend and ends with a two-letter consonant digraph.

Guide

- Write the word ***chunk*** on the chalkboard and ask students what they notice about how the word begins. Have students sound out the word with you.
- Give students the word lists from blackline master 2. Point out that the words on the lists contain either ***ch*** or ***sh*** digraphs. Have students sound out the first word on the first list while running a finger under the letters that stand for each sound.

Apply

- Have students independently sound out all or some of the remaining words on the lists. Students who are able to read the words without blending each sound should do so.
- For students who need more support in blending, guide them through blending some or all of the words on the lists before asking them to read the lists independently.

Teacher Tips

Assessment

Note whether students can suggest useful strategies for figuring out the words that you call attention to in the passage.

Comprehension

Use the following questions to discuss the information in the passage and to make sure students have understood what they read:

What kind of shop do Shep and Chad have?
(Level 1–facts and details)

Why do Shep and Chad put an ad in the mesh net?
(Level 2–cause/effect)

Why is this the last trip the fish will take?
(Level 3–make inferences)

Fluency

Intervene if students are having difficulty reading the passage, and model how to use word and meaning strategies to figure out the words. After students have had a chance to read the passage silently, have them read it orally for fluency. Model fluent reading of the passage. For some students, you may want to read the passage a second time and have them echo read along with you.

Spelling Words: ***smash, plush, shell, shop, much, which, chest, champ***

- Provide practice for students in segmenting words and associating sounds with spellings. Dictate the following words to students and have them write the words on their papers: ***smash***, ***plush***, ***shell***, ***shop***, ***much***, ***which***, ***chest***, ***champ***.
- Write the words on the board and have students self-correct their papers.
- Dictate the following sentence and have students write it on their papers: *Mitch had lunch and then put the fish, shells, and chips in the trash.*
- Write the sentence on the board and have students self-correct their papers.

P+A+M Develop Phonics and Word Strategies

Model

- Begin reading the overhead transparency passage aloud. Stop when you come to the word ***shop***. Model strategies you would use to read the word and figure out its meaning.
- **Think Aloud:** *Let's see if I can use what I know about sound/symbol relationships to read this word. Looking at how the word begins, I notice it starts with a blend: /**sh**/. The rest of the word looks like the end of the word **stop**, so the word must be **shop**. Hmmm, I wonder what kind of shop Shep and Chad own. I think it must have something to do with either a store that sells fish or sneaky tricks because of the title.*
- Model making a mistake and self-correcting it. For example, read ***cash*** instead of ***catch***.
- **Think Aloud:** *Wait a minute. This word can't be **cash** because that doesn't make any sense. I need to look at the whole word more carefully. Oh, I see–this word starts like **cash**, but it ends in /**tch**/, not /**sh**/. I think the word is **catch**, which makes more sense here. They catch fish, they don't cash them!*

Guide

- Continue reading, stopping at different words to ask students what strategies they would use to read the words and figure out their meanings.
- When students have read the passage with you, have volunteers come up and circle words they can find that end with blends. They could circle each final blend in a different color.

Apply

- Give students a copy of the reading passage on blackline master 3. Have them take turns reading the passage to a partner.
- Have students who need extra support practice reading the passage in a small group as you monitor their reading.

Lesson Objectives

Students will:

- Review consonant digraphs ***th***, ***wh***, ***ng***, ***ck***
- Practice blending words
- Use letter cards to spell words with consonant digraphs
- Read a word list and a reading passage containing words with consonant digraphs

Materials Needed

- Letter cards: **c**, **c**, **g**, **h**, **k**, **l**, **n**, **r**, **s**, **t**, **w**, **a**, **e**, **i**, **o**, **u**
- Word lists (BLM 2)
- Overhead transparency
- Reading passage (BLM 3)

Review Consonant Digraphs *th, wh, ng, ck*

Model

- Write the following words in a row along the board: ***neck***, ***cloth***, ***brick***, ***when***, ***hang***. Point out that each word has a consonant digraph at its begining, its end, or both. Remind students that a digraph is two letters that are combined to make one sound. Circle each digraph as you read it: ***ck***, ***th***, ***wh***, ***ng***.

Guide

- Have students brainstorm and suggest words containing ***th***, ***wh***, ***ng***, and ***ck*** digraphs. Record any words with short vowels on index cards. When students are finished with the brainstorming, mix up the index cards and have students tell you how to sort the words according to which digraph they contain.
- Give students the letter cards from blackline master 1.
- Say the word ***check***. Ask students what two letters they need to make the digraph at the beginning of ***check***. Have them find the letters and say the sound.
- Next, ask students what letter they need to make the /**e**/ sound, and have them find the letter and say the sound.
- Finally, ask students what two letters they need to make the digraph at the end of ***check***. Have them find the letters and say the sound.
- Have them read the word.

Apply

- Have students repeat the process independently with the words ***crack***, ***cluck***, ***sloth***, ***with***, ***thongs***, ***thick***, ***whisk***, ***sting***, ***rang***.

Blend Words

Model

- Write the word ***thick*** on the board. Model sounding out the word, blending each sound as you run your finger under the letters: **/th/ /iiii/ /k/**. Then say the whole word. Point out that the word begins and ends with two-letter digraphs.

Guide

- Write the word ***whim*** on the board and ask students what they notice about how the word begins. Have students sound out the word with you.
- Give students the word lists on blackline master 2. Point out that the words begin or end with consonant digraphs ***th***, ***wh***, ***ng***, ***ck***, and in some cases, the words both begin and end with consonant digraphs. Have students sound out the first word on the first list while running a finger under the letters that stand for each sound.

Apply

- Have students independently sound out all or some of the remaining words on the lists. Students who are able to read the words without blending each sound should do so.
- For students who need more support in blending, guide them through blending some or all of the words on the lists before asking them to read the lists independently.

Teacher Tips

Assessment

Note whether students can suggest useful strategies for figuring out the words that you call attention to in the passage.

Comprehension

Use the following questions to discuss the information in the passage and to make sure students have understood what they read:

Why do Seth, Beth and Whiz go to the dock?
(Level 1–facts and details)

Why does the duck kick the chick?
(Level 2–cause/effect)

Why did Seth want to leave so quickly?
(Level 3–make inferences)

Fluency

Intervene if students are having difficulty reading the passage, and model how to use word and meaning strategies to figure out the words. After students have had a chance to read the passage silently, have them read it orally for fluency. Model fluent reading of the passage. For some students, you may want to read the passage a second time and have them echo-read along with you.

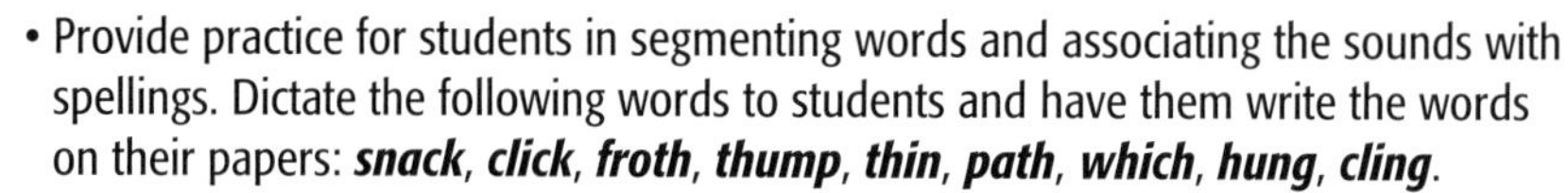

Spelling Words: *snack, click, froth, thump, thin, path, which, hung, cling*

- Provide practice for students in segmenting words and associating the sounds with spellings. Dictate the following words to students and have them write the words on their papers: ***snack***, ***click***, ***froth***, ***thump***, ***thin***, ***path***, ***which***, ***hung***, ***cling***.
- Write the words on the board and have students self-correct their papers.
- Dictate the following sentence and have students write it on their papers: *On a whim, Beth and the thin duck sang and ran on that long path.*
- Write the sentence on the board and have students self-correct their papers.

P+A+M Develop Phonics and Word Strategies

Model

- Begin reading the overhead passage aloud. Stop when you come to the word ***snacks***. Model strategies you would use to read the word and figure out its meaning.
- **Think Aloud:** *Let's see if I can use what I know about sound/symbol relationships to read this word. Looking at how the word begins, I notice the letters* **s** *and* **n**. *I remember that this is an s-family blend and that the sounds that each of these letters stands for are blended together:* **/sssnnn/**. *The root word ends like other words I know:* **back**, **pack**, *and* **rack**. *This makes it easy for me to read the word:* **snacks**.
- Model making a mistake and self-correcting it. For example, read ***ships*** instead of ***chips***.
- **Think Aloud:** *That doesn't sound right. Oh, I read the consonant digraph* **/sh/** *sound but it really is consonant digraph* **/ch/**: **chips**. *Yes,* **chips** *makes sense here.*

Guide

- Continue reading, stopping at different words to ask students what strategies they would use to read the words and figure out their meanings.
- When students have read the passage with you, have volunteers come up and circle words they can find that end with blends. They could circle each final blend in a different color.

Apply

- Give students a copy of the reading passage on blackline master 3. Have them take turns reading the passage to a partner.
- Have students who need extra support practice reading the passage in a small group as you monitor their reading.

Lesson Objectives
Students will:

- Review initial blends ***scr***, ***spl***, ***spr***, ***squ***, ***str***
- Practice blending words
- Use letter cards to spell words with initial blends
- Read a word list and a reading passage containing words with initial blends

Materials Needed
- Letter cards: **c**, **h**, **l**, **n**, **p**, **q**, **r**, **s**, **s**, **t**, **a**, **i**, **u**
- Word lists (BLM 2)
- Overhead transparency
- Reading passage (BLM 3)

Review Initial Blends *scr, spl, spr, squ, str*

Model
- Write the following words in a row along the board: ***scram***, ***splotch***, ***spritz***, ***squish***, ***strand***. Point out that each word starts with a three-letter blend. Remind students that a blend is a combination of two or three letters that stand for a blended sound. Circle each blend as you read it.

Guide
- Have students brainstorm and suggest words from each blend family. Record any words with short vowels on index cards. When students are finished with the brainstorming, mix up the index cards and have students tell you how to sort the words according to their initial blends.
- Give students the letter cards from blackline master 1.
- Say the word ***strap***. Ask students what three letters they need to make the s-family blend at the beginning of ***strap***. Have them find the letters and say the blended sound.
- Next, ask students what letter they need to make the /**a**/ sound, and have them find the letter and say the sound.
- Finally, ask students what letter they need to make the /**p**/ sound at the end of the word. Have them find the letter and say the sound.
- Have them read the word.

Apply
- Have students repeat the process independently with the words ***splash***, ***squint***, ***strip***, ***scrap***, and ***splat***.

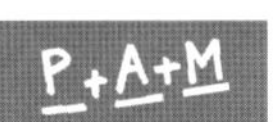

Blend Words

Model
- Write the word ***script*** on the board. Model sounding out the word, blending each sound as you run your finger under the letters: **/skr/ /iii/ /pt/**. Then say the whole word. Point out that the word starts with a three-letter, s-family blend.

Guide
- Write the word ***stress*** on the board and ask students what they notice about how the word begins. Have students sound out the word with you.
- Give students the word list on blackline master 2. Point out that the words begin with different three-letter blends, all beginning with the letter ***s***. Have students sound out the first word on the first list while running a finger under the letters that stand for each sound.

Apply
- Have students independently sound out all or some of the remaining words on the lists. Students who can read the words without blending each sound should do so.
- For students who need more support in blending, guide them through reading some or all of the words on the lists before asking them to read the lists independently.

REVIEW LESSON 5

Teacher Tips

Assessment

Note whether students can suggest useful strategies for figuring out the words that you call attention to in the passage.

Comprehension

Use the following questions to discuss the information in the passage and to make sure students have understood what they read:

What does Sam Squid do all day long?
(Level 1–facts and details)

What caused the big splash next to Sam?
(Level 2–cause/effect)

How do you think the chimp felt when Sam won the race?
(Level 3–make inferences)

Fluency

Intervene if students are having difficulty reading the passage, and model how to use word and meaning strategies to figure out the words. After students have had a chance to read the passage silently, have them read it orally for fluency. Model fluent reading of the passage. For some students, you may want to read the passage a second time and have them echo-read along with you.

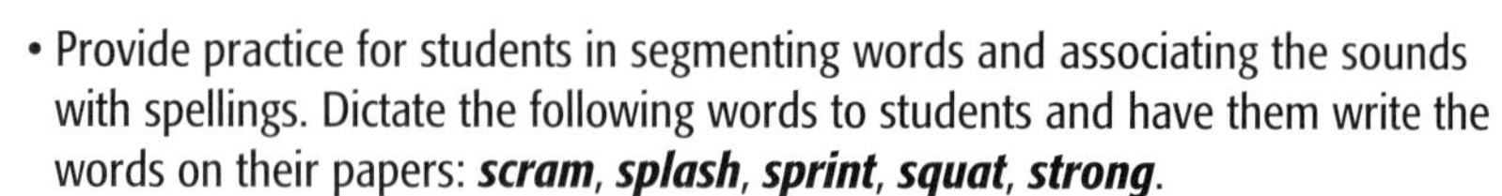

Spelling Words: *scram, splash, sprint, squat, strong*

- Provide practice for students in segmenting words and associating the sounds with spellings. Dictate the following words to students and have them write the words on their papers: ***scram***, ***splash***, ***sprint***, ***squat***, ***strong***.
- Write the words on the board and have students self-correct their papers.
- Dictate the following sentence and have students write it on their papers: *In the spring, I catch squid with strong string.*
- Write the sentence on the board and have students self-correct their papers.

P+A+M Develop Phonics and Word Strategies

Model

- Begin reading the overhead transparency passage aloud. Stop when you come to the word ***spring***. Model strategies you would use to read the word and figure out its meaning.
- **Think Aloud:** *Let's see if I can use what I know about sound/symbol relationships to read this word. Looking at how the word begins, I notice the letters* **s**, **p**, *and* **r**. *I remember that this is an s-family blend and the sounds that these three letters stand for are blended together:* **/sssprrr/**. *The word ends like other words I know:* **sing** *and* **wing**. *This makes it easy for me to read the word:* **spring**.
- Model making a mistake and self-correcting it. For example, read ***crimp*** instead of ***chimp***.
- **Think Aloud:** *That doesn't sound right. What is a* **crimp**? *Oh, I read* **/kr/** *instead of* **/ch/**. *The word should be* **chimp**. *Yes,* **chimp** *makes sense here.*

Apply

- Give students a copy of the reading passage on blackline master 3. Have them take turns reading the passage to a partner.
- Have students who need extra support practice reading the passage in a small group as you monitor their reading.

UNIT 1 Closed-syllable patterns

Unit Objectives

Students will:

- Recognize and read words with closed syllables
- Blend onset and rime
- Sort words according to their word families
- Read high-frequency words eat, food, sometimes, soon, watch
- Spell one- and two-syllable words with closed patterns: shock, fish, chunk, rock, trunk, dish, napkin, magnet, and basket
- Identify synonyms for selected words

Day 1

Letter Cards: **a, b, c, d, e, f, g, h, i, k, m, n, o, p, r, s, t, u**

Word Lists (BLM 2)

drill

Teacher Word Cards: **drill, duck, frog, grim, luck, truck, slim, smog, stamp, swim, trash**

Day 2

Word Lists (BLM 2)

Reading Passage 1 (BLM 3)

soon could
watch they
sometimes their
eat find
food are
have go
some with
like to

High-Frequency Word Cards for Unit 1 (BLM 7)

Day 3

Word Lists (BLM 2)

Reading Passages 1 & 2 (BLMs 3 & 4)

soon could
watch they
sometimes their
eat find
food are
have go
some with
like to

High-Frequency Word Cards for Unit 1 (BLM 7)

Day 4

Word Lists (BLM 2)

Reading Passages 1, 2, & 3 (BLMs 3, 4, & 5)

camp

Teacher Word Cards: **camp, champ, chum, chill, drill, drum, fed, pill, plum, prop, ramp, shed, shop, sled, stop**

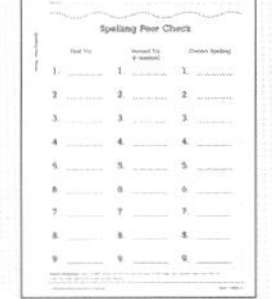
Spelling Peer Check (BLM 6)

Day 5

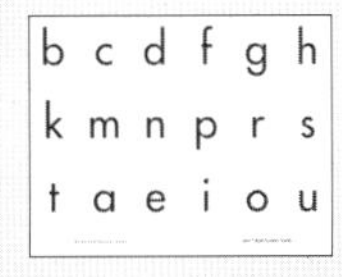

Letter Cards for Unit 1

Reading Passage 1 (BLM 3)

High-Frequency Word Cards for Unit 1 (BLM 7)

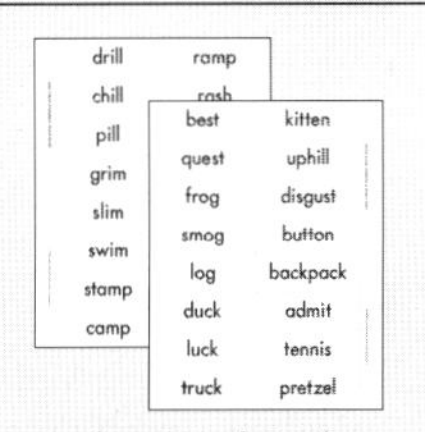

Student Word Cards (BLMs 8 & 9)

Quick-Check Student Sheet

Frieze Card

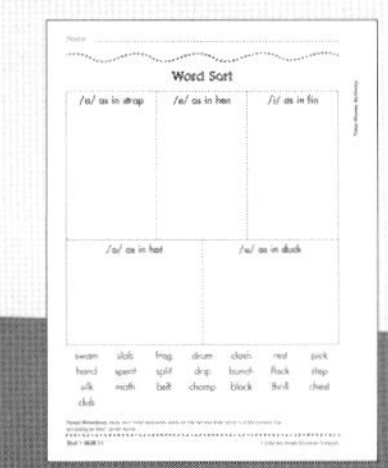

Take-Home Activity

Core Materials

All of these materials can be downloaded from http://phonicsresources.benchmarkeducation.com.

DAY 1

1 Syllable Introduce Closed-Syllable Patterns

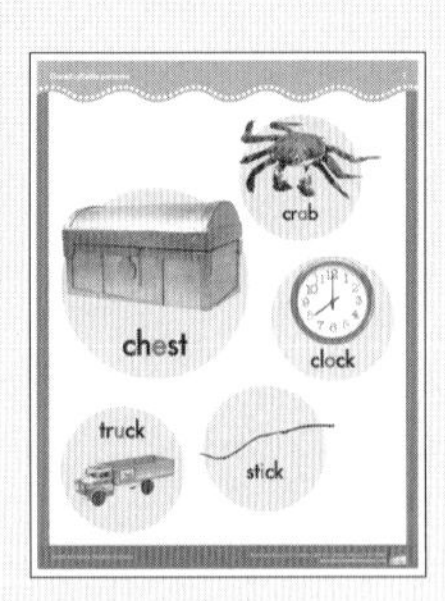

Frieze Card

Model

- Hold up the closed-syllable frieze card and have students name each object and read each word.
- Point out that the words have short vowel sounds. Explain that a syllable has only one vowel sound, so these are one-syllable words.
- Ask students what type of letter ends each syllable. Explain that these are examples of words that have a closed-syllable pattern because closed syllables have a short vowel sound and end with a consonant.

Guide

- Give students letter cards **b, c, d, f, g, h, k, m, n, p, r, s, t, a, e, i, o,** and **u,** and have them line up the letters in a row in front of them.
- Say the word ***fat.*** Ask students to make the word ***fat.*** Have them articulate why this is a closed syllable word.
- Have students remove the ***f.*** Ask what letters they need to replace it with to make the word ***brat.*** Have them make the word and read it.
- Have students take away the ***t*** at the end of the word and ask what letters they need to replace it with to make the word ***brand.***

Apply

- Repeat the procedure with the following words: ***dim, dish; net, neck; shop, stop; scrub, shrub.***

Assessment Tip: Watch to make sure students select the correct letters. Read the word. Note which students struggle with this activity, and provide reinforcement activities.

Sort Words: Blends, Vowel Sounds, Digraphs

- Give each student or pair of students one of the following teacher word cards: **drill, truck, grim, frog, trash, slim, swim, stamp, smog, luck, duck.** Have them hold up their card for the group to read. Have the group decide whether the card belongs in the group of words that start with blends or in the group of words that don't start with blends.
- Next, have students sort the words according to their vowel sounds, and finally according to those that end with a consonant digraph and those that don't.

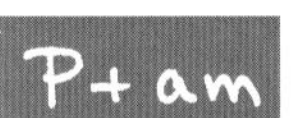

Blend Closed-Syllable Words

Model

- Write the word ***trap*** on the board, using a different color for the rime ***-ap.*** Point out that the word begins with a blend, has one vowel, and ends in a consonant. Model sounding out the word, blending onset and rime: ***/tr/ /ap/.*** Then say the whole word.

Guide

- Have students sound out the word with you. Repeat with other examples if you feel students need extra support.
- Give students blackline master 2. Have them use their fingers to frame the rime part of the first word on the list for Day One. Then have students read the word by blending the onset and rime.

Apply

- Have students independently sound out the remaining words on the list for Day One. Students who are able to read the words without blending each sound should do so.
- Guide students who need more support in blending by having them read some or all of the words on the list with you before asking them to read the list independently.

Assessment Tip: Note which students are able to read the words without blending each sound.

Spelling Words: *shock, fish, chunk*

Model

- Make a two-column spelling chart on chart paper. Label the first column "One-Syllable Words" and the second column "Two-Syllable Words." Tell students that they will be spelling words with the closed-syllable pattern. As you work through Unit One, you can add the spelling words to the chart and have students use the chart to check their spelling of the words.
- Say the word ***shock*** and model spelling it and writing it in the first column on the chart.
- **Think Aloud:** *I hear two parts in the word* **shock: /sh/** *and* **/ok/.** *I know that the letters* **s** *and* **h** *together stand for the* **/sh/** *sound. I hear short vowel* **/o/** *followed by the* **/k/** *sound. I write the letter* **o** *and then* **k,** *but this doesn't look right. I remember that the letters* **ck** *are often found at the ends of words and stand for the* **/k/** *sound. When I write* **ock,** *it looks right. I will blend the onset and rime to check the spelling of the word:* **/sh/ /ok/, shock.**

Guide

- Say the word ***fish.*** Have students identify the onset and rime in the word and the letters that stand for the sounds. Write the word in the first column on the chart as students tell you the word parts.
- Repeat with the word ***chunk.***

Apply

- Have students practice writing each of the words in their word study notebooks. After they write the word, have them check the spelling of the word by blending the onset and rime. Have students highlight the vowels in each of the words.

Our Spelling Words

One-Syllable Words	Two-Syllable Words
shock	napkin
fish	magnet
chunk	basket
rock	
trunk	
dish	

DAY 2

Teacher Tips

Reading Strategies

If students have difficulty applying strategies for challenging words, guide them to use the following strategies:

- look at how the words start and/or end
- look for familiar patterns or parts within the words
- separate the words into syllables and decode each part
- think about what familiar words look like the difficult words
- read forward to check the context
- reread the sentence or paragraph
- mark the words, substitute synonyms, and get on with reading–ask for help later

Comprehension

Use the following questions to ensure that students have understood the passage:

- *How many hens does this person have?* (Level 1–facts and details)
- *What are the chicks like now?* (Level 2–sequence of events)
- *What clues tell you that the chicks are happy?* (Level 3–draw conclusions)

Fluency

Intervene if students are having difficulty reading the passage. Model how to use word and meaning strategies to problem-solve the words. After students have had a chance to read the passage silently, have them read it aloud for fluency. Model fluent reading of the passage. For students who struggle, you may want to read the passage a second time and have them echo-read along with you.

P+ am Blend

- Have students blend the words from the first column of the list for Day Two, using the procedure for blending from Day One.

Develop Automaticity in Word Recognition

- Circle the following words on the overhead transparency: ***eat, food, sometimes, soon, watch.*** Tell students that practicing these words will help them recognize the words automatically and read more fluently.
- Read each word and point out that ***sometimes*** is made up of two smaller words.
- Have students read aloud with you the sentences in which the words are found, and then have them write each word in their word study notebooks.
- Give students a copy of blackline master 7. Point out the words from this lesson, as well as other words they have previously learned. Have students cut out the words, store them in an envelope, and use them for practice activities.

Build Fluency with Connected Text

Model

- Read the passage on the overhead transparency aloud. Stop when you come to the word ***chicks.*** Model strategies to read the word.
- **Think Aloud:** *This word ends with a consonant and has one vowel, so I know it's a closed syllable. Often the vowel in the closed syllable is short. I also recognize the word family* **-ick** *and I can blend this with the sounds at the beginning of the word:* **/ch/ /ick/, chick.** *There is an* **-s** *on the end, so this means there is more than one chick.*
- Continue reading. Model making a mistake and correcting it–for example, read ***wind*** instead of ***wings.***
- **Think Aloud:** *Hmm, "flap their wind" doesn't make sense. Let me look at this word again. I was right that the word starts with* **/w/** *and it has a short* **/i/** *sound. My mistake was that I didn't look at the ending. I see the blend* **/ng/** *and then a plural* **-s,** *so the word says* **wings** *and "flap their wings" makes sense.*

Guide

- Continue reading and stop at the word ***peck,*** this time asking students what strategies to use to read the word. Repeat with other words in the passage.

Apply

- Have students take turns reading blackline master 3 to a partner or in a small group as you monitor the reading. Use the teacher tips to check comprehension and fluency.

Spelling Words: *rock, trunk, dish*

- Have students practice writing the words from Day One in their word study notebooks. Have them refer to words on the spelling chart to check their spelling.
- Introduce the Day Two spelling words. Say the word ***rock*** and model spelling it and writing it on the spelling chart. Point to the word ***shock*** on the chart from the Day One spelling words, and highlight the word family. Model how to use the word family ***-ock*** to spell the new word and other words in the word family such as ***sock, block,*** and ***lock.***
- Repeat with the remaining words and have students practice writing the words in their word study notebooks.

Multisyllabic Words: Closed-Syllable Patterns

Model

- Write the word ***nap*** on the board and read it aloud. Point out that it has one vowel sound and one closed syllable.
- Write the word ***contest*** on the board. Explain to students that they can use what they know about vowel patterns and syllables to read longer words. Circle the two vowels in the word. Point out the two consonants between the vowels, and explain you will divide the word between them: ***con/test.***
- Point out that both syllables end with consonants and have a single vowel so they are closed syllables. Explain that since the vowels in closed syllables are often short, you will try the short sounds first.
- Model reading the two parts of the word and blending them together: ***/con/ /test/, contest.***

Guide

- Repeat with the word ***jacket.*** Ask what consonants are between the vowels. When students identify ***c*** and ***k,*** explain that ***c*** and ***k*** together make a consonant digraph that stands for the ***/k/*** sound. Explain that you don't divide consonant digraphs.
- Show students how you would divide the word: ***jack/et.*** Point out that the word has two closed syllables and have them sound it out using what they know about closed syllables.

Apply

- Have students independently blend the two-syllable words on the word list for Day Three. Provide support if necessary.

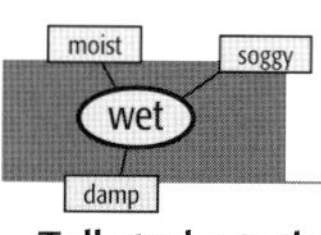

Develop Word Meanings

- Tell students that words that mean almost the same thing as another word are called synonyms.
- Write the following sentence on the board and underline the word ***bonnet:*** *She put her new <u>bonnet</u> on her head.* Read the sentence aloud. Explain that a bonnet is a kind of hat and that the word ***hat*** is a synonym for ***bonnet.***
- Write the following sentence on the board: *The glass was filled to the <u>brim</u>.* Read the sentence with students and have them suggest a synonym for ***brim.*** Reread the sentence using the synonym.
- Write the following sentences on the board: *The steps are very <u>slick</u>, so don't slip on them; The boy was <u>glad</u> to be back; His day was very <u>hectic</u> with all the things he had to do.* Have partners work to think of a synonym for each underlined word and use it in a written sentence.

Spelling Words: *napkin, magnet, basket*

- Have students practice spelling the words from Day One and Day Two by writing them several times in their word study notebooks.
- Say the word ***napkin.***
- **Think Aloud:** *When I spell this word, I need to think about how the word looks. I hear two syllables in the word, which means the syllables have one vowel and end with a consonant. I hear short* **a** *in the first syllable and short* **i** *in the second. I will write the word and see if it looks right.*
- Repeat with the remaining words and have students practice the words several times in their word study notebooks.

Build Fluency with Connected Text

- Have students read blackline master 4 to a partner or in a small group as you monitor their reading. Call attention to the following words in the reading passage before students read it: ***eat, even, food, it's, such.***

Teacher Tips

Digraphs

If necessary, provide extra practice in dividing words with digraphs into syllables, reminding students that the digraphs should not be separated. Use the following words: ***rocket, chicken, kitchen.***

Three-Syllable Words

Students can get a sense of achievement when they see they can apply what they know about closed syllables to read a three-syllable word such as ***fantastic.***

Develop Automaticity in Word Recognition

Have students write each high-frequency word on a self-stick note. Then have them search familiar books to find the words. When they find each word, have them mark the book with the self-stick note. When students have found all the words, have them read to a partner the sentences in which the words are found.

Repeated Reading

Have students read blackline master 3 repeatedly to develop fluency.

DAY 4

Teacher Tips

Develop Automaticity in Word Recognition

Have students search the reading passages on blackline masters 4 and 5 to find and circle any of the high-frequency words that they find. Encourage students to read the sentences that contain the high-frequency words.

Repeated Reading

Have students read blackline master 3 repeatedly to develop fluency.

P+ am Blend

- Have students blend the words on the list for Day Four, using the procedure for blending from Day One.

tea/cher Develop Phonics and Word Strategies: Word Families

- Place the following teacher word cards in a pocket chart: **drill, chill, pill, champ, camp, ramp, shed, sled, fed, stop, shop, prop, chum, drum, plum.**
- Tell students that you are going to sort the words and you want them to decide how the words in each group are alike. Sort the words into word families ***-ill, -amp, -ed, op,*** and ***-um.***
- Have students tell how you sorted the words. If students have difficulty, read the words in each group with them to see if they can hear something that is the same about the words.
- Have students help you sort the words another way: words that begin with one consonant and words that begin with two consonants.
- Have students work with a partner to sort their spelling words in their word study notebooks. Have the two students guess how their partner sorted the words.

Aa Spelling Words

- Provide practice for students in segmenting words and associating sounds with spellings. Dictate the following words to students and have them write the words on their papers: ***cat, rock, catnip, picnic.*** Remind students to use what they have learned about spelling closed-syllable words.
- Write the words on the board and have students self-correct their papers.
- Dictate the following sentence and have students write it on their papers: *The cat can get the catnip from the kitchen.*
- Write the sentence on the board and have students self-correct their papers.
- Give pairs of students blackline master 6. While one student reads the words, the other student writes them in the "First Try" column. After the student has spelled the words, the partner places a check mark next to words spelled correctly. For the second try, the partner may prompt the student by sounding out the words that were spelled incorrectly the first time. If the second spelling attempt is correct, the partner places a check mark in the "Second Try" column.

Assessment Tip: Use students' completed peer-check blackline masters to note which words gave students difficulty. Have students write the difficult words several times in their word study notebooks and have a partner check their spelling.

Build Fluency with Connected Text

- Give students the reading passage on blackline master 5. Have them take turns reading the passage to a partner. Call attention to the following words in the reading passage before students read it: ***eat, high, it's, play, soon, together, until***.
- Have students who need extra support practice reading the passage aloud in a small group as you monitor their reading.

Spelling Assessment

Use the following procedure to assess students' spelling of the Unit One words.
- Say each spelling word and use it in a sentence.
- Have students write the words on their papers.
- Continue with the next word on the list.
- When students have finished, collect their papers and analyze their spelling of the words.
- Use the assessment to plan small group or individual practice.

Small Group/Independent Activities

The following activities can be used to provide practice for students who need additional support.

PHONICS AND WORD STRATEGIES

Find the Words Have students search familiar books for examples of words with the closed-syllable pattern. Have them make a list in their word study notebooks.

Identify Syllables Have students copy the two-syllable words from the set of decodable words on blackline master 9 in their word study notebooks. Have them divide each word into syllables and write why they divided the words the way they did.

Word Sort Have students sort the student word cards from blackline masters 8 and 9 any way they choose. Have a partner read the words in the groups and tell how the groups were sorted.

AUTOMATICITY IN WORD RECOGNITION

Look and Say Laminate a set of word cards from blackline master 7 and place them in a stack. Have one student draw a card and show it to the group. The first student to read the word gets the card and chooses the next word to show to the group.

Make Sentences Place the high-frequency word cards in a paper bag. Have students work with a partner to draw a word card, read it, and use the word in an oral sentence.

BUILD FLUENCY WITH CONNECTED TEXT

Repeated Reading Have students practice reading blackline master 3 several times, until they feel they can read it fluently and accurately. Have them work with a partner to time each other as they read the passage aloud. Have them set a goal of reading ninety words per minute.

SPELLING

Make Words Provide a set of letter cards and the week's spelling words on index cards. You will need to provide an extra letter card for the letter ***n***. Have students use the letter cards to spell the words. They should check their spelling by blending the sounds and then looking at the words on the index cards.

Word Riddles Write the spelling words on the board. Then provide riddles for the words and have students write the words you have in mind. Say the following clues: *I am thinking of a word that names something that is electric; ... that you can use to wipe your hands; ... that Red Riding Hood carried; ... that you can put food on; ... that rhymes with* **clock**; *... that swims in water.*

Divide into Syllables Have students write the two-syllable words in their word study notebooks and divide them into syllables. Have them write why they divided the words the way they did.

Teacher Tips

Home Connection

Have students take blackline master 11 home to complete with a family member. Students can also take the reading passage on blackline master 3 home to share with their family.

Quick-Check

Assess students' mastery of closed syllables using the quick-check for Unit One in this Teacher Resource System.

ELL Support Tip

Two-column charts are a great way to help your ELL students master a specific skill and sort their spelling words. It gives them an opportunity to see the patterns in words and to process the syllables in their head. One way to help clarify the syllable patterns on the chart is to draw a visual next to the words that head each column; for example, a hand showing one finger for one-syllable words and two fingers for two-syllable words.

Quick-Check: Closed-syllable patterns

Student Name ______________________ Assessment Date __________

Segmenting and Blending

Directions: Explain that these words use sounds the student has been learning. Have the student point to each word on the corresponding student sheet, segment the word parts or syllables, and blend them together. Put a ✓ if the student successfully segments and blends the word or reads it as a complete unit. If the student misses the word, record the error. **Example:** trot

just		helmet		
miss		problem		
batch		ribbon		
tend		pencil		Score **/8**

Sight Words

Directions: Have the student point to the first word on the corresponding student sheet and read across the line, saying each word as quickly as possible. Put a ✓ if the student successfully reads the word and an **X** if the student hesitates more than a few seconds. If the student misses the word, record the error.

are		soon		
go		they		
with		could		
to		sometimes		
eat		watch		
food		some		
their		have		
find		like		Score **/16**

UNIT 2 CVCe syllable patterns

Unit Objectives

Students will:

- Recognize words with VCe syllable patterns
- Read two-syllable words with closed vowel pattern plus CVCe pattern
- Blend onset and rime words
- Sort words according to long and short vowel sounds and word families
- Read high-frequency words another, don't, kind, put, saw, sound
- Spell words with CVCe patterns: crate, stroke, glide, woke, plate, pride, reptile, naptime, mistake
- Recognize that some words can have multiple meanings

Day 1

Letter Cards: **a, c, d, e, n, o, p, r, t, u**

Word Lists (BLM 2)

cane

Teacher Word Cards: **can, cane, cop, cope, cut, cute, rip, ripe, shin, shine, tap, tape**

Day 2

Word Lists (BLM 2)

Reading Passage 1 (BLM 3)

High-Frequency Word Cards for Unit 2 (BLM 7)

Day 3

Word Lists (BLM 2)

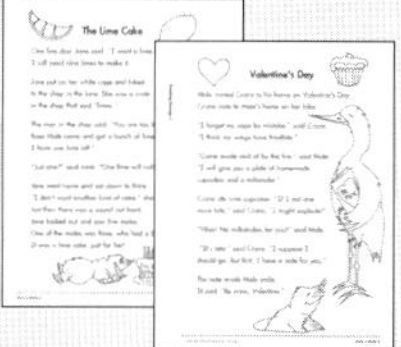

Reading Passages 1 & 2 (BLMs 3 & 4)

High-Frequency Word Cards for Unit 2 (BLM 7)

Day 4

Word Lists (BLM 2)

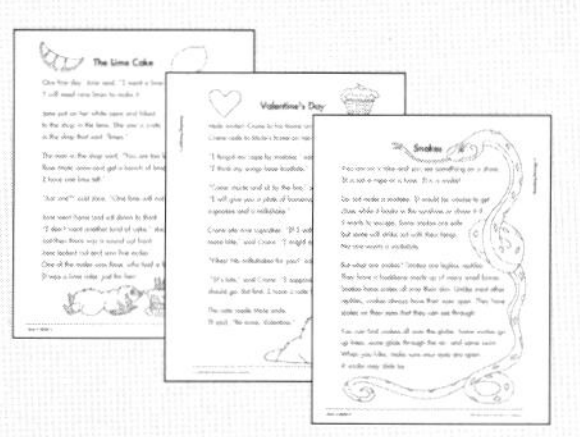

Reading Passages 1, 2, & 3 (BLMs 3, 4, & 5)

cane

Teacher Word Cards: **cane, cope, crane, cube, cute, flute, grape, gripe, hope, plane, ripe, shine, slope, spine, tape**

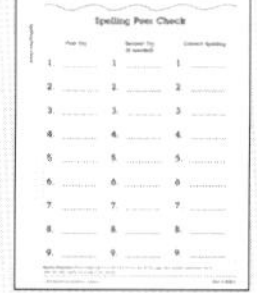

Spelling Peer Check (BLM 6)

Day 5

Letter Cards for Unit 2

Reading Passage 1 (BLM 3)

High-Frequency Word Cards for Unit 2 (BLM 7)

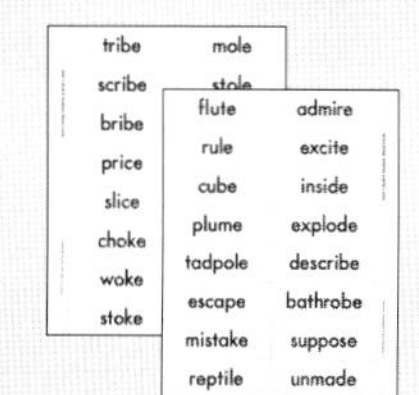

Student Word Cards (BLMs 8 & 9)

Quick-Check Student Sheet

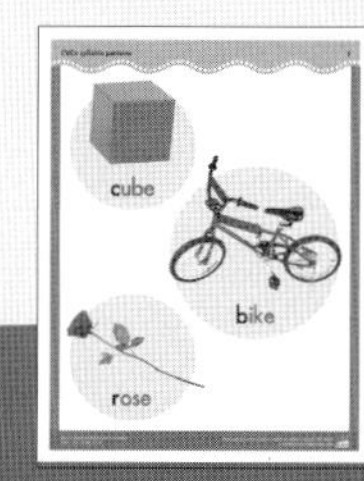

Frieze Card

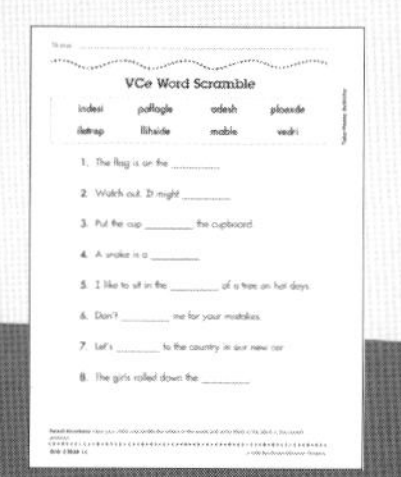

Take-Home Activity

Core Materials

All of these materials can be downloaded from http://phonicsresources.benchmarkeducation.com.

UNIT 2 CVCe syllable patterns

DAY 1

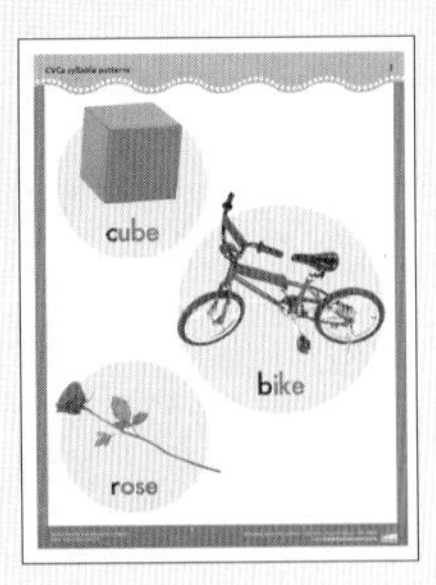

Frieze Card

1 Syllable Introduce CVCe Syllable Patterns

Model

- Hold up the CVCe frieze card and have students name each object.
- Point out that the vowel sound in each word is a long vowel sound. Remind students that words that have a vowel followed by a consonant and a final ***e***, as in ***snake***, often have the long vowel sound.
- Point out the CVCe pattern in each of the words on the frieze card.
- Have students read the words with you.
- Write the word ***cap*** on the board and remind students that this is a closed-syllable pattern and that the vowel sound is short.
- Add a final ***e*** to the word ***cap*** and model how changing the pattern to CVCe changes the sound of the vowel.

Guide

- Give students letter cards **c, d, n, p, r, t, a, e, o,** and **u,** and have them line up the letters in a row in front of them.
- Say the word ***can*** and ask students what letters they need to make the word. Have them push forward the letters to spell the word and then have them read the word.
- Ask students what letter they need to add to change the word ***can*** to ***cane***. Have students add a final ***e*** to the word ***can*** and read the new word.

Apply

- Have students repeat the process independently with the following words: ***tap, tape; rod, rode; not, note; cut, cute.***

Assessment Tip: Watch to make sure students select the correct letters and read the word. Note which students struggle with this activity, and provide reinforcement activities.

Sort Words: Long and Short Vowel Sounds

- Give students the following teacher word cards and have them sort the words according to their short and long vowel sounds: **can, cane, rip, ripe, shin, shine, tap, tape, cop, cope, cut, cute.** Have students explain why they grouped the words the way they did.

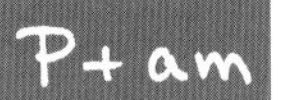

Blend Words with CVCe Patterns

Model

- Write the word ***blame*** on the board, using a different color for the rime ***-ame***. Point out that the word begins with a blend and ends with a CVCe pattern. Model sounding out the word, blending onset and rime: ***/bl/ /ame/***. Then say the whole word.

Guide

- Have students sound out the word with you. Repeat with other examples if you feel students need extra support.
- Give students blackline master 2. Have them use their fingers to frame the CVCe or rime part of the first word on the list for Day One. Then have students read the word by blending the onset and rime.

Apply

- Have students independently blend the remaining words on the list for Day One. Students who are able to read the words as a whole should do so.
- Note which students need more support in blending. Guide them as they read some or all of the words on the list by blending onset and rime before asking them to read the list independently.

Assessment Tip: Note which students are able to read the words without blending each sound.

Spelling Words: *crate, stroke, glide*

Model

- Make a two-column spelling chart on chart paper. Label the first column "One-Syllable Words" and the second column "Two-Syllable Words." Tell students that they will be spelling words with the CVCe syllable pattern. As you work through Unit Two, you can add the spelling words to the chart and have students use it to check their spelling of the words.
- Say the word ***crate*** and model spelling it and writing it on chart paper.
- **Think Aloud:** *I hear two parts in the word* **crate***: /***cr***/ and /***ā̄t***/. I know that the letters* **c** *and* **r** *stand for the blended sound /***cr***/. I will write these letters on the board. I hear long vowel /***ā***/ followed by /***t***/, so I will write the letters* **a** *and* **t***, which stand for these sounds. We are learning words with the CVCe pattern with a silent* **e** *at the end, so I will add the final* **e***. I will blend the onset and rime to check the spelling of the word: /***cr***/ /***āt***/,* **crate.**

Guide

- Say the word ***stroke***. Have students identify the onset and rime in the word and the letters that stand for the sounds. Write the word in the first column of the chart as students tell you the word parts.
- Repeat with the word ***glide***.

Apply

- Have students practice writing each of the words in their word study notebooks. After they write the word, have them check the spelling of the word by blending the onset and rime. Have students highlight the CVCe pattern in the words.

Our Spelling Words

One-Syllable Words	Two-Syllable Words
crate	reptile
stroke	naptime
glide	mistake
woke	
plate	
pride	

DAY 2

Teacher Tips

Reading Strategies

If students have difficulty applying strategies for challenging words, guide them to use the following strategies:

- look at how the words start and/or end
- look for familiar patterns or parts within the words
- separate the words into syllables and decode each part
- think about what familiar words look like the difficult words
- read forward to check the context
- reread the sentence or paragraph
- mark the words, substitute synonyms, and get on with reading–ask for help later

Comprehension

Use the following questions to ensure that students have understood the passage:

- *What did Jane want to make?* (Level 1–facts and details)
- *What did Jane do after she got home from the store?* (Level 2–sequence)
- *What will Jane and Rose probably do next?* (Level 3–make predictions)

Fluency

Intervene if students are having difficulty reading the passage. Model how to use word and meaning strategies to problem-solve the words. After students have had a chance to read the passage silently, have them read it aloud for fluency. Model fluent reading of the passage. For students who struggle, you may want to read the passage a second time and have them echo-read along with you.

P+ am Blend

- Have students blend the words on the word list for Day Two, using the procedure for blending from Day One.

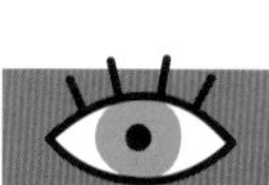

Develop Automaticity in Word Recognition

- Circle the following words on the overhead transparency: ***another, don't, kind, put, saw, sound***. Tell students that practicing these words will help them recognize the words automatically and make their reading more fluent.
- Read each word. Point out that ***don't*** is a contraction standing for ***do not.***
- Have students read aloud with you the sentences that contain the words and then write the words in their word study notebooks.
- Give students a copy of blackline master 7. Point out the words from this lesson, as well as other words they have learned previously. Have them cut out the words, store them in an envelope, and use them for practice activities.

Build Fluency with Connected Text

Model

- Read the passage on the overhead transparency aloud. Stop when you come to the word ***lime***. Model strategies to read the word.
- **Think Aloud:** *This word ends with a final* **e** *and has a CVCe pattern. I can use what I know about the pattern to read this word:* **lime**. *Hmmm, lime cake. You can make a lemon cake, so I guess you could make a lime cake too.*
- Continue reading. Model making a mistake and correcting it–for example, read ***crat*** instead of ***crate***.
- **Think Aloud:** *Whoops! I think something is wrong here. I said* **crat** *and that doesn't sound like a real word. Oh, I see. This word has the CVCe pattern, so the vowel sound is probably long. The word must be* **crate**. *A crate is a kind of box. Yes, that would make sense here.*

Guide

- Continue reading, stopping at other words and asking students what strategies they would use to read the words.

Apply

- Have students take turns reading blackline master 3 to a partner or in a small group as you monitor the reading. Use the teacher tips to check comprehension and fluency.

Spelling Words: *woke, plate, pride*

- Have students practice writing the spelling words from Day One in their word study notebooks.
- Introduce the Day Two spelling words. Say the word ***woke*** and model spelling it and writing it on the list of spelling words on chart paper. Point to the word ***stroke*** on the chart from the Day One spelling words, and highlight the word family. Model how to use the word family ***-oke*** to spell the new word and other words in the word family–for example: ***broke, spoke, poke.***
- Repeat with the remaining words, calling attention to the word families, and have students practice writing the words in their word study notebooks.

Multisyllabic Words: VCe Pattern

Model

- Write the word ***pole*** on the board and read it aloud. Point out that it has one syllable, one vowel sound, and a VCe pattern. Model blending the onset and rime: ***/p/ /ōl/, pole.***
- Write the word ***tadpole*** on the board. Explain to students that they can use what they know about vowel patterns and syllables to read longer words. Point out the silent final ***e***, and then tell students that there are two other vowels in the word. Circle the vowels ***a*** and ***o***.
- Ask students how many consonants they see between these two vowels. Explain that you will try dividing the word between the two consonants: ***tad/pole.*** Point out that the first syllable is a closed syllable, and the second syllable has a VCe pattern. Explain that you will try the long vowel sound first to see if that sounds right: ***/tad/ /pōl/, tadpole.***

Guide

- Repeat with the word ***explode***, this time guiding students to locate the consonants between the two vowels and divide the word.
- Then have them sound it out, using what they know about closed syllables and the VCe syllable pattern.

Apply

- Have students independently blend the two-syllable words on the word list for Day Three. Provide support if needed.

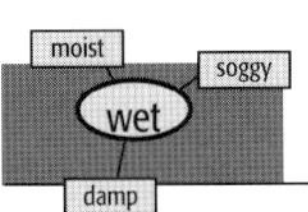

Develop Word Meanings

- Write the word ***strike*** on the board, read it, and tell students it has different meanings. Use the word in an oral sentence to demonstrate the meaning "to hit"—for example: *I will strike the nail with my hammer.*
- Model other meanings of the word by providing oral examples: *I can see the lightning strike the ground; Can you hear the clock strike midnight; The first pitch was a strike; Let's strike up the band and play some music.*
- Guide students to explain in their own words how the meanings of the words differ. Have them think of sentences that use the word.
- Have pairs of students choose one or more of the following words and write sentences illustrating the meanings of the word: ***race, shake, crane, date, rose, fire, mine, file.***

Spelling Words: *reptile, naptime, mistake*

- Have students practice spelling the words from Day One and Day Two by writing them several times in their word study notebooks.
- Introduce the new words, modeling how students can apply what they know about the VCe pattern to the spelling of words with more than one syllable.
- Write the word ***reptile*** on the board. Divide the word into syllables and use a different color to emphasize the first letter **e** and the ***i.***
- **Think Aloud:** *When I spell this word, I need to think about how the word looks. I hear two syllables. The first syllable is a closed syllable with short* **e**. *The second syllable has a long* **i** *sound. I must remember to write a final* **e** *at the end.*
- Repeat with the remaining words and then have students practice the words several times in their word study notebooks.

Build Fluency with Connected Text

- Have students read blackline master 4 to a partner or in a small group as you monitor their reading. Call attention to the following words in the reading passage before students read it: ***eat, it's, might, should.***

Teacher Tips

Word Meanings

If you give each pair or group of students a transparency, they can create their word webs on this and use the overhead projector to "teach" their words to the class.

Develop Automaticity in Word Recognition

Have students work with a partner to flash high-frequency words for each other.

Repeated Reading

Have students practice repeated readings of blackline master 3 to develop fluency.

DAY 4

Teacher Tips

Develop Automaticity in Word Recognition

Have students search the reading passages on blackline masters 4 and 5 for high-frequency words. Instruct students to circle the words they find. Encourage students to read the sentences that contain the high-frequency words.

Repeated Reading

Have students practice repeated readings of blackline master 3 to develop fluency.

Blend

- Have students blend the words on the list for Day Four, using the procedure for blending from Day One.

Sort: Word Families

- Use the following teacher word cards: **cane, plane, crane, gripe, ripe, shine, spine, tape, grape, cope, slope, hope, cube, cute, flute.** To begin, select the following word cards and place them in a pocket chart: **cope, hope; cane, plane; shine, spine.** Read the first two words and point out that they have the VCe pattern. Ask students what else they notice about the words. Once students have recognized that the two words are from the word family ***-ope***, have them brainstorm other words in this word family.
- Have students look at the remaining words in the pocket chart and tell you what other word families they recognize.
- Have students read the rest of the words with you, blending the onset and rime in each word.
- Give the above word cards to students. As a group, have students sort the words according to their vowel sounds.
- Have students sort the words according to their word families and list them by word family in their word study notebooks. Then have them write an explanation for why they grouped the words the way they did.

Spelling Words

- Provide practice for students in segmenting words and associating sounds with spellings. Dictate the following words to students and have them write the words on their papers: ***class, sun, classmate, sunshine***. Remind students to use what they have learned about spelling the VCe pattern.
- Write the words on the board and have students self-correct their papers.
- Dictate the following sentence and have students write it on their papers: *Jane likes the tadpole that her classmate put in the wide vase.*
- Write the sentence on the board and have students self-correct their papers.
- Give pairs of students blackline master 6. While one student reads the spelling words, the other student writes them in the "First Try" column. After the student has spelled the words, the partner places a check mark next to words spelled correctly. For the second try, the partner may prompt the student by sounding out the words that were spelled incorrectly the first time. If the second spelling attempt is correct, the partner places a check mark in the "Second Try" column.

Assessment Tip: Use students' completed peer-check blackline masters to note which words gave students difficulty.

Build Fluency with Connected Text

- Have students take turns reading blackline master 5 to a partner or in a small group as you monitor their reading. Call attention to the following words in the reading passage before students read it: ***always, eye(s), open, see, something.***
- Have students who need extra support practice reading the passage aloud in a small group as you monitor their reading.

Spelling Assessment

Use the following procedure to assess students' spelling of Unit Two words.
- Say each spelling word and use it in a sentence.
- Have students write the words on their papers.
- Continue with the next word on the list.
- When students have finished, collect their papers and analyze their spelling of the words.
- Use the assessment to plan small group or individual practice.

Small Group/Independent Activities

The following activities can be used to provide practice for students who need additional support.

PHONICS AND WORD STRATEGIES

Review Closed-Syllable Patterns Write the word ***nap*** on the board and ask students to identify the vowel. Have them tell why this word is a closed syllable. (one vowel; ends with consonant) Write the word ***napkin*** on the board. Circle the vowels and then point out the two consonants between them. Divide the word and have students identify the syllable patterns. Then blend the word.

Match the Words Have pairs or small groups of students combine sets of the student word cards (on blackline masters 8 and 9) so they have a pair for each word. Have students mix up the word cards and spread them facedown on the floor. Have them take turns turning over two cards and reading the words. If the words match, the student can keep the cards.

DEVELOP AUTOMATICITY IN WORD RECOGNITION

Word Flash Have pairs of students flash the high-frequency word cards for their partners to read.

Story Words Have students sit in a circle and place the high-frequency word cards facedown in a pile in the center. Going around the circle, have students take turns drawing a card. The first student to draw a card begins a story and uses the word. Once the word has been used, the student stops, and the next student draws a card and continues the story, using the new word. Students continue until all of the words have been used.

Make Sentences Place the high-frequency word cards in a paper bag. Have students work with a partner to draw a word card, read it, and use the word in an oral sentence.

BUILD FLUENCY WITH CONNECTED TEXT

Repeated Reading Have students practice reading blackline master 3 several times, until they feel they can read it fluently and accurately. Have them work with a partner to time each other as they read the passage aloud. Have them set a goal of reading ninety words per minute.

SPELLING

Make Words Provide a set of letter cards and the week's spelling words on index cards. Have students use the letter cards to spell the words. They should check their spelling by blending the sounds and then looking at the words on the index cards.

Spell and Write Have students write a sentence for each spelling word in their word study notebooks. Have them give their sentences to a partner to read and check.

Teacher Tips

Home Connection

Have students take blackline master 11 home to complete with a family member. Students can also take the reading passage on blackline master 3 home to share with their family.

Quick-Check

Assess students' mastery of CVCe syllable patterns using the quick-check for Unit Two in this Teacher Resource System.

ELL Support Tip

Ask students to act out the verbs with the VCe pattern in a game of charades. Have ELL students pair up with native English speakers, and give each pair one of the verbs written on a card. Allow time for practice before pairs perform for the class. Once the class guesses the word, write it on the board and label the VCe pattern.

UNIT 2 Quick-Check: CVCe syllable patterns

Student Name ______________________ Assessment Date ____________

Segmenting and Blending

Directions: Explain that these words use sounds the student has been learning. Have the student point to each word on the corresponding student sheet, segment the word parts or syllables, and blend them together. Put a ✔ if the student successfully segments and blends the word or reads it as a complete unit. If the student misses the word, record the error.
Example: shone

cute		handshake		
stripe		explode		
plane		sunrise		
froze		nickname		Score **/8**

Sight Words

Directions: Have the student point to the first word on the corresponding student sheet and read across the line, saying each word as quickly as possible. Put a ✔ if the student successfully reads the word and an **X** if the student hesitates more than a few seconds. If the student misses the word, record the error.

sound		very		have		again		
great		kind		another		put		
don't		saw		to		one		
want		that		said		you		Score **/16**

Unit Objectives

Students will:

- Recognize and read open-syllable words in print
- Review VCe syllable patterns
- Blend onset and rime
- Sort words according to their word families and vowel patterns
- Read high-frequency words because, done, don't, know, once, together
- Spell one- and two-syllable words with open-syllable patterns: cry, go, she, fly, we, so, baby, robot, tidy
- Identify pronouns and the words they refer to

Day 1

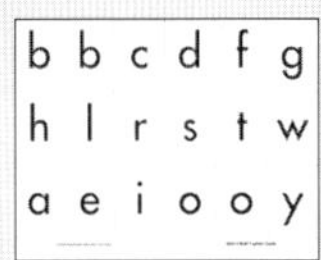

Letter Cards:
b, d, e, g, h, o, r, s, y

Word Lists (BLM 2)

be

Teacher Word Cards:
be, bed, go, got, he, hen, hot, no, not, she, so, we, wet

Day 2

Word Lists (BLM 2)

Reading Passage 1 (BLM 3)

High-Frequency Word Cards for Unit 3 (BLM 7)

Day 3

Word Lists (BLM 2)

Reading Passages 1 & 2 (BLMs 3 & 4)

High-Frequency Word Cards for Unit 3 (BLM 7)

Day 4

Word Lists (BLM 2)

Reading Passages 1 & 3 (BLMs 3 & 5)

funny

Teacher Word Cards:
funny, gravy, happy, iris, program, shady, shaky, shiny, robot, siren, total

because even don't large done saw know sound once soon together watch another eat early food

High-Frequency Word Cards for Unit 3 (BLM 7)

Spelling Peer Check (BLM 6)

Day 5

shaky label shady hazy robot crazy total bacon program raven siren focus silent open iris lilac

Student Word Cards (BLM 9)

Reading Passage 1 (BLM 3)

High-Frequency Word Cards for Unit 3 (BLM 7)

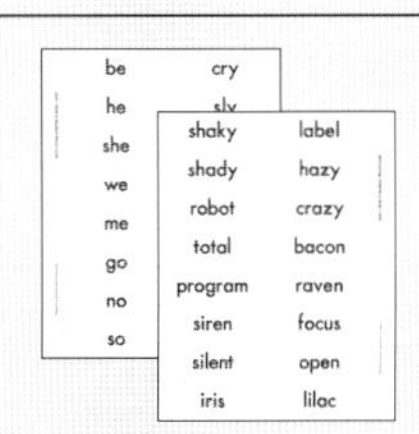

Student Word Cards (BLMs 8 & 9)

Quick-Check Student Sheet

Letter Cards for Unit 3

Frieze Card

Take-Home Activity

Core Materials

All of these materials can be downloaded from http://phonicsresources.benchmarkeducation.com.

UNIT 3 Open-syllable patterns

Introduce Open-Syllable Patterns

Frieze Card

Model

- Hold up the open-syllable frieze card and have students name each object and read the words. Ask students whether the vowels in the words are long or short, and how many vowel sounds they hear in each word.
- Tell students that every syllable in a word has only one vowel sound, so these are one-syllable words.
- Explain that these are examples of words that have open-syllable patterns because open syllables end with a vowel. Explain that these syllables often have a long vowel sound.

Guide

- Give students letter cards **b, d, g, h, r, s, e, o,** and **y,** and have them line up the letters in a row in front of them.
- Say the word ***be*** and ask students what two letters they need to make the word. Have them push the letters forward as they say the sounds. Have them read the word. Point out that the word is an open syllable.
- Have students take away the letter ***b*** and ask what letters they need to replace it with to make the word ***he***. Have them make the word and read it. Ask them if the new word is an open-syllable word.

Apply

- Repeat the steps with the following words: ***shy, dry; go, so***.

Assessment Tip: Watch to make sure students select the correct letters and read the word. Note which students struggle with this activity, and provide reinforcement activities.

Sort Words: Vowel Sounds

- Place the following teacher word cards in a pocket chart: **bed, hen, wet, got, not, hot, be, he, she, we, go, no, so.** Place the cards **bed** and **be** next to each other and separately from the other words. Ask students to tell you what is different about the two words.
- Have students tell you which words to sort under ***bed*** and which words under ***be***.
- Have students copy the words in groups in their word study notebook and explain why they grouped the words the way they did.

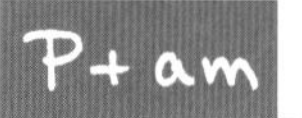

Blend Open-Syllable Words

Model

- Write the word ***try*** on the chalkboard. Point out that the word begins with a blend and that the word has an open syllable. Explain that the letter ***y*** at the end of a word can stand for the long ***i*** sound or the long ***e*** sound.
- Model sounding out the word, blending the onset and rime: ***/tr/ /ī/.*** Then say the whole word.

Guide

- Have students sound out the word with you. Repeat with other examples if you feel students need extra support.
- Give students blackline master 2. Have them read the words on the list for Day One by blending the onset and rime.

Apply

- Have students independently sound out the remaining words on the word list for Day One. Students who are able to read the words without blending each sound should do so.
- For students who need more support in blending, guide them as they read some or all of the words on the list before asking them to read the list independently.

Assessment Tip: Note which students are able to read the words without blending each sound.

Spelling Words: *cry, go, she*

Model

- Make a two-column chart on chart paper. Label the first column "One-Syllable Words" and the second column "Two-Syllable Words." Tell students that they will be spelling words with open-syllable patterns. As you work through Unit Three, you can add the spelling words to the chart and have students use the chart to check their spelling of the words.
- Say the word ***cry*** and model spelling it and writing it on the chart.
- **Think Aloud:** *I hear two parts in the word* **cry:** */***cr***/ and /* **ī** */. I know that the letters* **c** *and* **r** *stand for the blended sound /***cr***/. I know that the letter* **i** *stands for the /* **ī** */ sound, but I also know that the letter* **y** *at the end of a word also can stand for this sound. I will write the letter* **y** *next to the blend. Then I will blend the onset and rime to check the spelling of the word: /***cr***/ /* **ī** */,* **cry**. *Now that I know how to spell* **cry,** *I can also spell other words from this word family, such as* **try**, **fly**, *and* **why**.

Guide

- Say the word ***go.*** Have students identify the sounds in the word and the letters that stand for the sounds. Write the word in the first column of the chart as students tell you the word parts. Repeat with the word ***she.***

Apply

- Have students practice writing each of the words in their word study notebooks. After they write a word, have them check the spelling of the word by blending the onset and rime. Have students underline the vowels in the open syllable patterns.

Our Spelling Words

One-Syllable Words	Two-Syllable Words
cry go she fly we so	baby robot tidy

DAY 2

Teacher Tips

Reading Strategies

If students have difficulty applying strategies for challenging words, guide them to use the following strategies:

- look at how the words start and/or end
- look for familiar patterns or parts within the words
- separate the words into syllables and decode each part
- think about what familiar words look like the difficult words
- read forward to check the context
- reread the sentence or paragraph
- mark the words, substitute synonyms, and get on with reading–ask for help later

Comprehension

Use the following questions to ensure that students have understood the passage:

- *What kind of kite did Jo and Jill make?* (Level 1–facts and details)
- *Why did Chuck and Rick think Jill couldn't be in the contest?* (Level 2–cause and effect)
- *Who won the contest?* (Level 3–make inferences)

Fluency

Intervene if students are having difficulty reading the passage. Model how to use word and meaning strategies to problem-solve the words. After students have had a chance to read the passage silently, have them read it aloud for fluency. Model fluent reading of the passage. For students who struggle, you may want to read the passage a second time and have them echo-read along with you.

P+am Blend

- Have students blend the words in the list for Day Two, using the procedure for blending from Day One.

Develop Automaticity in Word Recognition

- Circle the following words on the overhead transparency: ***because, done, don't, know, once, together***. Tell students that practicing these words will help them recognize the words automatically so they can read more fluently.
- Read each word and point out that we don't hear the ***k*** in ***know***.
- Have students read aloud with you the sentences containing the words. Then have them write the words in their word study notebooks.
- Give students a copy of blackline master 7. Point out the words from this lesson, as well as other words they have previously learned. Have them cut out the words, store them in an envelope, and use them for practice activities.

Build Fluency with Connected Text

Model

- Read the passage on the overhead transparency aloud. Stop when you come to the word ***contest***. Model strategies to read it.
- **Think Aloud:** *It was easy for me to read this word because I recognized the two syllables in the word:* **con** *and* **test.** *I knew both were closed syllables so I tried the short vowel sounds for* **o** *and* **e.**
- Continue reading and stop at the word ***pro.***
- **Think Aloud:** *I know this word is an open syllable, so I can pronounce it:* **/prō/**. *I need to think about the meaning of the word in the sentence. I think Jo is saying she's good at making kites, so I think the word means someone who is very good at doing something.*
- Model making a mistake and correcting it–for example, read **/dōn/** instead of ***done.***
- **Think Aloud:** *What I read doesn't make sense. I saw the CVCe pattern and so I tried the long vowel sound. In this word, the rule doesn't apply. This is one of our high-frequency words. When I read the whole sentence, I know the word is* **done.**

Guide

- Continue reading and stop at other words in the passage. Guide students to read the words.

Apply

- Have students take turns reading blackline master 3 to a partner or in a small group as you monitor the reading. Use teacher tips to check comprehension and fluency.

Spelling Words: *fly, we, so*

- Have students practice writing the words from Day One in their word study notebooks. Have them refer to words on the spelling chart to check their spelling.
- Introduce the Day Two spelling words. Say the word ***fly*** and model spelling it and writing it on the chart of spelling words. Point to the word ***cry*** on the chart from the Day One spelling words and highlight how the words are similar. Model how to use ***cry*** to spell the new word and other words in the word family–for example: ***try, my, spy.***
- Repeat with the remaining words from Day Two and have students practice writing the words in their word study notebooks.

DAY 3

Multisyllabic Words: Open-Syllable Patterns

Model

- Say the word ***we*** and have students clap the syllables.
- Write the word ***we*** on the board and point out that it has one open syllable and one vowel sound.
- Say the word polite and have students clap the syllables.
- Write the word ***polite*** on the board. Show students how to use what they know about vowel patterns and syllables to read longer words.
- Point out the final silent ***e*** in the word and circle the two remaining vowels. Point out the single consonant between the vowels ***o*** and ***i***. Explain that when there is one consonant, they should first try dividing the word before the consonant: ***po/lite***.
- Point out the open syllable and the syllable with a VCe pattern. Tell students to first try the long vowel sounds in the open and VCe syllables and see if the word sounds right: ***/pō/ /līt/ polite.***

Guide

- Write the word ***label*** on the board and guide students to identify the two vowels and the number of consonants between the vowels.
- Guide students as they divide the word: ***la/bel***. Ask what syllable patterns they see and what clues this gives them about the vowel sounds in each syllable.

Apply

- Have students independently blend the two-syllable words on the word list for Day Three. If students need more support, guide them as they blend some or all of the words.

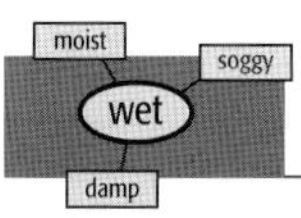

Develop Word Meanings

- Circle the pronouns ***you*** and ***I*** in paragraph two on the overhead transparency.
- **Think Aloud:** *Jo is talking to Jill in this sentence and she refers to herself as* **I**. *The pronoun* **I** *stands for the word* **Jo.** *When Jo says* **you**, *she is referring to Jill, and* **you** *stands for the word* **Jill.**
- Have students find and circle other pronouns in the passage. Ask what each pronoun stands for.

Spelling Words: *baby, robot, tidy*

- Have students practice spelling the words from Day One and Day Two by writing them several times in their word study notebooks.
- Introduce the new words, modeling how students can apply what they know about syllables to the spelling of words with more than one syllable.
- Say the word ***baby***.
- **Think Aloud:** *When I spell this word, I need to think about how it looks. I hear two syllables that both end with long vowel sounds: /ā/ and /ē/. I remember that the letter* **y** *stands for the long* **e** *sound at the end of a word. I will write the word and see if it looks right.*
- Repeat with the remaining words. As you introduce the word ***robot***, remind students that the closed syllable has a short vowel sound.
- Have students practice the words several times in their word study notebooks.

Build Fluency with Connected Text

- Have students read blackline master 4 to a partner or in small groups as you monitor their reading. call attention to the following words in the reading passage before students read it: ***learn, need, people, want.***

Teacher Tips

Exceptions to the Rule

If you feel your students are ready to work with exceptions to the open syllable rule, write the word ***alone*** on the board. Model how to apply the rule for dividing the word: ***a/lone***. Tell students that the letter ***a*** in this word does not stand for the long ***a*** sound, but the sound ***/u/***. Remind them that when they sound out words, they should also be thinking about what would make sense in the sentence. Using syllabication strategies will help them get close to the pronunciation of the word, which is often enough to help them recognize what the word is.

Challenge

For students who are ready for more of a challenge, have them apply what they know about open and closed syllables to read the word ***dragonfly: dra/gon/fly; dissatisfy: dis/sat/is/fy.***

Develop Automaticity in Word Recognition

Have students place their high-frequency word cards in alphabetical order, read them, and then copy them in their word study notebooks.

Repeated Reading

Have students practice repeated reading of blackline master 3 to develop fluency.

DAY 4

Teacher Tips

Develop Automaticity in Word Recognition

Have pairs of students combine their high-frequency word cards and spread them facedown on the table or floor to play concentration. Have them take turns turning over two words and reading them. If the words make a pair, the student gets another turn. If not, the student turns the cards back over and his/her partner takes a turn.

Repeated Reading

Have students practice repeated reading of blackline master 3 to develop fluency.

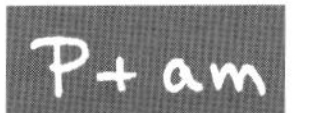

Blend

- Have students blend the words in the list for Day Four, using the procedure for blending from Day One.

Sort Words: Vowel Patterns

- Place the following teacher word cards in a pocket chart: **funny, happy, gravy, shiny, shaky, shady, robot, total, program, siren, iris**. Have students read each word with you.
- Make a three-column chart on chart paper with the following headings: "Closed/Open," "Open/Closed," "Open/Open." Place the chart on a table or on the floor. Give the word cards to students and have them sort the words according to their syllable patterns. Have students write an explanation in their word study notebooks for why they grouped the words the way they did.

Closed/Open	Open/Closed	Open/Open
funny happy	robot program total siren iris	gravy shiny shaky shady

Spelling Words

- Provide practice for students in segmenting words and associating sounds with spellings. Dictate the following words to students and have them write the words on their papers: ***sly, pro, relax, pupil***. Remind students to use what they have learned about spelling closed- and open-syllable words.
- Write the words on the board and have students self-correct their papers.
- Dictate the following sentence and have students write it on their papers: *We are not crazy about bagels.*
- Write the sentence on the board and have students self-correct their papers.
- Give pairs of students blackline master 6. While one student reads the spelling words, the other student writes them in the "First Try" column. After the student has spelled the words, the partner places a check mark next to words spelled correctly. For the second try, the partner may prompt the student by sounding out the words that were spelled incorrectly the first time. If the second spelling attempt is correct, the partner places a check mark in the "Second Try" column.

Assessment Tip: Use students' completed peer-check blackline masters to note which words gave students difficulty.

Build Fluency with Connected Text

- Have students take turns reading blackline master 5 to a partner or in a small group as you monitor their reading. Call attention to the following words in the reading passage before students read it: ***close, it's, let, open, put, side.***

Spelling Assessment

Use the following procedure to assess students' spelling of the Unit Three words.
- Say each spelling word and use it in a sentence.
- Have students write the words on their papers.
- Continue with the next word on the list.
- When students have finished, collect their papers and analyze their spelling of the words.
- Use the assessment to plan small group or individual practice.

Small Group/Independent Activities

The following activities can be used to provide practice for students who need additional support.

PHONICS AND WORD STRATEGIES

Review VCe Syllable Pattern Write the word ***bike*** on the board and ask students to tell you how many vowels they see. Ask them what the word ends with and how many consonants they see between the first vowel and the final ***e***. Have students read the words and ask them what happens to the final ***e***. Tell them that words that end in a vowel, consonant, and final ***e*** are called VCe syllables.

Open Sort Have partners think of different ways they can sort the word cards on blackline masters 8 and 9. Have them show their sort to another pair of students and ask these students to figure out how the words are sorted.

Sort Words Write the following words on the board in random order: ***hen, he, got, go, sod, so, went, we, met, me, shed, she, not, no, prod, pro, ski, skid.*** Have students make a T-chart in their word study notebooks and sort the words by long and short sounds. Have them write an explanation for how they sort the words.

AUTOMATICITY IN WORD RECOGNITION

Read the Word Have students use all of the words on blackline master 7 and a standard game board. Have them roll dice to find out how many spaces they can move. Then have them draw a card. If they read the word correctly, they can move ahead the number of spaces on the dice. If not, they must stay where they are.

Write a Paragraph Have students write one or two paragraphs using as many of the words on blackline master 7 as they can. Then have them exchange paragraphs with a partner and find and underline the high-frequency words in their partner's paragraph.

BUILD FLUENCY WITH CONNECTED TEXT

Repeated Reading Have students practice reading blackline master 3 several times, until they feel they can read it fluently and accurately. Have them work with a partner to time each other as they read the passage orally. Have them set a goal of reading ninety words per minute.

SPELLING

Make Words Provide a set of letter cards and the week's spelling words on index cards. Have students use the letter cards to spell the words. They should check their spelling by blending the sounds and then looking at the words on the index cards.

Around the Circle Have students sit in a circle. Say a spelling word and have a student say the first letter in the word. Have the next student say the next letter, and so on, until the word is spelled. Have the student who says the last letter write the word on the board.

Teacher Tips

Home Connection

Have students take blackline master 11 home to complete with a family member. Students can also take the reading passage on blackline master 3 home to share with their family.

Quick-Check

Assess students' mastery of open-syllable patterns using the quick-check for Unit Three in this Teacher Resource System.

ELL Support Tip

To help students make connections to the meanings of words, draw visuals on word cards to support the words. As you select words for the open-syllable pattern, try to select words for ELL students that they can use in their everyday speech. This will help them understand the concepts, build oral language, and transfer the concepts to their reading and writing.

Quick-Check: Open-syllable patterns

Student Name ______________________ Assessment Date __________

Segmenting and Blending

Directions: Explain that these words use sounds the student has been learning. Have the student point to each word on the corresponding student sheet, segment the word parts or syllables, and blend them together. Put a ✓ if the student successfully segments and blends the word or reads it as a complete unit. If the student misses the word, record the error. **Example:** shy

soda		wavy			
zero		silo			
pony		ply			
spry		whiny		Score	**/8**

Sight Words

Directions: Have the student point to the first word on the corresponding student sheet and read across the line, saying each word as quickly as possible. Put a ✓ if the student successfully reads the word and an **X** if the student hesitates more than a few seconds. If the student misses the word, record the error.

because		done			
once		another			
even		saw			
soon		eat			
don't		know			
together		early			
large		sound			
watch		food		Score	**/16**

UNIT 4 Long a digraph syllable patterns

Unit Objectives

Students will:

- Read words with long a digraphs
- Review open-syllable patterns
- Blend onset and rime
- Sort words according to long a digraphs and word families
- Read high-frequency words: along, both, idea, off, together, went, walk
- Spell one- and two-syllable words with long a digraphs: train, stay, eight, sprain, tray, freight, complain, obey, raisin.
- Recognize homophones and understand their meanings in context

Day 1

b c f g h l
m n p r s t
a e i i o y

Letter Cards:
a, b, e, g, h, i, l, m, n, p, r, s, t, y

Word Lists
(BLM 2)

bake

Teacher Word Cards:
bake, bat, braid, mad, made, maid, pain, pan, pane, plain, plan, plane

Day 2

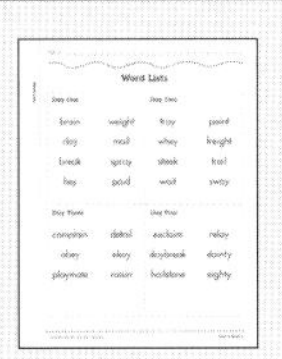

Word Lists
(BLM 2)

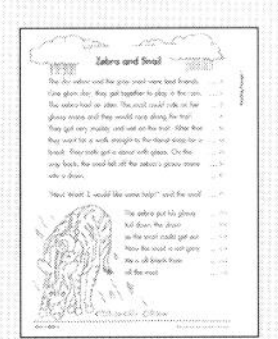

Reading Passage 1
(BLM 3)

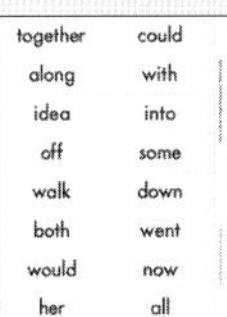

High-Frequency Word Cards for Unit 4 (BLM 7)

Day 3

Word Lists
(BLM 2)

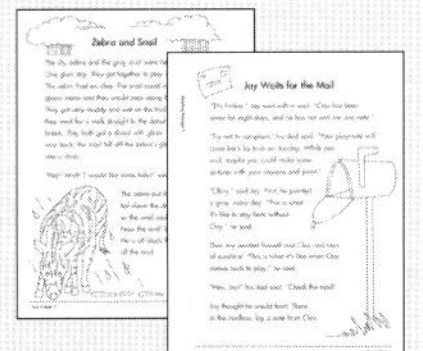

Reading Passages 1 & 2
(BLMs 3 & 4)

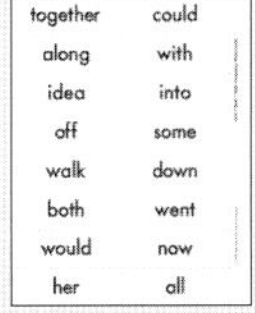

High-Frequency Word Cards for Unit 4 (BLM 7)

Day 4

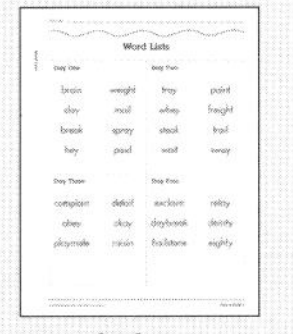

Word Lists
(BLM 2)

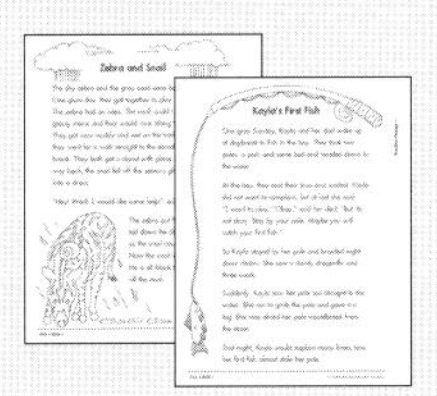

Reading Passages 1 & 3
(BLMs 3 & 5)

fray

Teacher Word Cards
fray, great, jail, nail, paint, pay, quaint, rail, say, tray

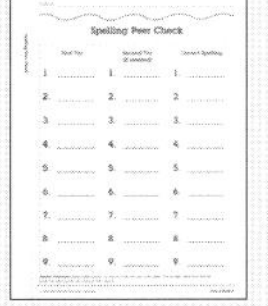

Spelling Peer Check
(BLM 6)

nail Friday
pay straighten
great contain
quail payment
they relay
jail subway
tray explain
weight detail

Student Word Cards (BLM 9)

together could
along with
idea into
off some
walk down
both went
would now
her all

High-Frequency Word Cards for Unit 4 (BLM 7)

Day 5

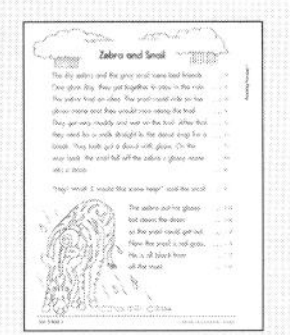

Reading Passage 1
(BLM 3)

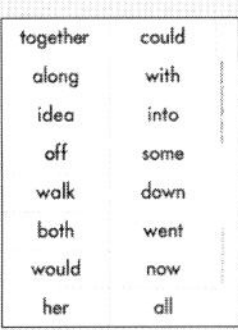

High-Frequency Word Cards for Unit 4 (BLM 7)

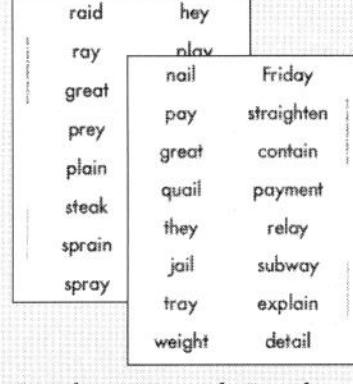

Student Word Cards
(BLMs 8 & 9)

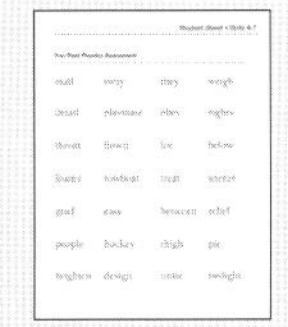

Quick-Check Student Sheet

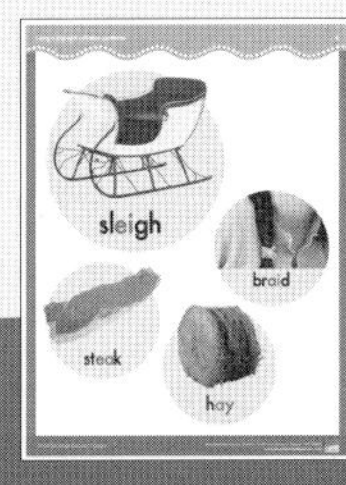

Frieze Card

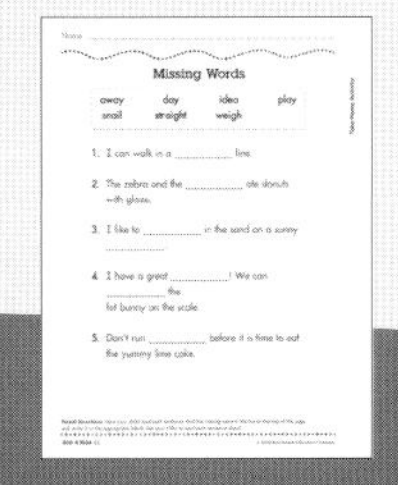

Take-Home Activity

Core Materials

All of these materials can be downloaded from http://phonicsresources.benchmarkeducation.com.

UNIT 4 Long a digraph syllable patterns

1 Syllable Introduce Long *a* Digraph Syllable Pattern

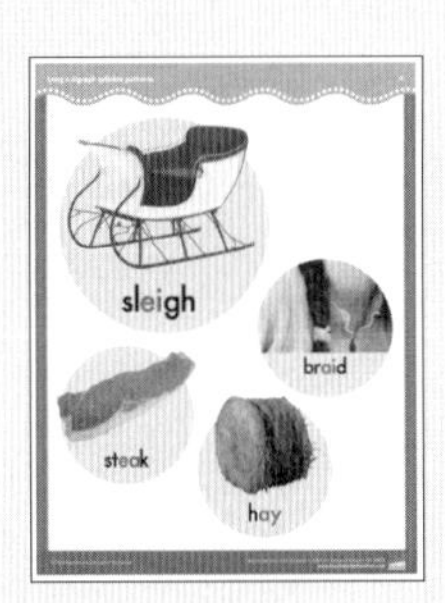

Frieze Card

Model

- Hold up the long ***a*** digraph frieze card and read the words. Point out the vowel digraphs and explain that although there are two vowels, there is only one vowel sound so the word has one syllable. Tell students that the digraph is not separated when dividing words into syllables.
- Point out that the ***gh*** in ***sleigh*** is silent.
- Write the word ***they*** on the board. Circle the ***ey*** pattern and explain that this is another example of a long ***a*** digraph.

Guide

- Give students letter cards **b, g, h, l, m, n, p, r, s, t, a, e, i,** and **y**, and have them line up the letters in a row in front of them.
- Say the word ***rain*** and ask students what letters they need to make the word. Remind them that they need two letters to stand for the **/ā/** sound. Have them choose from the spelling patterns on the frieze card. Have them push forward the letters to spell the word. If the word doesn't look right, have them try another spelling pattern.
- Have students replace the letter at the beginning to change the word from ***rain*** to ***plain***.
- Repeat with the words ***hey*** and ***they***, but point out that although these words have the long ***a*** vowel sound, they use different letters to stand for the sound.

Apply

- Have students repeat the process independently with the following pairs of words: ***main, grain; bay, ray***.

Assessment Tip: Watch to make sure students select the correct letters and say the correct sounds. Note which students struggle with this activity, and provide reinforcement activities.

Sort Words: Long and Short Vowels

- Place teacher word cards **pan, pain,** and **pane** in the pocket chart and read the words. Hold up the word card **bake** and model sorting the word.
- **Think Aloud: Pan/bake.** *No, they don't have the same vowel sound.* **Pain/bake.** *Yes, they have the same vowel sound but they don't have the same vowel pattern.* **Pane/Bake.** *Yes, they have the same vowel sound and the same vowel pattern. The word* **pane** *goes with* **bake.**
- Repeat with the following words, selecting them in random order. This time have students tell you where to place the word cards **bat, braid, plan, plane, plain, mad, maid,** and **made.**
- When the words are sorted, have students tell what the words in each column have in common.

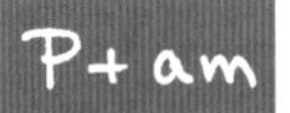

Blend Words with Long *a* Digraph

Model

- Write the word ***weight*** on the board, using a different color for the rime ***-eight***. Model sounding out the word, blending onset and rime: **/w/ /āt/**. Then say the whole word. Point out that the letters ***gh*** in the word are silent.

Guide

- Have students sound out the word with you. Repeat with other examples if you feel students need extra support.
- Give students blackline master 2. Have them read the words by blending the onset and rime.

Apply

- Have students independently read the remaining words on the word list for Day One. Guide students who need support to blend some or all of the words before reading them independently.

Assessment Tip: Note which students are able to read the words without blending each sound.

Spelling Words: *train, stay, eight*

Model

- Make a two-column spelling chart on chart paper. Label the first column "One-Syllable Words" and the second column "Two-Syllable Words." Tell students that they will be spelling words with long ***a*** digraphs. As you work through the unit, you can continue to add the spelling words to the chart and have students use the chart to check their spelling.
- Say ***train*** and model spelling and writing it on the chart.
- **Think Aloud:** *I hear two parts in the word* **train:** */***tr***/ and /***ān***/. I know that the letters* **t** *and* **r** *stand for the blended sound /***tr***/. I will write these letters on the board. I hear the long vowel sound /***ā***/ followed by /***n***/. I know there are several digraphs that can stand for the /***ā***/ sound. I will try* **ai** *and see if the word looks right.*

Guide

- Say the word ***stay***. Have students identify the onset and rime in the word and the letters that stand for the sounds. Remind students that the long ***a*** sound can be spelled in different ways and guide them to use the digraph ***ay***. Write the word in the first column of the chart as students tell you the word parts.
- Repeat with the word ***eight***.

Apply

- Have students practice writing each of the words in their word study notebooks. After they write the word, have them check the spelling of the word by blending the onset and rime. Have students highlight the vowel digraphs in the words.

Our Spelling Words

One-Syllable Words	Two-Syllable Words
train stay eight sprain tray freight	complain obey raisin

DAY 2

Blend

- Have students blend the words on the word list for Day Two, using the procedure for blending from Day One.

Develop Automaticity in Word Recognition

- Circle the following words on the overhead transparency: ***along, both, idea, off, together, went, walk.*** Tell students that practicing these words will help them recognize the words automatically so they can read more fluently.
- Read each word. Point out that ***together*** and ***idea*** each have three vowel sounds and three syllables.
- Have students read aloud with you the sentences in which the words are found, and then write the words in their word study notebooks.
- Give students a copy of blackline master 7. Point out the words from this lesson, as well as other words they have learned previously. Have them cut out the words, store them in an envelope, and use them for practice activities.

Build Fluency with Connected Text

Model

- Read the passage on the overhead transparency aloud. Stop when you come to the word ***gray***. Model strategies you would use to read the word.
- **Think Aloud:** *I see this word ends with the long* **a** *digraph,* **ay**, *like the word* **play** *in the next sentence. I can use what I know about the word pattern to read this word:* **gray**. *A gray snail. That makes sense. The snails I've seen in my yard are gray.*
- Continue reading. Model making a mistake and correcting it–for example, read ***street*** instead of ***straight***.
- **Think Aloud:** *This doesn't make sense. Let me look at the word again. Oh, I see. It has a long* **a** *digraph, not long* **e** *digraph. This is a tricky word. The tricky part is that, like in the word* **sleigh** *on the frieze card, the* **gh** *is silent. The word is* **straight** *Yes, that makes sense here.*

Guide

- Continue reading, stopping at other words and asking students what strategies they would use to read the words.

Apply

- Have students take turns reading blackline master 3 to a partner or in a small group as you monitor the reading. Use the teacher tips to check comprehension and fluency.

Spelling Words: *sprain, tray, freight*

- Have students practice writing the spelling words from Day One in their word study notebooks. Have them refer to words on the spelling chart to check their spelling.
- Introduce the Day Two spelling words. Say the word ***tray*** and model spelling it and writing it on the spelling words chart. Point to the word ***stay*** on the chart from the Day One spelling words, and model how to use the word family ***-ay*** to spell the new word and other words in the word family such as ***play, gray,*** and ***stray***.
- Repeat with the remaining words and have students practice writing the words in their word study notebooks.

Teacher Tips

Reading Strategies

If students have difficulty applying strategies for challenging words, guide them to use the following strategies:

- look at how the words start and/or end
- look for familiar patterns or parts within the words
- separate the words into syllables and decode each part
- think about what familiar words look like the difficult words
- read forward to check the context
- reread the sentence or paragraph
- mark the words, substitute synonyms, and get on with reading–ask for help later

Comprehension

Use the following questions to ensure that students have understood the passage:

- *What kind of day was it?* (Level 1–facts and details)
- *Why is the snail all black?* (Level 2–cause/effect)
- *How did the zebra help the snail?* (Level 3–analyze character)

Fluency

Intervene if students are having difficulty reading the passage. Model how to use word and meaning strategies to problem-solve the words. After students have had a chance to read the passage silently, have them read it aloud for fluency. Model fluent reading of the passage. For students who struggle, you may want to read the passage a second time and have them echo-read along with you.

Multisyllabic Words: Long *a* Digraphs

Model

- Write the word ***day*** on the board and point out that it has one open syllable and one vowel sound.
- Write the word ***Sunday*** on the board. Circle the vowels ***u*** and ***ay***, pointing out that the digraph ***ay*** stands for one vowel sound. Explain that you will divide the word between the two consonants that are between the vowels: ***Sun/day***.
- Point out that the first syllable is a closed syllable, with a short vowel sound. Model reading the word: **/sun/ /dā/, *Sunday***.

Guide

- Write the word ***explain*** on the board and guide students as they identify the long ***a*** digraph and the initial vowel.
- Point out that there are three consonants between the vowels, and because ***pl*** is a blend, you will divide the word between the ***x*** and the ***p: ex/plain***. Have students sound it out, using what they know about closed syllables and long ***a*** digraphs.

Apply

- Have students independently blend the two-syllable words on the word list for Day Three. Provide support if needed.

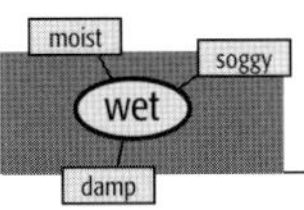

Develop Word Meanings

- Write the words ***way*** and ***weigh*** on the board and read them. Tell students the words are homophones, which means they sound the same but have different meanings and spellings. Explain the meaning of each word.
- Write the words ***hey, wait, break,*** and ***pray*** on the board. Have students read the words with you and then use the words in oral sentences. Challenge them to think of homophones for the words.
- Have students work with a partner to read the passage on blackline master 3 and see how many words in the passage have homophones. (***wait, break, mane, tail, way, so, one, to, for***)

Spelling Words: *complain, obey, raisin*

- Have students practice spelling the words from Day One and Day Two by writing them several times in their word study notebooks.
- Introduce the new words, modeling how students can apply what they know about long ***a*** digraph words to the spelling of words with more than one syllable.
- Say the word ***complain***.
- **Think Aloud:** *When I spell this word, I need to think about how the word looks. I hear two syllables. The first syllable is a closed syllable that has a short* **o** *sound and ends with /***m***/. The second syllable has a long* **a** *sound. I will look at the long* **a** *digraph patterns on the frieze card. I will try* **ai** *and see if the word looks right.*
- Repeat with the remaining words and then have students practice spelling the words several times in their word study notebooks.

Build Fluency with Connected Text

- Have students read blackline master 4 to a partner or in a small group as you monitor their reading. Call attention to the following words in the reading passage before students read it: ***away, it's, pictures, thought, try, while, without.***

Teacher Tips

Homophones

Encourage students to keep a list of homophones in their word study notebooks and continue to add to the list as they encounter other homophones in their reading.

Develop Automaticity in Word Recognition

Have pairs of students take turns doing speed drills together. One student will quickly show the other student the high-frequency word cards from blackline master 7, one at a time. Known words get put in one pile, unknown words in another pile. Have them repeat this several times.

Repeated Reading

Have students practice repeated readings of blackline master 3 to develop fluency.

DAY 4

Teacher Tips

Develop Automaticity in Word Recognition

Have students work with a partner to see how many times they can find the high-frequency words ***along, both, idea, off, together, walk, went*** in familiar books in the classroom.

Repeated Reading

Have students practice repeated readings of blackline master 3 to develop fluency.

Blend

Have students blend the words on the word list for Day Four, using the procedure for blending from Day One.

Sort: Guess My Sort

- Place the following teacher word cards randomly in a pocket chart: **rail, say, quaint, fray, nail, pay, great, tray, jail, paint**. Have students read the words aloud with you.
- Silently sort the words while the students watch. Do not tell the students how you are sorting them. Have students tell you how the words in each category are alike. Possible sorts include: words that begin with one consonant/words that begin with two consonants; words that describe actions/non-action words; words that name things that can be seen/words that name things that can't be seen.
- Give pairs or groups of students the set of words on blackline master 9 to cut out and use for their own rounds of "Guess My Sort."
- Monitor students to assess whether they understand the concept of sorting the words into different kinds of categories.

Spelling Words

- Provide practice for students in segmenting words and associating sounds with spellings. Dictate the following words to students and have them write the words on their papers: ***day, mail, daytime, mailbox***. Remind students to use what they have learned about spelling long ***a*** digraph words.
- Write the words on the board and have students self-correct their papers.
- Dictate the following sentence and have students write it on their papers: *When it is daytime, Gail and Ray check their mailbox for letters from Spain.*
- Write the sentence on the board and have students self-correct their papers.
- Give pairs of students blackline master 6. While one student reads the spelling words, the other student writes them in the "First Try" column. After the student has spelled the words, the partner places a check mark next to words spelled correctly. For the second try, the partner may prompt the student by sounding out the words that were spelled incorrectly the first time. If the second spelling attempt is correct, the partner places a check mark in the "Second Try" column.

Assessment Tip: Use students' completed peer-check blackline masters to note which words gave students difficulty.

Build Fluency with Connected Text

- Have students take turns reading the passage on blackline master 5 to a partner or in a small group as you monitor their reading. Call attention to the following words in the reading passage before students read it: ***almost, last, night, saw, took.***

Spelling Assessment

Use the following procedure to assess students' spelling of Unit Four words.
- Say each spelling word and use it in a sentence.
- Have students write the words on their papers.
- Continue with the next word on the list.
- When students have finished, collect their papers and analyze their spelling of the words.
- Use the assessment to plan small group or individual practice.

Small Group/Independent Activities

The following activities can be used to provide practice for students who need additional support.

PHONICS AND WORD STRATEGIES

Review Open-Syllable Patterns Write the word ***be*** on the board and ask students to identify the vowel and the vowel sound. Remind them that this is called an open syllable because it ends in a vowel. Write the word ***donate*** on the board. Circle the final ***e*** and remind students that this is a clue that there is a VCe pattern and that the vowel is probably long. Underline the remaining vowels and point to the consonant between them. Remind students that we usually divide the word before the consonant. Have a volunteer come up and divide the word into syllables. Then have students identify the syllable patterns and blend the word.

Word Sort Write the words ***pail, break, hey, day,*** and ***eight*** on separate paper bags. Have students choose a word card from blackline master 8 or 9, read the word, and place the word in the bag with the word that has the same spelling for the /ā/ sound.

AUTOMATICITY IN WORD RECOGNITION

Word Flash Have pairs of students use the set of cards from blackline master 7 to flash words for their partner to read.

Name That Word Place the set of high-frequency word cards faceup on a table. Have students take turns giving and answering clues about the words–for example: *There is only one consonant in this three-syllable word. What is it?* (idea)

Word Find Have students choose one high-frequency word from blackline master 7 and write it on an index card. Tell students that will be their special word for the day. Every time they see the word in print, they should make a tally mark on their card. At the end of the day have students total their tally marks and share their results with the group.

BUILD FLUENCY WITH CONNECTED TEXT

Repeated Reading Have students practice reading blackline master 3 several times, until they feel they can read it fluently and accurately. Have them work with a partner to time each other as they read the passage aloud. Have them set a goal of reading 90 words per minute.

SPELLING

Make Words Provide a set of magnetic letters and the week's spelling words on index cards. Have students use the magnetic letters to spell the words. They should check their spelling by blending the sounds and then looking at the words on the index cards.

Divide the Syllables Have students write the two-syllable words from the spelling list in their word study notebooks. Then have them divide the words into syllables and write why they divided the words the way they did.

Teacher Tips

Home Connection

Have students take blackline master 11 home to complete with a family member. Students can also take the reading passage on blackline master 3 home to share with their family.

Quick-Check

Assess students' mastery of long a digraph syllable patterns using the quick-check for Unit Four in this Teacher Resource System.

ELL Support Tip

Long digraphs can be tricky for ELL students. When you write them on the board, model with word cards, or write the spelling words on a chart, using two different color markers to identify the onset and the rime. Have ELL students do the same on the their blackline master. This process will encourage students to say the word and say the pattern, as well as to see the word and see the pattern. It will also guide them in blending.

UNIT 4 Quick-Check: Long a digraph syllable patterns

Student Name ______________________ Assessment Date __________

Segmenting and Blending

Directions: Explain that these words use sounds the student has been learning. Have the student point to each word on the corresponding student sheet, segment the word parts or syllables, and blend them together. Put a ✓ if the student successfully segments and blends the word or reads it as a complete unit. If the student misses the word, record the error.
Example: bait

maybe		delay		
grey		crayon		
mailman		frail		
sleigh		convey		Score **/8**

Sight Words

Directions: Have the student point to the first word on the corresponding student sheet and read across the line, saying each word as quickly as possible. Put a ✓ if the student successfully reads the word and an **X** if the student hesitates more than a few seconds. If the student misses the word, record the error.

together		could		
along		with		
idea		into		
off		some		
walk		down		
both		went		
would		now		
her		all		Score **/16**

UNIT 5 **Long o digraph syllable patterns**

Unit Objectives

Students will:

- Read words with long o vowel digraphs
- Review long a digraph syllable patterns
- Blend onset and rime words
- Sort words by long o digraphs and word families
- Read high-frequency words began, big, off, once, saw, went, while
- Spell words with different syllable patterns: float, doe, grown, boat, shown, toe, below, yellow, toenail
- Recognize that some words sound the same but are spelled differently and have different meanings

Day 1

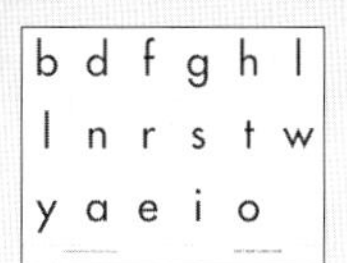

Letter Cards: **a, d, e, f, h, l, n, o, s, t, w**

Word Lists (BLM 2)

blond

Teacher Word Cards: **blond, boat, broke, choke, cloak, clock, moan, mop, mope roast, rob, robe**

Day 2

Word Lists (BLM 2)

Reading Passage 1 (BLM 3)

High-Frequency Word Cards for Unit 5 (BLM 7)

Day 3

Word Lists (BLM 2)

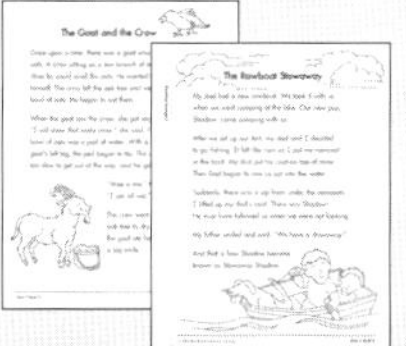
Reading Passages 1 & 2 (BLMs 3 & 4)

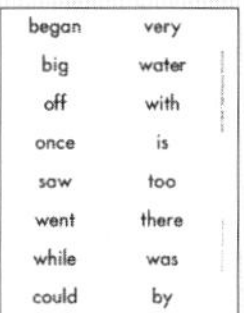

High-Frequency Word Cards for Unit 5 (BLM 7)

Day 4

Word Lists (BLM 2)

Reading Passages 1 & 3 (BLMs 3 & 5)

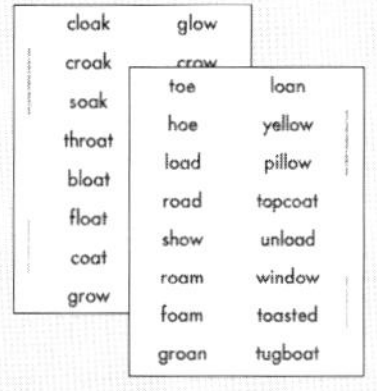

Student Word Cards (BLMs 8 & 9)

Spelling Peer Check (BLM 6)

Day 5

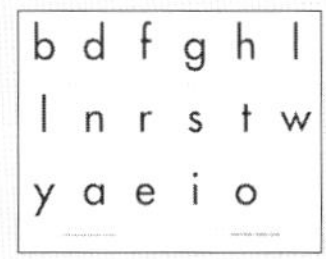

Letter Cards for Unit 5 (BLM 1)

Reading Passage 1 (BLM 3)

High-Frequency Word Cards for Unit 5 (BLM 7)

Quick-Check Student Sheet

Frieze Card

Take-Home Activity

Core Materials

All of these materials can be downloaded from http://phonicsresources.benchmarkeducation.com.

DAY 1

Frieze Card

1 Syllable Introduce Long *o* Digraph Syllable Patterns

Model

- Hold up the long ***o*** digraph frieze card and have students name each object.
- Point out that the vowel sound in each word is the long ***o,*** but that different letters in the words stand for the same vowel sound. Remind students that since there is one vowel sound, these words have one syllable.
- Have students read the words with you.

Guide

- Give students letter cards **d, f, h, l, n, s, t, w, a, e,** and **o,** and have them line up the letters in a row in front of them.
- Say the word ***hoe*** and ask students what letters they need to make the word. Remind them that they will need two letters to stand for the **/ō/** sound and have them look at the frieze card to decide which spelling pattern to use. Have them push forward the letters to spell the word and then decide whether the word looks right.
- Ask students what letter they need to use to replace the letter ***h*** at the beginning of ***hoe*** to make the word ***toe.***
- Repeat with the words ***snow*** and ***flow.*** Point out that although these words rhyme with ***toe*** and ***hoe,*** they use different letters to stand for the long ***o*** sound.

Apply

- Have students repeat the process independently with the words ***toad*** and ***load.***

Assessment Tip: Watch to make sure students select the correct letters and read the word. Note which students struggle with this activity, and provide reinforcement activities.

Sort Words: Long and Short Sounds

- Place teacher word cards **clock, cloak,** and **choke** in a pocket chart and read the words. Hold up the word card **robe** and model sorting the word.
- **Think Aloud: Clock/robe.** *No, they don't have the same vowel sound.* **Cloak/robe.** *Yes, they have the same vowel sound but they don't have the same digraph.* **Choke/robe.** *Yes, they have the same digraph and vowel sound. The word goes here.*
- Repeat with the following word cards, selecting them in random order: **blond, boat, broke, rob, roast, mop, moan,** and **mope.** This time have students tell you where to place the word cards.
- After the words are sorted, have students tell what the words in each column have in common.

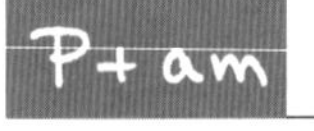

Blend Words with Long *o* Digraphs

Model

- Write the word ***coal*** on the board, using a different color for the rime ***-oal.*** Model sounding out the word, blending onset and rime: **/k/ /ōl/.** Then say the whole word.

Guide

- Have students sound out the word with you. Repeat with other examples if you feel students need extra support.
- Give students blackline master 2. Have them use their fingers to frame the rime of the first word on the list for Day One. Then have students read the word by blending the onset and rime.

Apply

- Have students independently read the remaining words on the list for Day One. Guide students who need support to blend some or all of the words on the list before they read the list independently.

Assessment Tip: Note which students are able to read the words without blending each sound.

Spelling Words: *float, doe, grown*

Model

- Make a two-column spelling chart on chart paper. Label the first column "One-Syllable Words" and the second column "Two-Syllable Words." Tell students that they will be spelling words with long o digraphs. As you work through the unit, you can continue to add the spelling words to the chart, and have students use the chart to check their spelling of the words.
- Say the word ***float*** and model spelling it and writing it on chart paper.
- **Think Aloud:** *I hear two parts in the word* **float:** **/fl/** *and* **/ōt/**. *I know that the letters* **f** *and* **l** *together stand for the blended sound* **/fl/**. *I will write these letters on the chart. I hear the long vowel sound* **/ō/** *followed by* **/t/**. *I know that the digraphs* **oa, oe,** *and* **ow** *can stand for the* **/ō/** *sound. I will try* **oa** *and see if the word looks right.*

Our Spelling Words

One-Syllable Words	Two-Syllable Words
float doe grown boat shown toe	below yellow toenail

Guide

- Say the word ***doe.*** Have students identify the onset and rime in the word. Remind students that the long ***o*** sound can be spelled in different ways, and guide them to use the digraph ***oe.*** Write the word in the first column of the chart as students tell you the word parts.
- Repeat with the word ***grown*** but write ***groan*** next to it. Tell students they need to use the context to tell which of the words is being used.

Apply

- Have students practice writing each of the words in their word study notebooks. After they write the word, have them check the spelling of the word by blending the onset and rime.

DAY 2

Teacher Tips

Reading Strategies

If students have difficulty applying strategies for challenging words, guide them to use the following strategies:

- look at how the words start and/or end
- look for familiar patterns or parts within the words
- separate the words into syllables and decode each part
- think about what familiar words look like the difficult words
- read forward to check the context
- reread the sentence or paragraph
- mark the words, substitute synonyms, and get on with reading–ask for help later

Comprehension

Use the following questions to ensure that students have understood the passage:

- *What did the crow want?* (Level 1–facts and details)
- *What happened at the end of the story?* (Level 2–sequence of events)
- *What is another good title for this story?* (Level 3–summarize)

Fluency

Intervene if students are having difficulty reading the passage. Model how to use word and meaning strategies to problem-solve the words. After students have had a chance to read the passage silently, have them read it aloud for fluency. Model fluent reading of the passage. For students who struggle, you may want to read the passage a second time and have them echo-read along with you.

Blend

- Have students blend the words in the list for Day Two, using the procedure for blending from Day One.

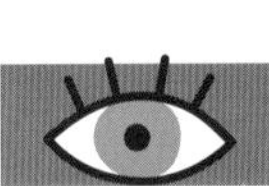

Develop Automaticity in Word Recognition

- Circle the following words on the overhead transparency: ***began, big, off, once, saw, went, while.*** Tell students that practicing these words will help them recognize the words automatically so they can read more fluently. Explain that they can sound out some of the words, but they will read more quickly if they don't have to stop and sound them out.
- Read each word. Point out that ***off*** has double consonants and that ***while*** ends with a silent ***e.***
- Have students read aloud with you the sentences in which the words are found, and then have them write the words in their word study notebooks.
- Give students a copy of blackline master 7. Point out the words from this lesson, as well as other words they have learned previously. Have students cut out the words, store them in an envelope, and use them for practice activities.

Build Fluency with Connected Text

Model

- Read the passage on the overhead transparency aloud. Stop when you come to the word ***wanted.*** Model strategies you would use to read the word.
- **Think Aloud:** *One way I can read this word is to break it into syllables. I look for the two vowels, and then check the number of consonants. I see two, so I divide the word between them. Now I have two closed syllables that I can sound out:* **/wan/ /ted/.**

Guide

- Continue reading. Model making a mistake and correcting it–for example, read ***low*** with an */**ou**/* sound.
- **Think Aloud:** *That word doesn't make sense. Let me look at it again. The letters* **ow** *sometimes stand for the /***ou***/ sound, but I know they can also be a long* **o** *digraph. If I try the long* **o** *sound, I get* **low.** *Now it makes sense.*
- Continue reading, stopping at other words and asking students what strategies they would use to read the words. You may want to call attention to the words ***soaked*** and ***groaned*** and guide students as they read the past tense ending.

Apply

- Have students take turns reading blackline master 3 to a partner or in a small group as you monitor the reading. Use the teacher tips to check comprehension and fluency.

Spelling Words: *boat, shown, toe*

- Have students practice writing the spelling words from Day One in their word study notebooks. Have them refer to words on the spelling chart to check their spelling.
- Introduce the Day Two spelling words. Say the word ***shown*** and model spelling it and writing it on the spelling chart. Point to the word ***grown*** on the chart from the Day One spelling words, and model how to use the word family ***-own*** to spell the new word and other words in the word family such as ***flown, blown,*** and ***thrown.***
- Repeat with the remaining words and have students practice writing the words in their word study notebooks.

DAY 3

Multisyllabic Words: Vowel Digraph Syllable Patterns

Model

- Write the word ***be*** on the board and point out that it has one open syllable and one vowel sound.
- Write the word ***below*** on the board. Circle the vowels ***e*** and ***o*** and point out that there is one consonant between them. Tell students you will divide the word before the consonant: ***be/low.***
- Point out the open syllable and that the second syllable has a vowel digraph. Explain that you will try the long vowel sound first when you blend the word and see if that sounds right. Model reading the word: **/bē/ /lō/, *below.***

Guide

- Write the word ***approach*** on the board and guide students as they identify the vowels and the consonants between them.
- Point out that they should divide the word between the double consonants: ***ap/proach.*** Have them sound it out, using what they know about closed syllables and the vowel digraph pattern.

Apply

- Have students independently blend the two-syllable words on the word list for Day Three. If students need more support, guide them as they blend some or all of the words.

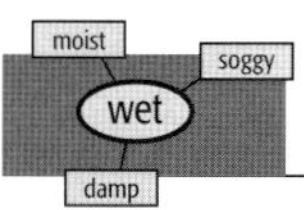

Develop Word Meanings

- Write the words ***toe*** and ***tow*** on the board and read them. Tell students the words are homophones, which sound the same but have different meanings and spellings.
- Use the words ***tow*** and ***toe*** in oral sentences to illustrate the difference in the meanings.
- Write the words ***toad*** and ***doe*** on the board, and ask students if they can think of homophones for these words. If they can't, write the words ***towed*** and ***dough*** on the board and use them in oral sentences that demonstrate their meanings.
- Challenge students to think of other homophone pairs they could add to the list.

Spelling Words: *below, yellow, toenail*

- Have students practice spelling the words from Day One and Day Two by writing them several times in their word study notebooks.
- Introduce the new words, modeling how students can apply what they know about syllable patterns to the spelling of words with more than one syllable.
- Write the word ***yellow*** on the board. Divide the word into syllables and use a different color to emphasize the vowels. Model how the double consonants allow for a closed syllable with a short vowel sound.
- **Think Aloud:** *When I spell this word, I need to remember how the word looks. There are double* **l**'*s in* **yellow.** *If there were only one* **l,** *I would divide it like this* **(ye/low)** *and the first vowel would be long.*
- Repeat with the remaining words. Have students practice the words several times in their word study notebooks.

Build Fluency with Connected Text

- Have students read blackline master 4 to a partner or in small groups as you monitor their reading. Call attention to the following words in the reading passage before students read it: ***began, put, took, under, us, went.***

Teacher Tips

Homophone Game

To provide practice in using homophones, play the following game with students: Send one student out of the room while the group decides on a homophone pair or group. Call the student back in. Students in the classroom then provide oral sentences in which they substitute the word ***buzz*** for one of the homophones. The student has to guess what the homophone group is. For example, if the homophone group is ***two, too,*** and ***to,*** an oral sentence might be: *I am going* ***buzz*** *the picnic.*

Develop Automaticity in Word Recognition

Have students place all 16 high-frequency word cards from blackline master 7 in alphabetical order. Have a partner check the order. Then have partners alternate reading the words in the list.

Repeated Reading

Have students practice repeated readings of blackline master 3 to develop fluency.

DAY 4

Teacher Tips

Develop Automaticity in Word Recognition

Have students write these high-frequency words on self-stick notes: ***began, big, off, once, saw, went, while.*** Then have them search old magazines and newspapers for examples of each word. Have them mark the examples with the self-stick notes. Then have them cut out the words they find and paste them on a page in their word study notebooks. When the words are pasted in, have them exchange notebooks with a partner and read all the words on the page.

Repeated Reading

Have students practice repeated readings of blackline master 3 to develop fluency.

Blend

- Have students blend the words on the list for Day Four, using the procedure for blending from Day One.

Sort Words: Open Sort

- Give each student a set of student word cards from blackline masters 8 and 9. Have students sort the words any way they want, but tell them they have to be able to explain how they sorted the words.
- Have students share their sorts with a partner, who must decide how the words are sorted.
- Call the group together and have students share different ways to sort these words (number of vowels, number of letters, beginning blends, digraphs for long ***o,*** etc.). As students make suggestions, arrange the words in the pocket chart into the sorts they suggest.

Spelling Words

- Provide practice for students in segmenting words and associating sounds with spellings. Dictate the following words to students and have them write the words on their papers: ***blow, window, toast, toasted.*** Remind students to use what they have learned about spelling syllables with long ***o*** digraphs.
- Write the words on the board and have students self-correct their papers.
- Dictate the following sentence and have students write it on their papers: *Show me the soapy yellow foam in the bowl.*
- Write the sentence on the board and have students self-correct their papers.
- Give pairs of students blackline master 6. While one student reads the spelling words, the other student writes them in the "First Try" column. After the student has spelled the words, the partner places a check mark next to words spelled correctly. For the second try, the partner may prompt the student by sounding out the words that were spelled incorrectly the first time. If the second spelling attempt is correct, the partner places a check mark in the "Second Try" column.

Assessment Tip: Use students' completed peer-check blackline masters to note which words gave students difficulty.

Build Fluency with Connected Text

- Give students the reading passage on blackline master 5. Have them take turns reading the passage to a partner. Call attention to the following words in the reading passage before students read it: ***big, kinds, might, sea, sometimes, watch.***
- Have students who need extra support practice reading the passage aloud in a small group as you monitor their reading.

Spelling Assessment

Use the following procedure to assess students' spelling of Unit Five words.
- Say each spelling word and use it in a sentence.
- Have students write the words on their papers.
- Continue with the next word on the list.
- When students have finished, collect their papers and analyze their spelling of the words.
- Use the assessment to plan small group or individual practice.

Small Group/Independent Activities

The following activities can be used to provide practice for students who need additional support.

PHONICS AND WORD STRATEGIES

Build Words Write the words ***throw*** and ***boat*** on the board and have students copy them in their word study notebooks. Challenge them to write as many words as they can from each of the word families.

Review Long *a* Digraph Syllable Patterns Write the word ***tray*** on the board and ask students to identify the vowels and the vowel sound. Point out that the letter ***y*** is a vowel in this word and that ***ay*** is a vowel digraph, which stands for one sound. Explain that this kind of syllable is called a vowel digraph syllable. Explain that it is not a closed syllable because a closed syllable has one vowel, and it is not an open syllable because open syllables end with a vowel. Write the word ***betray*** on the board. Underline each vowel and then point to the consonants between them. Point out that since there are two consonants between the vowels, you will keep the blend ***tr*** together and divide the word before the ***t***. Have a volunteer come up and divide the word into syllables. Then have students identify the syllable patterns (open and vowel digraph) and blend the word.

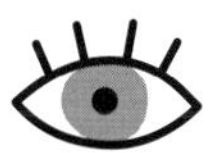

AUTOMATICITY IN WORD RECOGNITION

Read Words Have pairs of students place a set of high-frequency word cards in a stack. Have them take turns drawing a card, reading the word, and using the word in a sentence.

Read and Write Place the high-frequency word cards in a stack. Have a volunteer choose one of the words, say it, and write it on the board, using the card as a model. While the student writes the word on the board, the other students write the word in their word study notebooks, and then check their spelling by looking at the word on the board.

BUILD FLUENCY WITH CONNECTED TEXT

Repeated Reading Have students practice reading blackline master 3 several times, until they feel they can read it fluently and accurately. Have them work with a partner to time each other as they read the passage aloud. Have them set a goal of reading 90 words per minute.

SPELLING

Make Words Provide a set of letter cards and the week's spelling words on index cards. Have students use the letter cards to spell the words. They should check their spelling by blending the sounds and then looking at the words on the index cards.

Spell On Have students sit in a circle. Say a spelling word and the first letter of the word. Have the student next to you say the next letter, the next student the third letter, and so on until the word is spelled. Repeat with another spelling word.

Teacher Tips

Home Connection

Have students take blackline master 11 home to complete with a family member. Students can also take the reading passage on blackline master 3 home to share with their family.

Quick-Check

Assess students' mastery of long o digraph syllable patterns using the quick-check for Unit Five in this Teacher Resource System.

ELL Support Tip

ELL students can benefit from singing or creating silly songs. To practice long o digraphs, create songs to the tune of "Row, Row, Row Your Boat"; for example, "Load, load, load the boat, as it floats along," or "Yellow, yellow is the boat, as it floats along."

UNIT 5 Quick-Check: Long o digraph syllable patterns

Student Name ______________________ Assessment Date ____________

Segmenting and Blending

Directions: Explain that these words use sounds the student has been learning. Have the student point to each word on the corresponding student sheet, segment the word parts or syllables, and blend them together. Put a ✓ if the student successfully segments and blends the word or reads it as a complete unit. If the student misses the word, record the error.
Example: loaf

boast		rainbow		
fishbowl		poach		
known		bestow		
floe		coax		Score **/8**

Sight Words

Directions: Have the student point to the first word on the corresponding student sheet and read across the line, saying each word as quickly as possible. Put a ✓ if the student successfully reads the word and an **X** if the student hesitates more than a few seconds. If the student misses the word, record the error.

began		with		
big		is		
off		too		
once		there		
saw		was		
went		by		
while		down		
could		went		
very		now		
water		all		Score **/20**

UNIT 6

Long e digraph syllable patterns

Unit Objectives

Students will:

- Recognize and read one- and two-syllable words with long e vowel digraphs
- Review long o digraph syllable patterns
- Blend onset and rime words
- Sort words by long e digraphs and word families
- Read high-frequency words always, far, play, put, school, sometimes, while
- Spell one- and two-syllable words with different syllable patterns: dream, feel, yield, cream, wheel, field, greedy, increase, relief
- Find synonyms

Day 1

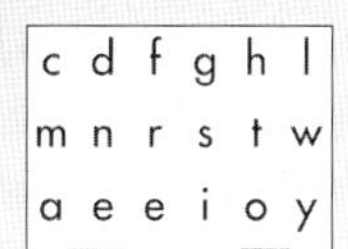

Letter Cards:
a, d, e, e, f, g, h, i, l, m, r, s, t,

Word Lists
(BLM 2)

bed

Teacher Word Cards:
bed, bead, bet, bleach, cheap, chief, field, green, heal, hen, least, let, meet, met, shield, sped, speed

Day 2

Word Lists
(BLM 2)

Reading Passage 1
(BLM 3)

High-Frequency Word Cards for Unit 6 (BLM 7)

Day 3

Word Lists
(BLM 2)

Reading Passages 1 & 2
(BLMs 3 & 4)

High-Frequency Word Cards for Unit 6 (BLM 7)

Day 4

Word Lists
(BLM 2)

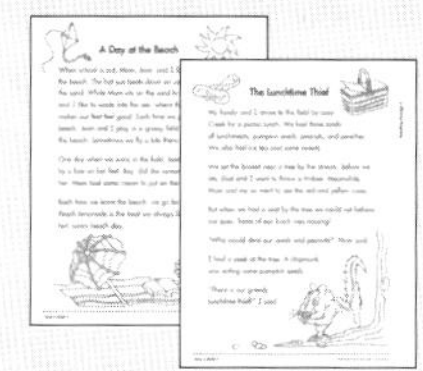

Reading Passages 1 & 3
(BLMs 3 & 5)

beach

Teacher Word Cards:
beach, between, canteen, donkey, field, key, neat, peanut, peep, reason, relief, repeat, sixteen, thief, weak, week

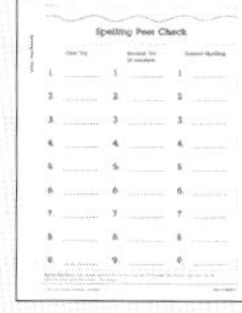

Spelling Peer Check (BLM 6)

High-Frequency Word Cards for Unit 6 (BLM 7)

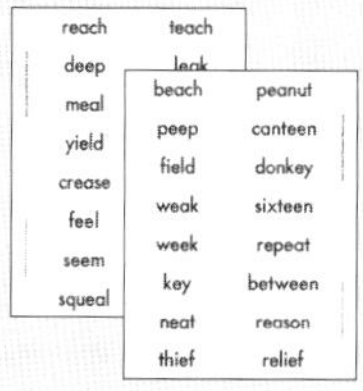

Student Word Cards
(BLMs 8 & 9)

Day 5

Letter Cards for Unit 6

Reading Passage 1
(BLM 3)

High-Frequency Word Cards for Unit 6 (BLM 7)

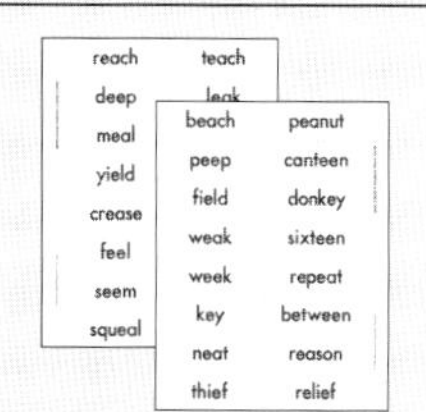

Student Word Cards
(BLMs 8 & 9)

Quick-Check Student Sheet

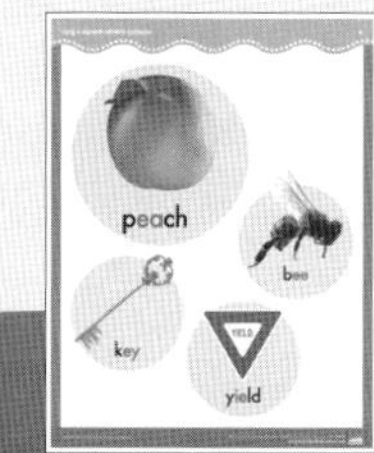

Frieze Card

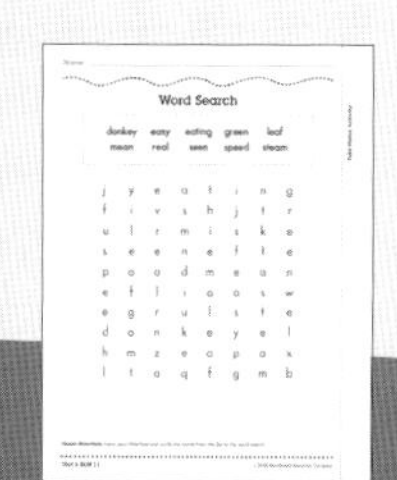

Take-Home Activity

Core Materials

All of these materials can be downloaded from http://phonicsresources.benchmarkeducation.com.

UNIT 6 Long e digraph syllable patterns

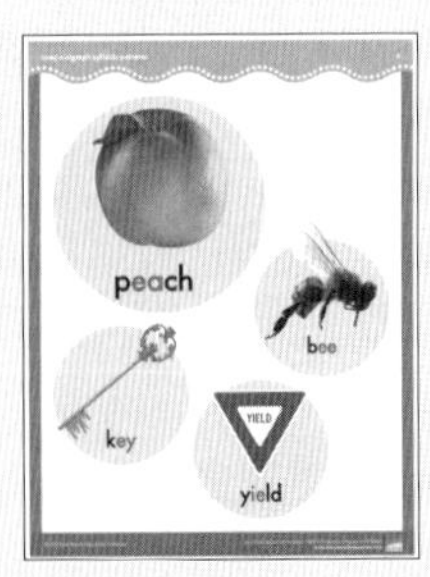

Frieze Card

1 Syllable Introduce Long Digraph Syllable Patterns

Model

- Hold up the long ***e*** digraph frieze card and have students name each object.
- Point out that the vowel sound in each word is the long ***e,*** but that different letters in the words stand for the sound. Remind students that each syllable has one vowel sound, and point out the letters that stand for the /ē/ sound.
- Have students read the words with you.

Guide

- Give students letter cards **d, f, g, h, l, m, r, s, t, a, e, e,** and **i,** and have them line up the letters in a row in front of them.
- Say the word ***feet*** and ask students what letters they need to make the word. Remind them that they will need two letters to stand for the /ē/ sound and have them choose from the spelling patterns on the frieze card. Have them push forward the letters to spell the word and then check to make sure the word looks right.
- Ask students what letters they need to use to replace the letter ***f*** at the beginning of ***feet*** to make the word ***greet.***
- Repeat with the words ***heat*** and ***meat.*** Point out that although these words rhyme with ***feet*** and ***greet,*** they use different letters to stand for the long ***e*** sound.

Apply

- Have students repeat the process independently with the words ***field*** and ***shield.***

Assessment Tip: Watch to make sure students select the correct letters and read the words. Note which students struggle with this activity and provide reinforcement activities.

Sort Words: Long and Short Sounds

- Place teacher word cards **bed, green, field,** and **bead** in a pocket chart and read the words. Hold up the word card **heal** and model sorting the word.
- **Think Aloud: Bed/heal.** *No, they don't have the same vowel sound.* **Green/heal.** *Yes, they have the same vowel sound but they don't have the same digraph.* **Field/heal.** *Again, they have the same vowel sound but not the same digraph.* **Bead/heal.** *Yes, they have the same digraph and vowel sound. The word goes here.*
- Repeat with the following word cards, selecting them in random order. This time have students tell you where to place the word: **bet, hen, let, met, sped, bleach, cheap, least, meet, speed, chief, shield.**
- When the words are sorted, have students tell what the words in each column have in common.

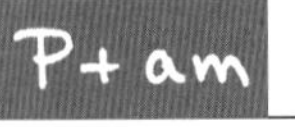

Blend Words with Long Digraphs

Model

- Write the word ***real*** on the board, using a different color for the rime ***-eal.*** Model sounding out the word, blending onset and rime: **/r/ /ēl/.** Then say the whole word.

Guide

- Have students sound out the word with you. Repeat with other examples if you feel students need extra support.
- Give students blackline master 2. Have them use their fingers to frame the rime of the first word on the list for Day One. Then have students read the word by blending the onset and rime.

Apply

- Have students independently blend the remaining words on the list for Day One. Students who are able to read the words as a whole should do so.
- Guide students who need support as they read some or all of the words by blending onset and rime.

Assessment Tip: Note which students are able to read the words without blending each sound.

Spelling Words

Model

- Make a two-column spelling chart on chart paper. Label the first column "One-Syllable Words" and the second column "Two-Syllable Words." Tell students that they will be spelling words with long ***e*** digraphs. As you work through the unit, you can continue to add the spelling words to the chart, and have students use the chart to check their spelling of the words.
- Say the word ***dream*** and model spelling it and writing it on chart paper.
- **Think Aloud:** *I hear two parts in the word* **dream:** **/dr/** *and* **/ē m/**. *I know that the letters* **d** *and* **r** *together stand for the blended sound* **/dr/**. *I hear the long vowel sound* **/ē/** *followed by* **/m/**. *I know that the digraphs* **ea, ee,** *and* **ie** *can stand for the* **/ē/** *sound. I will try* **ea** *and see if the word looks right.*

Guide

- Say the word ***feel.*** Have students identify the onset and rime in the word and the letters that stand for the sounds. Remind students that the long ***e*** sound can be spelled in different ways and guide them to use the digraph ***ee.*** Write the word in the first column of the chart as students tell you the word parts.
- Repeat with the word ***yield.***

Apply

- Have students practice writing each of the words in their word study notebooks, checking spelling by blending onset and rime. Have them highlight the long ***e*** digraphs in the words.

Our Spelling Words

One-Syllable Words	Two-Syllable Words
dream feel yield cream wheel field	greedy increase relief

DAY 2

Teacher Tips

Reading Strategies

If students have difficulty applying strategies for challenging words, guide them to use the following strategies:

- look at how the words start and/or end
- look for familiar patterns or parts within the words
- separate the words into syllables and decode each part
- think about what familiar words look like the difficult words
- read forward to check the context
- reread the sentence or paragraph
- mark the words, substitute synonyms, and get on with reading–ask for help later

Comprehension

Use the following questions to ensure that students have understood the passage:

- *What does Mom do at the beach?* (Level 1–facts and details)
- *Why did Jean scream?* (Level 2–cause/effect)
- *What words tell you that the people go to the beach often?* (Level 3–draw conclusions)

Fluency

Intervene if students are having difficulty reading the passage. Model how to use word and meaning strategies to problem-solve the words. After students have had a chance to read the passage silently, have them read it aloud for fluency. Model fluent reading of the passage. For students who struggle, you may want to read the passage a second time and have them echo-read along with you.

Blend

- Have students blend the words on the word list for Day Two, using the procedure for blending from Day One.

Develop Automaticity in Word Recognition

- Circle the following words on the overhead transparency: ***always, far, play, put, school, sometimes,*** and ***while.*** Tell students that practicing these words will help them recognize the words automatically and make their reading more fluent. Explain that they can sound out some of the words, but they will read more quickly if they don't have to stop and sound them out.
- Read each word. Point out that the ***s*** in ***always*** stands for the **/z/** sound and that ***sometimes*** is made up of the words ***some*** and ***times.***
- Have students read aloud with you the sentences that contain the words and then write the words in their word study notebooks.
- Give students a copy of blackline master 7. Point out the words from this lesson as well as words from previous lessons. Have students cut out the words, store them in an envelope, and use them for practice activities.

Build Fluency with Connected Text

Model

- Read the passage on the overhead transparency aloud. Stop when you come to the word ***beats.*** Model strategies you would use to read the word.
- **Think Aloud:** *I can tell by looking at this word that it is a one-syllable word and that it has an* **ea** *digraph, so the vowel sound is probably* **/ē/**. *I notice an* **s** *on the end, so I think this word is* **beats.**
- Continue reading. Model making a mistake and correcting it–for example, read **/red/** instead of **/rēd/**.
- **Think Aloud:** **/red/** *doesn't sound right because this passage is not in the past tense. I see the* **ea** *digraph, which can stand for the long* **e** *sound. I know that this word can be pronounced* **/red/** *or* **/rēd/** *but the context tells me it should be* **/rēd/**.

Guide

- Continue reading, stopping at other words and asking students what strategies they would use to read the words.

Apply

- Have students take turns reading blackline master 3 to a partner or in a small group as you monitor the reading. Use the teacher tips to check comprehension and fluency.

Spelling Words

- Have students practice writing the spelling words from Day One in their word study notebooks.
- Introduce the Day Two spelling words. Say the word ***wheel*** and model spelling it and writing it on the spelling chart. Point to the word ***feel*** on the chart from the Day One spelling words, and model how to use the word family ***-eel*** to spell the new word and other words in the word family, such as ***heel, peel,*** and ***steel.***
- Repeat with the remaining words and have students practice writing the words in their word study notebooks.

DAY 3

Multisyllabic Words: Vowel Digraph Syllable Patterns

Model

- Write the word ***be*** on the board and point out that it has one open syllable and one vowel sound.
- Write the word ***beneath*** on the board. Circle the vowels ***e*** and ***ea*** and point out that there is one consonant between them. Tell students you will divide the word before the consonant: ***be/neath.***
- Point out the open syllable and that the second syllable has a vowel digraph. Explain that you will try the long vowel sound first when you blend the word and see if that sounds right. Model reading the word: **/bē/ /nēth/**, ***beneath.***

Guide

- Write the word ***appeal*** on the board and guide students as they identify the vowels and the consonants between them.
- Point out that they should divide the word between the double consonants: ***ap/peal.*** Have them sound it out, using what they know about closed syllables and the vowel digraph pattern.

Apply

- Have students independently blend the two-syllable words on the word list for Day Three. If students need more support, guide them as they blend some or all of the words.

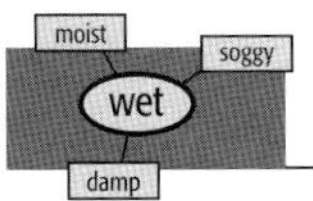

Develop Word Meanings

- Write the following sentences on the board: *A soft breeze made the leaves sway in the trees. The wind from the east kept the kite up in the sky for a long time.* Read the sentences with students and discuss what is similar in the two sentences.
- Switch ***breeze*** and ***wind*** in the two sentences. Read the sentences again, explaining that these words are called synonyms, which are words that mean the same or almost the same thing.
- Write the following words on the board: ***scream, weep, clean,*** and ***leap.*** Have students think of synonyms for the words and use them in oral sentences.

Spelling Words

- Have students practice spelling the words from Day One and Day Two by writing them several times in their word study notebooks.
- Introduce the new words, modeling how students can apply what they know about syllable patterns to the spelling of words with more than one syllable.
- Say the word ***greedy.***
- *When I spell this word, I need to think about how the word looks. I hear two syllables. The first syllable has a long* **e** *and ends with* **/d/**. *will look at the frieze card to decide which spelling pattern I will use for the long* **e** *digraph. The second syllable also has a long* **e.** *I remember that the letter* **y** *usually stands for the long* **e** *sound at the end of a word.*
- Repeat with the remaining words. Have students practice the words several times in their word study notebooks.

Build Fluency with Connected Text

- Have students read blackline master 4 to a partner or in small groups as you monitor their reading. Call attention to the following words in the reading passage before students read it: ***again, hear, night, thought, well, went.***

Teacher Tips

Uncommon Digraph

Write the word ***people*** on the board, and circle the vowel digraph ***eo.*** Explain to students that this is also an example of a long ***e*** digraph syllable pattern, but a very unusual one. Tell students this is a word they should practice reading automatically because it is one they will come across a lot in their reading.

Develop Automaticity in Word Recognition

Give partners the high-frequency word cards ***always, far, play, put, school, sometimes,*** and ***while.*** As one student reads blackline master 3 aloud, another student holds up the appropriate card when the word is read in the story.

Repeated Reading

Have students practice repeated readings of blackline master 3 to develop fluency.

DAY 4

Blend

- Have students blend the words on the word list for Day Four, using the procedure for blending from Day One.

Sort Words: Speed Sort

- Put the following teacher word cards in the pocket chart: **beach, peep, field, weak, week, key, neat, thief, peanut, canteen, donkey, sixteen, repeat, between, reason, relief.**
- Read the words aloud with students. Ask students what they notice about the words. Point out that two of the words are homophones and make sure students understand the meanings of the words.
- To establish the time necessary to "beat the teacher," set a timer and then quickly sort the words according to their long ***e*** digraph patterns (***ea/ee/ie/ey***) while students watch.
- Have students sort their own word cards from blackline master 9 and try to beat your time.

Spelling Words

- Provide practice for students in segmenting words and associating sounds with spellings. Dictate the following words to students and have them write the words on their papers: ***green, squeak, field, yield.*** Remind students to use what they have learned about spelling syllables with long ***e*** digraphs.
- Write the words on the board and have students self-correct their papers.
- Dictate the following sentence and have students write it on their papers: *I like to eat crunchy green beans with snappy sweet peas for dinner.* Write the sentence on the board and have students self-correct their papers.
- Give pairs of students blackline master 6. While one student reads the spelling words, the other student writes them in the "First Try" column. After the student has spelled the words, the partner places a check mark next to words spelled correctly. For the second try, the partner may prompt the student by sounding out the words that were spelled incorrectly the first time. If the second spelling attempt is correct, the partner places a check mark in the "Second Try" column.

Assessment Tip: Use students' completed peer-check blackline masters to note which words gave students difficulty.

Build Fluency with Connected Text

- Give students the reading passage on blackline master 5. Have them take turns reading the passage to a partner. Call attention to the following words in the reading passage before students read it: ***eye(s), family, kind(s), miss(ing), near, set, went.***
- Have students who need extra support practice reading the passage aloud in a small group as you monitor their reading.

Teacher Tips

Develop Automaticity in Word Recognition

Have students work with a partner and take turns using magnetic letters to make, mix, and remake each high-frequency word from blackline master 7. Remind them to spell and read each word aloud as they make it.

Repeated Reading

Have students practice repeated readings of blackline master 3 to develop fluency.

Spelling Assessment

Use the following procedure to assess students' spelling of Unit Six words.

- Say each spelling word and use it in a sentence.
- Have students write the words on their papers.
- Continue with the next word on the list.
- When students have finished, collect their papers and analyze their spelling of the words.
- Use the assessment to plan small group or individual practice.

Small Group/Independent Activities

The following activities can be used to provide practice for students who need additional support.

PHONICS AND WORD STRATEGIES

Review Long *o* Digraph Syllable Patterns Write the word ***boat*** on the board and ask students to identify the vowels and the vowel sound. Point out that it is a vowel digraph, which means it stands for one sound, and that this kind of syllable is called a vowel digraph syllable. Explain that it is not a closed syllable because a closed syllable has one vowel, and it is not an open syllable because open syllables end with a vowel. Write the word ***below*** on the board. Underline each vowel and then point to the consonant between them. Ask students where you should divide the word. Have a volunteer come up and divide the word into syllables. Then have students identify the syllable patterns (open and vowel digraph) and blend the word.

Digraph Spin Have students sit in a circle with the student word cards (from blackline masters 8 and 9) facedown in a stack in the middle. One student spins a plastic bottle. Whomever the bottle points to selects a word card, reads the word, and identifies the long ***e*** vowel digraph pattern.

Identify Syllables Have students copy into their word study notebooks the two-syllable words from the set of decodable words on blackline master 9. Have them divide each word into syllables and write why they divided the words the way they did.

AUTOMATICITY IN WORD RECOGNITION

Build Sentences Partners use the student word cards (from blackline masters 8 and 9) and the high-frequency word cards to make sentences. They can write other words they need on index cards.

Practice Makes Perfect Pairs of students take the set of high-frequency word cards and put the words in alphabetical order. Then they practice reading and spelling the words.

BUILD FLUENCY WITH CONNECTED TEXT

Repeated Reading Have students practice reading blackline master 3 several times, until they feel they can read it fluently and accurately. Have them work with a partner to time each other as they read the passage aloud. Have them set a goal of reading 90 words per minute.

SPELLING

Make Words Provide a set of letter cards and the week's spelling words on index cards. Have students use the letter cards to spell the words. They should check their spelling by blending the sounds and then looking at the words on the index cards.

Board Spelling Ask several students to stand at the board. Say a spelling word and have the students write it. Continue until all students have had a chance to write a spelling word.

Teacher Tips

Home Connection

Have students take blackline master 11 home to complete with a family member. Students can also take the reading passage on blackline master 3 home to share with their family.

Quick-Check

Assess students' mastery of long e digraph syllable patterns using the quick-check for Unit Six in this Teacher Resource System.

ELL Support Tip

As you teach multi-syllabic words to ELL students, first say the word, and then ask students to say it with you. Write the word in syllable parts, and have the students read each part.

UNIT 6 Quick-Check: Long e digraph syllable patterns

Student Name ______________________ Assessment Date ____________

Segmenting and Blending

Directions: Explain that these words use sounds the student has been learning. Have the student point to each word on the corresponding student sheet, segment the word parts or syllables, and blend them together. Put a ✓ if the student successfully segments and blends the word or reads it as a complete unit. If the student misses the word, record the error.
Example: knead

reveal		chief		
pinwheel		seacoast		
monkey		upkeep		
screech		belief		Score **/8**

Sight Words

Directions: Have the student point to the first word on the corresponding student sheet and read across the line, saying each word as quickly as possible. Put a ✓ if the student successfully reads the word and an **X** if the student hesitates more than a few seconds. If the student misses the word, record the error.

always		like		
far		down		
play		into		
put		where		
sometimes		water		
when		our		
while		good		
school		from		Score **/16**

UNIT 7 Long i digraph syllable patterns

Unit Objectives

Students will:

- Recognize and read one- and two-syllable words with long i vowel digraphs
- Review long e digraph syllable patterns
- Blend onset and rime
- Sort words by word families
- Read high-frequency words: always, even, idea, later, still, took, went
- Spell one- and two-syllable words with a variety of syllable patterns: bright, brightly, pie, lightning, sigh, tighten, high, flight, lie
- Find antonyms for words in context

Day 1

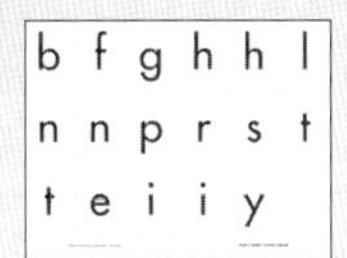

Letter Cards:
e, f, g, h, i, l, p, s, t

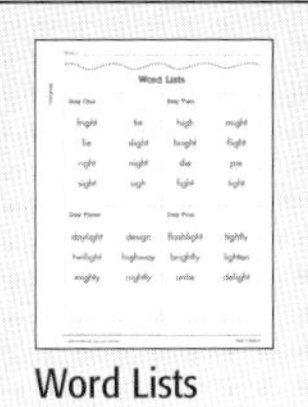

Word Lists
(BLM 2)

dig

Teacher Word Cards:
dig, fig, fit, flight, high, hit, lie, pie, right, sigh, sight, sit, thigh

Day 2

Word Lists
(BLM 2)

Reading Passage 1
(BLM 3)

High-Frequency Word Cards for Unit 7
(BLM 7)

Day 3

Word Lists
(BLM 2)

Reading Passages 1 & 2
(BLMs 3 & 4)

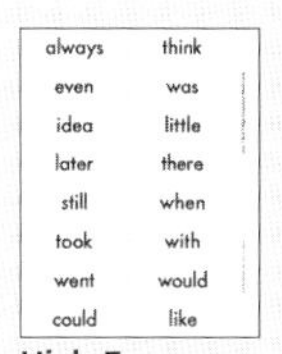

High-Frequency Word Cards for Unit 7 (BLM 7)

Day 4

Word Lists
(BLM 2)

Reading Passages 1 & 3
(BLMs 3 & 5)

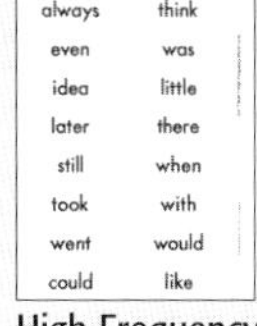

High-Frequency Word Cards for Unit 7 (BLM 7)

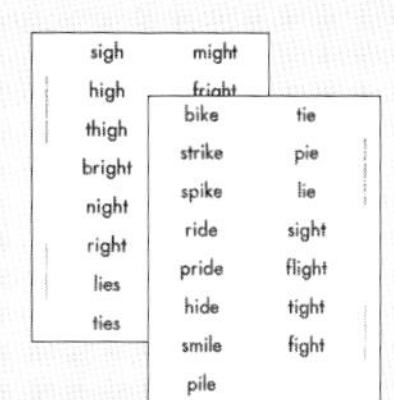

Student Word Cards for Unit 7
(BLMs 8 & 9)

Spelling Peer Check
(BLM 6)

Day 5

Letter Cards for Unit 7

Reading Passage 1
(BLM 3)

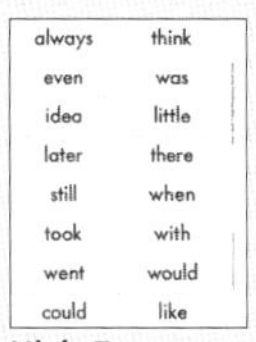

High-Frequency Word Cards for Unit 7 (BLM 7)

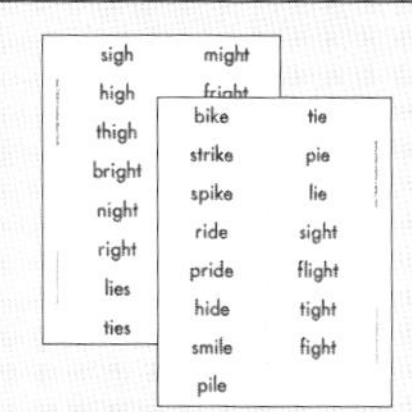

Student Word Cards

Quick-Check Student Sheet

Frieze Card

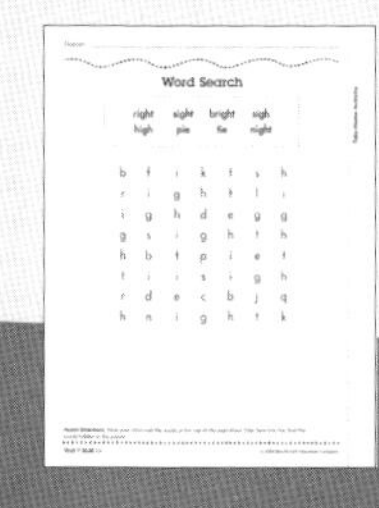

Take-Home Activity

Core Materials

All of these materials can be downloaded from http://phonicsresources.benchmarkeducation.com.

UNIT 7 Long i digraph syllable patterns

1 Syllable Introduce Long *i* Digraph Syllable Patterns

Frieze Card

Model

- Point to the pictures of ***night*** and ***pie*** on the long ***i*** digraph frieze card, name them, and read the words.
- Point out that the vowel sound in each word is long ***i,*** but that different letters in the words stand for the sound. Point out that ***ie*** stands for the sound /ī/ in ***pie,*** while the letters ***igh*** stand for the sound /ī/ in ***night.***
- Remind students that a syllable has one vowel sound and that the vowel digraphs stand for one vowel sound.

Guide

- Give students letter cards **f, g, h, l, p, s, t, e,** and **i,** and have them line up the letters in a row in front of them.
- Say the word ***tie*** and ask students what letters they need to make the word. If necessary, tell them ***tie*** comes from the same word family as the word ***pie*** on the frieze card.
- Ask students what letter they need to replace in ***tie*** to make the word ***lie.*** Have students make the word.
- Repeat with the ***-ight*** family word ***fight.***

Apply

- Have students repeat the process independently with the words ***flight, sight,*** and ***slight.***

Assessment Tip: Watch to make sure students select the correct letters and read the word. Note which students struggle with this activity, and provide reinforcement activities.

Sort Words: Long *i* Word Families

- Read each word as you place the following teacher word cards in a pocket chart in random order: **sigh, high, thigh, flight, right, sight, tie, pie, lie, fig, dig, sit, fit, hit.**
- Set the word card **sigh** apart from the other words. Ask students what other words you could group with the word ***sigh*** and have them explain why.
- Once you have sorted words into the ***-igh*** family, ask students how you could sort the other words.
- Have students sort the words into those with long ***i*** and those with short ***i*** sounds.

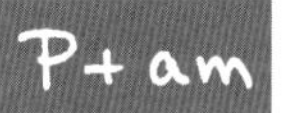

Blend Words with Long *i* Digraphs

Model

- Write the word ***thigh*** on the board, using a different color for the rime, ***-igh.*** Model sounding out the word, blending onset and rime: **/th/ /ī/.** Then say the whole word.

Guide

- Have students sound out the word with you. Repeat with other examples if you feel students need extra support.
- Give students blackline master 2. Have them use their fingers to frame the rime part of the first word on the list for Day One. Then have students read the word by blending the onset and rime.

Apply

- Have students independently blend the remaining words on the list for Day One. Students who are able to read the words as a whole should do so.
- Note which students need more support in blending. Guide them as they read some or all of the words on the list by blending onset and rime before asking them to read the list independently.

Assessment Tip: Note which students are able to read the words without blending each sound.

Spelling Words: *bright, pie, sigh*

Model

- Make a two-column spelling chart on chart paper. Label the first column "One-Syllable Words" and the second column "Two-Syllable Words." Tell students that they will be spelling words with long ***i*** digraphs. As you work through the unit, you can continue to add the spelling words to the chart and have students use it to check their spelling of the words.
- Say the word ***bright*** and model spelling it and writing it on the chart paper.
- **Think Aloud:** *When I say the word* **bright,** *I hear two parts in the word: /***br***/ and /***īt***/. I know that the letters* **b** *and* **r** *stand for the blended sound /***br***/. I will write these letters on the chart. I hear long vowel* **i** *followed by /***t***/. I know that the digraphs* **ie** *and* **igh** *can stand for the /ī/ sound. I will try* **igh** *and see if the word looks right.*

Guide

- Say the word ***pie.*** Have students identify the onset and rime in the word and the letters that stand for the sounds. Remind students that the long ***i*** sound can be spelled in different ways and guide them to use the digraph ***ie.*** Write the word in the first column of the chart as students tell you the word parts.
- Repeat with the word ***sigh***.

Apply

- Have students practice writing each of the words in their word study notebooks. After they write the word, have them check the spelling of the word by blending the onset and rime. Have students highlight the long ***i*** digraph spelling patterns.

Teacher Tips

You may want to show students other spellings for long ***i.*** Review the VCe long ***i*** pattern, as well as looking at words such as ***wild, child, find, kind, bye, eye,*** and ***rye.***

Our Spelling Words

One-Syllable Words	Two-Syllable Words
bright pie sigh high flight lie	brightly lightning tighten

DAY 2

Teacher Tips

Reading Strategies

If students have difficulty applying strategies for challenging words, guide them to use the following strategies:

- look at how the words start and/or end
- look for familiar patterns or parts within the words
- separate the words into syllables and decode each part
- think about what familiar words look like the difficult words
- read forward to check the context
- reread the sentence or paragraph
- mark the words, substitute synonyms, and get on with reading–ask for help later

Comprehension

Use the following questions to ensure that students have understood the passage:

- *What was Brent's idea about his problem?* (Level 1–facts/details)
- *Why did Brent sleep with the light on?* (Level 2–cause/effect)
- *What does the story tell you about Brent?* (Level 3–analyze character)

Fluency

Intervene if students are having difficulty reading the passage. Model how to use word and meaning strategies to problem-solve the words. After students have had a chance to read the passage silently, have them read it aloud for fluency. Model fluent reading of the passage. For students who struggle, you may want to read the passage a second time and have them echo-read along with you.

Blend

- Have students blend the words on the word list for Day Two, using the procedure for blending from Day One.

Develop Automaticity in Word Recognition

- Circle the following words on the overhead transparency: ***always, even, idea, later, still, took, went.*** Tell students that practicing these words will help them recognize the words automatically so they can read more fluently. Explain that they can sound out some of the words, but they will read more quickly if they don't have to stop and sound them out.
- Read each word. Point out the two- and three-syllable words.
- Have students read aloud with you the sentences that contain the words, and then have them write the words in their word study notebooks.
- Give students a copy of blackline master 7. Point out the words from this lesson, as well as other words students have learned previously. Have them cut out the words, store them in an envelope, and use them for practice activities.

Build Fluency with Connected Text

Model

- Read the passage on the overhead transparency aloud. Stop when you come to the two-syllable word ***wanted.*** Model strategies you would use to read the word.
- **Think Aloud:** *One way I can read this word is to break it into syllables. I see two vowels,* **a** *and* **e,** *and two consonants between them. I will divide the word between the two consonants. I have two closed CVC syllables that I can sound out:* **wan/ted.**
- Continue reading. Model making a mistake and correcting it–for example, attempt to sound out ***sigh*** using a short sound: **/s/ /i/ /g/.**
- **Think Aloud:** *Wait a minute. This looked like a closed syllable, so I tried the short sound, but that didn't work. Looking carefully at the word, I see that it has the* **-igh** *pattern. The vowel sound is /ī/ and the word is* **sigh.** *That makes sense. I see another word in the sentence that has the same pattern.*

Guide

- Continue reading, stopping at other words and asking students what strategies they would use to read the words.

Apply

- Have students take turns reading blackline master 3 to a partner or in a small group as you monitor the reading. Use the teacher tips to check comprehension and fluency.

Spelling Words: *high, flight, lie*

- Have students practice writing the spelling words from Day One in their word study notebooks. Have them refer to words on the spelling chart to check their spelling.
- Introduce the Day Two spelling words. Say the word ***high*** and model spelling it and writing it on the list of spelling words on chart paper. Point to the word ***sigh*** on the chart from the Day One spelling words, and model how to use the word family ***-igh*** to spell the new word.
- Repeat with the remaining words and have students practice writing the words in their word study notebooks.

Multisyllabic Words: Vowel Digraph Pattern

Model

- Write the word ***neck*** on the board and point out that it has one closed syllable and one vowel sound.
- Write the word ***necktie*** on the board. Circle the **e** and the digraph ***ie,*** and point out that there is a consonant digraph and another consonant between the vowels. Tell students you will divide the word after the consonant digraph because that digraph shouldn't be divided: ***neck/tie.***
- Remind students that the first syllable is a closed syllable with a short vowel sound, and that the second syllable has a vowel digraph. Model reading the word: **/nek/ /tī/,** ***necktie.***

Guide

- Write the word ***nightly*** on the board and guide students as they identify the vowels and the consonants between the vowels. In this word, tell students that the ***-ight*** stays together and the word is divided after the letter ***t.***
- Have students identify the syllable patterns and read the word.

Apply

- Have students independently blend the two-syllable words on the word list for Day Three. If students need more support, guide them as they blend some or all of the words.

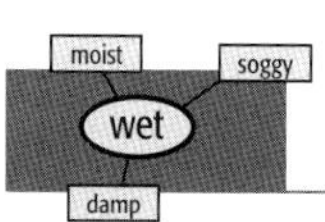

Develop Word Meanings

- Write the following sentences on the board: *I turned to the right at the stoplight; Is this the right answer?* Read the sentences with students and discuss the two meanings of the word ***right.***
- Write the words ***left*** and ***wrong*** on the board. Have students substitute the words for ***right*** in the sentences. Explain that these words are called antonyms and that antonyms are words with opposite meanings.
- Write the following words on the board: ***bright, high, night, tight.*** Have students think of antonyms for the words and use them in oral sentences.

Spelling Words: *brightly, lightning, tighten*

- Have students practice spelling the words from Day One and Day Two by writing them several times in their word study notebooks.
- Introduce the new words, modeling how students can apply what they know about syllable patterns to the spelling of words with more than one syllable.
- Say the word ***brightly.***
- **Think Aloud:** *When I spell this word, I need to think about how the word looks. I hear a long* **i** *in the first syllable, and the second syllable ends with a long* **e** *sound. I remember that this sound at the end of a word is usually the letter* **y.** *I will look at the frieze card to check the spelling patterns. I think I will try the* **-igh** *pattern and see if the word looks right.*
- Repeat with the remaining words. Have students practice the words several times in their word study notebooks.

Build Fluency with Connected Text

- Have students read blackline master 4 to a partner or in small groups as you monitor their reading. Call attention to the following words in the reading passage before students read it: ***away, does, Earth, move, set(s), side, turn(s).***

Teacher Tips

Antonyms

Have students work in small groups to list antonym pairs. Have the group write the pairs one per index card. Then have them play concentration and match the word pairs.

Develop Automaticity in Word Recognition

Have students divide a piece of paper into a 4 x 3 grid. Have them write a high-frequency word from blackline master 7 in each of the squares on the grid. Have the students play bingo in small groups or pairs. Have them take turns to draw a word card and read the word. If students have the word on their grid, they cover it with a marker. The first students to cover all the words wins.

Repeated Reading

Have students practice repeated readings of blackline master 3 to develop fluency.

DAY 4

Teacher Tips

Develop Automaticity in Word Recognition

Make a simple jigsaw puzzle by drawing shapes on cardboard, writing a high-frequency word inside the shape and then cutting up the shape. Place the cut-up pieces in envelopes and have students put together the puzzles and then read the words. Students could also make their own jigsaw puzzles using the high-frequency words.

Repeated Reading

Have students practice repeated readings of blackline master 3 to develop fluency.

Blend

- Have students blend the words from the word list for Day Four, using the procedure for blending from Day One.

Sort Words: Open Sort

- Give each student blackline master 9. As a group, read through the words. Ask students what one thing it is that all the words have in common.
- Have students sort the words any way they want but they have to be able to explain how they sorted them.
- Have students share their sorts with a partner, who must decide how the words are sorted.
- Call the group together and have students share different ways to sort these words. As students make suggestions, arrange the words in the pocket chart into the groups they suggest.

Spelling Words

- Provide practice for students in segmenting words and associating sounds with spellings. Dictate the following words to students and have them write the words on their papers: ***tight, tighten, light, lighten.*** Remind students to use what they have learned about spelling syllables with long ***i*** digraphs.
- Write the words on the board and have students self-correct their papers.
- Dictate the following sentence and have students write it on their papers: *The bright light gave him a fright last night.*
- Write the sentence on the board and have students self-correct their papers.
- Give pairs of students blackline master 6. While one student reads the spelling words, the other student writes them in the "First Try" column. After the student has spelled the words, the partner places a check mark next to words spelled correctly. For the second try, the partner may prompt the student by sounding out the words that were spelled incorrectly the first time. If the second spelling attempt is correct, the partner places a check mark in the "Second Try" column.

Assessment Tip: Use students' completed peer-check blackline masters to note which words gave students difficulty.

Build Fluency with Connected Text

- Give students the reading passage on blackline master 5. Have them take turns reading the passage to a partner. Call attention to the following words in the reading passage before students read it: ***begin(s), face, girl(s), hard, hear(s), need, story.***
- For students who need extra support, have them practice reading the passage aloud in a small group as you monitor their reading.

Spelling Assessment

Use the following procedure to assess students' spelling of Unit Seven words.
- Say each spelling word and use it in a sentence.
- Have students write the words on their papers.
- Continue with the next word on the list.
- When students have finished, collect their papers and analyze their spelling of the words.
- Use the assessment to plan small group or individual practice.

Small Group/Independent Activities

The following activities can be used to provide practice for students who need additional support.

PHONICS AND WORD STRATEGIES

Sort Words Write the following words on index cards: ***bit, side, high, hid, find, sight, write, sigh, like, mitt, lid, drive, night.*** Make a two-column chart with the headings "Long *i*" and "Not Long *i*." Have volunteers take a card and hold it up for the group to read. Have the group decide which column each word belongs in.

Review Long *e* Digraph Syllable Patterns Write the word ***beach*** on the board and ask students to identify the vowels and the vowel sound. Point out that ***ea*** is a vowel digraph, which stands for one sound, and that this kind of syllable is called a vowel digraph syllable. Explain that it is not a closed syllable because a closed syllable has one vowel, and it is not an open syllable because open syllables end with a vowel. Write the word ***easy*** on the board. Underline each vowel and then point to the consonant between them. Ask students where you should divide the word. Have a volunteer come up and divide the word into syllables. Then have students identify the syllable patterns (open and vowel digraph) and blend the word.

AUTOMATICITY IN WORD RECOGNITION

Silly Story Place the high-frequency word cards in a bag. Have students sit in a circle. The first student draws a word from the bag, reads the word, and uses the word in a sentence to begin a story. The next student chooses another card and continues the story, using the new word.

What's the Word? Have students work in small groups and place the high-frequency words from blackline master 7 facedown in the center of the circle. Have students take turns providing clues about a word. The other students race to guess the word.

BUILD FLUENCY WITH CONNECTED TEXT

Repeated Reading Have students practice reading blackline master 3 several times, until they feel they can read it fluently and accurately. Have them work with a partner to time each other as they read the passage aloud. Have them set a goal of reading 90 words per minute.

SPELLING

Make Words Provide a set of letter cards and the week's spelling words on index cards. Have students use the letter cards to spell the words. They should check their spelling by blending the sounds and then looking at the words on the index cards.

Write On Have students write a paragraph that uses as many of the spelling words as possible. Have a partner read the story, circle the spelling words used, and check the spelling.

Word Families Have students write each spelling word in its word family. Then have them add as many words as they can to each word family.

Teacher Tips

Home Connection

Have students take blackline master 11 home to complete with a family member. Students can also take the reading passage on blackline master 3 home to share with their family.

Quick-Check

Assess students' mastery of long i digraph syllable patterns using the quick-check for Unit Seven in this Teacher Resource System.

ELL Support Tip

Help ELL students recognize word patterns by having them complete a word search. Give each student a set of the word cards that are in the word search, a set of letter tiles, and the word search. Have students match the letter tiles with the word, and then ask them to locate the word in the word search. Keep the word search simple at first by not presenting words diagonally. As students' language proficiency grows, create diagonal and more advanced word searches.

Quick-Check: Long i digraph syllable patterns

Student Name ______________________ Assessment Date __________

Segmenting and Blending

Directions: Explain that these words use sounds the student has been learning. Have the student point to each word on the corresponding student sheet, segment the word parts or syllables, and blend them together. Put a ✓ if the student successfully segments and blends the word or reads it as a complete unit. If the student misses the word, record the error.
Example: knight

potpie		highlight		
blight		nigh		
frighten		weeknight		
insight		lie		Score **/8**

Sight Words

Directions: Have the student point to the first word on the corresponding student sheet and read across the line, saying each word as quickly as possible. Put a ✓ if the student successfully reads the word and an **X** if the student hesitates more than a few seconds. If the student misses the word, record the error.

always		think		
even		was		
idea		little		
later		there		
still		when		
took		with		
went		would		
could		like		Score **/16**

Unit Objectives

Students will:

- Read words with r-controlled a syllables
- Review long i digraph syllable patterns
- Blend onset and rime
- Sort words according to word families and vowel sounds
- Read high-frequency words away, idea, left, near, play, until
- Spell words with r-controlled a syllable patterns: smart, scar, shark, start, star, spark, market, garlic, party
- Identify multiple meanings for words

Day 1

Letter Cards:
a, c, d, h, k, m, p, r, s, t,

Word Lists
(BLM 2)

carp

Teacher Word Cards:
carp, dart, harp, mark, park, shark, sharp, smart, tart

Day 2

Word Lists
(BLM 2)

Reading Passage 1
(BLM 3)

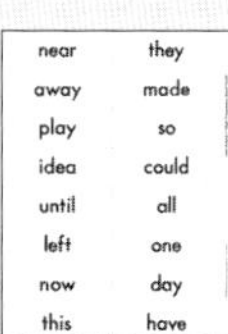

High-Frequency Word Cards for Unit 8 (BLM 7)

Day 3

Word Lists
(BLM 2)

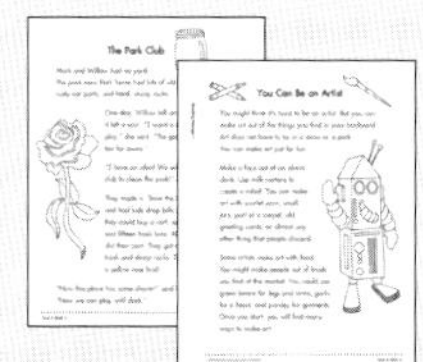

Reading Passages 1 & 2
(BLMs 3 & 4)

Day 4

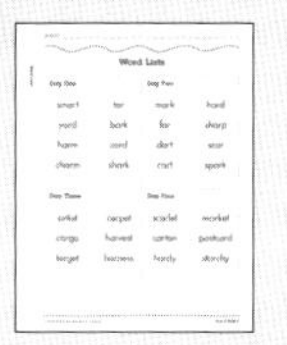

Word Lists (BLM 2)

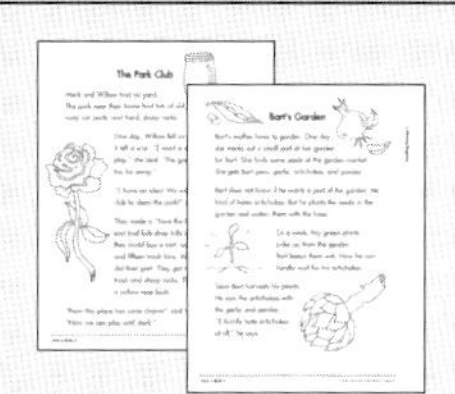

Reading Passages 1 & 3
(BLMs 3 & 5)

bake

Teacher Word Cards:
bake, ban, barn, cart, cat, had, hard, lad, laid, lard, late, main

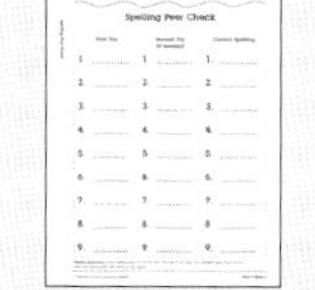

Spelling Peer Check
(BLM 6)

High-Frequency Word Cards for Unit 8 (BLM 7)

Day 5

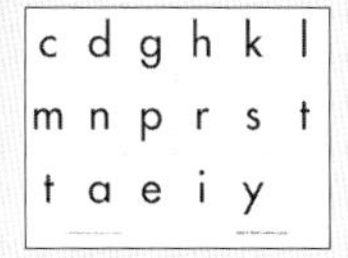

Letter Cards for Unit 8

Reading Passage 1
(BLM 3)

High-Frequency Word Cards for Unit 8 (BLM 7)

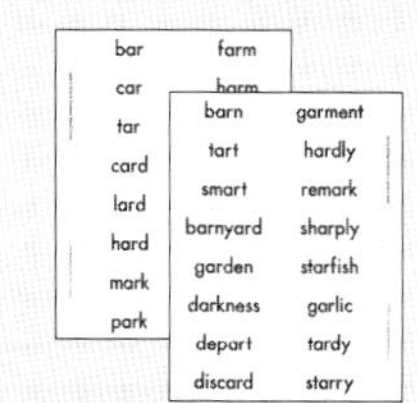

Student Word Cards
(BLMs 8 & 9)

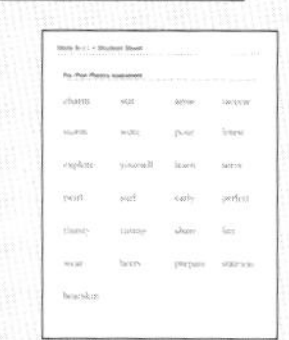

Quick-Check Student Sheet

UNIT 8 r-controlled a syllable patterns

Frieze Card

Take-Home Activity

Core Materials

All of these materials can be downloaded from http://phonicsresources.benchmarkeducation.com.

1 Syllable Introduce r-Controlled *a* Syllable Patterns

Frieze Card

Model

- Hold up the r-controlled ***a*** frieze card and have students name the picture and read the word.
- Remind students that the vowel is neither long nor short, and that when the letter ***r*** follows a vowel, it affects the sound that the vowel stands for.
- Remind students that every syllable in a word has only one vowel sound, so ***shark*** is an example of a one-syllable word. Explain that when words with r-controlled vowels are divided into syllables, the vowel plus the ***r*** usually stay in the same syllable.

Guide

- Give students letter cards **c**, **d**, **h**, **k**, **m**, **p**, **r**, **s**, **t**, and **a**, and have them line up the letters in a row in front of them.
- Say the word ***dark*** and ask students what letter they need to start the word. Then ask what three letters they need to make the **/ärk/** sound. Have them push the letters forward as they say the sounds. Have them read the word. Point out that the word has an r-controlled vowel.
- Have students take away the letter ***d*** and ask what letter they need to replace it with to make the word ***mark.*** Have them make the word and read it. Then have them take away the ***m*** and replace it with a blend to make the word ***stark.***

Apply

- Repeat the steps with the following words: ***harm***, ***charm; part***, ***chart; spark***, ***shark.***

Assessment Tip: Watch to make sure students select the correct letters and read the word. Note which students struggle with this activity, and provide reinforcement activities.

Sort Words: Word Families

- Give each student or pair of students one of the following teacher word cards: **shark**, **park**, **mark**, **sharp**, **carp**, **harp**, **tart**, **smart**, **dart.** Have them hold up their cards for the group to read.
- Have the group decide what word family the word belongs in. Have students with the same word family words stand together. After the words have been sorted, have students read the words in each grouping to check the word family.

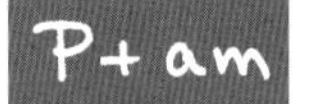

Blend Words with r-Controlled *a*

Model

- Write the word ***charm*** on the board. Point out that the word begins with a consonant digraph.
- Model sounding out the word, blending the onset and rime: **/ch/ /ärm/.** Then say the whole word. Point out that it has one r-controlled vowel sound and one syllable.

Guide

- Guide students as they sound out the word ***cart.*** Repeat with other examples if you feel students need extra support.

- Give students blackline master 2. Have them read each word on the list for Day One by blending the onset and rime.

Apply

- Have students independently sound out the remaining words on the list for Day One. Students who are able to read the words without blending each sound should do so.
- Note which students need more support in blending. Guide them as they read some or all of the words on the list before asking them to read the list independently.

Assessment Tip: Note which students are able to read the words without blending each sound.

Spelling Words: *smart, scar, shark*

Model

- Make a two-column chart on chart paper. Label the first column "One-Syllable Words" and the second column "Two-Syllable Words." Tell students that they will be spelling words with the r-controlled ***a.*** As you work through Unit Eight, you can add the spelling words to the chart and have students use the chart to check their spelling of the words.
- Say the word ***smart*** and model spelling it and writing it on the chart.
- **Think Aloud:** *I hear two parts in the word* **smart: /sm/** *and* **/art/.** *I know that the letters* **s** *and* **m** *stand for the blended sound* **/sm/.** *I will write these letters on the board. I hear* **/art/**, *so I will write the letters* **a**, **r**, *and* **t.** *Then I will blend the onset and rime to check the spelling of the word:* **/sm/ /ärt/**, **smart.** *Now that I know how to spell* **smart**, *I can also spell other words from this word family, such as* **part**, **chart**, *and* **dart.**

Guide

- Say the word ***scar.*** Have students identify the sounds in the word and the letters that stand for the sounds. Write the word in the first column of the chart as students tell you the word parts. Repeat with the word ***shark.***

Apply

- Have students practice writing each of the words in their word study notebooks. After they write the word, have them check the spelling of the word by blending the onset and rime. Have students circle the r-controlled vowel patterns in the words.

Our Spelling Words

One-Syllable Words	Two-Syllable Words
smart scar shark start star spark	market garlic party

DAY 2

Teacher Tips

Reading Strategies

If students have difficulty applying strategies for challenging words, guide them to use the following strategies:

- look at how the words start and/or end
- look for familiar patterns or parts within the words
- separate the words into syllables and decode each part
- think about which familiar words look like the difficult words
- read forward to check the context
- reread the sentence or paragraph
- mark the words, substitute synonyms, and get on with reading–ask for help later

Comprehension

Use the following questions to ensure that students have understood the passage:

- *What was wrong with the park near Mark and Willow's home?* (Level 1–facts and details)
- *How was the park different from the beginning of the story to the end of the story?* (Level 2–compare/contrast)
- *What might happen next?* (Level 3–make predictions)

Fluency

Intervene if students are having difficulty reading the passage. Model how to use word and meaning strategies to problem-solve the words. After students have had a chance to read the passage silently, have them read it aloud for fluency. Model fluent reading of the passage. For students who struggle, you may want to read the passage a second time and have them echo-read along with you.

P+ am Blend

- Have students blend the words on the list for Day Two, using the procedure for blending from Day One.

Develop Automaticity in Word Recognition

- Circle the following words on the overhead transparency: ***away***, ***idea***, ***left***, ***near***, ***play***, ***until.*** Tell students that practicing these words will help them recognize the words automatically so they can read more fluently. Explain that students can sound out some of these words, but they will read more quickly if they don't have to stop and sound them out each time they see them.
- Read each word. Point out that ***play*** and ***away*** end with the same sounds and that ***idea*** has three vowel sounds and three syllables.
- Have students read aloud with you the sentences in the passage that contain the words. Then have them write the words in their word study notebooks.
- Give students a copy of blackline master 7. Point out the words from this lesson, as well as other words they have learned previously. Have them cut out the words, store them in an envelope, and use them for practice activities.

Build Fluency with Connected Text

Model

- Read the passage on the overhead transparency aloud. Stop at the word ***Willow***. Model strategies you would use to read it.
- **Think Aloud:** *This is a name I don't recognize. When I divide it into syllables between the two letter* **ls**, *I get two smaller word parts that I know:* **wil** *and* **low**. *Her name is* **Willow.** *That's a nice name.*
- Model making a mistake and correcting it–for example, read ***scare*** instead of ***scar.***
- **Think Aloud:** *"It left a scare." I don't think that makes sense. Let me see. Oh, the word ends with* **/r/** *and there is an r-controlled vowel so I'll try the* **/är/** *sound:* **scar.** *"It left a scar." Yes, that makes sense.*

Guide

- Continue reading and stop at other words in the passage. Guide students as they read the words.

Apply

- Have students take turns reading blackline master 3 to a partner or in a small group as you monitor the reading. Use the teacher tips to check comprehension and fluency.

Spelling Words: *start, star, spark*

- Have students practice writing the spelling words from Day One in their word study notebooks. Have them refer to words on the spelling chart to check their spelling.
- Introduce the Day Two spelling words. Say the word ***star*** and model spelling it and writing it on the chart of spelling words. Point to the word ***scar*** on the chart from the Day One spelling words and highlight how the words are similar. Model how to use ***scar*** to spell the new word and other words in the word family–for example: ***far***, ***spar***, ***tar.***
- Repeat with the remaining spelling words for Day Two and have students practice writing the words in their word study notebooks.

Multisyllabic Words: r-Controlled *a* Syllables

Model

- Write the word ***card*** on the board and point out that it has one syllable.
- Write the word ***garden*** on the board. Show students how to use what they know about vowel patterns and syllables to read longer words. Highlight the two consonants between the vowels ***a*** and ***e***, and divide the word between the consonants: **gar/den.**
- Point out the r-controlled syllable and the closed syllable before sounding out the syllables: **/gar/ /den/**, ***garden.***

Guide

- Write the word ***harvest*** on the board and guide students to identify the two vowels and the number of consonants between the vowels.
- Guide students as they divide the word: ***har/vest.*** Ask what syllable patterns they see and what clues this gives them about the vowel sounds in each syllable.

Apply

- Have students independently blend the two-syllable words on the word list for Day Three. If students need more support, guide them as they blend some or all of the words.

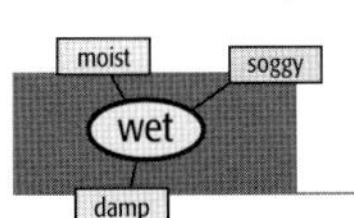

Develop Word Meanings

- Tell students that words can have more than one meaning. Using the overhead, point out the word ***park*** and ask students what the word means in this passage. Challenge them to think of another meaning for the word. Provide an example sentence if students have difficulty: I will park the car in the driveway.
- Highlight the following words in the passage: ***club***, ***bills***, ***part***, ***bark***, ***play.*** Have students read aloud the sentences in which the words are found. Have them tell what each word means in the passage.
- Assign pairs of students one or more of these words from the passage and have them write sentences illustrating the different meanings of the word(s). Have students share their sentences and discuss the different meanings of the words.

Spelling Words: *market, garlic, party*

- Have students practice spelling the words from Day One and Day Two by writing them several times in their word study notebooks.
- Introduce the new spelling words, modeling how students can apply what they know about syllables to the spelling of words with more than one syllable.
- Say the word ***party.***
- **Think Aloud:** *When I spell this word, I need to think about how the word looks. I hear two syllables in the word. The first syllable has an r-controlled* **a** *sound. The second syllable is an open syllable that ends with /ē/. I know that the letter* **y** *stands for the long* **e** *sound at the end of a word. I will write the word and see if it looks right.*
- Repeat with the remaining words.
- Have students practice the words several times in their word study notebooks.

Build Fluency with Connected Text

- Have students read blackline master 4 to a partner or in small groups as you monitor their reading. Call attention to the following words in the reading passage before students read it: ***almost***, ***does***, ***food***, ***head***, ***it's***, ***might***, ***once.***

Teacher Tips

Multiple Meanings

After students have read the words in the passage and talked about their meanings, have them work with a partner to show the multiple meanings of one or more of the words, using illustrations instead of words. The pairs could show their drawings to the group and have them guess which word they have illustrated.

Develop Automaticity in Word Recognition

Have students cut out letters from newspaper headlines to spell the high-frequency words ***away, idea, left, near, play,*** and ***until.*** Have them paste the letters on a sheet of paper or in their word study notebooks. Challenge them to make as many of the words as they can.

Repeated Reading

Have students practice repeated readings of blackline master 3 to develop fluency.

DAY 4

Teacher Tips

Develop Automaticity in Word Recognition

Have students use the word cards from blackline master 7 in small groups. Have them spread one set of words faceup on the floor. Place another set of cards facedown in a stack. Have one student draw a card and read it. The rest of the students race to find the matching word in the words spread out on the floor.

Repeated Reading

Have students practice repeated readings of blackline master 3 to develop fluency.

P+am Blend

- Have students blend the words on the word list for Day Four, using the procedure for blending from Day One.

Sort Words: Short, Long, and r-Controlled *a*

- Place the following teacher word cards in random order in a pocket chart: **ban**, **barn**, **cat**, **cart**, **had**, **hard**, **lad**, **lard**, **bake**, **late**, **laid**, **main.** Have students read each word with you.
- Place the word cards **ban**, **barn**, and **bake** apart from the rest of the cards. Ask students why each card is in a different group. Ask students if you should put the word card **cat** with **ban**, **barn**, or **bake.**
- Ask students where to put the remaining word cards.
- Challenge students to think of other ways the word cards could be sorted. (by beginning letter, final letter, number of letters, etc.)

Spelling Words

- Provide practice for students in segmenting words and associating sounds with spellings. Dictate the following words to students and have them write the words on their papers: ***car***, ***carpet***, ***mark***, ***remark.*** Remind students to use what they have learned about spelling words with more than one syllable.
- Write the words on the board and have students self-correct their papers.
- Dictate the following sentence and have students write it on their papers: *I got a chart, a charm, and a jar of lard at the market.*
- Write the sentence on the board and have students self-correct their papers.
- Give pairs of students blackline master 6. While one student reads the spelling words, the other student writes them in the "First Try" column. After the student has spelled the words, the partner places a check mark next to words spelled correctly. For the second try, the partner may prompt the student by sounding out the words that were spelled incorrectly the first time. If the second spelling attempt is correct, the partner places a check mark in the "Second Try" column.

Assessment Tip: Use students' completed peer-check blackline masters to note which words gave students difficulty.

Build Fluency with Connected Text

- Have students take turns reading blackline master 5 to a partner or in a small group as you monitor their reading. Call attention to the following words in the reading passage before students read it: ***does***, ***eat(s)***, ***keep(s)***, ***kind***, ***mother***, ***plant(s)***, ***soon.***

Spelling Assessment

Use the following procedure to assess students' spelling of the Unit Eight words.

- Say each spelling word and use it in a sentence.
- Have students write the words on their papers.
- Continue with the next word on the list.
- When students have finished, collect their papers and analyze their spelling of the words.
- Use the assessment to plan small group or individual practice.

Small Group/Independent Activities

The following activities can be used to provide practice for students who need additional support.

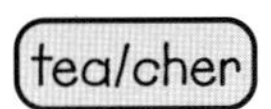

PHONICS AND WORD STRATEGIES

Review Long *i* Digraph Syllable Patterns Write the word ***pie*** on the board and ask students to identify the vowel and the vowel sound. Point out it is a vowel digraph, which stands for one sound, and that this kind of syllable is called a vowel digraph syllable. Explain that it is not a closed syllable because a closed syllable has one vowel. Explain that although it ends with a vowel, it is not an open syllable because open syllables have one vowel. Write the word ***magpie*** on the board. Underline each vowel and then point to the consonants between them. Ask students where you should divide the word. Have a volunteer come up and divide the word into syllables. Then have students identify the syllable patterns (closed and vowel digraph) and blend the word.

Sort Words Write the following words on the board in random order: ***cap***, ***part***, ***pat***, ***fad***, ***bar***, ***date***, ***dart***, ***had***, ***cape***, ***hard***, ***barb***, ***fade***, ***late***, and ***carp.*** Have students make a three-column chart in their word study notebooks with the headings "Long ***a***," "Short ***a***," and "r-controlled ***a***." Have them sort the words into the correct columns.

AUTOMATICITY IN WORD RECOGNITION

Read the Word Have students select several high-frequency words and write sentences using the words, leaving blanks in place of the words. Have students exchange sentences with a partner and fill in the missing high-frequency words.

Write the Words Have students work with a partner and an envelope containing the high-frequency word cards. Have one student take out a word from the envelope and read it while the partner writes the word in his or her word study notebook. The reader then checks the writer's spelling of the word. The partners then change roles.

BUILD FLUENCY WITH CONNECTED TEXT

Repeated Reading Have students practice reading blackline master 3 several times, until they feel they can read it fluently and accurately. Have them work with a partner to time each other as they read the passage aloud. Have them set a goal of reading 90 words per minute.

SPELLING

Make Words Provide a set of letter cards and the week's spelling words on index cards. Have students use the letter cards to spell the words. They should check their spelling by blending the sounds and then looking at the words on the index cards.

Unscramble Write the following spelling words on the board by scrambling the letters: ***arksh***, ***tyarp***, ***karmet***, ***tars***, ***matrs***, ***ligarc.*** Have students unscramble the letters and write the words in their word study notebooks.

Teacher Tips

Home Connection

Have students take blackline master 11 home to complete with a family member. Students can also take the reading passage on blackline master 3 home to share with their family.

Quick-Check

Assess students' mastery of r-controlled a syllable patterns using the quick-check for Unit Eight in this Teacher Resource System.

ELL Support Tip

To continue developing oral language, have students form language buddy partnerships. These partnerships should pair ELL students with someone slightly more proficient. Language buddies will help build confidence and give less proficient language learners more opportunity to hear and say the word patterns. As you say a word, buddies can turn to each other and say the word together. When working with letter cards, buddies can work together, with one partner saying the word and the other finding the letter cards. They can switch roles for the next word. During the word sorts, language buddies can discuss where to put the words.

Quick-Check: r-controlled a syllable patterns

Student Name ______________________ Assessment Date __________

Segmenting and Blending

Directions: Explain that these words use sounds the student has been learning. Have the student point to each word on the corresponding student sheet, segment the word parts or syllables, and blend them together. Put a ✓ if the student successfully segments and blends the word or reads it as a complete unit. If the student misses the word, record the error.
Example: chart

embark		arch		
alarm		arctic		
yarn		pardon		
boxcar		radar		Score **/8**

Sight Words

Directions: Have the student point to the first word on the corresponding student sheet and read across the line, saying each word as quickly as possible. Put a ✓ if the student successfully reads the word and an **X** if the student hesitates more than a few seconds. If the student misses the word, record the error.

near		they		
away		made		
play		so		
idea		could		
until		all		
left		one		
now		day		
this		have		Score **/16**

UNIT 9 **r-controlled o syllable patterns**

Unit Objectives

Students will:

- Recognize and read words with r-controlled o syllables
- Review r-controlled a syllables
- Blend onset and rime
- Sort words according to word families and vowel sounds
- Read high-frequency words began, don't, here, never, next, second, went
- Spell one- and two-syllable words with r-controlled o syllable patterns: score, fort, horn, shore, short, thorn, before, forest, hornet
- Use context clues to figure out word meanings

UNIT 9 r-controlled o syllable patterns

Day 1

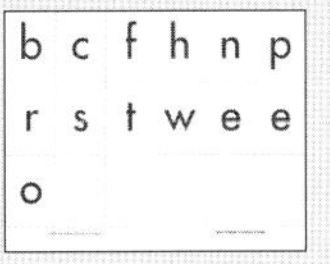

Letter Cards for Unit 9

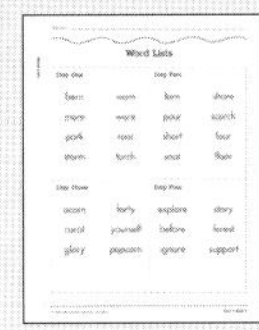
Word Lists (BLM 2)

barn

Teacher Word Cards: **barn, chore, fort, mark, port, scar, scorch, snore, starch, yard**

Day 2

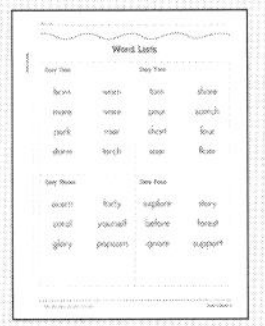
Word Lists (BLM 2)

Reading Passage 1 (BLM 3)

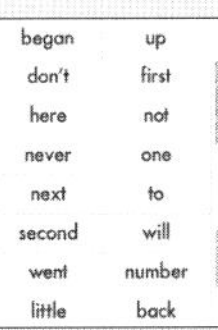

High-Frequency Word Cards for Unit 8 (BLM 7)

Day 3

Word Lists (BLM 2)

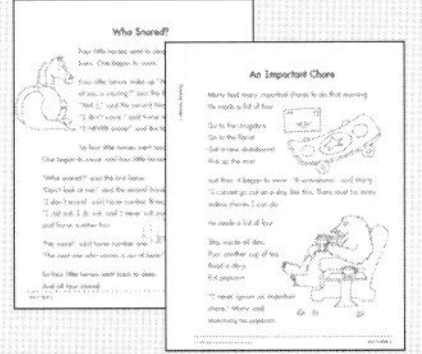
Reading Passages 1 & 2 (BLMs 3 & 4)

Day 4

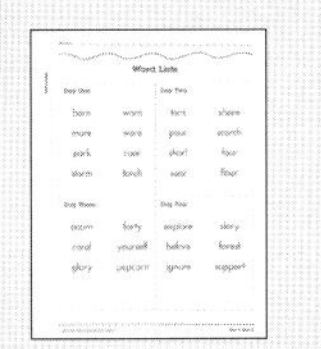
Word Lists (BLM 2)

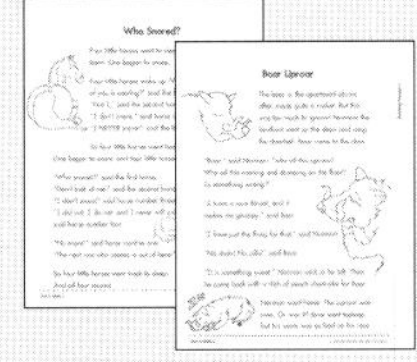
Reading Passages 1 & 3 (BLMs 3 & 5)

blond

Teacher Word Cards: **blond, born, bone, chore, cod, cop, cord, corn, moan, mop, more, stock, stop, stork, storm, stove**

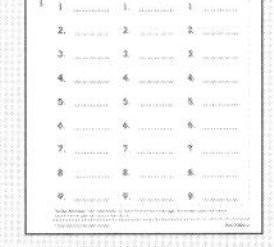
Spelling Peer Check (BLM 6)

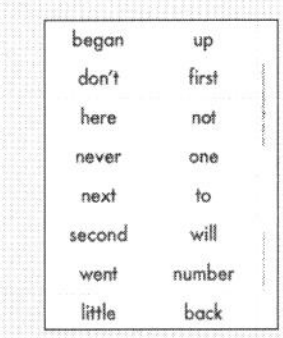

High-Frequency Word Cards for Unit 8 (BLM 7)

Day 5

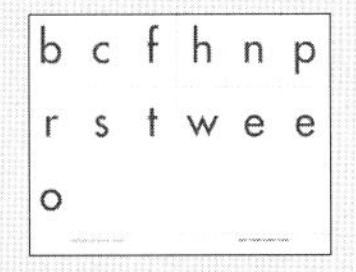

Letter Cards for Unit 8

Reading Passage 1 (BLM 3)

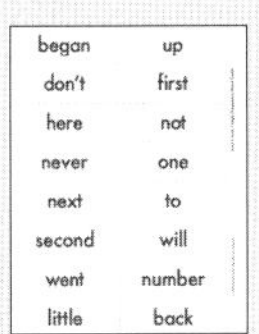

High-Frequency Word Cards for Unit 8 (BLM 7)

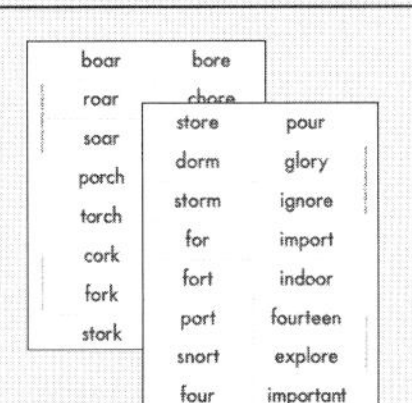

Student Word Cards (BLMs 8 & 9)

Quick-Check Student Sheet

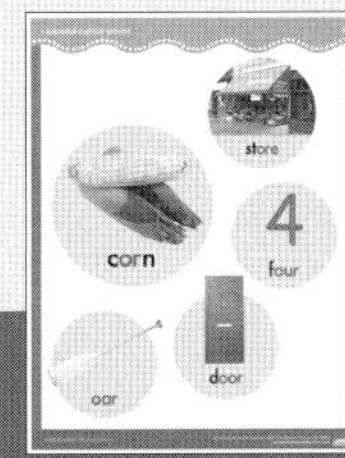

Frieze Card

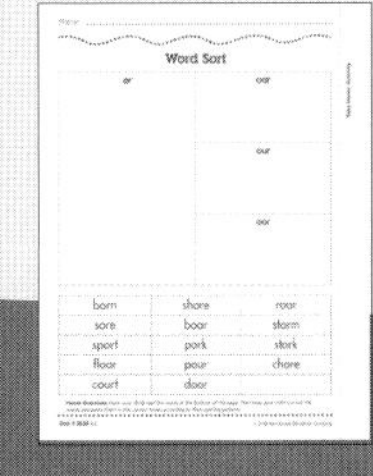
Take-Home Activity

Core Materials

All of these materials can be downloaded from http://phonicsresources.benchmarkeducation.com.

DAY 1

Frieze Card

1 Syllable — Introduce r-Controlled *o* Syllable Patterns

Model

- Hold up the r-controlled ***o*** frieze card and have students read the words.
- Remind students that the vowels in the words are not long or short, but are affected by the letter ***r***. Point out that in the words ***door***, ***oar***, and ***four***, the letter ***r*** affects the sound of the vowel digraphs.
- Explain that when words with r-controlled vowels are divided into syllables, the vowel (or vowel digraph) plus the ***r*** usually stay in the same syllable.

Guide

- Give students letter cards **b**, **c**, **h**, **n**, **p**, **r**, **s**, **t**, **w**, **e**, and **o**, and have them line up the letters in a row in front of them.
- Say the word ***born*** and ask students what letter they need to start the word. Then ask what three letters they need to make the sound **/ôrn/**. Have them decide which r-controlled pattern shown on the frieze card they will use. Have them push the letters forward and read the word.
- Have students take away the letter card **b** and ask what two letters they need to replace it with to make the word ***sworn.*** Have them make the word and read it. Then have them change the blend to spell the word ***scorn.***

Apply

- Repeat the steps with the following words: ***sort***, ***snort***, ***sport***, ***bore***, ***chore***, ***snore.***

Assessment Tip: Watch to make sure students select the correct letters and read the word. Guide those who need support.

Sort Words: r-Controlled Vowels *o, a*

- Place the following teacher word cards in a pocket chart: **barn**, **mark**, **scar**, **starch**, **yard**, **chore**, **scorch**, **snore**, **port**, **fort.** Read each word with students.
- Give each student or pair of students one of the word cards. Have them hold up their cards for the group to read.
- Ask students to stand to your right if they have a word with r-controlled ***a***, and to the left if they have a word with r-controlled ***o.*** Have students in the group on the right hold up their cards while the students on the left read the words to check that they all have r-controlled ***a.*** Repeat with the words students on the left are holding–have them check that all words are r-controlled ***o.***
- Place the cards back in the pocket chart and ask students what other ways they can think of to sort the words. Have them write their sorts in their word study notebooks and write why they sorted the words the way they did.

P+am — Blend Words with r-Controlled *o*

- Write the word ***chore*** on the board. Point out that the word begins with a consonant digraph.
- Model sounding out the word, blending the onset and rime: **/ch/ /ôr/.** Then say the whole word. Point out that it has one r-controlled vowel sound and one syllable.

Guide

- Guide students as they sound out the word ***roar.*** Repeat with other examples if you feel students need extra support.
- Give students blackline master 2. Have them read each word on the word list for Day One by blending the onset and rime.

Apply

- Have students independently sound out the remaining words on the list for Day One. Guide students who need support to read some or all of the words before asking them to read the list independently.

Assessment Tip: Note which students are able to read the words without blending each sound.

Spelling Words: *score, fort, horn*

Model

- Make a two-column chart on chart paper. Label the first column "One-Syllable Words" and the second column "Two-Syllable Words." Tell students that they will be spelling words with an r-controlled ***o***. As you work through Unit Nine, add the daily spelling words to the chart, and have students use the chart to check their spelling of the words.
- Say the word ***score*** and model spelling it and writing it on the chart.
- **Think Aloud:** *I hear two parts in the word* **score:** */***sk***/ and /***ôr***/. I know that the letters* **s** *and* **c** *stand for the blended sound /***sk***/. I hear /***ôr***/, so I write the letters* **o** *and* **r.** *Then I blend the onset and rime to check the spelling of the word: /***sk***/ /***ôr***/,* **scor.** *This doesn't look right. I think I need to add a final* **e** *like I see in the word* **store** *on the frieze card.*

Guide

- Say the word ***fort.*** Have students identify the sounds in the word and the letters that stand for the sounds. Write the word in the first column of the chart as students tell you the word parts. Repeat with the word ***horn.***

Apply

- Have students practice writing each of the words in their word study notebooks. Have them highlight the r-controlled ***o*** patterns in the words.

Our Spelling Words

One-Syllable Words	Two-Syllable Words
score fort horn shore short thorn	before forest hornet

DAY 2

Teacher Tips

Reading Strategies

If students have difficulty applying strategies for challenging words, guide them to use the following strategies:

- look at how the words start and/or end
- look for familiar patterns or parts within the words
- separate the words into syllables and decode each part
- think about what familiar words look like the difficult words
- read forward to check the context
- reread the sentence or paragraph
- mark the words, substitute synonyms, and get on with reading–ask for help later

Comprehension

Use the following questions to ensure that students have understood the passage:

- *Where does this story take place?* (Level 1–story elements)
- *What happened after the horses went back to sleep?* (Level 2–sequence)
- *What might happen next?* (Level 3–make predictions)

Fluency

Intervene if students are having difficulty reading the passage. Model how to use word and meaning strategies to problem-solve the words. After students have had a chance to read the passage silently, have them read it aloud for fluency. Model fluent reading of the passage. For students who struggle, you may want to read the passage a second time and have them echo-read along with you.

P+ am Blend

- Have students blend the words on the word list for Day Two, using the procedure for blending from Day One.

Develop Automaticity in Word Recognition

- Circle the following words on the overhead transparency: ***began***, ***don't***, ***here***, ***never***, ***next***, ***second***, ***went.***
- Tell students that practicing these words will help them recognize the words automatically so they can read more fluently. Explain that students can sound out some of these words, but they will read more quickly if they don't have to stop and sound out the words each time they see them.
- Read each word. Point out that ***don't*** is a contraction meaning ***do not.***
- Have students read aloud with you the sentences in the passage that contain the words. Then have them write the words in their word study notebooks.
- Give students a copy of blackline master 7. Point out the words from this lesson as well as other words they have learned previously. Have them cut out the words, store them in an envelope, and use them for practice activities.

Build Fluency with Connected Text

Model

- Read the passage on the overhead transparency aloud. Stop at the word ***barn.*** Call attention to the r-controlled syllables.
- **Think Aloud:** *This word has two examples of r-controlled* **a** *syllable patterns, which we learned about in the last unit. I divide the word between the* **n** *and the* **y** *because the letter* **r** *stays with the letter* **a.** *This breaks the word into two smaller parts that are easier for me to read.*
- Model making a mistake and correcting it–for example, read ***went*** instead of ***woke.***
- **Think Aloud:** *Oh, that's not right. I just looked at the beginning letter. I need to look at the word more carefully. I see it is a VCe word, so I will try the long* **o** *sound:* **woke.** *Yes, that sounds better.*

Guide

- Continue reading and stop at other words in the passage. Guide students as they read the words.

Apply

- Have students take turns reading blackline master 3 to a partner or in a small group as you monitor the reading. Use the teacher tips to check comprehension and fluency.

Spelling Words: *shore, short, thorn*

- Have students practice writing the spelling words from Day One in their word study notebooks. Have them refer to words on the spelling chart to check their spelling.
- Introduce the Day Two spelling words. Say the word ***short*** and model spelling it and writing it on the chart of spelling words. Point to the word ***fort*** on the chart from the Day One spelling words and highlight how the words are similar. Model how to use ***fort*** to spell the new word and other words in the word family–for example: ***port***, ***sort***, and ***snort.***
- Repeat with the remaining spelling words for Day Two and have students practice writing the words in their word study notebooks.

DAY 3

Multisyllabic Words: r-Controlled *o*

Model
- Write the word ***for*** on the board, read it, and point out that it has one syllable.
- Write the word ***forget*** on the board. Show students how to use what they know about vowel patterns and syllables to read longer words. Highlight the two consonants between the vowels ***o*** and ***e***, and divide the word between the consonants: ***for/get.*** Before sounding out the syllables, point out that the word has an r-controlled syllable and a closed syllable: **/for/ /get/**, ***forget.***

Guide
- Write the word ***resort*** on the board and guide students to identify the single consonant between the two vowels ***e*** and ***o.***
- Guide students as they divide the word: ***re/sort.*** Ask what syllable patterns they see and what clues this gives them about the vowel sounds in each syllable.

Apply
- Have students independently blend the two-syllable words on the word list for Day Three. If students need more support, guide them as they blend some or all of the words.

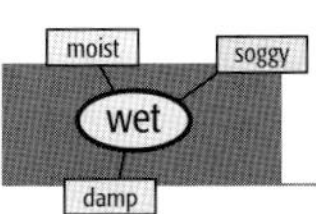

Develop Word Meanings

- Write the following sentence on the board and underline the word ***hornet:*** *A hornet is also known as a paper wasp.* Model how to divide ***hornet*** into two syllables and then sound out the parts.
- Ask students how they could figure out the meaning of the word ***hornet*** if they didn't know what it meant. Point out the context clue "also known as." Tell students that as they begin to read larger words with several syllables, it is important that they both sound out the words and use the context clues in sentences around the words to figure out their meanings.
- Repeat the process with the following sentences, having students sound out the two-syllable words and confirm their meanings through the context of the sentences: *I went to the florist to buy some roses; She was mourning because her pet goldfish died; The hot sun was scorching the plants; When the nose on the doll was chipped, her face looked deformed.*

Spelling Words: *before, forest, hornet*

- Have students practice spelling the words from Day One and Day Two by writing them several times in their word study notebooks.
- Introduce the new spelling words, modeling how students can apply what they know about syllables to the spelling of words with more than one syllable.
- Say the word ***forest.***
- **Think Aloud:** *When I spell this word, I need to think about how it looks. I hear two syllables. The first one has an r-controlled vowel and the second one has a short* **e** *sound and ends with consonant blend. I will look at the frieze card to check the r-controlled patterns. I think I will try the* **or** *spelling pattern and see if the word looks right.*
- Repeat with the remaining words.
- Have students practice the words several times in their word study notebooks.

Build Fluency with Connected Text

- Have students read blackline master 4 to a partner or in small groups as you monitor their reading. Call attention to the following words in the reading passage before students read it: ***another***, ***began***, ***eat***, ***list***, ***must***, ***never***, ***read.***

Teacher Tips

Context Clues

Give students extra practice in using context clues by providing them with sentences in which you have deleted a key word.

Develop Automaticity in Word Recognition

Have students work with a partner to flash the high-frequency words on blackline master 7.

Repeated Reading

Have students practice repeated readings of blackline master 3 to develop fluency.

DAY 4

Teacher Tips

Climb the Ladder

Have pairs of students draw a ladder on a sheet of paper. Have them place a set of high-frequency words from blackline master 7 in a stack. Have the students take turns drawing a card and reading the word. If the word is read correctly, the student can move a marker up one rung on the ladder. Continue until one of the students in the pairs reaches the top of the ladder.

Repeated Reading

Have students practice repeated readings of blackline master 3 to develop fluency.

Blend

- Have students blend the words on the word list for Day Four, using the procedure for blending from Day One.

Sort Words: Short, Long, and r-Controlled *o*

- Place the following teacher word cards in random order in the pocket chart: **blond**, **stock**, **stop**, **cop**, **cod**, **mop**, **born**, **stork**, **storm**, **corn**, **chore**, **cord**, **more**, **bone**, **moan**, **stove.** Have students read each word with you.
- Set the word cards **cop**, **born**, and **moan** apart from the rest of the cards. Ask students why these words should be in different groups.
- Once students recognize that one word has short ***o***, one has a long ***o***, and the other has an r-controlled ***o***, have them tell you which words you should group under the three words.
- Challenge students to think of other ways the word cards could be sorted. (by beginning letter, final letter, number of letters, etc.)

Spelling Words

- Provide practice for students in segmenting words and associating sounds with spellings. Dictate the following words to students and have them write the words on their papers: ***corn***, ***four***, ***fourteen***, ***popcorn.*** Remind students to use what they have learned about spelling words with more than one syllable.
- Write the words on the board and have students self-correct their papers.
- Dictate the following sentence and have students write it on their papers: *I had a sore throat before I went indoors.*
- Write the sentence on the board and have students self-correct their papers.
- Give pairs of students blackline master 6. While one student reads the spelling words, the other student writes them in the "First Try" column. After the student has spelled the words, the partner places a check mark next to words spelled correctly. For the second try, the partner may prompt the student by sounding out the words that were spelled incorrectly the first time. If the second spelling attempt is correct, the partner places a check mark in the "Second Try" column.

Assessment Tip: Use students' completed peer-check blackline masters to note which words gave students difficulty.

Build Fluency with Connected Text

- Have students take turns reading blackline master 5 to a partner or in a small group as you monitor their reading. Call attention to the following words in the reading passage before students read it: ***above***, ***home***, ***left***, ***often***, ***something***, ***went***, ***why.***

Spelling Assessment

Use the following procedure to assess students' spelling of the Unit Nine words.

- Say each spelling word and use it in a sentence.
- Have students write the words on their papers.
- Continue with the next word on the list.
- When students have finished, collect their papers and analyze their spelling of the words.
- Use the assessment to plan small group or individual practice.

Small Group/Independent Activities

The following activities can be used to provide practice for students who need additional support.

PHONICS AND WORD STRATEGIES

Review r-Controlled *a* Syllable Patterns Write the word ***harm*** on the board and ask students to identify the vowel and the vowel sound. Point out that the vowel is neither long nor short and that it is affected by the letter ***r***. Explain that this kind of syllable is called an r-controlled syllable. Explain that it is not a closed syllable because even though a closed syllable has one vowel like this word does, this word also has the letter ***r***, which affects the vowel sound. Write the word ***garden*** on the board. Underline each vowel and then point to the consonants between them. Ask students where you should divide the word. Have a volunteer come up and divide the word into syllables. Then have students identify the syllable patterns (closed and r-controlled) and blend the word.

Word Search Have students make a two-column chart labeled "One-Syllable Words" and "Two-Syllable Words" in their word study notebooks. Have them search through familiar books in the classroom to find examples of words with r-controlled ***o*** and write them in their charts.

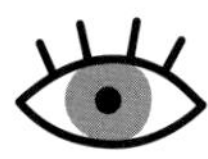

AUTOMATICITY IN WORD RECOGNITION

Write a Sentence Have students write a sentence, using as many of the following high-frequency words as they can: ***began***, ***don't***, ***here***, ***never***, ***next***, ***second***, ***went***. Have each student give his/her sentence to a partner to read.

Make Sentences Have students or groups of students sit in a circle and place the high-frequency words in a stack. Have a student draw a word, read it, and use it in an oral sentence. Have the student pass the word to the next student in the circle who uses the word in a different oral sentence. Continue around the circle until every student has made up a sentence. Repeat with the remaining words.

BUILD FLUENCY WITH CONNECTED TEXT

Repeated Reading Have students practice reading blackline master 3 several times, until they feel they can read it fluently and accurately. Have them work with a partner to time each other as they read the passage aloud. Have them set a goal of reading 90 words per minute.

SPELLING

Make Words Provide a set of letter cards and the week's spelling words on index cards. Have students use the letter cards to spell the words. They should check their spelling by blending the sounds and then looking at the words on the index cards.

Beat the Teacher Draw blanks on the board for the number of letters in one of the spelling words. Draw a circle next to it. Have students guess one of the letters. If the letter is incorrect, add an eye. Continue having students guess, adding facial features if they are incorrect–for example, two eyes and ears, a nose, and a mouth. If students can fill in the blanks before the face is complete, they beat the teacher.

Teacher Tips

Home Connection

Have students take blackline master 11 home to complete with a family member. Students can also take the reading passage on blackline master 3 home to share with their family.

Quick-Check

Assess students' mastery of r-controlled o syllable patterns using the quick-check for Unit Nine in this Teacher Resource System.

ELL Support Tip

Give groups of students two sets of word cards to play concentration, as well as a T-chart that matches the spelling chart. Each time a student gets a matched pair of word cards, have the rest of the group say the word, clap out the syllables, and write the word on the spelling chart in either the one- or two-syllable column.

Quick-Check: r-controlled o syllable patterns

Student Name ______________________________ Assessment Date ______________

Segmenting and Blending

Directions: Explain that these words use sounds the student has been learning. Have the student point to each word on the corresponding student sheet, segment the word parts or syllables, and blend them together. Put a ✓ if the student successfully segments and blends the word or reads it as a complete unit. If the student misses the word, record the error.
Example: porch

distort		inform		
implore		adorn		
pore		carport		
format		ashore		Score **/8**

Sight Words

Directions: Have the student point to the first word on the corresponding student sheet and read across the line, saying each word as quickly as possible. Put a ✓ if the student successfully reads the word and an **X** if the student hesitates more than a few seconds. If the student misses the word, record the error.

began		up		
don't		first		
here		not		
never		one		
next		to		
second		will		
went		number		
little		back		Score **/16**

Unit Objectives

Students will:

- Recognize and read words with r-controlled e, i, u syllable patterns
- Review r-controlled o syllable patterns
- Blend onset and rime
- Sort words according to word families and vowel sounds
- Read high-frequency words another, because, got, head, really, saw, thought
- Spell words with r-controlled e, i, u syllable patterns: learn, girl, turn, heard, twirl, churn, person, dirty, turnip
- Recognize and use descriptive words and their antonym pairs

Day 1

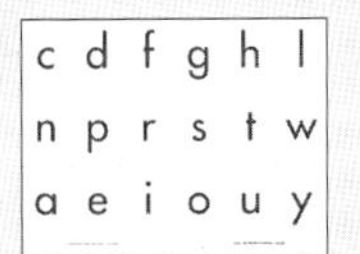

Letter Cards: **d, e, f, h, i, l, n, p, r, s, t, u**

Word Lists (BLM 2)

bit

Teacher Word Cards: **bit, bite, earth, eat, nurse, nut, skirt, skit, team, ten, term, tune, turn**

Day 2

Word Lists (BLM 2)

Reading Passage 1 (BLM 3)

High-Frequency Word Cards for Unit 10 (BLM 7)

Day 3

Word Lists (BLM 2)

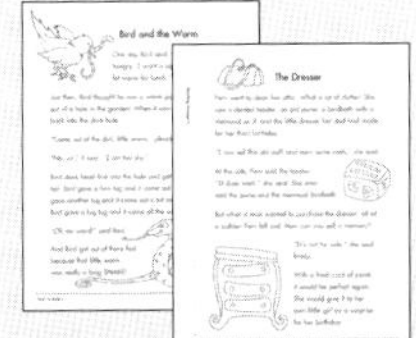

Reading Passages 1 & 2 (BLMs 3 & 4)

Day 4

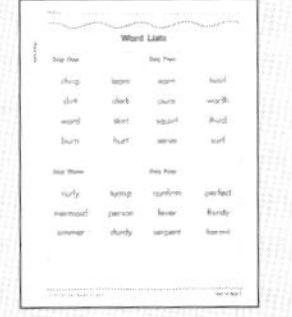

Word Lists (BLM 2)

Reading Passages 1 & 3 (BLMs 3 & 5)

blurb

Teacher Word Cards: **blurb, burn, churn, clerk, curb, dirt, fir, germ, jerk, perk, sir, squirt, stir, term, turn**

Spelling Peer Check (BLM 6)

High-Frequency Word Cards for Unit 10 (BLM 7)

Day 5

Letter Cards for Unit 10

Reading Passage 1 (BLM 3)

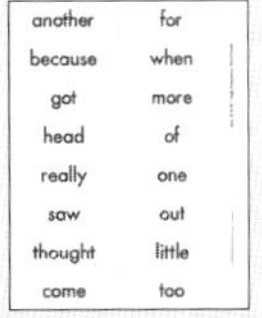

High-Frequency Word Cards for Unit 10 (BLM 7)

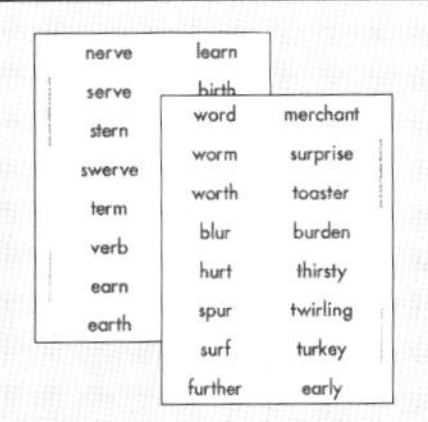

Student Word Cards (BLMs 8 & 9)

Quick-Check Student Sheet

Frieze Card

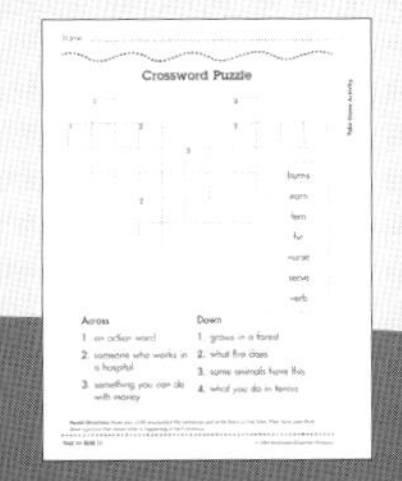

Take-Home Activity

Core Materials

All of these materials can be downloaded from http://phonicsresources.benchmarkeducation.com.

UNIT 10 r-controlled e, i, u syllable patterns

DAY 1

Introduce r-Controlled *e, i, u* Syllable Patterns

1 Syllable

Frieze Card

Model

- Hold up the r-controlled ***e, i, u*** frieze card and have students name the pictures and read the words.
- Remind students that the vowel is neither long nor short when it is followed by the letter ***r.***
- Point out that every syllable in a word has only one vowel sound, so the words on the frieze card are examples of one-syllable words. Explain that when words with r-controlled vowels are divided into syllables, the vowel plus the ***r*** usually stay in the same syllable.
- Explain that the ***ea*** in the word ***earth*** is a vowel digraph that is affected by the letter ***r.***

Guide

- Give students letter cards **d, f, h, l, n, p, r, s, t, e, i,** and **u,** and have them line up the letters in a row in front of them.
- Say the word ***dirt*** and ask students what letter they need to start the word. Then ask what three letters they need to make the **/ûrt/** sound. Have them decide which r-controlled pattern on the frieze card they will use. Have them push the letters forward as they say and read the word. Have them check to see if the word looks right. Point out that the word is a closed syllable with an r-controlled vowel.
- Have students take away the letter ***d*** and ask what letters they need to replace it with to make the word ***flirt.*** Have them make the word and read it. Then have them replace the ***fl*** to make the word ***shirt.***

Apply

- Repeat the steps with the following words: ***nurse, purse; fern, stern; hurt, spurt.***

Assessment Tip: Watch to make sure students select the correct letters and say the correct sounds. Note which students struggle with this activity, and provide reinforcement activities.

Sort Words: Vowel Sounds

- Place teacher word cards **bit, bite,** and **skirt** next to each other in a pocket chart. Tell students you have made three groups from the cards and ask them to tell you how they think you have grouped the words.
- Once students have identified the groupings (short, long, r-controlled vowels) hold up the card **skit.** Ask students under which word you should place this card. Have them tell why.
- Repeat with the remaining word cards: **tune, turn, nut, nurse, term, ten, team, earth, eat.**

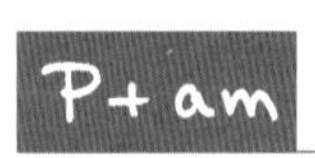

Blend Words with r-controlled *e, i, u*

Model

- Write the word ***chirp*** on the board and point out the initial digraph.
- Model sounding out the word, blending the onset and rime: **/ch/ /ûrp/.** Then say the whole word. Point out that it has an r-controlled vowel sound and one syllable.

Guide

- Guide students as they sound out the word ***fern.*** Repeat with other examples if you feel students need extra support.
- Give students blackline master 2. Have them read each word on the list for Day One by blending the onset and rime.

Apply

- Have students independently sound out the remaining words on the word list for Day One. Students who are able to read the words without blending each sound should do so.
- Note which students need more support in blending. Guide them as they read some or all of the words on the list before asking them to read the list independently.

Assessment Tip: Note which students are able to read the words without blending each sound.

Spelling Words: *learn, girl, turn*

Model

- Make a two-column chart on chart paper. Label the first column "One-Syllable Words" and the second column "Two-Syllable Words." Tell students that they will be spelling words with r-controlled ***e, i,*** and ***u*** syllable patterns. As you work through Unit Ten, you can add the spelling words to the chart and have students use the chart to check their spelling of the words.
- Say the word ***learn*** and model spelling it and writing it on the chart.
- **Think Aloud:** *I hear two parts in the word* **learn:** */***l***/ and /***ûrn***/. I know the word starts with the letter* **l.** *I wonder if the vowels are* **e, i,** *or* **u,** *or if there is an* **ea** *digraph like in the word* **earth.** *I will try* **er.** *That doesn't look right. I will try* **ea***–that looks better.*

Our Spelling Words

One-Syllable Words	Two-Syllable Words
learn girl turn heard twirl churn	person dirty turnip

Guide

- Say the word ***girl.*** Have students identify the sounds and the letters that stand for the sounds. Have them decide which vowel to combine with ***r*** to make the r-controlled pattern. Write the word in the first column of the chart as students tell you the word parts. Repeat with the word ***turn.***

Apply

- Have students practice writing each of the words in their word study notebooks. After they write the word, have them check the spelling of the word by blending the onset and rime. Have students highlight the r-controlled vowels in the words.

DAY 2

Teacher Tips

Reading Strategies

If students have difficulty applying strategies for challenging words, guide them to use the following strategies:

- look at how the words start and/or end
- look for familiar patterns or parts within the words
- separate the words into syllables and decode each part
- think about what familiar words look like the difficult words
- read forward to check the context
- reread the sentence or paragraph
- mark the words, substitute synonyms, and get on with reading–ask for help later

Comprehension

Use the following questions to ensure that students have understood the passage:

- *What did Bird want for lunch?* (Level 1–facts/details)
- *What happened when Bird gave a big tug?* (Level 2–cause/effect)
- *What is the story mainly about?* (Level 3–main idea)

Fluency

Intervene if students are having difficulty reading the passage. Model how to use word and meaning strategies to problem-solve the words. After students have had a chance to read the passage silently, have them read it aloud for fluency. Model fluent reading of the passage. For students who struggle, you may want to read the passage a second time and have them echo-read along with you.

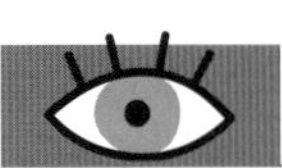

Blend

- Have students blend the words on the word list for Day Two, using the procedure for blending from Day One.

Develop Automaticity in Word Recognition

- Circle the following words on the overhead transparency: ***another, because, got, head, really, saw, thought.*** Tell students that practicing these words will help them recognize the words automatically so they can read more fluently. Explain that students can sound out some of these words, but they will read more quickly if they don't have to stop and sound them out each time they see them.
- Read each word. Point out that the ***gh*** in ***thought*** is silent and that the word ***another*** ends with an r-controlled ***e*** sound.
- Have students read aloud with you the sentences in the passage that contain the words. Then have them write the words in their word study notebooks.
- Give students a copy of blackline master 7. Point out the words from this lesson, as well as other words they have learned previously. Have them cut out the words, store them in an envelope, and use them for practice activities.

Build Fluency with Connected Text

Model

- Read the passage on the overhead transparency aloud. Stop at the word ***hungry*** and model strategies to read it.
- **Think Aloud:** *I knew this word was* **hungry** *because I recognized the open vowel at the end and I knew the first part of the word had a short vowel sound. I also knew how to read* **squishy** *because of the open vowel at the end and the short vowel sound in the closed syllable.*
- Model making a mistake and correcting it–for example, read ***slide*** instead of ***slid.***
- **Think Aloud:** *I knew right away that* **slide** *wasn't right because the rest of the story is in the past tense. Also, there is no final* **e** *in the word, so it doesn't have a VCe pattern. It has a closed-syllable pattern, so the vowel is short.*

Guide

- Continue reading and stop at other words in the passage. Guide students as they read the words.

Apply

- Have students take turns reading blackline master 3 to a partner or in a small group as you monitor the reading. Use the teacher tips to check comprehension and fluency.

Spelling Words: *heard, twirl, churn*

- Have students practice writing the spelling words from Day One in their word study notebooks. Have them refer to words on the spelling chart to check their spelling.
- Introduce the Day Two spelling words. Say the word ***twirl*** and model spelling it and writing it on the chart of spelling words. Point to the word ***girl*** on the chart from the Day One spelling words and highlight how the words are similar. Model how to use ***girl*** to spell the new word and other words in the word family–for example: ***twirl, swirl, whirl.***
- Repeat with the remaining spelling words for Day Two and have students practice writing the words in their word study notebooks. Have students highlight the r-controlled vowels.

DAY 3

Multisyllabic Words: r-Controlled *e, i, u* Syllables

Model

- Write the word ***fur*** on the board, read it, and point out that it has one syllable with an r-controlled vowel.
- Write the word ***further*** on the board. Show students how to use what they know about vowel patterns and syllables to read longer words. Highlight the consonant ***r*** and the digraph the between the vowels ***u*** and ***e,*** and divide the word after the first ***r,*** keeping the consonant digraph ***th*** together: ***fur/ther.***
- Point out the r-controlled syllables before sounding them out.

Guide

- Write the word ***perfect*** on the board and guide students as they identify the two vowels and the number of consonants between the vowels.
- Guide students as they divide the word: ***per/fect.*** Ask what syllable patterns they see and what clues this gives them about the vowel sounds in each syllable.

Apply

- Have students independently blend the two-syllable words on the word list for Day Three. If students need more support, guide them as they blend some or all of the words.

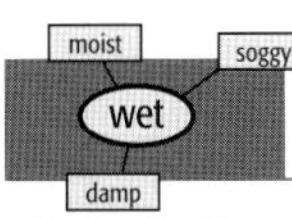

Develop Word Meanings

- Refer to the second sentence in the overhead passage and ask students what kind of worm Bird wanted. Use the word ***fat*** and ask students what word they could use to describe the worm if he was the opposite of ***fat.*** Guide them to think of words such as ***skinny*** and ***thin.***
- Point out the following words in the passage: ***dark, fast, long.*** Guide students as they think of opposites for each word.
- As a group, brainstorm a list of descriptive words and their antonyms.

Spelling Words: *person, dirty, turnip*

- Have students practice spelling the words from Day One and Day Two by writing them several times in their word study notebooks.
- Introduce the new spelling words, modeling how students can apply what they know about syllables to the spelling of words with more than one syllable.
- Say the word ***person.***
- **Think Aloud:** *When I spell this word, I need to think about how the word looks. I hear two syllables in the word. I hear an r-controlled vowel in the first syllable and a short* **o** *in the second syllable. The r-controlled vowel pattern might be* **ear, er, ir,** *or* **ur.** *I will try* **er** *and see if the word looks right.*
- Repeat with the remaining words.
- Have students practice the words several times in their word study notebooks.

Build Fluency with Connected Text

- Have students read blackline master 4 to a partner or in small groups as you monitor their reading. Call attention to the following words in the reading passage before students read it: ***does, even, father, it's, own, saw, went.***

Teacher Tips

Antonyms

Have students rewrite sentences from the passage, using opposites of words used in the story.

Develop Automaticity in Word Recognition

Have students use as many of the high-frequency words ***another, because, got, head, really, saw,*** and ***thought*** as they can in one or two sentences. Have them read their sentences to a partner.

Repeated Reading

Have students practice repeated readings of blackline master 3 to develop fluency.

DAY 4

Teacher Tips

Develop Automaticity in Word Recognition

Have partners flash a set of high-frequency word cards for each other to read. Words that are read incorrectly are placed in a pile and read again. Once students feel confident, have them time themselves while the partner flashes the words. Have them try to beat their own time as they read the words again.

Repeated Reading

Have students practice repeated readings of blackline master 3 to develop fluency.

Blend

- Have students blend the words on the word list for Day Four, using the procedure for blending from Day One.

Sort Words: Word Families

- Place the following teacher word cards in random order in a pocket chart: **jerk, clerk, perk, germ, term, curb, blurb, burn, turn, churn, dirt, squirt, stir, fir, sir.** Have students read each word with you.
- Place the word cards **stir, fir,** and **sir** together in a group. Ask students why you grouped these words together.
- Once students recognize that the words are from the same word family, have them tell you how to sort the remaining words. Once the words are sorted, read each group and have students identify the word family.

Spelling Words

- Provide practice for students in segmenting words and associating sounds with spellings. Dictate the following words to students and have them write the words on their papers: ***burn, sunburn, birth, birthday.*** Remind students to use what they have learned about spelling words with more than one syllable.
- Write the words on the board and have students self-correct their papers.
- Dictate the following sentence and have students write it on their papers: *The girl got hurt when she fell in the dirt.*
- Write the sentence on the board and have students self-correct their papers.
- Give pairs of students blackline master 6. While one student reads the spelling words, the other student writes them in the "First Try" column. After the student has spelled the words, the partner places a check mark next to words spelled correctly. For the second try, the partner may prompt the student by sounding out the words that were spelled incorrectly the first time. If the second spelling attempt is correct, the partner places a check mark in the "Second Try" column.

Assessment Tip: Use students' completed peer-check blackline masters to note which words gave students difficulty.

Build Fluency with Connected Text

- Have students take turns reading blackline master 5 to a partner or in small groups as you monitor their reading. Call attention to the following words in the reading passage before students read it: ***again, don't, head, saw, took, try, went.***

DAY 5

Spelling Assessment

Use the following procedure to assess students' spelling of the Unit Ten words.
- Say each spelling word and use it in a sentence.
- Have students write the words on their papers.
- Continue with the next word on the list.
- When students have finished, collect their papers and analyze their spelling of the words.
- Use the assessment to plan small group or individual practice.

Small Group/Independent Activities

The following activities can be used to provide practice for students who need additional support.

PHONICS AND WORD STRATEGIES

Sort the Words Have students sort the decodable words on blackline masters 8 and 9 with a partner. After they have sorted the words, have them take turns reading the words in the groups.

Review r-Controlled *o* Syllable Patterns Write the word ***corn*** on the board and ask students to identify the vowel and the vowel sound. Point out that the vowel is neither long nor short and that it is affected by the letter ***r.*** Explain that this kind of syllable is called an r-controlled syllable. Explain that it is not a closed syllable because even though a closed syllable has one vowel like this word does, this word also has the letter ***r,*** which affects the vowel sound. Write the word ***forest*** on the board. Underline each vowel and then point out the single consonant between them. Point out that in this word, you do not divide the word before the consonant, because this would give you an open syllable: ***fō/ rest.*** Have a volunteer come up and divide the word into syllables. Then have students identify the syllable patterns (r-controlled and closed) and blend the word.

AUTOMATICITY IN WORD RECOGNITION

Be the Teacher Place students in small groups and have one student in the group choose three of the high-frequency word cards and hold them up one at a time for the group to read. Then have that student choose another student to be the teacher and choose the high-frequency words for the group to read.

Hopscotch Make a hopscotch pattern on the floor and put a high-frequency word card inside each square. As students hop on the grid, they must read the words in the squares they land on.

BUILD FLUENCY WITH CONNECTED TEXT

Repeated Reading Have students practice reading blackline master 3 several times, until they feel they can read it fluently and accurately. Have them work with a partner to time each other as they read the passage aloud. Have them set a goal of reading ninety words per minute.

SPELLING

Make Words Provide a set of letter cards and the week's spelling words on index cards. Have students use the letter cards to spell the words. They should check their spelling by blending the sounds and then looking at the words on the index cards.

Finish the Word Write the beginning and ending letters of the spelling words on the board, leaving blanks for the medial sounds. Have students fill in the missing r-controlled vowels–for example: ***l_ _ _ n = learn; p_ _ son = person.***

Teacher Tips

Home Connection

Have students take blackline master 11 home to complete with a family member. Students can also take the reading passage on blackline master 3 home to share with their family.

Quick-Check

Assess students' mastery of r-controlled ***e, i, u*** syllable patterns using the quick-check for Unit Ten in this Teacher Resource System.

ELL Support Tip

Using gestures during lessons helps students make sense of the skill being taught. Keep the gestures simple, but try to repeat the same gesture for key activities. For example, when modeling the letters that stand for the sounds in the word learn, say the word once. Then say it again and point to the word with one hand. With the other hand, count out with your fingers the ***/l/*** and ***/urn/*** sounds so students are visually seeing the word and seeing the two fingers that represent the sounds they hear. Have them do the same when they are practicing.

Quick-Check: r-controlled e, i, u syllable patterns

Student Name ______________________ Assessment Date __________

Segmenting and Blending

Directions: Explain that these words use sounds the student has been learning. Have the student point to each word on the corresponding student sheet, segment the word parts or syllables, and blend them together. Put a ✓ if the student successfully segments and blends the word or reads it as a complete unit. really If the student misses the word, record the error.
Example: yearn

squirm		bird		
occur		disturb		
adverb		prefer		
earn		return		Score **/8**

Sight Words

Directions: Have the student point to the first word on the corresponding student sheet and read across the line, saying each word as quickly as possible. Put a ✓ if the student successfully reads the word and an **X** if the student hesitates more than a few seconds. If the student misses the word, record the error.

another		got		
really		saw		
for		more		
one		out		
because		head		
thought		come		
when		of		
little		too		Score **/16**

UNIT 11

r-controlled /âr/ syllable patterns

Unit Objectives

Students will:

- Read words with r-controlled /âr/ syllable patterns
- Review r-controlled e, i, u syllable patterns
- Blend onset and rime
- Sort words according to word families and vowel sounds
- Read high-frequency words big, important, left, need, off, together, took
- Spell one- and two-syllable words with r-controlled /âr/ syllable patterns: blare, hair, bear, flare, pair, wear, repair, cherry, barely
- Identify multiple meanings and pronunciations for words

Day 1

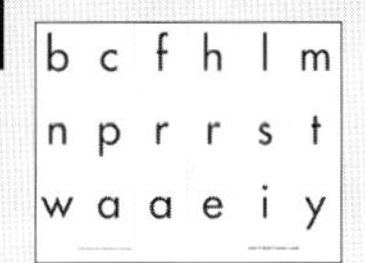

Letter Cards: **a, b, c, e, f, i, l, r, s, t**

Word Lists (BLM 2)

air

Teacher Word Cards: **air, fair, gain, hair, heard, learn, main, pain, pearl, search, stair, strain**

Day 2

Word Lists (BLM 2)

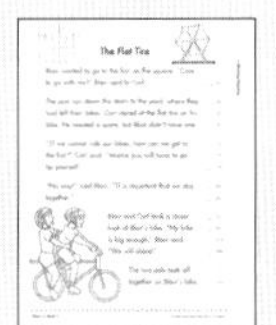

Reading Passage 1 (BLM 3)

important, took, off, need, left, together, big, down, with, where, their, have, will, by, look, how

High-Frequency Word Cards for Unit 11 (BLM 7)

Day 3

Word Lists (BLM 2)

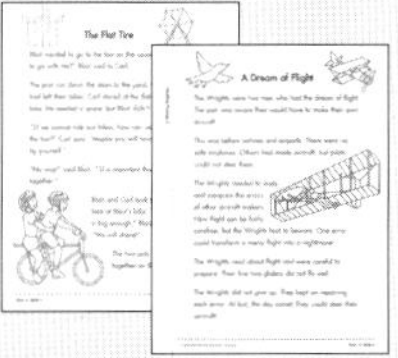

Reading Passages 1 & 2 (BLMs 3 & 4)

important, took, off, need, left, together, big, down, with, where, their, have, will, by, look, how

High-Frequency Word Cards for Unit 11 (BLM 7)

Day 4

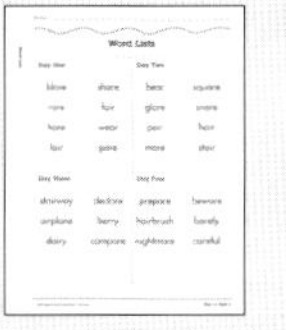

Word Lists (BLM 2)

Reading Passages 1 & 3 (BLMs 3 & 5)

berry

Teacher Word Cards **berry, blur, chair, cherry, ferry, fur, mark, pair, pare, park, shark, spur, square, stare, stair**

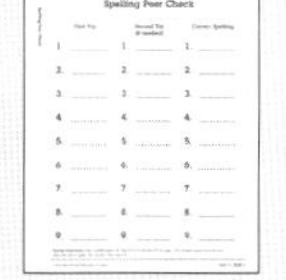

Spelling Peer Check (BLM 6)

important, took, off, need, left, together, big, down, with, where, their, have, will, by, look, how

High-Frequency Word Cards for Unit 11 (BLM 7)

Day 5

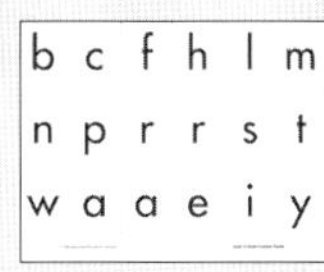

Letter Cards for Unit 11

Reading Passage 1 (BLM 3)

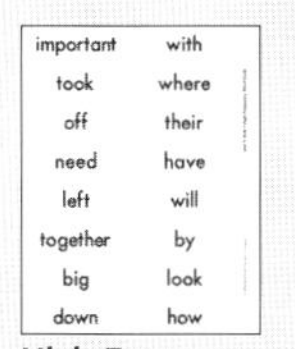

High-Frequency Word Cards for Unit 11 (BLM 7)

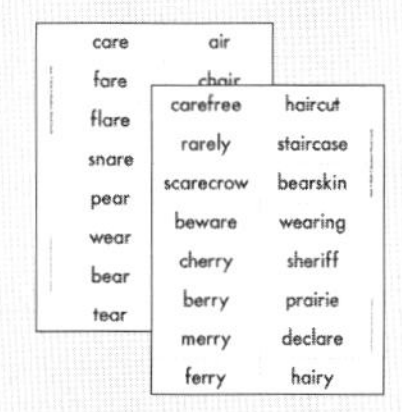

Student Word Cards (BLMs 8 & 9)

Quick-Check Student Sheet

Frieze Card

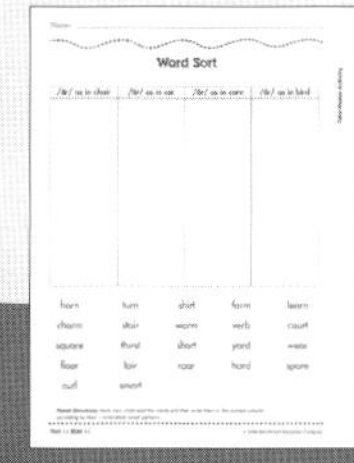

Take-Home Activity

Core Materials

All of these materials can be downloaded from http://phonicsresources.benchmarkeducation.com.

UNIT 11 r-controlled /âr/ syllable patterns

DAY 1

Frieze Card

Introduce r-Controlled /âr/ Syllable Patterns

Model

- Hold up the r-controlled /**âr**/ frieze card and have students name the pictures and read the words. Emphasize each r-controlled syllable spelling pattern.
- Remind students that the vowel is neither long nor short, and that when the letter ***r*** follows a vowel, it affects the sound that the vowel stands for. Point out that the words ***bear*** and ***chair*** have vowel digraphs affected by an ***r***. Remind students that these are one-syllable words because they have one vowel sound.

Guide

- Give students letter cards **b**, **c**, **f**, **l**, **r**, **s**, **t**, **a**, **e**, and **i**, and have them line up the letters in front of them.
- Say the word ***scare*** and ask students what letter they need to start the word. Have them decide which r-controlled pattern on the frieze card they will use. Then ask what letters they need to make the /**âr**/ sound. Have them push the letters forward as they say and read the word ***scare.*** Have them check to see if the word looks right. Point out that the word is a closed syllable with an r-controlled vowel.
- Have students take away the letter ***c*** and ask what they need to replace it with to make the word ***stare.*** Have them make the word and read it. Then have them take away the ***st*** and replace it with another blend to make the word ***flare.***

Apply

- Repeat the steps with the following words: ***fair***, ***flair; bear***, ***tear.***

Assessment Tip: Make sure students select the correct letters and read the word. Note which students struggle with this activity, and provide reinforcement activities.

Sort Words: Vowel Sounds

- Place teacher word cards **pain**, **pearl**, and **fair** next to each other in a pocket chart. Tell students you have made three groups from the cards and ask them to tell you how they think you have grouped the words.
- Once students have identified the groupings (long ***a*** digraph, r-controlled vowels /**ĭr**/ and /**âr**/), hold up the card **pair**. Ask students under which word you should place this card. Have them tell why.
- Repeat with the remaining word cards: **strain**, **main**, **gain**, **learn**, **search**, **heard**, **stair**, **air**, **hair.**

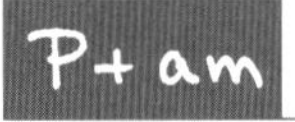

Blend Words with r-Controlled /âr/

Model

- Write the word ***share*** on the board. Point out the consonant digraph that begins the word.
- Model sounding out the word, blending the onset and rime: /**sh**/ /**âr**/. Say the whole word, pointing out that it has one vowel sound and one syllable.

Guide

- Guide students as they sound out the word ***chair.*** Repeat with other examples if you feel students need extra support.
- Give students blackline master 2. Have them read each word for Day One by blending the onset and rime.

Apply

- Have students independently sound out the remaining words for Day One. Students who are able to read the words without blending each sound should do so.
- Note which students need more support in blending. Guide them as they read some or all of the words on the list before asking them to read the list independently.

Assessment Tip: Note which students are able to read the words without blending each sound.

Spelling Words: *blare, hair, bear*

Model

- Make a two-column chart on chart paper. Label the first column "One-Syllable Words" and the second column "Two-Syllable Words." Tell students that they will be spelling words with the r-controlled pattern sound /**âr**/. As you work through Unit Eleven, add the spelling words to the chart, which students can use to check their spelling of the words.
- Say the word ***blare*** and model spelling it and writing it on the chart.
- **Think Aloud:** *I hear two parts in the word* **blare:** /**bl**/ *and* /**âr**/. *I know that the letters* **b** *and* **l** *stand for the blended sound* /**bl**/. *I also hear* /**âr**/. *I wonder which of the r-controlled vowel patterns to use–***are**, **air**, *or* **ear**. *I will try the* **-are** *pattern and see if it looks right:* /**bl**/ /**âr**/, **blare.** *Now that I can spell* **blare**, *I can also spell other words from this word* family, *such as* **dare**, **snare**, *and* **share.**

Our Spelling Words

One-Syllable Words	Two-Syllable Words
blare hair bear flare pair wear	repair cherry barely

Guide

- Say the word ***hair.*** Have students identify the sounds in the word and the letters that stand for the sounds. Have them check the frieze card to choose the spelling pattern. Write the word in the first column of the chart as students tell you the word parts. Repeat with the word ***bear.***

Apply

- Have students practice writing each of the words in their word study notebooks. After they write the word, have them check the spelling of the word by blending the onset and rime.

DAY 2

Teacher Tips

Reading Strategies

If students have difficulty applying strategies for challenging words, guide them to use the following strategies:

- look at how the words start and/or end
- look for familiar patterns or parts within the words
- separate the words into syllables and decode each part
- think about what familiar words look like the difficult words
- read forward to check the context
- reread the sentence or paragraph
- mark the words, substitute synonyms, and get on with reading–ask for help later

Comprehension

Use the following questions to ensure that students have understood the passage:

- *Where did Blair want to go with Carl?* (Level 1–facts and details)
- *What was the problem they had?* (Level 2–problem/solution)
- *Why do you think Blair didn't want to go to the fair by himself?* (Level 3–make inferences)

Fluency

Intervene if students are having difficulty reading the passage. Model how to use word and meaning strategies to problem-solve the words. After students have had a chance to read the passage silently, have them read it aloud for fluency. Model fluent reading of the passage. For students who struggle, you may want to read the passage a second time and have them echo-read along with you.

Blend

- Have students blend the words on the word list for Day Two, using the procedure for blending from Day One.

Develop Automaticity in Word Recognition

- Circle the following words on the overhead transparency: ***big***, ***important***, ***left***, ***need(ed)***, ***off***, ***together***, and ***took.*** Tell students that practicing these words will help them recognize the words automatically so they can read more fluently. Explain that students can sound out some of these words, but they will read more quickly if they don't have to stop and sound them out each time they see them. Point out that in the passage, the word ***need*** has an ***-ed*** ending.
- Read each word. Point out that there are two letter ***f***'s in ***off***, and the letters ***gh*** in ***enough*** make the **/f/** sound.
- Have students read aloud with you the sentences in the passage that contain the words. Then have them write the words in their word study notebooks.
- Give students a copy of blackline master 7. Point out the words from this lesson, as well as other words they have learned previously. Have them cut out the words, store them in an envelope, and use them for practice activities.

Build Fluency with Connected Text

Model

- Read the passage on the overhead transparency aloud. Stop at the word ***care*** and model strategies to read the word.
- **Think Aloud:** *I've already come across three words in this passage that have the* **/âr/** *sound–***fair**, **square**, *and* **Blair.** *I also notice that there are two different spellings for* **/âr/** *in these three words.*
- Continue reading. Model making a mistake and correcting it–for example, read ***starred*** instead of ***stared.***
- **Think Aloud:** *Oops. I saw the little word* **star** *in this word, so I thought it said* **starred**, *which doesn't make sense. I have to remember that* **ar** *followed by* **e** *is an r-controlled syllable pattern, so that in this case, the word is* **stared**, *which makes sense here.*

Guide

- Continue reading and stop at other words in the passage. Guide students as they read the words.

Apply

- Have students take turns reading blackline master 3 to a partner or in a small group as you monitor the reading. Use the teacher tips to check comprehension and fluency.

Spelling Words: *flare, pair, wear*

- Have students practice writing the spelling words from Day One in their word study notebooks. Have them refer to words on the spelling chart to check their spelling.
- Introduce the Day Two spelling words. Say the word ***pair*** and model spelling it and writing it on the chart of spelling words. Point to the word ***hair*** on the chart from the Day One spelling words and highlight how the words are similar. Model how to use hair to spell the new word and other words in the word family–for example, ***fair***, ***chair***, and ***Blair.***
- Repeat with the remaining spelling words for Day Two and have students practice writing the words in their word study notebooks.

DAY 3

Multisyllabic Words: r-Controlled /âr/ Syllable Patterns

Model

- Write the word ***air*** on the board, read it, and point out that it has one vowel sound and one syllable.
- Write the word ***airport*** on the board. Show students how to use what they know about vowel patterns and syllables to read longer words. Remind students that ***ai*** is a digraph and highlight the two consonants between the vowels ***ai*** and ***o.*** Divide the word between the consonants: ***air/port***, and point out the r-controlled syllables before sounding it out.

Guide

- Write the word ***prairie*** on the board and guide students to identify the two sets of vowel digraphs and the consonant between them. Remind them that the digraphs each stand for one vowel sound.
- Guide students as they divide the word: ***prair/ie.*** Point out that the second ***r*** stays with the first digraph when the word is divided.

Apply

- Have students independently blend the two- and three-syllable words on the word list for Day Three. If students need more support, guide them as they blend some or all of the words.

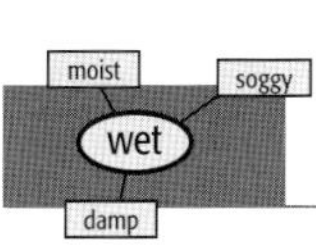

Develop Word Meanings: Homophones

- Write the words ***pair***, ***pare***, and ***pear*** on the board. Read the words and tell students that these three words sound the same but are spelled differently and mean different things. Provide definitions of the words and use them in oral sentences.
- Provide sentences using the words, and after each sentence have a volunteer come up and point to the word on the board that is used in the sentence. Example sentences are: *Will you pare my apple for me; She made pear crumble for dessert; I need a new pair of shoes.*
- Guide students as they list /âr/ words that are homophones. (***fair/fare; flare/flair; bear/ bear; hair/hare; wear/ware; stare/stair***) Discuss the meanings of the words and have students use them in oral sentences.

Spelling Words: *repair, cherry, barely*

- Have students practice spelling the words from Days One and Two by writing them several times in their word study notebooks.
- Introduce the new spelling words, modeling how students can apply what they know about syllables to the spelling of words with more than one syllable.
- Say the word ***barely.***
- **Think Aloud:** *When I spell this word, I need to think about how the word looks. I hear two syllables in the word. I hear an r-controlled vowel in the first syllable, and the second syllable ends with the vowel sound /ē/. I remember that* **y** *often stands for this sound at the end of a word. I will look at the frieze card and decide which spelling pattern I will use for the r-controlled syllable. I will try* **are** *and see if the word looks right.*
- Repeat with the remaining words.
- Have students practice writing the words several times in their word study notebooks.

Build Fluency with Connected Text

- Have students read blackline master 4 to a partner or in small groups as you monitor their reading. Call attention to the following words in the reading passage before students read it: ***last, men, need(ed), own, read, study, well.***

Teacher Tips

Three-Syllable Words

Model for students how they can read words with three or more syllables by dividing them into syllables and applying what they know about syllable patterns–for example, ***chair/ per/son***.

Develop Automaticity in Word Recognition

Have students work in pairs. Give students a copy of blackline master 7. Have partners take turns to hold up a high-frequency word card and read the word, while the other partner repeats the word and writes it in his or her word study notebook.

Repeated Reading

Have students practice repeated readings of blackline master 3 to develop fluency.

DAY 4

Teacher Tips

Develop Automaticity in Word Recognition

Have students work in pairs, using the words from blackline master 7. Partner One closes his or her eyes and holds out a hand. Partner Two gives Partner One a high-frequency word card. Partner One opens his or her eyes and reads the word. Partners switch roles.

Repeated Reading

Have students practice repeated readings of blackline master 3 to develop fluency.

Blend

- Have students blend the words on the word list for Day Four, using the procedure for blending from Day One.

Sort Words: Word Families

- Place the following teacher word cards in random order in the pocket chart: **square**, **stare**, **pare**, **chair**, **stair**, **pair**, **cherry**, **berry**, **ferry**, **blur**, **fur**, **spur**, **park**, **shark**, **mark.** Have students read each word with you.
- Place the word cards **cherry**, **berry**, and **ferry** together in a group. Ask students why you grouped these words together.
- Once students recognize that the words are from the same r-controlled vowel word family, have them tell you how to sort the remaining words. Once the words are sorted, read each group and have students identify the word family.

Spelling Words

- Provide practice for students in segmenting words and associating sounds with spellings. Dictate the following words to students and have them write the words on their papers: ***ware***, ***beware***, ***fair***, ***fairly.*** Remind students to use what they have learned about spelling words with more than one syllable.
- Write the words on the board and have students self-correct their papers.
- Dictate the following sentence and have students write it on their papers: *The fairy with golden hair glared at the merry bear.*
- Write the sentence on the board and have students self-correct their papers.
- Give pairs of students blackline master 6. While one student reads the spelling words, the other student writes them in the "First Try" column. After the student has spelled the words, the partner places a check mark next to words spelled correctly. For the second try, the partner may prompt the student by sounding out the words that were spelled incorrectly the first time. If the second spelling attempt is correct, the partner places a check mark in the "Second Try" column.

Assessment Tip: Use students' completed peer-check blackline masters to note which words gave students difficulty.

Build Fluency with Connected Text

- Have students take turns reading blackline master 5 to a partner or in a small group as you monitor their reading. Call attention to the following words in the reading passage before students read it: ***don't***, ***enough***, ***even***, ***grow***, ***might***, ***need***, ***plant.***

Spelling Assessment

Use the following procedure to assess students' spelling of the Unit Eleven words.
- Say each spelling word and use it in a sentence.
- Have students write the words on their papers.
- Continue with the next word on the list.
- When students have finished, collect their papers and correct them.
- Use the assessment to plan small group or individual practice.

Small Group/Independent Activities

The following activities can be used to provide practice for students who need additional support.

PHONICS AND WORD STRATEGIES

Review r-Controlled Vowel Patterns Write the words ***dirt*** and ***hurt*** on the board and read the words. Point out they each have an r-controlled vowel syllable pattern. Remind students that an r-controlled vowel stands for one sound that is neither long nor short, and that when words with r-controlled vowels are divided into syllables, the vowel plus the ***r*** usually stays in the same syllable. Write the word ***merchant*** on the board. Underline each vowel and point out the three consonants between them. Tell students that the letters ***ch*** are a digraph that stay together, so you divide the word before the letter ***c.*** Divide the word and have students identify the syllable patterns.

Bingo Have each student divide a sheet of paper by drawing a three-row by three-column grid. Have them select words from blackline masters 8 and 9 to write in the grid. Have a student draw a student word card and read the word aloud. If students have the word on their paper, they can place a counter over the word. Continue with the next word. The first student to cover all of his or her words wins.

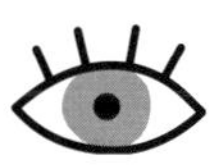

AUTOMATICITY IN WORD RECOGNITION

Write a Paragraph Have students write one or two paragraphs using as many of the week's high-frequency words as they can. Then have them exchange paragraphs with a partner and find and underline the high-frequency words in the partner's paragraph.

High-Frequency Word Toss Place the high-frequency word cards in cups, one per cup. Have students toss a button into a cup, take the card out of the cup and read it, and then use the word in an oral sentence.

BUILD FLUENCY WITH CONNECTED TEXT

Repeated Reading Have students practice reading blackline master 3 several times, until they feel they can read it fluently and accurately. Have them work with a partner to time each other as they read the passage aloud. Have them set a goal of reading 90 words per minute.

SPELLING

Make Words Provide a set of letter cards and the week's spelling words on index cards. Have students use the letter cards to spell the words. They should check their spelling by blending the sounds and then looking at the words on the index cards.

Around the Circle Have students sit in a circle. Say a spelling word and have a student say the first letter in the word. Have the next student say the next letter, and so on, until the word is spelled. Have the student who says the last letter write the word on the board.

Teacher Tips

Home Connection

Have students take blackline master 11 home to complete with a family member. Students can also take the repeated reading passage on blackline master 3 home to share with their family.

Quick-Check

Assess students' mastery of r-controlled /âr/ syllable patterns using the quick-check for Unit Eleven in this Teacher Resource System.

ELL Support Tip

Giving English Language Learners hands-on activities is a great way to reinforce skills and strategies. Write the new **/âr/** words on cards. Give students the cards and some yarn and have them glue the yarn to the words on the cards. Students can then read the words while tracing over the yarn with a finger, providing a tactile experience as well as visual experience.

Quick-Check: r-controlled /âr/ syllable patterns

Student Name ______________________ Assessment Date __________

Segmenting and Blending

Directions: Explain that these words use sounds the student has been learning. Have the student point to each word on the corresponding student sheet, segment the word parts or syllables, and blend them together. Put a ✓ if the student successfully segments and blends the word or reads it as a complete unit. If the student misses the word, record the error.
Example: lair

rainwear		impair			
compare		swear			
sparrow		parish			
airfare		aware		Score	**/8**

Sight Words

Directions: Have the student point to the first word on the corresponding student sheet and read across the line, saying each word as quickly as possible. Put a ✓ if the student successfully reads the word and an **X** if the student hesitates more than a few seconds. If the student misses the word, record the error.

important		with			
took		where			
off		their			
need		have			
left		will			
together		by			
big		look			
down		how		Score	**/16**

UNIT 12 Vowel diphthong /oi/ syllable patterns

Unit Objectives

Students will:

- Recognize and read one- and two-syllable words with vowel diphthong /oi/ syllable patterns
- Review r-controlled /âr/ syllable patterns
- Blend onset and rime words
- Sort words by vowel sounds
- Read high-frequency words big, both, left, must, plant, play
- Spell one- and two-syllable words with different syllable patterns: point, broil, boy, joint, spoil, toy, enjoy, poison, oyster
- Identify and use synonyms

Day 1

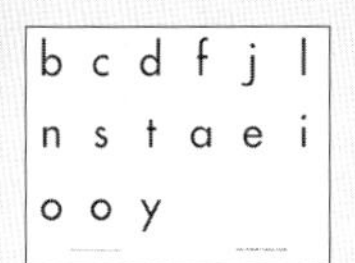

Letter Cards:
b, c, f, i, j, l, n, , o, s, t, y

Word Lists (BLM 2)

boat

Teacher Word Cards:
boat, coin, crow, fox, globe, hope, hot, job, moan, mop, point, toe, toil, toy

Day 2

Word Lists (BLM 2)

Reading Passage 1 (BLM 3)

High-Frequency Word Cards for Unit 12 (BLM 7)

Day 3

Word Lists (BLM 3)

Reading Passages 1 & 2 (BLMs 3 & 4)

big what
left was
must have
both been
plant time
play did
out have
with you

High-Frequency Word Cards for Unit 12 (BLM 7)

Day 4

Word Lists (BLM 2)

Reading Passages 1, & 3 (BLMs 3, & 5)

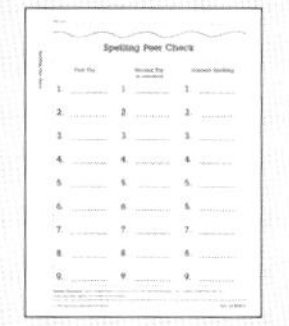
Spelling Peer Check (BLM 6)

big what
left was
must have
both been
plant time
play did
out have
with you

High-Frequency Word Cards for Unit 12 (BLM 7)

Day 5

Letter Cards for Unit 12

Reading Passage 1 (BLM 3)

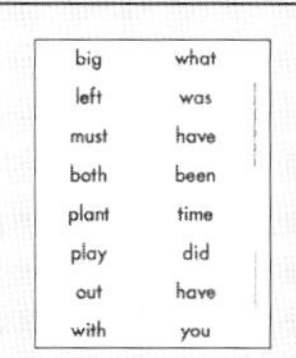

High-Frequency Word Cards for Unit 12 (BLM 7)

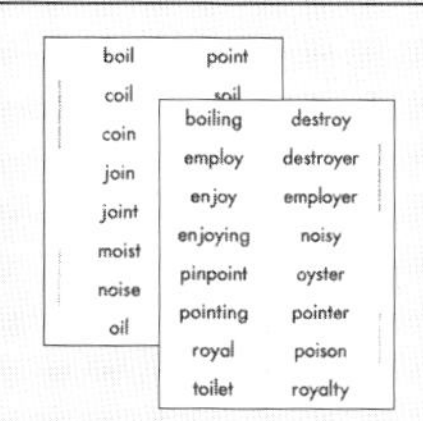

Student Word Cards (BLMs 8 & 9)

Quick-Check Student Sheet

Frieze Card

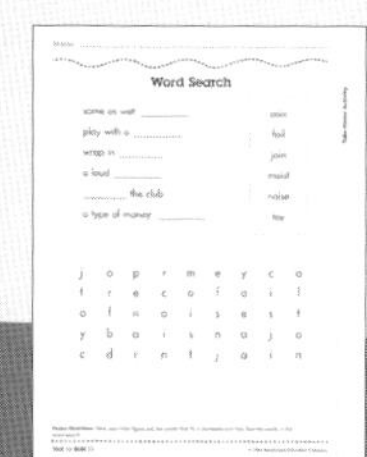
Take-Home Activity

Core Materials

All of these materials can be downloaded from http://phonicsresources.benchmarkeducation.com.

UNIT 12 Vowel diphthong /oi/ syllable patterns

Frieze Card

Introduce Vowel Diphthong /oi/ Syllable Patterns

1 Syllable

Model

- Hold up the vowel diphthong **/oi/** frieze card and point out that the vowel sound in each word is **/oi/**, but that different letters in the words stand for the sound. Remind students that each syllable has one vowel sound, and point out that ***oy*** and ***oi*** stand for one sound.

Guide

- Give students letter cards **b**, **c**, **f**, **j**, **l**, **n**, **s**, **t**, **i**, **o**, and **y**, and have them line up the letters in a row in front of them.
- Say the word ***coin*** and ask students what letters they need to make the word. Remind them that they will need two letters to stand for the **/oi/** sound. Have them decide which spelling pattern on the frieze card they will use. Have them push forward the letters to spell and read the word. Have them decide whether the word looks right and, if not, try the other spelling pattern.
- Ask students what letter they need to use to replace the letter ***c*** at the beginning of coin to make the word ***join.***
- Repeat with the words ***boy*** and ***toy***. Point out that these use different letters to stand for the **/oi/** sound.

Apply

- Have students independently make the words ***foil*** and ***soil***.

Assessment Tip: Watch to make sure students select the correct letters and read the word. Note which students struggle with this activity, and provide reinforcement activities.

Sort Words: Vowel Sounds

- Write each of the following three headings on an index card and place the cards at the top of a pocket chart: "Short o," "Long o," "Vowel Diphthong /oi/." Give students an oral example of each sound: ***not***, ***rope***, ***oil.***
- Hold up the teacher word card **globe** and read it. Model placing the card under the right heading.
- **Think Aloud:** *When I say this word, I do not hear a short sound or a vowel diphthong. I hear a long* **o** *sound. I will place it under long* **o.**
- Hold up the following word cards one at a time: **mop**, **moan**, **hope**, **coin**, **hot**, **boat**, **crow**, **job**, **point**, **toil**, **fox**, **toy**, **toe.** Have students read each word and tell where you should place the word card.
- When the words are sorted, have students tell what spelling patterns they see for the different sounds.

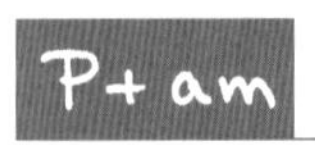

Blend Words with Vowel Diphthong /oi/

Model

- Write the word ***boil*** on the board, using a different color for the rime ***-oil***. Model sounding out the word, blending onset and rime: **/b/ /oil/**. Then say the whole word.

Guide

- Have students sound out the word with you. Repeat with other examples if you feel students need extra support.
- Give students blackline master 2. Have them use their fingers to frame the rime of the first word on the list for Day One. Then have students read the word by blending the onset and rime.

Apply

- Have students independently read the remaining words on the list for Day One. Guide students who need support to blend some or all of the words on the list before they read the list independently.

Assessment Tip: Note which students are able to read the words without blending each sound.

Spelling Words: *point, broil, boy*

Model

- Make a two-column spelling chart on chart paper. Label the first column "One-Syllable Words" and the second column "Two-Syllable Words." Tell students that they will be spelling words with vowel diphthong **/oi/.** As you work through the unit, you can continue to add the spelling words to the chart and have students use the chart to check their spelling of the words.
- Say the word ***point*** and model spelling it and writing it on chart paper.
- **Think Aloud:** *I hear two parts in the word* **point***: /***p***/ and /***oint***/. I know that the letter* **p** *stands for /***p***/. I hear the vowel diphthong followed by the blend /***nt***/ in the second part. I know that the letters* **oi** *and* **oy** *can stand for the /***oi***/ sound. I will try* **oi** *and see if the word looks right.*

Our Spelling Words

One-Syllable Words	Two-Syllable Words
point broil boy joint spoil toy	enjoy poison oyster

Guide

- Say the word ***broil.*** Have students identify the onset and rime in the word. Remind students that the vowel diphthong **/oi/** sound can be spelled in different ways and guide them to use the letters ***oi.*** Write the word in the first column of the chart as students tell you the word parts.
- Repeat with the word ***boy***, guiding students to use the letters ***oy*** for the diphthong sound.

Apply

- Have students practice writing each of the words in their word study notebooks. After they write the word, have them check the spelling of the word by blending the onset and rime. Have students highlight the letters in each word that make the diphthong sound.

DAY 2

Teacher Tips

Reading Strategies

If students have difficulty applying strategies for challenging words, guide them to use the following strategies:

- look at how the words start and/or end
- look for familiar patterns or parts within the words
- separate the words into syllables and decode each part
- think about what familiar words look like the difficult words
- read forward to check the context
- reread the sentence or paragraph
- mark the words, substitute synonyms, and get on with reading–ask for help later

Comprehension

Use the following questions to ensure that students have understood the passage:

- *What did the boys find on the floor?* (Level 1–facts and details)
- *What happened after the boys heard footsteps on the stairs?* (Level 2–sequence)
- *Why do you think the boys were relieved when they found out the mess came from the plant?* (Level 3–draw conclusions)

Fluency

Intervene if students are having difficulty reading the passage. Model how to use word and meaning strategies to problem-solve the words. After students have had a chance to read the passage silently, have them read it aloud for fluency. Model fluent reading of the passage. For students who struggle, you may want to read the passage a second time and have them echo-read along with you.

Blend

- Have students blend the words in the list for Day Two, using the procedure for blending from Day One.

Develop Automaticity in Word Recognition

- Circle the following words on the overhead transparency: ***big***, ***both***, ***left***, ***must***, ***plant***, and ***play(ing)***. Tell students that practicing these words will help them recognize the words automatically so they can read more fluently. Explain that they can sound out some of the words, but they will read more quickly if they don't have to stop and sound them out. Point out that the word ***play*** has an ***-ing*** ending.
- Read each word. Point out that ***both*** has a long ***o*** sound, even though it is in the middle of the syllable. Point out that ***plant*** and ***play*** both start with the ***pl*** blend.
- Have students read aloud with you the sentences in which the words are found, and then have them write the words in their word study notebooks.
- Give students a copy of blackline master 7. Point out the words from this lesson, as well as other words they have learned previously. Have students cut out the words, store them in an envelope, and use them for practice activities.

Build Fluency with Connected Text

Model

- Read the first sentence on the overhead transparency aloud. Then point to the word ***heard***. Model strategies you would use to read the word.
- **Think Aloud:** *I saw the letter* **r** *in this word and realized it had an r-controlled syllable. I know that* **ea** *is a digraph, and I remembered how the r-controlled digraph sounds in the word* **earth.** *This helped me read the word.*
- Continue reading. Model making a mistake and correcting it–for example, read ***cones*** instead of ***coins.***
- **Think Aloud:** *Hmmmm, would he be playing with cones? Oh, I see. The word has a diphthong, not a long* **o** *digraph. The word is* **coins**. *I guess that makes sense because he could be playing with some coins.*

Guide

- Continue reading, stopping at other words and asking students what strategies they would use to read the words.

Apply

- Have students take turns reading blackline master 3 to a partner or in a small group as you monitor the reading. Use the teacher tips to check comprehension and fluency.

Spelling Words: *joint, spoil, toy*

- Have students practice writing the spelling words from Day One in their word study notebooks. Have them refer to words on the spelling chart to check their spelling.
- Introduce the Day Two spelling words. Say the word ***spoil*** and model spelling it and writing it on the spelling chart. Point to the word ***broil*** on the chart from the Day One spelling words, and model how to use the word family ***-oil*** to spell the new word and other words in the word family such as ***oil***, ***soil***, and ***toil***.
- Repeat with the remaining words and have students practice writing the words in their word study notebooks.

Multisyllabic Words: Vowel Diphthong /oi/ Syllable Patterns

Model

- Write the word ***joy*** on the board, read it, and point out that it has one vowel sound and one syllable.
- Write the word ***enjoy*** on the board. Show students how to use what they know about vowel patterns and syllables to read longer words. Highlight the two consonants between the vowels ***e*** and ***oy*** and divide the word between the consonants: ***en/joy***.
- Point out that the first syllable is a closed syllable, and the second syllable has a vowel diphthong. Model reading the word: **/en/ /joi/**, ***enjoy.***

Guide

- Write the word ***broiler*** on the board and guide students as they identify the vowel diphthong **/oi/** in the first half of the word and the r-controlled vowel pattern in the second half.
- Highlight the vowels, pointing out that ***oi*** stands for one vowel sound, which leaves one consonant between the vowel sounds. Apply the rule of dividing the word before the consonant. Have students sound it out, using what they know about diphthongs and r-controlled vowels.

Apply

- Have students independently blend the two-syllable words on the word list for Day Three. If students need more support, guide them as they blend some or all of the words.

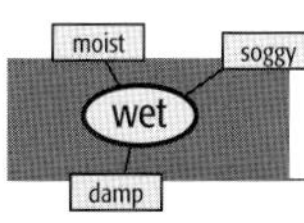

Develop Word Meanings: Synonyms

- Read the first sentence in the second paragraph on the overhead. Call attention to the words ***moist*** and ***soil.*** Explain that you can replace these words with two words that mean almost the same thing. Write the following sentence on the board or at the bottom of the overhead: *It looks like wet dirt*. Have students read the sentence.
- Guide students as they read the following sentences in the passage and think of synonyms for the underlined words: *He left . . . to see what the <u>noise</u> was about; We did not <u>spoil</u> the rug.*
- Have pairs of students go through blackline master 3, substituting synonyms where they can. Have pairs read the passage aloud with their synonyms. Have the group decide if the meaning has changed.

Spelling Words: *enjoy, poison, oyster*

- Have students practice spelling the words from Day One and Day Two by writing them several times in their word study notebooks.
- Introduce the new words, modeling how students can apply what they know about syllable patterns to spell multisyllabic words.
- Say the word ***enjoy.***
- **Think Aloud:** *I think about how the word looks and sounds. I hear two syllables, and the first syllable sounds like a closed syllable with a short* **e** *sound. The second syllable has the diphthong sound* **/oi/***, which can be spelled* **oi** *or* **oy***. I think I will try the* **oy** *pattern and see if the word looks right.*
- Repeat with the remaining words. Have students practice the words several times in their word study notebooks.

Build Fluency with Connected Text

- Have students read blackline master 4 to a partner or in small groups as you monitor their reading. Call attention to the following words before students read: ***began, idea, later, next, plant, why.***

Teacher Tips

Three-Syllable Words

Provide a challenge for students by having them use syllable patterns to read three-syllable words. Example words are: ***employee, destroyer, royalty.***

Develop Automaticity in Word Recognition

Have students work with a partner and a set of high-frequency words from blackline master 7. Have each student take a turn drawing a card and reading it while his or her partner writes the word or spells it aloud. Have the partner check the spelling.

Repeated Reading

Have students practice repeated readings of blackline master 3 to develop fluency.

DAY 4

Teacher Tips

Develop Automaticity in Word Recognition

Have students sort the words on blackline master 7 into groups according to the number of letters in the words. After the words are sorted, have them work with a partner to read the groups of words to each other.

Repeated Reading

Have students practice repeated readings of blackline master 3 to develop fluency.

Blend

- Have students blend the words on the list for Day Four, using the procedure for blending from Day One.

be
hope

Sort Words: Blind Sort

- Write the words ***point***, ***rode***, and ***top*** on the board. Read the words with students and have them identify the categories. (diphthong, long ***o***, short ***o***) Say a word and model sorting it under one of the words on the board.
- **Think Aloud: Pole**. *This word has a long* **o** *sound like the word* **rode.** *I will write it under the word* **rode**.
- Have students copy the three words in their word study notebooks. Say the following words one at a time and have them write the word under the correct word in their notebook: ***hot***, ***oil***, ***join***, ***broke***, ***rope***, ***top***, ***foil.*** After students write each word, write the word on the board and have them check whether they wrote the word in the correct column.

Spelling Words

- Provide practice for students in segmenting words and associating sounds with spellings. Dictate the following words to students and have them write the words on their papers: ***joy***, ***enjoy***, ***noise***, ***noisy.*** Remind students to use what they have learned about spelling syllables with vowel sound /**oi**/.
- Write the words on the board and have students self-correct their papers.
- Dictate the following sentence and have students write it on their papers: *Roy pointed to the oil on the soil.* Write the sentence on the board and have students self-correct their papers.
- Give pairs of students blackline master 6. While one student reads the spelling words, the other student writes them in the "First Try" column. After the student has spelled the words, the partner places a check mark next to words spelled correctly. For the second try, the partner may prompt the student by sounding out the words that were spelled incorrectly the first time. If the second spelling attempt is correct, the partner places a check mark in the "Second Try" column.

Assessment Tip: Use students' completed peer-check blackline masters to note which words gave students difficulty.

Build Fluency with Connected Text

- Give students the reading passage on blackline master 5. Have them take turns reading the passage to a partner. Call attention to the following words in the reading passage before students read it: ***began***, ***food***, ***home***, ***left***, ***put(ting)***, ***went***, ***without.***
- Have students who need extra support practice reading the passage aloud in a small group as you monitor their reading.

DAY 5

Spelling Assessment

Use the following procedure to assess students' spelling of Unit Twelve words.
- Say each spelling word and use it in a sentence.
- Have students write the words on their papers.
- Continue with the next word on the list.
- When students have finished, collect their papers and correct their spelling.
- Use the assessment to plan small group or individual practice.

Small Group/Independent Activities

The following activities can be used to provide practice for students who need additional support.

PHONICS AND WORD STRATEGIES

Build Words Write the words ***boil*** and ***coy*** on the board and have students copy them in their word study notebooks. Challenge them to write as many words as they can from each of the word families.

Review r-Controlled /âr/ Syllable Patterns Write the word ***chair*** on the board and ask students to identify the vowel sound. Remind students that the letters ***a*** and ***i*** make a vowel digraph that is affected by the letter ***r***. Write the word ***chairlift*** on the board. Point out the r-controlled ***ai***, the vowel ***i***, and the two consonants between them. Explain that the word is divided between the two consonants, which makes a two-syllable word with a closed syllable pattern and an r-controlled pattern. Have students read the word.

Onset and Rime Laminate a set of words from blackline master 8 and cut them into onset and rime. Have students make words by putting together onset and rime.

Word Sort Have students sort the words on blackline master 9 any way they want. Have them write their sort in their word study notebooks and explain why they sorted the words the way they did.

AUTOMATICITY IN WORD RECOGNITION

Stand Up Hand out three sets of high-frequency word cards. Say one of the words. Students who have the word stand up. The first one to stand up gets a point.

Around the Circle Place students in groups and give each group the high-frequency words from blackline master 7. Have students stand in a circle and choose somebody to go first. Beginning with that student, the students go around the circle reading the words as quickly as they can.

BUILD FLUENCY WITH CONNECTED TEXT

Repeated Reading Have students practice reading blackline master 3 several times, until they feel they can read it fluently and accurately. Have them work with a partner to time each other as they read the passage aloud. Have them set a goal of reading 90 words per minute.

SPELLING

Divide the Syllables Have students write the two-syllable words from the spelling list in their word study notebooks. Then have them divide the words into syllables and write why they divided the words the way they did.

Spell the Words Have students use the letter cards to make each of the spelling words and then copy each word in their word study notebook.

Teacher Tips

Home Connection

Have students take blackline master 11 home to complete with a family member. Students can also take the repeated reading passage on blackline master 3 home to share with their family.

Quick-Check

Assess students' mastery of vowel diphthong /oi/ syllable patterns using the quick-check for Unit Twelve in this Teacher Resource System.

ELL Support Tip

When introducing new skills to ELL students, provide them with sufficient wait-and-think time before asking them to orally state their answers. While students may have the concepts, they might not have the vocabulary and command of language to express them. If they make a mistake, validate the fact that they made the effort to answer the question. If they say the correct answer, but use poor English, repeat the answer modeling good English, while at the same time validating that the answer was correct.

UNIT 12 Quick-Check: Vowel diphthong/oi/ syllable patterns

Student Name ______________________ Assessment Date __________

Segmenting and Blending

Directions: Explain that these words use sounds the student has been learning. Have the student point to each word on the corresponding student sheet, segment the word parts or syllables, and blend them together. Put a ✓ if the student successfully segments and blends the word or reads it as a complete unit. If the student misses the word, record the error.
Example: spoil

annoy		turquoise			
sirloin		ploy			
loyal		rejoice			
charbroil		decoy		Score	**/8**

Sight Words

Directions: Have the student point to the first word on the corresponding student sheet and read across the line, saying each word as quickly as possible. Put a ✓ if the student successfully reads the word and an **X** if the student hesitates more than a few seconds. If the student misses the word, record the error.

big		what			
left		was			
must		have			
both		been			
plant		time			
play		did			
out		you			
with				Score	**/15**

UNIT 13 Vowel diphthong /ou/ syllable patterns

Unit Objectives

Students will:

- Read one- and two-syllable words with vowel diphthong /ou/ syllable patterns
- Review vowel diphthong /oi/ syllable patterns
- Blend onset and rime words
- Sort words by vowel sounds and word families
- Read high-frequency words don't, head, last, put, saw, school, took
- Spell words with different syllable patterns: down, shout, mouth, town, sprout, south, surround, powder, outside
- Identify prepositions that tell where something is

Day 1

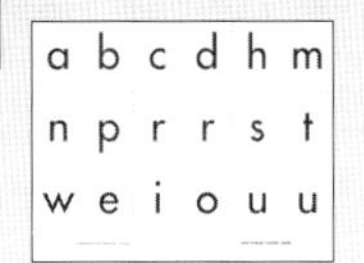

Letter Cards:
c, d, h, n, o, r, s, t, u, w

Word Lists
(BLM 2)

brown

Teacher Word Cards:
brown, crow, crowd, crown, howl, mouse, rough, shown, snout, throw, trout

Day 2

Word Lists
(BLM 2)

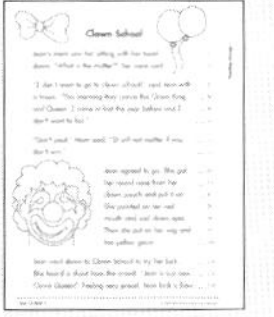

Reading Passage 1
(BLM 3)

High-Frequency Word Cards for Unit 13 (BLM 7)

Day 3

Word Lists
(BLM 2)

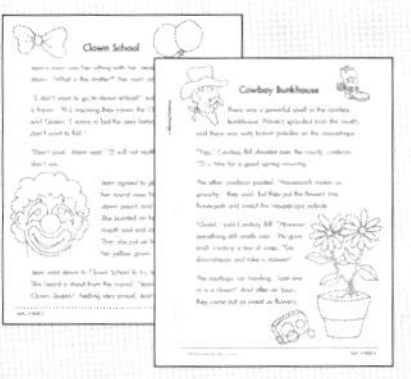

Reading Passages 1 & 2
(BLMs 3 & 4)

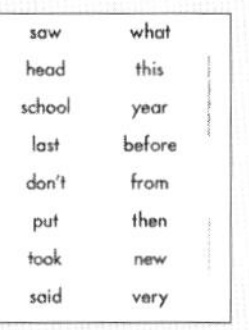

High-Frequency Word Cards for Unit 13 (BLM 7)

Day 4

Word Lists
(BLM 2)

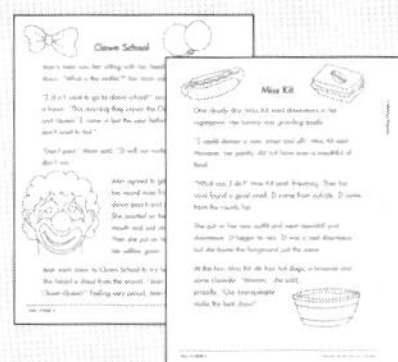

Reading Passages 1 & 3
(BLMs 3 & 5)

Spelling Peer Check
(BLM 6)

Student Word Cards (BLM 8)

Day 5

Reading Passage 1
(BLM 3)

saw what
head this
school year
last before
don't from
put then
took new
said very

High-Frequency Word Cards for Unit 13 (BLM 7)

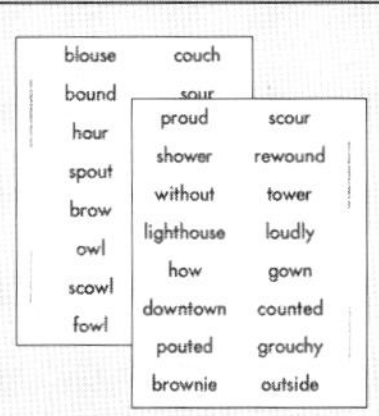

Student Word Cards
(BLMs 8 & 9)

Quick-Check Student Sheet

Frieze Card

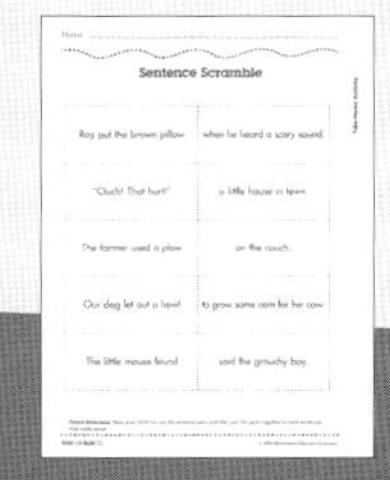

Take-Home Activity

Core Materials

All of these materials can be downloaded from http://phonicsresources.benchmarkeducation.com.

Frieze Card

1 Syllable Introduce Vowel Diphthong /ou/ Syllable Patterns

Model

- Hold up the vowel diphthong **/ou/** frieze card and point out that the vowel sound in each word is **/ou/**, but that different letters in the words stand for the sound. Remind students that each syllable has one vowel sound, and point out that ***ou*** and ***ow*** stand for one sound.

Guide

- Give students letter cards **c, d, h, n, r, s, t, w, o**, and **u**, and have them line up the letters in a row in front of them.
- Say the word ***town*** and ask students what letters they need to make the word. Remind them that they will need two letters to stand for the **/ou/** sound. Have them decide which spelling pattern on the frieze card they will use. Have them push forward the letters to spell and read the word. Have them decide whether the word looks right and if not, have them try the other spelling pattern.
- Ask students what letter they need to use to replace the letter ***t*** at the beginning of ***town*** to make the word ***down***.
- Repeat with the words ***round*** and ***sound***. Point out that these words use different letters to stand for the **/ou/** sound.

Apply

- Have students repeat the process independently with the words ***scour*** and ***hour.***

Assessment Tip: Watch to make sure students select the correct letters and read the word. Note which students struggle with this activity, and provide reinforcement activities.

Sort Words: Vowel Sounds

- Place teacher word cards **crow, mouse,** and **howl** in a pocket chart and read the words. Hold up the **crown** card and model sorting the word.
- **Think Aloud: Crown/crow.** *They do have the letters* **ow** *but they don't have the same vowel sound.* **Crown/mouse.** *No–they do have the same vowel sound, but they don't have the same spelling pattern.* **Crown/howl.** *Yes–they have the same vowel sound and spelling pattern. The word goes here.*
- Repeat with the following word cards, selecting them in random order. This time have students tell you where to place the word cards **snout, trout, crowd, brown, shown, throw,** and **rough.**
- As you have students sort the word ***rough***, guide them to recognize that this word does not match the vowel sounds of any of the other words.
- When the words are sorted, have students tell what the words in each column have in common.

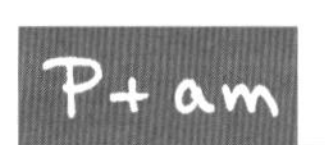

Blend Words with Vowel Diphthong /ou/

Model

- Write the word ***scout*** on the board, using a different color for the rime ***-out.*** Model sounding out the word, blending onset and rime: **/sk/ /out/.** Then say the whole word.

Guide

- Have students sound out the word with you. Repeat with other examples if you feel students need extra support.
- Give students blackline master 2. Have them use their fingers to frame the rime of the first word on the list for Day One. Then have students read the word by blending the onset and rime.

Apply

- Have students independently read the remaining words on the list for Day One. Guide students who need support to blend some or all of the words on the list before they read the list independently.

Assessment Tip: Note which students are able to read the words without blending each sound.

Spelling Words: *down, shout, mouth*

Model

- Make a two-column spelling chart on chart paper. Label the first column "One-Syllable Words" and the second column "Two-Syllable Words." Tell students that they will be spelling words with vowel diphthong /**ou**/. As you work through the unit, you can continue to add the spelling words to the chart, and have students use the chart to check their spelling of the words.
- Say the word ***down*** and model spelling and writing it.
- **Think Aloud:** *I hear two parts in the word* **down:** */***d***/ and /***oun***/. I know that the letter* **d** *stands for /***d***/. I hear the vowel diphthong followed by /***n***/ in the second part. I know that the letters* **ou** *and* **ow** *can stand for the /***ou***/ sound. I will try* **ow** *and see if the word looks right.*

Guide

- Say the word ***shout***. Have students identify the onset and rime in the word. Remind students that the vowel diphthong /**ou**/ sound can be spelled in different ways. Guide them to use the letters ***ou.*** Write the word in the first column of the chart as students tell you the word parts.
- Repeat with the word ***mouth.***

Apply

- Have students practice writing each of the words in their word study notebooks. After they write the word, have them check the spelling of the word by blending the onset and rime. Have students highlight the letters that make the diphthong sound in each word.

Our Spelling Words

One-Syllable Words	Two-Syllable Words
down shout mouth town sprout south	surround powder outside

DAY 2

Blend

- Have students blend the words on the word list for Day Two, using the procedure for blending from Day One.

Develop Automaticity in Word Recognition

- Circle the following words on the overhead transparency: ***don't, head, last, put, saw, school,*** and ***took.*** Tell students that practicing these words will help them recognize the words automatically so they can read more fluently. Explain that they can sound out some of the words, but they will read more quickly if they don't have to stop and sound them out.
- Read each word. Tell students that ***head*** has a short **ea** digraph. Point out that the letters ***oo*** stand for different sounds in ***took*** and ***school***.
- Have students read aloud with you the sentences that contain the words, and then have them write the words in their word study notebooks.
- Give students a copy of blackline master 7. Point out the words from this lesson, as well as other words they have learned previously. Have students cut out the words, store them in an envelope, and use them for practice activities.

Build Fluency with Connected Text

Model

- Read the passage on the overhead transparency aloud. Stop when you come to the word ***matter.*** Model strategies you would use to read the word.
- **Think Aloud:** *To help me read this word, I divided it into syllables. I looked for the two vowels, and there were two consonants between them. I divided between the consonants, and I had a closed syllable and an r-controlled* **e** *syllable.*
- Continue reading. Model making a mistake and correcting it–for example, read **/frōn/** instead of **/froun/**.
- **Think Aloud:** *That word doesn't make sense. Let me look at it again. The letters* **ow** *sometimes stand for the* **/ō/** *sound, but I know they can also stand for the* **/ou/** *sound. If I try the* **/ou/** *sound, I get* **frown.** *Now it makes sense.*

Guide

- Continue reading, stopping at other words and asking students what strategies they would use to read the words.

Apply

- Have students take turns reading blackline master 3 to a partner or in small groups as you monitor the reading. Use the teacher tips to check comprehension and fluency.

Spelling Words: *town, sprout, south*

- Have students practice writing the spelling words from Day One in their word study notebooks. Have them refer to words on the spelling chart to check their spelling.
- Introduce the Day Two spelling words. Say the word ***sprout*** and model spelling it and writing it on the spelling chart. Point to the word ***shout*** on the chart from the Day One spelling words, and model how to use the word family ***-out*** to spell the new word and other words in the word family such as ***scout, trout,*** and ***pout.***
- Repeat with the remaining words and have students practice writing the words in their word study notebooks.

Teacher Tips

Reading Strategies

If students have difficulty applying strategies for challenging words, guide them to use the following strategies:

- look at how the words start and/or end
- look for familiar patterns or parts within the words
- separate the words into syllables and decode each part
- think about what familiar words look like the difficult words
- read forward to check the context
- reread the sentence or paragraph
- mark the words, substitute synonyms, and get on with reading–ask for help later

Comprehension

Use the following questions to ensure that students have understood the passage:

- *What kind of school did Jean go to?* (Level 1–facts and details)
- *What things did Jean need to do before she could go to school?* (Level 2–sequence)
- *What do you think Jean's mom will say when she hears that Jean won?* (Level 3–make predictions)

Fluency

Intervene if students are having difficulty reading the passage. Model how to use word and meaning strategies to problem-solve the words. After students have had a chance to read the passage silently, have them read it aloud for fluency. Model fluent reading of the passage. For students who struggle, you may want to read the passage a second time and have them echo-read along with you.

Multisyllabic Words: Vowel Diphthong /ou/ Syllable Patterns

Model

- Write the word ***gown*** on the board, read it, and point out that it has one vowel sound and one syllable.
- Write the word ***nightgown*** on the board. Show students how to use what they know about vowel patterns and syllables to read longer words. Highlight the two consonants between the vowel digraph ***igh*** and the letters for the vowel diphthong (***ow***), and divide the word between the consonants: ***night/gown.***
- Point out the closed syllable and that the second syllable has a vowel diphthong. Model reading the word: **/nīt/goun/**, ***nightgown.***

Guide

- Write the word ***downstairs*** on the board and guide students as they identify the vowel diphthong **/ou/** in the first half of the word and the r-controlled vowel pattern in the second half.
- Point out that there are three consonants between the vowels, and because ***st*** is a blend, you will divide the word between the ***n*** and the ***s: down/stairs.*** Have students sound it out, using what they know about closed syllables and r-controlled vowel patterns.

Apply

- Have students independently blend the two-syllable words on the word list for Day Three. If students need more support, guide them as they blend some or all of the words.

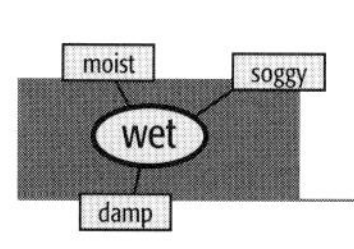

Develop Word Meanings: Prepositions

- Write the words ***down, out,*** and ***around*** on the board and read them aloud. Tell students these words are often used to tell where something is.
- Write the following sentences on the board: *Ben walked around the block; Amy ran down the stairs to catch her puppy; She ran out the door.* Read the sentences aloud to students. Ask students where each person in the sentences went and the words that tell them this.
- Guide students as they make a list of other words that tell where something or someone is–for example: ***in, under, over, through.***

Spelling Words: *surround, powder, outside*

- Have students practice spelling the words from Day One and Day Two by writing them several times in their word study notebooks.
- Introduce the new words, modeling how students can apply what they know about syllable patterns to the spelling of words with more than one syllable.
- Say the word ***surround.***
- **Think Aloud:** *When I spell this word, I need to think about how the word looks and sounds. I hear two syllables, and the first syllable has an r-controlled vowel. The second syllable has the diphthong sound* **/ou/**, *which can be spelled* **ow** *or* **ou.** *I think I will try the* **-ou** *pattern and see if the word looks right.*
- Repeat with the remaining words. Have students practice writing the words several times in their word study notebooks.

Build Fluency with Connected Text

- Have students read blackline master 4 to a partner or in small groups as you monitor their reading. Call attention to the following words in the reading passage before students read it: ***last, put, something, still, us.***

Teacher Tips

Teacher Tips

Preposition Game To provide practice in using prepositions, play the following game with students. Pick an object that can be seen from anywhere in the room. Have students sit in a circle. Say, for example, "I spy a blue pen." Students take turn asking questions that must have prepositions in them, such as "Is it on Ian's desk?" and "Is it over by the drinking fountain?" Encourage them to refer to the list of prepositions made earlier. The first student to identify the object you had in mind gets to lead the next round.

Develop Automaticity in Word Recognition

Have students place all sixteen high-frequency word cards from blackline master 7 in alphabetical order. Have a partner check the order. Then have partners alternate reading the words on the list.

Repeated Reading

Have students practice repeated readings of blackline master 3 to develop fluency.

DAY 4

Teacher Tips

Develop Automaticity in Word Recognition

Have students write these high-frequency words on self-stick notes: ***don't, head, last, put, saw, school,*** and ***took***. Then have them search old magazines and newspapers for examples of each word. Have them mark the examples with the self-stick notes. Then have them cut out the words they find and paste them on a page in their word study notebooks. When the words are pasted in, have them exchange notebooks with a partner and read all the words on the page.

Repeated Reading

Have students practice repeated readings of blackline master 3 to develop fluency.

P+ am Blend

- Have students blend the words on the word list for Day Four, using the procedure for blending from Day One.

Sort Words: Open Sort

- Give each student a set of student word cards from blackline master 8. Have students sort the words any way they want, but tell them they have to be able to explain how they sorted the words.
- Have students share their sorts with a partner, who must decide how the words are sorted.
- Call the group together and have students share different ways to sort these words. (number of vowels, number of letters, beginning blends, spellings for vowel diphthong **/ou/**, etc.) As students make suggestions, arrange the words in the pocket chart into the sorts they suggest.

Spelling Words

- Provide practice for students in segmenting words and associating sounds with spellings. Dictate the following words to students and have them write the words on their papers: ***down, sundown, count, counter.*** Remind students to use what they have learned about spelling syllables with vowel sound **/ou/.**
- Write the words on the board and have students self-correct their papers.
- Dictate the following sentence and have students write it on their papers: *The cow next door was too loud, so the mouse left his house.* Write the sentence on the board and have students self-correct their papers.
- Give pairs of students blackline master 6. While one student reads the spelling words, the other student writes them in the "First Try" column. After the student has spelled the words, the partner places a check mark next to words spelled correctly. For the second try, the partner may prompt the student by sounding out the words that were spelled incorrectly the first time. If the second spelling attempt is correct, the partner places a check mark in the "Second Try" column.

Assessment Tip: Use students' completed peer-check blackline masters to note which words gave students difficulty.

Build Fluency with Connected Text

- Give students the reading passage on blackline master 5. Have them take turns reading the passage to a partner. Call attention to the following words in the reading passage before students read it: ***began, even, food, four, miss, put, went.***
- Have students who need extra support practice reading the passage aloud in a small group as you monitor their reading.

Spelling Assessment

Use the following procedure to assess students' spelling of Unit Thirteen words.
- Say each spelling word and use it in a sentence.
- Have students write the words on their papers.
- Continue with the next word on the list.
- When students have finished, collect their papers and correct their spelling.
- Use the assessment to plan small group or individual practice.

Small Group/Independent Activities

The following activities can be used to provide practice for students who need additional support.

PHONICS AND WORD STRATEGIES

Build Words Write the words ***house*** and ***clown*** on the board and have students copy them in their word study notebooks. Challenge them to write as many words as they can from each of the word families.

Review Vowel Diphthong /oi/ Syllable Patterns Write the word ***join*** on the board and ask students to identify the vowel sound. Remind students that the letters ***o*** and ***i*** in this word combine to make the sound **/oi/**. Write the word ***enjoy*** on the board. Underline each vowel and then point to the two consonants between the ***e*** and the ***oy.*** Point out that the word should be divided between the two consonants. Have students identify the syllable patterns (closed and vowel diphthong) and blend the word.

Sort Have students sort the words on blackline master 9 any way they want. Then ask a partner to tell how the words were sorted.

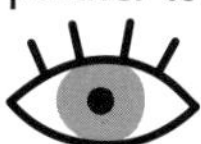

AUTOMATICITY IN WORD RECOGNITION

Read Words Have pairs of students place a set of high-frequency word cards in a stack. Have them take turns drawing a card, reading the word, and using the word in a sentence.

Look and Say Laminate a set of words from blackline master 7 and place them in a stack. Have one student draw a card and show it to the group. The first student to read the word gets the card and chooses the next word to show to the group.

BUILD FLUENCY WITH CONNECTED TEXT

Repeated Reading Have students practice reading blackline master 3 several times, until they feel they can read it fluently and accurately. Have them work with a partner to time each other as they read the passage aloud. Have them set a goal of reading 90 words per minute.

SPELLING

Divide the Syllables Have students write the two-syllable words from the spelling list in their word study notebooks. Then have them divide the words into syllables and write why they divided the words the way they did.

Word Riddles Write the spelling words on the board. Then provide riddles for the words and have students write the words you have in mind. Say the following clues: *I'm thinking of a word . . . that names what I smile with; . . . that is what baby plants do; . . . that is where birds fly in the winter; . . . that means* **yell;** *. . . that is the opposite of* **up;** *. . . that is a place people live; . . . that is where you go for fresh air; . . . that rhymes with* **chowder;** *. . . that means* **to close in around**.

Teacher Tips

Home Connection

Have students take blackline master 11 home to complete with a family member. Students can also take the repeated reading passage on blackline master 3 home to share with their family.

Quick-Check

Assess students' mastery of vowel diphthong /ou/ syllable patterns using the quick-check for Unit Thirteen in this Teacher Resource System.

ELL Support Tip

Give ELL students letter tiles and word cards with **/oi/** words. Have them make word chains by using the tiles to build off other words. Students can work independently or in pairs.

Quick-Check: Vowel diphthong /ou/ syllable patterns

Student Name ______________________ Assessment Date __________

Segmenting and Blending

Directions: Explain that these words use sounds the student has been learning. Have the student point to each word on the corresponding student sheet, segment the word parts or syllables, and blend them together. Put a ✓ if the student successfully segments and blends the word or reads it as a complete unit. If the student misses the word, record the error.
Example: crouch

aloud		scowl		
chowder		bouncy		
flounce		turnout		
greyhound		account		Score **/8**

Sight Words

Directions: Have the student point to the first word on the corresponding student sheet and read across the line, saying each word as quickly as possible. Put a ✓ if the student successfully reads the word and an **X** if the student hesitates more han a few seconds. If the student misses the word, record the error.

saw		what		
head		before		
school		year		
last		this		
don't		from		
said		new		
took		very		
put		then		Score **/16**

UNIT 14 Variant vowel /o͞o/ syllable patterns

Unit Objectives

Students will:

- Recognize and read words with variant vowel /o͞o/ syllable patterns
- Review vowel diphthong /ou/ syllable patterns
- Blend onset and rime
- Sort words according to word families and vowel sounds
- Read high-frequency words through, enough, off, soon, try, why
- Spell words with variant vowel /o͞o/ syllable patterns: brew, soup, blue, clue, blew, group, cashew, cartoon, pursue
- Identify irregular past tense verbs

Day 1

b c g h l m
n p r s t w
a e o o u u

Letter Cards:
b, c, e, g, h, l, m, n, o, o, p, r, s, t, u, u, w

Word Lists (BLM 2)

count

Teacher Word Cards:
count, do, down, due, ground, group, hoot, howl, mouth, scout, soon, stew, who

Day 2

Word Lists (BLM 2)

Reading Passage 1 (BLM 3)

High-Frequency Word Cards for Unit 14 (BLM 7)

Day 3

Word Lists (BLM 2)

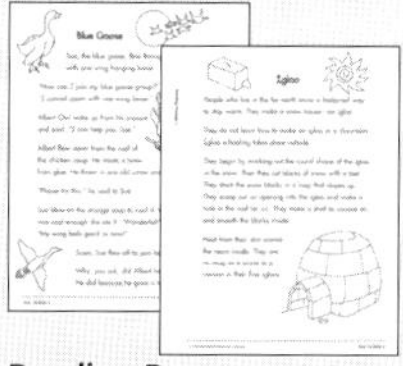

Reading Passages 1 & 2 (BLMs 3 & 4)

High-Frequency Word Cards for Unit 14 (BLM 7)

Day 4

Word Lists (BLM 2)

Reading Passages 1 & 3 (BLMs 3 & 5)

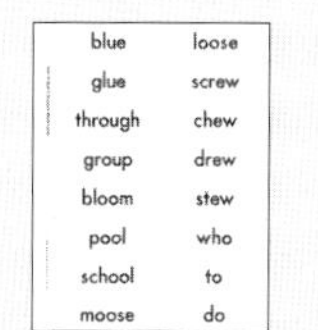

Student Word Cards (BLM 8)

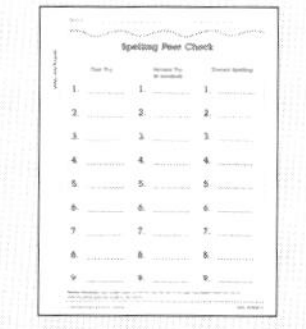

Spelling Peer Check (BLM 6)

High-Frequency Word Cards for Unit 14 (BLM 7)

Day 5

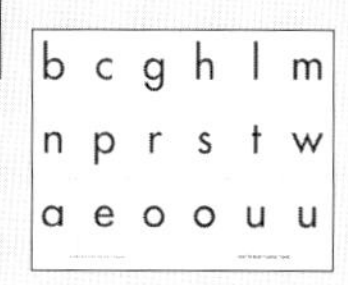

Letter Cards for Unit 14

Reading Passage 1 (BLM 3)

High-Frequency Word Cards for Unit 14 (BLM 7)

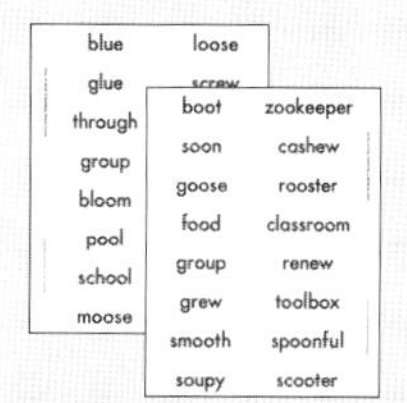

Student Word Cards (BLMs 8 & 9)

Quick-Check Student Sheet

Frieze Card

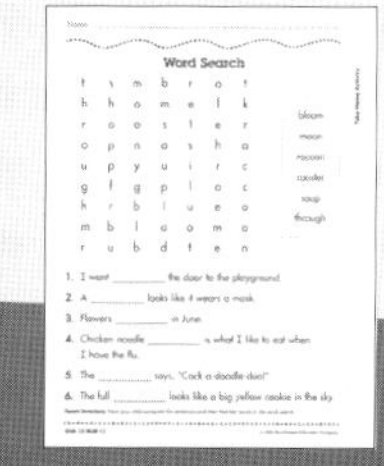

Take-Home Activity

Core Materials

All of these materials can be downloaded from http://phonicsresources.benchmarkeducation.com.

UNIT 14 Variant vowel /o͞o/ syllable patterns

Frieze Card

Introduce Variant Vowel /o͞o/ Syllable Patterns

Model

- Point out the variant vowel /o͞o/ words on the frieze card. Explain that the variant vowel /o͞o/ is neither long nor short, and that the sound can be spelled in different ways. Point out each spelling pattern for /o͞o/.

Guide

- Give students letter cards **b, c, g, h, l, m, n, p, r, s, t, w, e, o, o, u** and **u,** and have them line up the letters in a row in front of them.
- Say the word ***bloom*** and ask students what letters they need to start the word. Then ask what three letters they need to make the /o͞om/ sound. Have them choose from the vowel patterns on the frieze card. Have them push the letters forward as they say the sounds. Have them read the word and decide if it looks right.
- Have students take away the letter ***l*** and ask what letter they need to replace it with to make the word ***broom.*** Have them make the word and read it. Then have them take away the ***/br/*** and replace it with another blend to make the word ***gloom.***

Apply

- Repeat the steps with the following words: ***soon, spoon; chew, threw.***

Assessment Tip: Watch to make sure students select the correct letters and read the word. Note which students struggle with this activity, and provide reinforcement activities.

Sort Words: Variant Vowel /o͞o/ and Diphthong /ou/

- Place the following teacher word cards in a pocket chart: **soon, who, hoot, do, due, stew, group, ground, scout, down, howl, mouth, count.** Read each word with students.
- Give each student or pair of students one of the word cards. Have them hold up their cards for the group to read.
- Ask students to stand to your right if they have a word with a diphthong ***/ou/*** and to the left if they have a word with variant vowel ***/o͞o/.*** Have students in the group on the right hold up their cards while the students on the left read the words to check that they all have a diphthong ***/ou/*** sound. Repeat with the words students on the left are holding–have students on the right check that all words have variant vowel /o͞o/.

Blend Words with Variant Vowel /o͞o/

Model

- Write the word ***proof*** on the board. Point out that the word begins with a consonant blend.
- Model sounding out the word, blending the onset and rime: ***/pr/ /o͞of/.*** Say the whole word. Point out that it has one variant vowel sound and one syllable.

Guide

- Guide students as they sound out the word ***hoop.*** Repeat with other examples if you feel students need extra support.
- Give students blackline master 2. Have them read each word on the list for Day One by blending the onset and rime.

Apply

- Have students independently sound out the remaining words on the list for Day One. Guide students who need help to read some or all of the words before asking them to read the list independently.

Assessment Tip: Note which students are able to read the words without blending each sound.

Spelling Words: *brew, soup, blue*

Model

- Make a two-column chart on chart paper. Label the first column "One-Syllable Words" and the second column "Two-Syllable Words." Tell students that they will be spelling words with the variant vowel /o͞o/. As you work through Unit Fourteen, you can add the spelling words to the chart and have students use the chart to check their spelling of the words.
- Say the word ***brew*** and model spelling it and writing it on the chart.
- **Think Aloud:** *I hear two parts in the word brew:* /**br**/ *and* /**o͞o**/. *I know that the letters* **b** *and* **r** *stand for the blended sound* /**br**/. *I will write these letters on the board. I hear variant vowel* /**o͞o**/ *at the end. I know that* **ew, oo, o, ou,** *and* **ue** *can stand for the* /**o͞o**/ *sound. I will try* **oo** *and see if the word looks right.*
- Model deciding that the word doesn't look right and trying the pattern ***ew*** to spell the word.

Guide

- Say the word ***soup.*** Have students identify the sounds in the word and the letters that stand for the sounds. Write the word in the first column of the chart as students tell you the word parts. Repeat with the word ***blue.***

Apply

- Have students practice writing each of the words in their word study notebooks. After they write the word, have them check the spelling of the word by blending the onset and rime. Have students highlight the variant vowel /o͞o/ patterns in the words.

Our Spelling Words

One-Syllable Words	Two-Syllable Words
brew soup blue clue blew group	cashew cartoon pursue

DAY 2

Teacher Tips

Reading Strategies

If students have difficulty applying strategies for challenging words, guide them to use the following strategies:

- look at how the words start and/or end
- look for familiar patterns or parts within the words
- separate the words into syllables and decode each part
- think about what familiar words look like the difficult words
- read forward to check the context
- reread the sentence or paragraph
- mark the words, substitute synonyms, and get on with reading–ask for help later

Comprehension

Use the following questions to ensure that students have understood the passage:

- *What was wrong with Sue's wing?* (Level 1–facts and details)
- *What did Sue do after the soup was cool?* (Level 2–sequence of events)
- *What does this passage tell you about Albert Owl?* (Level 3–analyze character)

Fluency

Intervene if students are having difficulty reading the passage. Model how to use word and meaning strategies to problem-solve the words. After students have had a chance to read the passage silently, have them read it aloud for fluency. Model fluent reading of the passage. For students who struggle, you may want to read the passage a second time and have them echo-read along with you.

Blend

- Have students blend the words on the list for Day Two, using the procedure for blending from Day One.

Develop Automaticity in Word Recognition

- Circle the following words on the overhead transparency: ***through, enough, off, soon, try, why.*** Tell students that practicing these words will help them recognize the words automatically so they can read more fluently. Explain that students can sound out some of these words, but they'll read more quickly if they don't have to stop and sound them out each time they see them.
- Read each word. Point out that ***try*** and ***why*** end with the same open vowel and that ***because*** is a compound word: ***be + cause.***
- Have students read aloud with you the sentences in the passage that contain the words. Then have them write the words in their word study notebooks.
- Give students a copy of blackline master 7. Point out the words from this lesson, as well as other words they have learned previously. Have them cut out the words, store them in an envelope, and use them for practice activities.

Build Fluency with Connected Text

Model

- Read the passage on the overhead transparency aloud. Stop at the word ***blue*** and model strategies to read it.
- **Think Aloud:** /**Bl$\overline{oo}$**/ *is one of those words that has two spellings and two meanings. I can tell which meaning is correct here by reading the context. I can tell that in this sentence, the word describes the goose's color.*
- Model making a mistake and correcting it–for example, read ***lose*** instead of ***loose.***
- **Think Aloud:** *". . . one wing hanging lose." I don't think that makes sense. Let me see. Oh, this is one of those tricky words I have to memorize because even though I know the rules, they're not helping me with this word. I remember now that* **loose** *has two* **o***s, and* **lose** *has only one* **o** *and ends with a /***z***/ sound. ". . . one wing hanging loose" makes sense.*

Guide

- Continue reading and stop at other words in the passage. Guide students as they read the words.

Apply

- Have students take turns reading blackline master 3 to a partner or in a small group as you monitor the reading. Use teacher tips to check comprehension and fluency.

Spelling Words: *clue, blew, group*

- Have students practice writing the spelling words from Day One in their word study notebooks. Have them refer to words on the spelling chart to check their spelling.
- Introduce the Day Two spelling words. Say the word ***clue*** and model spelling it and writing it on the chart of spelling words. Point to the word ***blue*** on the chart from the Day One spelling words and highlight how the words are similar. Model how to use ***blue*** to spell the new word and other words in the word family–for example: ***glue, due,*** and ***sue.***
- Repeat with the remaining spelling words for Day Two and have students practice writing the words in their word study notebooks.

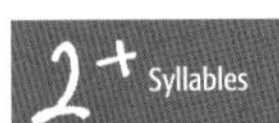

Multisyllabic Words: Variant Vowel /o͞o/ Syllables

Model

- Write the word ***moon*** on the board, read it, and point out that it has one vowel sound and one syllable.
- Write the word ***moonbeam*** on the board. Show students how to use what they know about vowel patterns and syllables to read longer words. Highlight the two consonants between the variant vowel /o͞o/ and the vowel digraph ***ea,*** and divide the word between the consonants: ***moon/beam.***
- Point out the variant vowel /o͞o/ syllable pattern and the vowel digraph ***ea*** syllable pattern before sounding out the syllables: **/moon/ /beam/,** ***moonbeam.***

Guide

- Write the word ***carpool*** on the board and guide students to identify the two vowel patterns and the number of consonants between the vowel patterns.
- Guide students as they divide the word: ***car/pool.*** Ask what syllable patterns they see and what clues this gives them about the vowel sounds in each syllable.

Apply

- Have students independently blend the two-syllable words on the word list for Day Three. If students need more support, guide them as they blend some or all of the words.

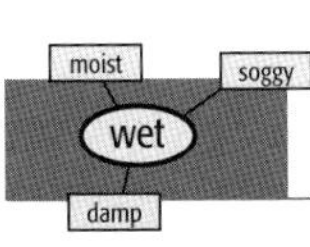

Develop Word Meanings: Irregular Verbs

- Using the overhead, point out the word ***flew*** and ask students what the word means. Tell students ***flew*** is the past tense of the verb ***fly*** and that it is irregular because it doesn't follow the usual rules of changing verbs to the past tense. For example, if ***fly*** were a regular verb, the past tense would be ***fly + ed, flyed,*** instead of ***flew.***
- Highlight the following words in the passage: ***threw, blew.*** Have students read aloud the sentences in which the words are found. Have them tell the present tense verb of each of these irregular verbs.
- Assign pairs of students one or more of these words from the passage and have them write sentences using the present tense of the verb(s). Have students share their sentences.

Spelling Words: *cashew, cartoon, pursue*

- Have students practice spelling the words from Day One and Day Two by writing them several times in their word study notebooks.
- Introduce the new spelling words, modeling how students can apply what they know about syllables to spelling multisyllabic words.
- Say the word ***cashew.***
- **Think Aloud:** *When I spell this word, I need to think about how the word looks. I hear two syllables in the word. The first syllable is a closed syllable with a short* **a** *vowel sound. The second syllable is an open syllable that ends with* **/o͞o/***. I know that the* **/o͞o/** *sound can be spelled in different ways. I think I will try the letters* **ew** *and see if it looks right.*
- Repeat with the remaining Day Three spelling words.
- Have students practice writing the words in their word study notebooks.

Build Fluency with Connected Text

- Have students read blackline master 4 to a partner or in small groups as you monitor their reading. Call attention to the following words in the reading passage before students read it: ***air, cut, far, house, learn, open(ing).***

Teacher Tips

Passage Riddles

Have one partner give a riddle based on the passage, using /o͞o/ words–for example: *What does Albert put in his brew?* The other partner reads the sentence(s) that provide(s) the answer to the riddle.

Develop Automaticity in Word Recognition

Give partners the high-frequency word cards from blackline master 7. As one student reads the passage from blackline master 3 aloud, another student holds up the appropriate high-frequency word card when that word is read in the story.

Repeated Reading

Have students practice repeated readings of blackline master 3 to develop fluency.

DAY 4

Teacher Tips

Develop Automaticity in Word Recognition

Write the high-frequency words from blackline master 7 on cutouts of footprints and place them in a path through the classroom. Have students follow the path by stepping on the footprints and reading the high-frequency words.

Repeated Reading

Have students practice repeated readings of blackline master 3 to develop fluency.

Blend

- Have students blend the words on the word list for Day Four, using the procedure for blending from Day One.

Sort Words: Open Sort

- Give each student blackline master 8. As a group, read through the words. Ask students what one thing it is that all the words have in common.
- Have students sort the words any way they want but tell them they will need to explain how they sorted them.
- Have students share their sorts with a partner, who must decide how the words are sorted.
- Call the groups together and have students share different ways to sort the words. As students make suggestions, arrange the words in the pocket chart into the groups they suggest.

Spelling Words

- Provide practice for students in segmenting words and associating sounds with spellings. Dictate the following words to students and have them write the words on their papers: ***zoo, zookeeper, room, classroom.*** Remind students to use what they have learned about spelling words with more than one syllable.
- Write the words on the board and have students self-correct their papers.
- Dictate the following sentence and have students write it on their papers: *The blue moon grew and grew and lit up the gloomy night sky.*
- Write the sentence on the board and have students self-correct their papers.
- Give pairs of students blackline master 6. While one student reads the spelling words, the other student writes them in the "First Try" column. After the student has spelled the words, the partner places a check mark next to words spelled correctly. For the second try, the partner may prompt the student by sounding out the words that were spelled incorrectly the first time. If the second spelling attempt is correct, the partner places a check mark in the "Second Try" column.

Assessment Tip: Use students' completed peer-check blackline masters to note which words gave students difficulty.

Build Fluency with Connected Text

- Have students take turns reading blackline master 5 to a partner or in a small group as you monitor their reading. Call attention to the following words in the reading passage before students read it: ***because, don't, found, must, off.***

Spelling Assessment

Use the following procedure to assess students' spelling of the Unit Fourteen words.
- Say each spelling word and use it in a sentence.
- Have students write the words on their papers.
- Continue with the next word on the list.
- When students have finished, collect their papers and analyze their spelling of the words.
- Use the assessment to plan small group or individual practice.

Small Group/Independent Activities

The following activities can be used to provide practice for students who need additional support.

PHONICS AND WORD STRATEGIES

Review Diphthong /ou/ Syllable Patterns Write the word ***pound*** on the board and ask students to identify the vowel sound. Remind students that the letters ***o*** and ***u*** in this word combine to make the sound /ou/ and that this syllable has a diphthong pattern. Write the word ***downhill*** on the board. Underline each vowel, reminding students that ***ow*** stands for one vowel sound and the letter ***i*** for another. Point out the consonants between them. Ask students where you should divide the word. Have a volunteer come up and divide the word into syllables. Then have students identify the syllable patterns (vowel diphthong and closed vowel) and blend the word.

Sort Words Have students make a four-column chart in their word study notebooks with the headings "ew," "ue," "oo," and "o." Have them sort the words from blackline masters 8 and 9 into the correct columns.

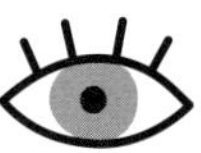

AUTOMATICITY IN WORD RECOGNITION

Make Sentences Put half the high-frequency word cards in one paper bag and the other half in another paper bag. Partners take turns choosing and reading a word from each bag and then using both words in an oral sentence.

Trace and Read Give each student a high-frequency word card. Have students trace the letters with their fingers and read the word. Give another high-frequency word to each student and repeat the procedure.

BUILD FLUENCY WITH CONNECTED TEXT

Repeated Reading Have students practice reading blackline master 3 several times, until they feel they can read it fluently and accurately. Have them work with a partner to time each other as they read the passage aloud. Have them set a goal of reading ninety words per minute.

SPELLING

Find the Missing Letter Write a spelling word on the board, omitting one of the letters. Tell students that a letter is missing and needs to be added for the word to be spelled correctly. Say the word and have students use letter cards to spell the word correctly before writing it in their word study notebooks.

Make Words Provide a set of letter cards and the week's spelling words on index cards. Have students use the letter cards to spell the words. Have them check their spelling by blending the sounds and then looking at the words on the index cards.

Teacher Tips

Home Connection

Have students take blackline master 11 home to complete with a family member. Students can also take the repeated reading passage on blackline master 3 home to share with their family.

Quick-Check

Assess students' mastery of variant vowel /$\overline{oo}$/ syllable patterns using the quick-check for Unit Fourteen in this Teacher Resource System.

ELL Support Tip

Give ELL students plenty of opportunities to summarize their learning as you proceed through the lessons. "What do we know now?" is a good question to ask to get them to think about what they have learned. Have students turn and share with a partner before sharing with the whole group.

Quick-Check: Variant vowel /o͞o/ syllable patterns

Student Name ______________________ Assessment Date __________

Segmenting and Blending

Directions: Explain that these words use sounds the student has been learning. Have the student point to each word on the corresponding student sheet, segment the word parts or syllables, and blend them together. Put a ✓ if the student successfully segments and blends the word or reads it as a complete unit. If the student misses the word, record the error.
Example: crew

roomy		flue		
mildew		foolish		
soundproof		blue		
subdue		moody		Score **/8**

Sight Words

Directions: Have the student point to the first word on the corresponding student sheet and read across the line, saying each word as quickly as possible. Put a ✓ if the student successfully reads the word and an **X** if the student hesitates more than a few seconds. If the student misses the word, record the error.

try		enough		off		soon		
because		why		from		through		
made		help		down		this		
old		said		one		other		Score **/16**

Variant vowel /o͝o/ syllable patterns

Unit Objectives

Students will:

- Recognize and read words with variant vowel /o͝o/ syllable patterns
- Review variant vowel /o͞o/ syllable patterns
- Blend onset and rime
- Sort words according to word families and vowel sounds
- Read high-frequency words away, got, head, later, leave, read, saw
- Spell one- and two-syllable words with variant vowels: brook, push, pull, bush, look, full, bully, bookshop, seagull
- Learn about onomatopoeia and make a list.

Day 1

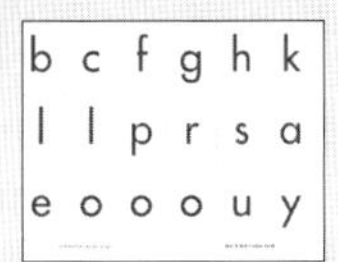

Letter Cards:
b, c, f, g, h, k, l, l, o, o, r, u

Word Lists
(BLM 2)

bull

Teacher Word Cards:
bull, bun, cook, cool, cut, food, foot, good, goof, push, rush, stood, stool

Day 2

Word Lists
(BLM 2)

Reading Passage 1
(BLM 3)

High-Frequency
Word Cards (BLM 7)

Day 3

Word Lists
(BLM 2)

Reading Passages 1 & 2
(BLMs 3 & 4)

High-Frequency
Word Cards (BLM 7)

Day 4

Word Lists
(BLM 2)

Reading Passages 1 & 3
(BLMs 3 & 5)

boy

Teacher Word Cards:
boy, bush, coin, count, crowd, hook, moist, moon, mouth, proof, proud, prowl, pull, soup, threw, through, wood

Spelling Peer Check
(BLM 6)

High-Frequency
Word Cards (BLM 7)

Day 5

Reading Passage 1
(BLM 3)

High-Frequency
Word Cards (BLM 7)

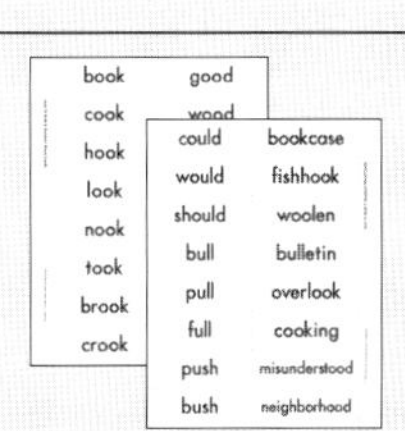

Student Word Cards
(BLMs 8 & 9)

Quick-Check
Student Sheet

Frieze Card

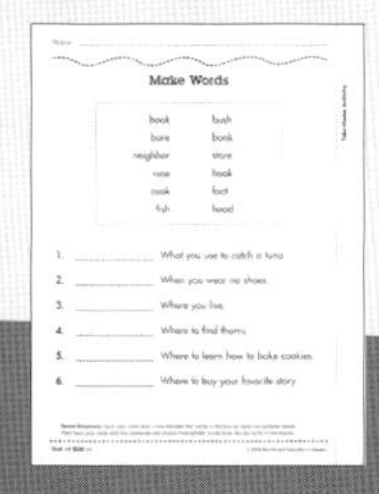

Take-Home Activity

Core Materials

All of these materials can be downloaded from http://phonicsresources.benchmarkeducation.com.

UNIT 15 Variant vowel /o͝o/ syllable patterns

DAY 1

Introduce Variant Vowel /o͝o/ Syllable Patterns

1 Syllable

Frieze Card

Model

- Hold up the variant vowel /o͝o/ frieze card and have students read the words.
- Point out the different spelling patterns for the sound /o͝o/. Write the word ***could*** on the board, and highlight the letters ***ou.*** Explain that this is another spelling pattern for the sound.
- Explain to students that some words with variant vowel /o͝o/, like ***push*** and ***bull,*** look as though they are closed syllables with a short vowel, but they are exceptions. The ***u*** in these words is not the short sound.
- Remind students that a syllable has one vowel sound and that the variant vowels stand for one vowel sound.

Guide

- Give students letter cards **b, c, f, g, h, k, l, l, r, o, o,** and **u,** and have them line up the letters in a row in front of them.
- Say the word ***hook*** and ask students what letter they need to start the word. Then ask what three letters they need to make the sound /o͝o/. Have students decide which variant vowel pattern shown on the frieze card they will use. Have them push the letters forward and read the word.
- Have students take away the letter card **h** and ask what two letters they need to replace it with to make the word ***crook.***

Apply

- Repeat the steps with the following words: ***cook, book; full, gull.***

Assessment Tip: Watch to make sure students select the correct letters and read the word. Guide those who need support.

Sort Words: Vowel Sounds and Variant Vowel Patterns

- Place teacher word cards **cut, cook,** and **cool** next to each other in a pocket chart. Tell students you have made three groups from the cards and ask them to tell you how they think you have grouped the words.
- Once students have identified the groupings (short ***u***, variant vowels /o͝o/ and /o͞o/), hold up the **goof** word card. Ask students under which word you should place this card. Have them tell why.
- Repeat with the following teacher word cards: **stood, stool, foot, food, bun, rush, push, bull, good.**

Blend Words with Variant Vowel /o͝o/

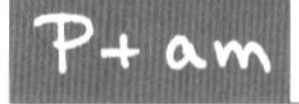

Model

- Write the word ***crook*** on the board. Point out that the word begins with a blend.
- Model sounding out the word, blending the onset and rime: **/cr/ /o͝ok/**. Then say the whole word. Point out that it has one variant vowel sound and one syllable.

Guide

- Guide students as they sound out the word ***should.*** Remind them that the ***l*** is silent. Repeat with other examples if you feel students need extra support.

- Give students blackline master 2. Have them read each word on the word list for Day One by blending the onset and rime.

Apply

- Have students independently sound out the remaining words on the list for Day One. Guide students who need support to read some or all of the words before asking them to read the list independently.

Assessment Tip: Note which students are able to read the words without blending each sound.

Spelling Words: *brook, push, pull*

Model

- Make a two-column chart on chart paper. Label the first column "One-Syllable Words" and the second column "Two-Syllable Words." Tell students that they will be spelling words with a variant vowel . As you work through Unit Fifteen, add the daily spelling words to the chart and have students use the chart to check their spelling of the words.
- Say the word ***brook*** and model spelling it and writing it on the chart.
- **Think Aloud:** *I hear two parts in the word brook: /**br**/ and /**o͝ok**/. I know that the letters* **br** *stand for the sound /**br**/. I hear /**o͝ok**/, and I know that this sound can be spelled in different ways. I will check the frieze card to decide which spelling pattern to use. I write the variant vowel pattern* **oo** *like I see in the word* **book** *on the frieze card.*

Guide

- Say the word ***push.*** Have students identify the sounds in the word and the letters that stand for the sounds. Have them choose from the variant vowel patterns on the frieze card and on the board. Write the word in the first column of the chart as students tell you the word parts. Repeat with the word ***pull.***

Apply

- Have students practice writing each of the words in their word study notebooks. Have them highlight the variant vowel /**o͝o**/ patterns in the words.

Our Spelling Words

One-Syllable Words	Two-Syllable Words
brook	bully
push	bookshop
pull	seagull
bush	
look	
full	

DAY 2

Teacher Tips

Reading Strategies

If students have difficulty applying strategies for challenging words, guide them to use the following strategies:

- look at how the words start and/or end
- look for familiar patterns or parts within the words
- separate the words into syllables and decode each part
- think about what familiar words look like the difficult words
- read forward to check the context
- reread the sentence or paragraph
- mark the words, substitute synonyms, and get on with reading–ask for help later

Comprehension

Use the following questions to ensure that students have understood the passage:

- *Who are the characters in this story?* (Level 1–story elements)
- *What happened after Terry started pulling weeds?* (Level 2–sequence)
- *What words could you use to describe Arliss the dog?* (Level 3–analyze character)

Fluency

Intervene if students are having difficulty reading the passage. Model how to use word and meaning strategies to problem-solve the words. After students have had a chance to read the passage silently, have them read it aloud for fluency. Model fluent reading of the passage. For students who struggle, you may want to read the passage a second time and have students echo-read along with you.

Blend

- Have students blend the words on the word list for Day Two, using the procedure for blending from Day One.

Develop Automaticity in Word Recognition

- Circle the following words on the overhead transparency: ***away, got, head, later, leave, read,*** and ***saw.***
- Tell students that practicing these words will help them recognize the words automatically so they can read more fluently. Explain that students can sound out some of these words, but they will read more quickly if they don't have to stop and sound out the words each time they see them.
- Read each word. Point out that the ***ea*** digraph is short in the word ***head*** and long in the word ***leave.*** Have students read aloud with you the sentences in the passage that contain the words. Then have them write the words in their word study notebooks.
- Give students a copy of blackline master 7. Point out the words from this lesson as well as other words they have learned previously. Have students cut out the words, store them in an envelope, and use them for practice activities.

Build Fluency with Connected Text

Model

- Begin reading the passage on the overhead transparency aloud, stopping at the word ***cool.*** Call attention to the variant vowel /o͞o/ syllables.
- **Think Aloud:** *This word has an example of the variant vowel /o͝o/ that we learned about in the last unit. I tried out the /o͝o/ sound first, but when that didn't make sense, I knew that the letters* **oo** *must stand for the /o͞o/ sound.*
- Model making a mistake and correcting it–for example, read **/hēd/** instead of **/hed/.**
- **Think Aloud:** *Oh, that's not right. I know that the letters* **ea** *often stand for the long* **e** *digraph, but* **/hēd/** *doesn't make sense here. This must be one of the exceptions where the letters* **ea** *are a short* **e** *digraph, like in* **/red/**, *so this word must be* **head.** *That makes more sense. I need to look at the context of the word more carefully.*

Guide

- Continue reading and stop at other words in the passage. Guide students as they read the words.

Apply

- Have students take turns reading blackline master 3 to a partner or in a small group as you monitor the reading. Use the teacher tips to check comprehension and fluency.

Spelling Words: ***bush, look, full***

- Have students practice writing the spelling words from Day One in their word study notebooks. Have them refer to words on the spelling chart to check their spelling.
- Introduce the Day Two spelling words. Say the word ***full*** and model spelling it and writing it on the chart of spelling words. Point to the word ***pull*** on the chart from the Day One spelling words and highlight how the words are similar. Model how to use ***pull*** to spell the new word and one other word–***bull.***
- Repeat with the remaining spelling words for Day Two and have students practice writing the words in their word study notebooks.

Multisyllabic Words: Variant Vowel / o͝o /

Model

- Write the word ***book*** on the board, read it, and point out that it has one vowel sound and one syllable.
- Write the word ***bookmark*** on the board. Show students how to use what they know about vowel patterns and syllables to read longer words. Highlight the two consonants between the vowels ***oo*** and the r-controlled ***a,*** and divide the word between the consonants: ***book/ mark.*** Before sounding out the syllables, point out that the word has two syllables, one with a variant vowel and the other with an r-controlled vowel: **/bo͝ok/ /mârk/, *bookmark.***

Guide

- Write the word ***pushy*** on the board and guide students to identify the consonant digraph between the two vowels ***u*** and ***y.***
- Guide students as they divide the word, reminding them that the letters in the digraph stay together when the word is divided: ***push/y.*** Ask what syllable patterns they see and what clues this gives them about the vowel sounds in each syllable.

Apply

- Have students independently blend the two-syllable words on the word list for Day Three. If students need more support, guide them as they blend some or all of the words.

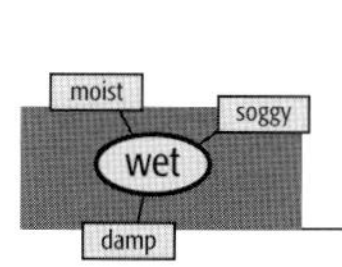

Develop Word Meanings: Onomatopoeia

- Write the following sentence from blackline master 3 on the board and underline the word ***woof:*** *"Yes!" said Arliss with a woof and a wag of his tail.*
- Ask students what they notice about the word ***woof.*** Tell students that this is an example of onomatopoeia, which is the use of a word that sounds like the thing it is describing. Other common examples are ***boom, beep,*** and ***click.***
- Ask students for other examples of onomatopoeia and make a list on chart paper.

Spelling Words: *bully, bookshop, seagull*

- Have students practice spelling the words from Day One and Day Two by writing them several times in their word study notebooks.
- Introduce the new spelling words, modeling how students can apply what they know about syllables to the spelling of words with more than one syllable.
- Say the word ***bully.***
- **Think Aloud:** *When I spell this word, I need to think about how it looks. I hear two syllables. The first syllable begins with a* **b** *and has a variant vowel* **/o͝o/** *sound. The second syllable is an open syllable, and I remember that the letter* **y** *often stands for the* **/ē/** *sound at the end of a word. For the first syllable, I will look at the frieze card to check the variant vowel pattern spellings. I think I will try* **b-u-l-l-y** *and see if the word looks right.*
- Repeat with the remaining words.
- Have students practice the words several times in their word study notebooks.

Build Fluency with Connected Text

- Have students read blackline master 4 to a partner or in small groups as you monitor their reading. Call attention to the following words in the reading passage before students read it: ***animal(s), because, got, land(ed), picture(s), soon, us.***

Teacher Tips

Cloze Activity

Give students extra practice in using the context to figure out words by providing them with sentences in which you have deleted a key word.

Develop Automaticity in Word Recognition

Have students work with a partner to flash the high-frequency word cards from blackline master 7.

Repeated Reading

Have students practice repeated readings of blackline master 3 to develop fluency.

DAY 4

Teacher Tips

Practice Makes Perfect

Have students place their high-frequency words in alphabetical order. Have partners check the list as they read each of the words.

Repeated Reading

Have students practice repeated readings of blackline master 3 to develop fluency.

Blend

- Have students blend the words on the word list for Day Four, using the procedure for blending from Day One.

Sort Words: Diphthongs /oi/ and /ou/ and Variant Vowels /o͞o/ and /o͝o/

- Place the following teacher word cards in random order in the pocket chart: **moist, coin, boy, count, proud, mouth, crowd, prowl, soup, through, threw, moon, proof, hook, wood, bush, pull.** Have students read each word with you.
- Set the word cards **coin, count, hook,** and **moon** apart from the rest of the cards. Ask students why these words should be in different groups.
- Once students recognize that one word has diphthong **/oi/,** one has diphthong **/ou/,** one has variant vowel **/o͝o/,** and the last has variant vowel **/o͞o/,** have them tell you which words you should group under the four words.
- Challenge students to think of other ways the word cards could be sorted. (by beginning letter, final letter, number of letters, etc.)

Spelling Words

- Provide practice for students in segmenting words and associating sounds with spellings. Dictate the following words to students and have them write the words on their papers: ***look, stood, understood, lookout.*** Remind students to use what they have learned about spelling words with more than one syllable.
- Write the words on the board and have students self-correct their papers.
- Dictate the following sentence and have students write it on their papers: *The bull should have boots and a hood with holes in it for the cold weather.*
- Write the sentence on the board and have students self-correct their papers.
- Give pairs of students blackline master 6. While one student reads the spelling words, the other student writes them in the "First Try" column. After the student has spelled the words, the partner places a check mark next to words spelled correctly. For the second try, the partner may prompt the student by sounding out the words that were spelled incorrectly the first time. If the second spelling attempt is correct, the partner places a check mark in the "Second Try" column.

Assessment Tip: Use students' completed peer-check blackline masters to note which words gave students difficulty.

Build Fluency with Connected Text

- Have students take turns reading blackline master 5 to a partner or in a small group as you monitor their reading. Call attention to the following words in the reading passage before students read it: ***always, began, food, found, play, put, read.***

Spelling Assessment

Use the following procedure to assess students' spelling of the Unit Fifteen words.
- Say each spelling word and use it in a sentence.
- Have students write the words on their papers.
- Continue with the next word on the list.
- When students have finished, collect their papers and analyze their spelling of the words.
- Use the assessment to plan small group or individual practice.

Small Group/Independent Activities

The following activities can be used to provide practice for students who need additional support.

PHONICS AND WORD STRATEGIES

Review Variant Vowel /o͝o/ Write the word ***tooth*** on the board and ask students to identify the vowel sound and what letters stand for the vowel sound. Remind students that although there are two letters representing the vowel sound, they stand for just one sound, making it a one-syllable word. Write the word ***raccoon*** on the board. Underline each vowel sound and then point to the two consonants between them. Ask students where you should divide the word. Have a volunteer come up and divide the word into syllables. Then have students identify the syllable patterns (closed and variant vowel) and blend the word.

Word Sort Write the words ***book, could,*** and ***bush*** on separate paper bags. Have students sort the student word cards from blackline masters 8 and 9 by reading each word and placing it in the bag with the word that has the same spelling for the variant vowel /o͝o/ sound.

AUTOMATICITY IN WORD RECOGNITION

Word Find Have students choose one high-frequency word from blackline master 7 and write it on an index card. Tell students that will be their special word for the day. Every time they see the word in print, they should make a tally mark on their card. At the end of the day, have students total their tally marks and share their results with the group.

Write a Paragraph Have students write one or two paragraphs using as many of the words from blackline master 7 as they can. Then have them exchange paragraphs with a partner and find and underline the high-frequency words in their partner's paragraph.

BUILD FLUENCY WITH CONNECTED TEXT

Repeated Reading Have students practice reading blackline master 3 several times, until they feel they can read it fluently and accurately. Have them work with partners to time one another as they read the passage aloud. Have them set a goal of reading 90 words per minute.

SPELLING

Divide the Syllables Have students write the words with more than one syllable from the spelling list in their word study notebooks. Then have them divide the words into syllables and write why they divided the words the way they did.

Around the Circle Have students sit in a circle. Say a spelling word and have a student say the first letter in the word. Have the next student say the next letter, and so on, until the word is spelled. Have the student who says the last letter write the word on the board.

Teacher Tips

Home Connection

Have students take blackline master 11 home to complete with a family member. Students can also take the repeated reading passage on blackline master 3 home to share with their family.

Quick-Check

Assess students' mastery of Variant vowel /o͝o/ syllable patterns using the quick-check for Unit Fifteen in this Teacher Resource System.

ELL Support Tip

Use a three-prong folder to store reading passages and create personal readers for students. Place cut-out words in baggies attached to the folder. Students can then practice matching words that are in a passage in order to build fluency and reinforce skills. The personal readers can be read with a buddy, or can be taken home to be read with families.

Quick-Check: Variant vowel /o͝o/ syllable patterns

Student Name ______________________________ Assessment Date ______________

Segmenting and Blending

Directions: Explain that these words use sounds the student has been learning. Have the student point to each word on the corresponding student sheet, segment the word parts or syllables, and blend them together. Put a ✓ if the student successfully segments and blends the word or reads it as a complete unit. If the student misses the word, record the error.
Example: wooly

skull		sullen		
childhood		mistook		
bushy		pulley		
checkbook		output		Score **/8**

Sight Words

Directions: Have the student point to the first word on the corresponding student sheet and read across the line, saying each word as quickly as possible. Put a ✓ if the student successfully reads the word and an **X** if the student hesitates more than a few seconds. If the student misses the word, record the error.

away		back		
got		good		
head		now		
later		over		
leave		want		
read		take		
saw		right		
work		all		Score **/16**

UNIT 16 **Variant vowel /ô/ syllable patterns**

Unit Objectives

Students will:

- Read words with variant vowel /ô/ syllable patterns
- Review variant vowel /o͞o/ syllable patterns
- Blend onset and rime
- Sort words by vowel sounds
- Read high-frequency words head, last, near, really, school, under, us
- Spell one- and two-syllable words with variant vowel /ô/ syllable patterns: claw, small, boss, draw, stall, gloss, salty, bossy, jigsaw
- Identify present and past tense verbs

Day 1

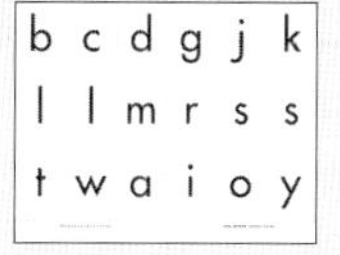

Letter Cards: **a, b, c, k, l, o, r, s, t, w**

Word Lists (BLM 2)

brought

Teacher Word Cards: **brought, could, count, ought, should, shout, soup, south, thought, through, you, would**

Day 2

Word Lists (BLM 2)

Reading Passage 1 (BLM 3)

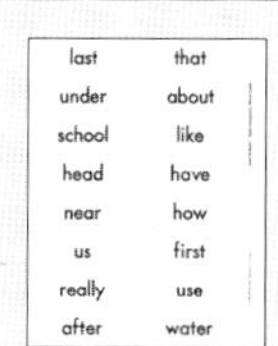

High-Frequency Word Cards (BLM 7)

Day 3

Word Lists (BLM 2)

Reading Passages 1 & 2 (BLMs 3 & 4)

High-Frequency Word Cards (BLM 7)

Day 4

Word Lists (BLM 2)

Reading Passages 1 & 3 (BLMs 3 & 5)

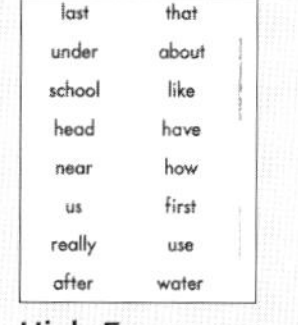

High-Frequency Word Cards (BLM 7)

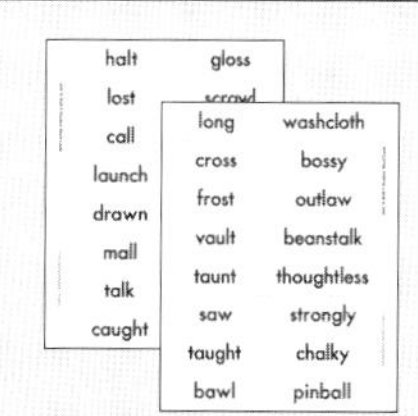

Student Word Cards (BLMs 8 & 9)

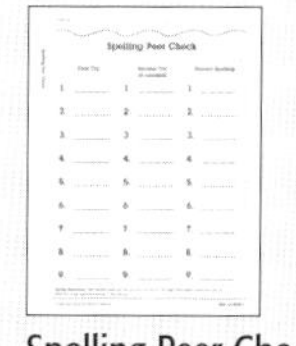

Spelling Peer Check (BLM 6)

Day 5

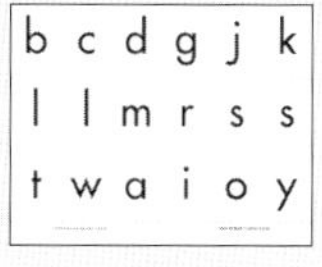

Letter Cards for Unit 16

Reading Passage 1 (BLM 3)

bawl

Teacher Word Cards: **bawl, boss, caught, crawl, cross, halt, malt, moss, salt, scrawl, taught**

High-Frequency Word Cards (BLM 7)

Quick-Check Student Sheet

Frieze Card

Take-Home Activity

Core Materials

All of these materials can be downloaded from http://phonicsresources.benchmarkeducation.com.

DAY 1

1 Syllable Introduce Variant Vowel /ô/ Syllable Patterns

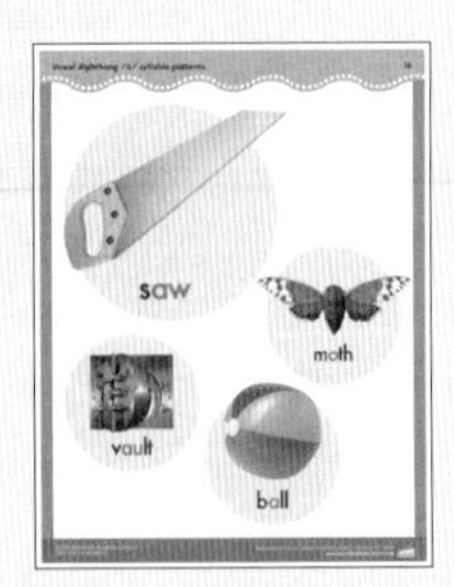

Frieze Card

Model

- Show students the variant vowel /ô/ frieze card and point out the spelling patterns for the /ô/ sound. Write the word ***bought*** on the board and point out that the letters ***ou*** can also stand for the /ô/ sound.
- Remind students that the words on the frieze card are one-syllable words because they have one vowel sound.

Guide

- Give students letter cards **b**, **c**, **k**, **l**, **r**, **s**, **t**, **w**, **a**, and **o**, and have them line up the letters in a row in front of them.
- Say the word ***talk*** and ask students what letter they need to start the word. Then ask what three letters they need to make the /**ôk**/ sound. Have them decide which spelling pattern they will use from the frieze card or from the one on the board. Have them make the word. Ask whether the word looks right, and if not, have them try other spelling patterns.
- Have students take away the letter ***t*** and ask what letter they need to replace it with to make the word ***walk***. Have them make the word and read it. Then have them take away the w and replace it with a blend to make the word ***stalk***.

Apply

- Repeat the steps with the following words: ***crawl***, ***bawl***; ***cost***, ***lost***.

Assessment Tip: Watch to make sure students select the correct letters and read the word. Note which students struggle with this activity, and provide reinforcement activities.

Sort Words: Vowel Sounds

- Place the teacher word cards **you**, **ought**, **would**, and **shout** next to each other in a pocket chart. Read each word and point out that although all the words have the letters ***ou***, they stand for different sounds in each word.
- Hold up the word card **could** and model placing it under the words in the pocket chart.
- **Think Aloud: You/could**. *No, not the same sound.* **Ought/could**. *No, not the same sound.* **Would/could**. *Yes. These words have the same sound.*
- Hold up the following word cards one at a time and have students help you sort them under the correct card in the pocket chart: **should**, **soup**, **through**, **thought**, **brought**, **count**, **south**.
- Have students copy the words in groups in their word study notebooks and explain how the words are sorted.

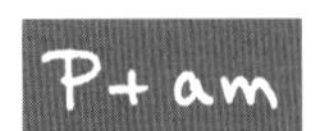

Blend Words with Variant Vowel /ô/

Model

- Write the word ***stall*** on the board. Point out that the word begins with a consonant blend.

Model sounding out the word, blending the onset and rime: /**st**/ /**ôl**/. Then say the whole word. Point out that it has one variant vowel sound and one syllable.

Guide

- Guide students as they sound out the word ***strong***. Repeat with other examples if you feel students need extra support.
- Give students blackline master 2. Have them read each word on the list for Day One by blending the onset and rime.

Apply

- Have students independently sound out the remaining words on the list for Day One. If students need more help, guide them as they blend some or all of the words on the list before asking them to read the list independently.

Assessment Tip: Note which students are able to read the words without blending each sound.

Spelling Words: *claw, small, boss*

Model

- Make a two-column chart on chart paper. Label the first column "One-Syllable Words" and the second column "Two-Syllable Words." Tell students that they will be spelling words with the variant vowel /**ô**/. As you work through Unit Sixteen, add the spelling words to the chart and have students use the chart to check their spelling.
- Say the word ***claw*** and model spelling it and writing it on the chart.
- **Think Aloud:** *I hear two parts in the word* **claw:** /**kl**/ *and* /**ô**/. *I know that the letters* **c** *and* **l** *stand for the blended* sound /**kl**/. *I will write these letters on the board. I hear* /**ô**/ *and I know that this sound can be spelled using* **aw, au, al,** *or just* **o**. *I will try* **aw** *and see if it looks right. It looks right and looks like words I know from this* **aw** *word family:* **jaw** *and* **paw**.

Our Spelling Words

One-Syllable Words	Two-Syllable Words
claw small boss draw stall gloss	salty bossy jigsaw

Guide

- Say the word ***small***. Have students identify the sounds in the word and the letters that stand for the sounds. Have them check the frieze card for /**ô**/ spelling patterns. Write the word in the first column of the chart as students tell you the letters. Ask if the word looks right. Repeat with the word ***boss***.

Apply

- Have students practice writing each of the words in their word study notebooks. After they write the word, have them check the spelling of the word by blending the onset and rime. Have students highlight the letters that make the variant vowel /**ô**/ sound in each word.

DAY 2

Teacher Tips

Reading Strategies

If students have difficulty applying strategies for challenging words, guide them to use the following strategies:

- look at how the words start and/or end
- look for familiar patterns or parts within the words
- separate the words into syllables and decode each part
- think about what familiar words look like the difficult words
- read forward to check the context
- reread the sentence or paragraph
- mark the words, substitute synonyms, and get on with reading–ask for help later

Comprehension

Use the following questions to ensure that students have understood the passage:

- *What is special about the park?* (Level 1–facts and details)
- *What happened after the boat was launched?* (Level 2–sequence)
- *What do you think is the main idea of this passage?* (Level 3–infer main idea)

Fluency

Intervene if students are having difficulty reading the passage. Model how to use word and meaning strategies to problem-solve the words. After students have had a chance to read the passage silently, have them read it aloud for fluency. Model fluent reading of the passage. For students who struggle, you may want to read the passage a second time and have them echo-read along with you.

P+ am

Blend

- Have students blend the words on the word list for Day Two, using the procedure for blending from Day One.

Develop Automaticity in Word Recognition

- Circle the following words on the overhead transparency: ***head***, ***last***, ***near***, ***really***, ***school***, ***under***, ***us***. Tell students that practicing these words will help them recognize the words automatically so they can read more fluently. Explain that students can sound out most of these words, but they will read more quickly if they don't have to stop and sound them out each time they see them.
- Read each word. Point out that the ***ea*** digraph in ***head*** is short while the ***ea*** digraphs in near and really are long.
- Have students read aloud with you the sentences in the passage that contain the words. Then have them write the words in their word study notebooks.
- Give students a copy of blackline master 7. Point out the words from this lesson, as well as other words they have learned previously. Have them cut out the words, store them in an envelope, and use them for practice activities.

Build Fluency with Connected Text

Model

- Begin reading aloud the passage on the overhead transparency, stopping at the word ***completely*** and modeling strategies to read the word.
- **Think Aloud:** *This looks like a big word, but I can divide it into syllables and this will make it easier to read. I divide first between the* **m** *and the* **p**. *This makes the first syllable a closed syllable and easy to read:* **com**. *The second syllable is a* VCe *syllable, so the vowel is probably long:* /**plēt**/. *The last syllable is open and I know that* **y** *at the end of a word can stand for the* /ē/ *sound. Putting it all together, the word says* **completely**, *which makes sense.*
- Model making a mistake and correcting it–for example, read ***lunch*** instead of ***launch***.
- **Think Aloud:** *"After the boat lunch." I don't think that's right. Let me see. Oh, there's an* **a** *before the* **u**, *and I know that* **au** *can make the* /ô/ *sound:* /**lônch**/. *"After the boat launch."* **Launch** *means when the boat leaves or takes off.*

Guide

- Continue reading and stop at other words in the passage. Guide students as they read the words.

Apply

- Have students take turns reading blackline master 3 to partners or in small groups as you monitor their reading. Use the teacher tips to check comprehension and fluency.

Spelling Words: *draw, stall, gloss*

- Have students practice writing the spelling words from Day One in their word study notebooks. Have them refer to words on the spelling chart to check their spelling.
- Introduce the Day Two spelling words. Say the word ***stall*** and model spelling it and writing it on the chart of spelling words. Point to the word ***small*** on the chart from the Day One spelling words and model how to use ***small*** to spell the new word and other words in the word family–for example: ***call***, ***fall***, ***wall***.
- Repeat with the remaining spelling words for Day Two and have students practice writing the words in their word study notebooks.

Multisyllabic Words: Variant Vowel /ô/ Syllable Patterns

Model

- Write the word ***frost*** on the board, read it, and point out that it has one variant vowel sound and one syllable.
- Write the word ***frosty*** on the board. Highlight the two consonants between the two vowels and divide the word between the consonants: ***fros/ty***. Point out the variant vowel syllable and the open syllable before sounding out the word.

Guide

- Write the word ***install*** on the board and guide students as they identify the two vowels and the number of consonants between the vowels. Point out that since there are three consonants, they should keep the blend ***st*** together and divide the word before the ***s: in/stall***.
- Ask what syllable patterns they see and what clues this gives them about the vowel sounds in each syllable.

Apply

- Have students independently blend the two- and three-syllable words on the word list for Day Three. If students need more support, guide them as they blend some or all of the words.

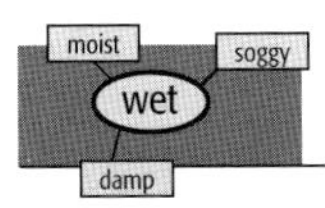

Develop Word Meanings

- Tell students that verbs are words that show action. Using the overhead, point out the word ***bought***. Tell students that ***bought*** is the past tense of the verb ***buy.***
- Highlight the following words in the passage: ***saw***, ***yawn***, ***thought***, ***ought***. Have students read aloud the sentences in which the words are found. Have them tell which verbs are present tense and which are past tense. (Point out that some verbs, like ***ought***, are helping verbs that are neither present nor past tense.) For those verbs that are past tense, have them tell you the present tense forms of the verbs.
- Assign pairs of students the task of circling the remaining verbs in the passage, using yellow circles to mark present tense verbs, and red circles for past tense verbs.

Spelling Words: *salty, bossy, jigsaw*

- Have students practice spelling the words from Day One and Day Two by writing them several times in their word study notebooks.
- Introduce the new spelling words, modeling how students can apply what they know about syllables to the spelling of words with more than one syllable.
- Say the word ***salty***.
- **Think Aloud:** *When I spell this word, I need to think about how the word looks. I hear two syllables in the word. The first syllable has the variant vowel sound /***ô***/, which can have different spellings. Looking at the patterns on the frieze card, I think I will use* **al** *and see if that looks right. The second syllable is open and has a long* **e** *sound. I know that the letter* **y** *often stands for this sound at the end of a word.*
- Repeat with the remaining words.
- Have students practice spelling the words several times in their word study notebooks.

Build Fluency with Connected Text

- Have students read blackline master 4 to partners or in small groups as you monitor their reading. Call attention to the following words in the reading passage before students read it: ***eat***, ***hear(ing)***, ***high***, ***keep(s)***, ***last***, ***well***.

Teacher Tips

Three-Syllable Words

Provide a challenge for students by having them use syllable patterns to read three-syllable words. Example words are: ***somersault, lawnmower, wallpaper, basketball, strawberry, jawbreaker.***

Develop Automaticity in Word Recognition

Draw a set of steps on the board and write the high-frequency words from blackline master 7 on the steps. Have students take turns seeing how high they can climb by reading the high-frequency words correctly. Change the high-frequency words and repeat.

Repeated Reading

Have students practice repeated readings of blackline master 3 to develop fluency.

DAY 4

Independent Activities

Develop Automaticity in Word Recognition

Have small groups of students use two sets of words from blackline master 7. Have them spread one set of the words faceup on the floor. Have them place another set of the words facedown in a stack. Have one student draw a card and read it. The rest of the students race to find the matching word in the words spread out on the floor.

Repeated Reading

Have students practice repeated readings of blackline master 3 to develop fluency.

P+ am Blend

- Have students blend the words on the word list for Day Four, using the procedure for blending from Day One.

Sort Words: Open Sort

- Give each student a set of words from blackline masters 8 and 9. Have students sort the words any way they want, but tell them they have to be able to explain how they sorted the words.
- Have each student share his or her sorts with a partner who must decide how the words are sorted.
- Call the group together and have students share different ways to sort these words. (number of vowels, number of letters, beginning blends, variant vowel syllable patterns, etc.) As students make suggestions, arrange the words in the pocket chart into the sorts they suggest.

Aa Spelling Words

- Provide practice for students in segmenting words and associating sounds with spellings. Dictate the following words to students and have them write the words on their papers: ***saw***, ***seesaw***, ***cloth***, ***washcloth***. Remind students to use what they have learned about spelling words with more than one syllable.
- Write the words on the board and have students self-correct their papers.
- Dictate the following sentence and have students write it on their papers: *Ross bought a moss green shawl and a glass ball for his mother.*
- Write the sentence on the board and have students self-correct their papers.
- Give pairs of students blackline master 6. While one student reads the spelling words, the other student writes them in the "First Try" column. After the student has spelled the words, the partner places a check mark next to words spelled correctly. For the second try, the partner may prompt the student by sounding out the words that were spelled incorrectly the first time. If the second spelling attempt is correct, the partner places a check mark in the "Second Try" column.

Assessment Tip: Use students' completed peer-check blackline masters to note which words gave students difficulty.

Build Fluency with Connected Text

- Have students take turns reading blackline master 5 to partners or in small groups as you monitor their reading. Call attention to the following words in the reading passage before students read it: ***began***, ***got***, ***last***, ***let***, ***soon***, ***turn***, ***while***.

Spelling Assessment

Use the following procedure to assess students' spelling of the Unit Sixteen words.

- Say each spelling word and use it in a sentence.
- Have students write the words on their papers.
- Continue with the next word on the list.
- When students have finished, collect their papers and analyze their spelling of the words.
- Use the assessment to plan small group or individual practice.

Small Group/Independent Activities

The following activities can be used to provide practice for students who need additional support.

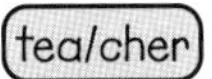

PHONICS AND WORD STRATEGIES

Review Variant Vowel /o͝o/ Syllable Patterns Write the word ***stood*** on the board and ask students to identify the vowel and the vowel sound. Point out that the word has a variant vowel syllable pattern. Write the word ***fishhook*** on the board. Underline each vowel and then point to the consonants between them. Point out that there are three consonants, but that ***sh*** is a digraph that doesn't get split up when words are divided. Ask students where you should divide the word. Have a volunteer come up and divide the word into syllables. Then have students identify the syllable patterns (closed and variant vowel) and blend the word.

Sort Words Give each student or pair of students one of the following word cards: **salt**, **malt**, **halt**, **bawl**, **crawl**, **scrawl**, **boss**, **cross**, **moss**, **caught**, **taught**. Have them hold up their card for the group to read. Have the group decide what word family the word belongs in. Have students with the same word family words stand together. After the words have been sorted, have students read the words in each grouping to check the word family.

AUTOMATICITY IN WORD RECOGNITION

Make Sentences Place the high-frequency word cards in a paper bag. Have students work with a partner to draw a word card, read it, and use the word in an oral sentence.

Match the Words Have pairs or small groups of students combine sets of high-frequency word cards so they have a pair for each word. Have them mix up the cards and spread them facedown on the floor. Have students take turns turning over two cards and reading the words. If the words match, the student can keep the cards.

BUILD FLUENCY WITH CONNECTED TEXT

Repeated Reading Have students practice reading blackline master 3 several times, until they feel they can read it fluently and accurately. Have them work with a partner to time each other as they read the passage aloud. Have them set a goal of reading 90 words per minute.

SPELLING

Help with Spelling Say a spelling word. Ask a volunteer to suggest a way to remember how to spell the word with the variant vowel /**ô**/ pattern. Have students write the word. Continue with other spelling words.

Spell the Words Have students use the letter cards to make each of the spelling words and then copy each word in their word study notebooks.

Teacher Tips

Home Connection

Have students take blackline master 11 home to complete with a family member. Students can also take the repeated reading passage on blackline master 3 home to share with their family.

Quick Check

Assess students' mastery of variant vowel /**ô**/ syllable patterns using the quick-check for Unit Sixteen in this Teacher Resource System.

ELL Support Tip

When giving directions to ELL students, show what you mean rather than simply telling them. Your students need to see what they will be learning and doing. Using the show-not-tell method gives students a purpose, especially if their language proficiency is at a lower level. Be sure to supplement visuals with strong body language and gestures.

Quick-Check: Variant vowel /ô/ syllable patterns

Student Name ______________________________ Assessment Date __________

Segmenting and Blending

Directions: Explain that these words use sounds the student has been learning. Have the student point to each word on the corresponding student sheet, segment the word parts or syllables, and blend them together. Put a ✔ if the student successfully segments and blends the word or reads it as a complete unit. If the student misses the word, record the error. **Example:** straw

exhaust		halter		
cobalt		mall		
lawful		withdraw		
gauze		fault		Score **/8**

Sight Words

Directions: Have the student point to the first word on the corresponding student sheet and read across the line, saying each word as quickly as possible. Put a ✔ if the student successfully reads the word and an **X** if the student hesitates more than a few seconds. If the student misses the word, record the error.

last		that		
under		about		
school		like		
head		have		
near		how		
us		first		
really		us		
after		water		Score **/16**

UNIT 17 **Consonant + le, al, or el syllable patterns**

Unit Objectives

Students will:

- Review hard and soft c and g
- Read words with consonant + le, al, or el syllable patterns
- Review variant vowel /â/ syllable patterns
- Sort words according to hard and soft c and g and syllable patterns
- Read high-frequency words along, never, run, second, tree, under
- Spell words with consonant + le syllable patterns: puddle, saddle, bottle, table, noble, bridle, purple, marble, turtle
- Identify synonyms

UNIT 17 Consonant + le, al, or el syllable patterns

Day 1

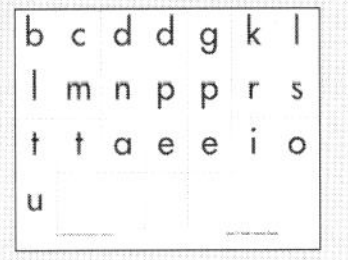

Letter Cards:
a, b, d, d, e, i, l, m, r, t, t

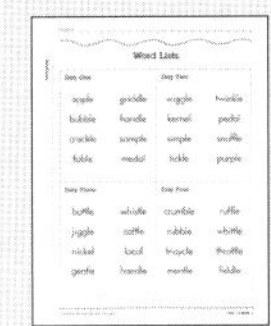

Word Lists
(BLM 2)

cape

Teacher Word Cards:
cape, car, cent, coat, edge, fudge, goat, gone, greedy, hug, huge, large, peace, picnic, race, since, slice

Day 2

Word Lists
(BLM 2)

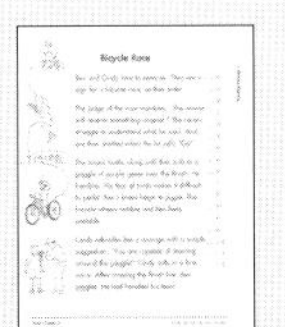

Reading Passage 1
(BLM 3)

High-Frequency Word Cards for Unit 17 (BLM 7)

Day 3

Word Lists
(BLM 2)

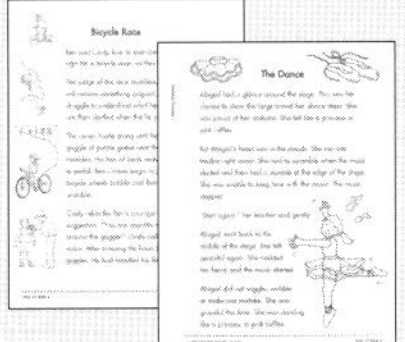

Reading Passages 1 & 2
(BLMs 3 & 4)

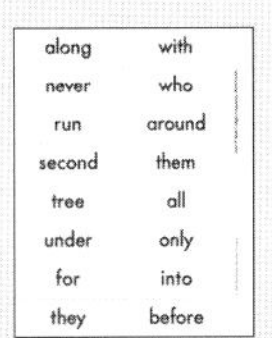

High-Frequency Word Cards for Unit 17 (BLM 7)

Day 4

Word Lists
(BLM 2)

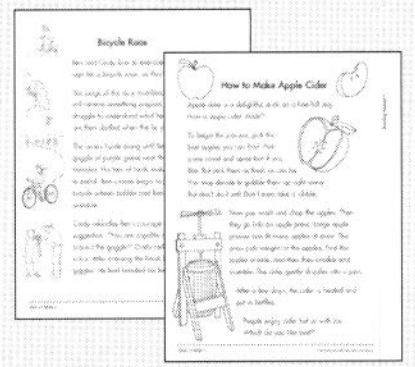

Reading Passages 1 & 3
(BLMs 3 & 5)

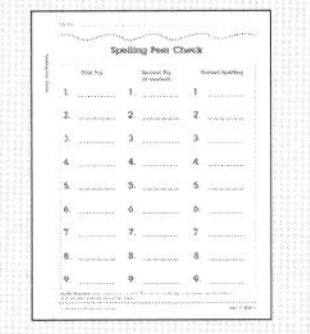

Spelling Peer Check
(BLM 6)

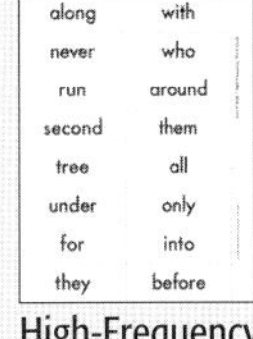

High-Frequency Word Cards for Unit 17 (BLM 7)

admit

Teacher Word Cards:
admit, basic, bedside, dislike, essay, escape, even, explain, freckle, grumble, hello, middle, rabbit, raisin, tennis

Day 5

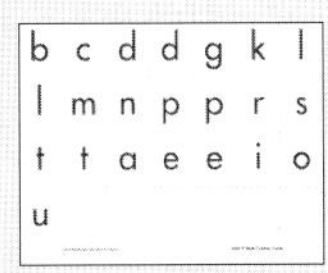

Letter Cards for Unit 17

Reading Passage 1
(BLM 3)

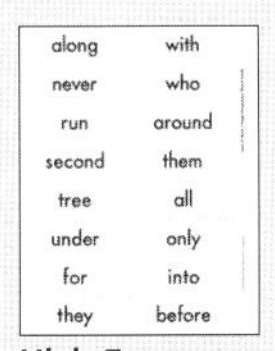

High-Frequency Word Cards for Unit 17 (BLM 7)

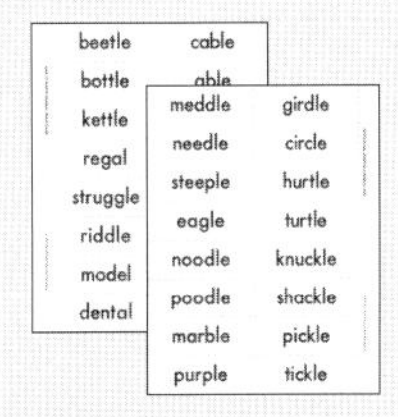

Student Word Cards
(BLMs 8 & 9)

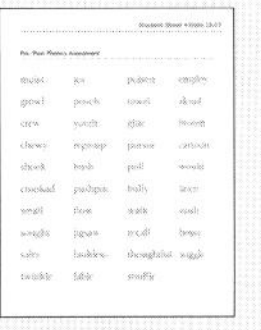

Quick-Check Student Sheet

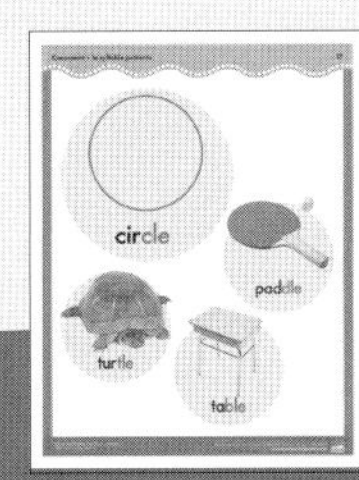

Frieze Card

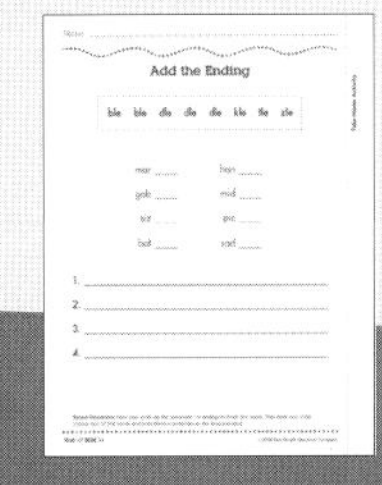

Take-Home Activity

Core Materials

All of these materials can be downloaded from http://phonicsresources.benchmarkeducation.com.

DAY 1

Review Hard and Soft *c* and *g*

- Write the words ***face*** and ***cat*** on the board and read the words. Remind students that the letter ***c*** can stand for **/s/** and **/k/.** Review that when the vowel ***i*** or ***e*** follows the letter ***c,*** the sound is usually soft: **/s/.** When the vowel ***o*** or ***a*** follows the letter ***c,*** the sound is usually hard: **/k/** as in ***coat*** or ***cat.***
- Write the words ***huge*** and ***gate*** on the board. Remind students that the letter ***g*** can stand for **/g/** and **/j/.** When a silent final ***e*** follows the letter ***g,*** the sound is usually **/j/.** Review that the letter ***g*** also stands for the soft sound when followed by ***i,*** as in the word ***giraffe.***

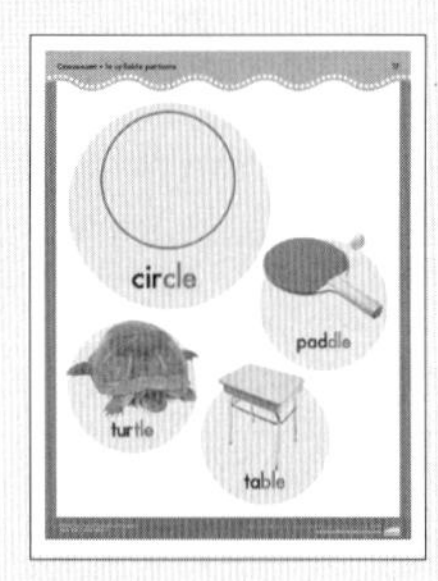

Frieze Card

Sort Words: Hard and Soft *c* and *g*

- Read each of the following teacher word cards as you place them in a row in a pocket chart: **cent, car, goat, large**. Point out that the words contain both hard and soft sounds for ***c*** and ***g***.
- Hold up the word card **race** and model sorting it.
- **Think Aloud:** *I need to decide if the letter* **c** *in* **race** *has the hard sound as in* **car** *or the soft sound as in* **cent.** *I hear the soft sound, so I will place it under the word* **cent.**
- Repeat with the following word cards, having students tell you where to place the cards according to the sound of the letters ***c*** and ***g:*** **slice, cape, edge, gone, peace, huge, hug, coat, picnic, greedy, fudge, since.**
- After students have sorted the words, have them generalize about when ***c*** and ***g*** have the soft sound and when they have the hard sound.

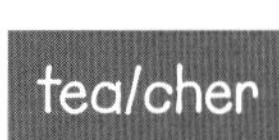

Introduce Consonant + *le, al, el* Syllable Patterns

Model

- Show students the frieze card. Read each word and have students listen for the two syllables. Point out that the first ***c*** in ***circle*** is the soft ***c*** sound.
- Point out the double consonant in ***paddle.*** Explain that to make the first syllable a closed syllable, it needs to end with a consonant. Then another consonant is needed to make the consonant + ***le*** ending.
- Point out the words that end with ***-al*** and ***-el*** and explain that they have the same ending sound as words that end with ***-le***.

Guide

- Give students letter cards **b, d, d, l, m, r, t, t, a, e,** and **i,** and have them line up the letters in a row in front of them.
- Say the word ***rattle*** and ask students to say the two syllables. Ask what they need at the end of the first syllable to make a closed syllable. Have them push forward the letters to make the closed syllable. Then ask what letters they need to spell the second syllable, and have them push forward ***t*** and ***le.***

Apply

- Have students use the letters to spell ***riddle*** and ***medal*** independently. If students have difficulty, remind them to listen to the first syllable and decide whether it is closed or open. Have them make the first syllable and then add consonant + ***le.***

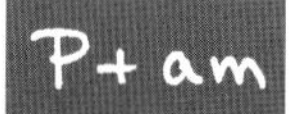

Blend Words

Model

- Write the word ***poodle*** on the board. Model sounding out the word, using what you know about syllable patterns. Then say the whole word.

Guide

- Give students blackline master 2. Guide them to sound out the first word on the word list for Day One.

Apply

- Have students independently sound out the remaining words on the list for Day One. Guide students who need more support to blend some or all of the words on the list before asking them to read the list independently.

Assessment Tip: Note which students are able to read the words without blending each sound.

Spelling Words: *puddle, saddle, bottle*

Model

- Begin a list of the week's spelling words on chart paper. As you work through Unit Seventeen, add the spelling words to the chart, and have students use the chart to check their spelling of the words.
- Say the word ***puddle*** and model spelling it and writing it on the chart.
- **Think Aloud:** *I hear two syllables in the word* **puddle.** *The first syllable sounds like a closed syllable that has a short /***u***/ and ends with /***d***/. The second syllable is the consonant* **d** *plus* **le**.

Guide

- Say the word ***saddle.*** Have students identify the two syllables and spell the word while you write it on the list. Repeat with the word ***bottle.*** Point out that these words have a double consonant.

Apply

- Have students practice writing each of the words in their word study notebooks. Have students highlight the consonant + ***le*** syllable.

Our Spelling Words

puddle
saddle
bottle
table
noble
bridle
nickel
label
global

DAY 2

Teacher Tips

Reading Strategies

If students have difficulty applying strategies for challenging words, guide them to use the following strategies:

- look at how the words start and/or end
- look for familiar patterns or parts within the words
- separate the words into syllables and decode each part
- think about what familiar words look like the difficult words
- read forward to check the context
- reread the sentence or paragraph
- mark the words, substitute synonyms, and get on with reading–ask for help later

Comprehension

Use the following questions to ensure that students have understood the passage:

- *What kind of race was it?* (Level 1–facts and details)
- *What happened after the race started?* (Level 2–sequence)
- *What do you think Ben will do next time he sees a bird?* (Level 3–make predictions)

Fluency

Intervene if students are having difficulty reading the passage. Model how to use word and meaning strategies to problem-solve the words. After students have had a chance to read the passage silently, have them read it aloud for fluency. Model fluent reading of the passage. For students who struggle, you may want to read the passage a second time and have them echo-read along with you.

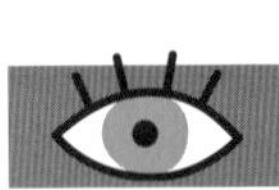

Blend

- Have students blend the words on the list for Day Two, using the procedure for blending from Day One.

Develop Automaticity in Word Recognition

- Circle the following words on the overhead transparency: ***along, winner, racer, steering, fear, finish.*** Tell students that practicing these words will help them recognize the words automatically so they can read more fluently. Explain that students can sound out some of these words, but they will read more quickly if they don't have to stop and sound out the words each time they see them.
- Read each word and point out the words with two syllables.
- Have students read aloud with you the sentences in the passage containing the words. Then have them write the words in their word study notebooks.
- Give students a copy of blackline master 7. Point out the words from this lesson, as well as other words they have learned previously. Have them cut out the words, store them in an envelope, and use them for practice activities.

Build Fluency with Connected Text

Model

- Begin reading aloud the passage on the overhead transparency, stopping after the first two sentences to model strategies.
- **Think Aloud:** *I read three words with soft* **c.** *I noticed that the letter* **c** *was followed by either* **i, e,** *or* **y** *so this told me to try the soft sound, and the words made sense.*
- Model making a mistake and correcting it–for example, read ***hug*** instead of ***huge.***
- **Think Aloud:** *No, that's not right. I thought the word said* **hug,** *but it doesn't make sense. I forgot about the VCe pattern and the silent* **e** *after the letter* **g.** *The* **g** *has a soft sound and the letter* **u** *stands for a long sound:* **huge**. *"A huge sign" sounds right.* **Huge** *means the same thing as* **big.**

Guide

- Continue reading and stop at other words in the passage. Guide students as they read the words.

Apply

- Have students take turns reading blackline master 3 to partners or in small groups as you monitor their reading. Use the teacher tips to check comprehension and fluency.

Spelling Words: *table, noble, bridle*

- Have students practice writing the spelling words from Day One in their word study notebooks. Have them refer to words on the spelling chart to check their spelling.
- Introduce the Day Two spelling words. Say the word ***table*** and model spelling it and writing it on the list of spelling words. Point out that the first syllable ends with a long vowel and is an open syllable.
- Repeat with the remaining spelling words for Day Two and have students practice writing the words in their word study notebooks. Have them underline the consonant + ***le*** syllable.

Blend

- Have students blend the words on the word list for Day Three, using the procedure for blending from Day One.

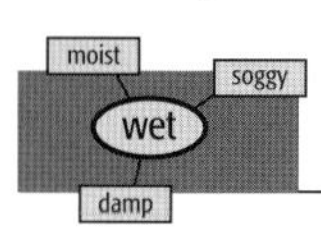

Develop Word Meanings

- Using the overhead point to the first sentence in paragraph three. Highlight the word ***hustle***. Ask students for ideas for other words you could use in place of ***hustle*** that would mean the same thing. As students suggest words, record them and then have students read the sentence, substituting a different word for ***hustle*** each time. Explain that words that mean almost the same thing are called synonyms.
- Have students think of synonyms for these other words in the passage: ***trembles, jiggle, simple, bobble.*** Have them reread the sentences, substituting the synonyms. Have them decide which words sound best in the story.

Spelling Words: *nickel, label, global*

- Have students practice spelling the words from Day One and Day Two by writing them several times in their word study notebooks.
- Introduce the spelling words for Day Three. Say the word ***nickel.***
- **Think Aloud:** *The first syllable is a closed syllable with short /**i**/. I hear /**k**/ and I think the letters* **ck** *stand for the /**k**/ sound in* **nickel.** *I wonder if the /**l**/ sound is spelled* **el, al,** *or* **le.** *I think I will try* **el** *and see if it looks right.*
- Repeat with the remaining words, pointing out the spellings for the /**l**/ sound in each word.
- Have students practice the words several times in their word study notebooks.

Build Fluency with Connected Text

- Have students read blackline master 4 to partners or in small groups as you monitor their reading. Call attention to the following words in the reading passage before students read it: ***again, away, head, keep, start, stop(ped), went.***

Teacher Tips

Three-Syllable Words

Have students apply what they know about syllable patterns to read the following three-and four-syllable words: ***honeysuckle, resemble, timetable, quadruple.***

Develop Automaticity in Word Recognition

Cut up sets of laminated high-frequency word cards (from blackline master 7) to make jigsaw puzzles. Place the pieces in envelopes. Have pairs of students put the puzzle pieces together and then read the words on the page.

Repeated Reading

Have students practice repeated readings of blackline master 3 to develop fluency.

Teacher Tips

Develop Automaticity in Word Recognition

Wad up word cards from blackline master 7 and put them in a bag. Have small groups of students take turns drawing a word from the bag, smoothing the paper, and reading the word. Once the word is read, the student wads up the word, puts it back in the bag, and the next student takes a turn. To turn the activity into a game, write numbers from one to ten on each of the cards before wadding them up. Have each student grab a fistful of words, unfold them, and read each one. Have them keep score for each word read correctly. When the words are read, they are wadded up and returned to the bag for the next student.

Repeated Reading

Have students practice repeated readings of blackline master 3 to develop fluency.

Blend

- Have students blend the words on the word list for Day Four, using the procedure for blending from Day One.

Sort Words: Syllable Patterns

- Place the following teacher word cards in the pocket chart in random order: **tennis, rabbit, admit, bedside, dislike, escape, basic, even, hello, essay, explain, raisin, middle, freckle, grumble.** Have students read each word with you.
- Tell students that each word has at least one syllable that is a closed syllable. Hold up the **raisin** card and have students identify the closed syllable. Point out that the other syllable has a vowel digraph. Ask students to sort the other words that also have closed and vowel digraph syllable patterns under the word card **raisin.**
- Repeat with the word cards **dislike** (closed and VCe), **essay** (open and closed), **freckle** (closed and consonant + ***le***), and **admit** (closed and closed).
- Once the words are sorted, have students explain how to identify each syllable pattern.

Spelling Words

- Provide practice for students in segmenting words and associating sounds with spellings. Dictate the following words to students and have them write the words on their papers: ***bubble, fable, sample, thistle.*** Remind students to use what they have learned about spelling words with more than one syllable.
- Write the words on the board and have students self-correct their papers.
- Dictate the following sentence and have students write it on their papers: *The gentle giant likes to nibble purple pickles.*
- Write the sentence on the board and have students self-correct their papers.
- Give pairs of students blackline master 6. While one student reads the spelling words, the other student writes them in the "First Try" column. After the student has spelled the words, the partner places a check mark next to words spelled correctly. For the second try, the partner may prompt the student by sounding out the words that were spelled incorrectly the first time. If the second spelling attempt is correct, the partner places a check mark in the "Second Try" column.

Assessment Tip: Use students' completed peer-check blackline masters to note which words gave students difficulty.

Build Fluency with Connected Text

- Have students take turns reading blackline master 5 to partners or in small groups as you monitor their reading. Call attention to the following words in the reading passage before students read it: ***away, begin, don't, even, few, once, put(s).***

DAY 5

Spelling Assessment

Use the following procedure to assess students' spelling of the Unit Seventeen words.

- Say each spelling word and use it in a sentence.
- Have students write the words on their papers.
- Continue with the next word on the list.
- When students have finished, collect their papers and analyze their spelling of the words.
- Use the assessment to plan small group or individual practice.

Small Group/Independent Activities

The following activities can be used to provide practice for students who need additional support.

PHONICS AND WORD STRATEGIES

Review Variant Vowel Syllable Patterns Write the word ***salty*** on the board. Point out the two vowels ***a*** and ***y*** and the two consonants between them. Divide the word between the consonants and point out the open syllable at the end. Explain that the first syllable ends with a consonant but it is not a regular closed syllable because it has a variant vowel sound instead of a short vowel sound. Contrast the short sound **/a/** with variant sound **/ô/**. Repeat with the word ***basketball,*** having students find the vowels, identify the consonants between them, and divide the word into three syllables. Point out the two closed syllables with short vowel sounds, and the syllable with a variant vowel.

Sort Words Have students use the words on blackline masters 8 and 9 and sort them into their syllable patterns–for example, open and consonant + ***le,*** r-controlled and consonant +***le,*** etc.

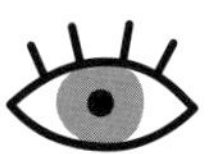

AUTOMATICITY IN WORD RECOGNITION

Read the Word Have students select several high-frequency words and write sentences using the words, leaving blanks in place of the words. Have students exchange sentences with partners and fill in the missing high-frequency words.

Write the Words Have each student work with a partner and an envelope containing the high-frequency word cards. Have them time how fast they can read the words in the envelope.

BUILD FLUENCY WITH CONNECTED TEXT

Repeated Reading Have students practice reading blackline master 3 several times, until they feel they can read it fluently and accurately. Have partners time each other as they read the passage aloud. Have them set a goal of reading 90 words per minute.

SPELLING

Make Words Provide a set of letter cards and the week's spelling words on index cards. Have students use the letter cards to spell the words. They should check their spelling by blending the sounds and then looking at the words on the index cards.

Teacher Tips

Home Connection

Have students take blackline master 11 home to complete with a family member. Students can also take the repeated reading passage on blackline master 3 home to share with their family.

Quick-Check

Assess students' mastery of consonant plus -le, -al, or -el syllable patterns using the quick-check for Unit Seventeen in this Teacher Resource System.

ELL Support Tip

To assist ELL students in remembering the difference between the hard and soft sounds, provide pictures of a face, cat, gate, and giraffe. As you introduce the words or ask ELL students to find the words in their reading, they will have the pictures to help them make connections between the sounds and the words. Students can also use the pictures for word sorts.

UNIT 17 Quick-Check: Consonant + le, al, or el syllable patterns

Student Name ______________________________ Assessment Date ____________

Segmenting and Blending

Directions: Explain that these words use sounds the student has been learning. Have the student point to each word on the corresponding student sheet, segment the word parts or syllables, and blend them together. Put a ✓ if the student successfully segments and blends the word or reads it as a complete unit. If the student misses the word, record the error.
Example: bauble

treble		straggle			
quibble		speckle			
topple		trifle			
shuffle		bubble		Score	**/8**

Sight Words

Directions: Have the student point to the first word on the corresponding student sheet and read across the line, saying each word as quickly as possible. Put a ✓ if the student successfully reads the word and an **X** if the student hesitates more than a few seconds. If the student misses the word, record the error.

along		with			
never		who			
run		around			
second		them			
tree		all			
under		only			
for		into			
they		before		Score	**/16**

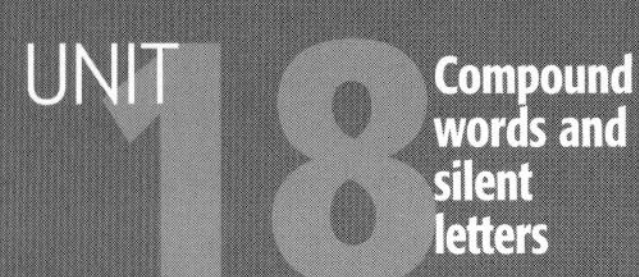

Unit Objectives

Students will:

- Recognize three different types of compound words and how they are constructed
- Review silent letters
- Read high-frequency words ask(ed), face, it's, large, next, saw, watch(ed)
- Spell compound words: softball, someone, nighttime, cherry pie, fire drill, high school, good-bye, part-time, ice-skater
- Write a recount that uses compound words

Day 1

b c d f g h h h
k l l m n p r
r s t t w a e e
e i i o o y -

Letter Cards:
a, b, c, d, e, g, h, i, l, m, n, o, p, r, s, t, w, y

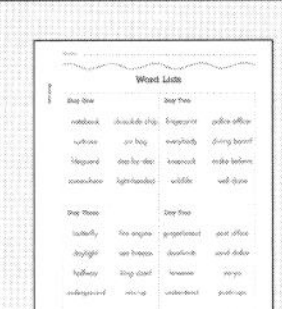

Word Lists
(BLM 2)

fire drill

Teacher Word Cards:
fire drill, fire engine, fire-eater, firefly, fireworks, hand puppet, hand-feed, handmade, handshake, hands-on, playground, playhouse, play-offs, playpen

Day 2

Word Lists
(BLM 2)

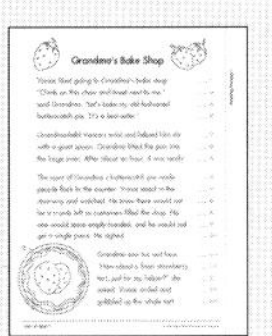

Reading Passage 1
(BLM 3)

ask	about
it's	made
face	there
large	would
next	one
saw	be
watch	with
after	to

High-Frequency Word Cards for Unit 18 (BLM 7)

Day 3

Word Lists
(BLM 2)

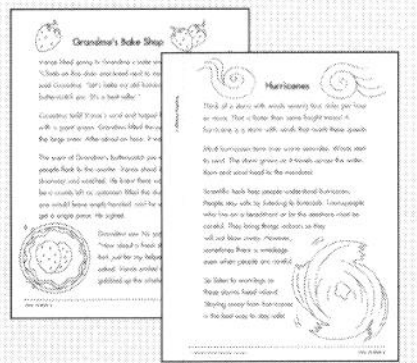

Reading Passages 1 & 2
(BLMs 3 & 4)

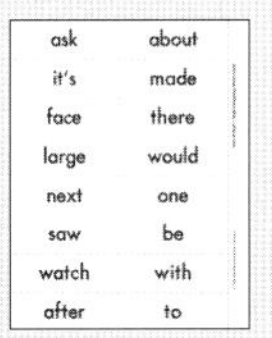

ask	about
it's	made
face	there
large	would
next	one
saw	be
watch	with
after	to

High-Frequency Word Cards for Unit 18 (BLM 7)

Day 4

Word Lists
(BLM 2)

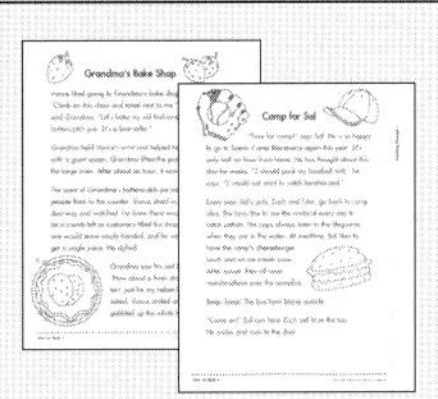

Reading Passages 1 & 3
(BLMs 3 & 5)

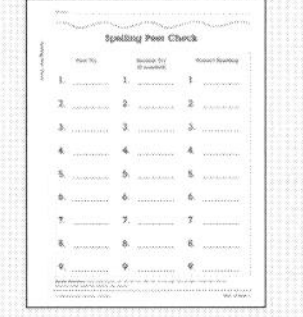

Spelling Peer Check
(BLM 6)

ask	about
it's	made
face	there
large	would
next	one
saw	be
watch	with
after	to

High-Frequency Word Cards for Unit 18 (BLM 7)

Day 5

b c d f g h h h
k l l m n p r
r s t t w a e e
e i i o o y -

Letter Cards for Unit 18

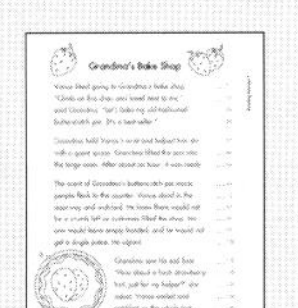

Reading Passage 1
(BLM 3)

ask	about
it's	made
face	there
large	would
next	one
saw	be
watch	with
after	to

High-Frequency Word Cards for Unit 18 (BLM 7)

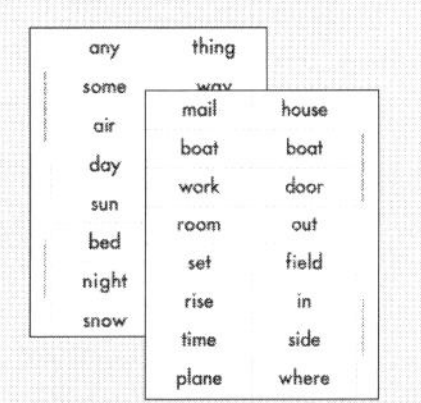

any	thing
some	way
air	
day	
sun	
bed	
night	
snow	

mail	house
boat	boat
work	door
room	out
set	field
rise	in
time	side
plane	where

Student Word Cards
(BLMs 8 & 9)

Quick-Check Student Sheet

Open	Closed	Hyphenated
air mattress	anybody	merry-go-round
grocery store	backyard	forty-five
fire drill	bluebird	grown-ups
sea horse	wristwatch	well-known
high jump	sunflower	time-out

Frieze Card

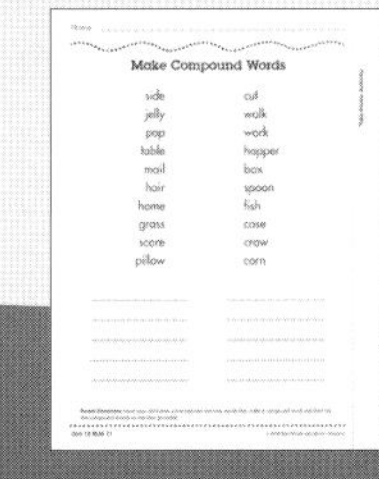

Make Compound Words

side	cut
jelly	walk
pop	work
table	hopper
mail	box
hair	spoon
home	fish
grass	case
score	crow
pillow	corn

Take-Home Activity

Core Materials

All of these materials can be downloaded from http://phonicsresources.benchmarkeducation.com.

Frieze Card

tea/cher Review Silent Letters

- Write the word ***write*** on the board and read it. Explain that certain words have silent letters. Explain that ***w*** is silent when it appears before ***r***.
- Write the following words on the board: ***wreck***, ***wrap***, ***wrist***, ***wren***, ***wrong.*** Have students read the words and circle the silent letter.
- Repeat with the letter ***b***, explaining it is silent in one-syllable words before a ***t*** and after an ***m. (debt***, ***doubt***, ***lamb***, ***dumb***, ***thumb)***
- Repeat with the letter ***k***, explaining it is silent at the beginning of some words or syllables. ***(knew***, ***knife***, ***knot)***

tea/cher Introduce Compound Words

Model

- Show students the compound words frieze card and explain that each of the words on the card is a compound word that is made up of two or more words. Tell students that the meaning of a compound word can often be figured out from the meaning of the two smaller words.
- Point out the three different kinds of compound words shown on the frieze card: open (made up of two separate words), closed (made up of two or more words that are combined), and hyphenated (made up of two or more words separated by a hyphen or hyphens).
- Ask students to find the words with the silent letters. (***wristwatch***, ***well-known***)

Guide

- Give students letter cards **b**, **c**, **d**, **g**, **h**, **l**, **m**, **m**, **n**, **p**, **r**, **s**, **t**, **w**, **a**, **e**, **e**, **e**, **i**, **o**, **o**, and **y.** Explain that they are going to spell compound words from the "some" family.
- Say the word ***someday*** and ask students what two words make up the compound word. Have students find the letters to spell the word ***some***, reminding them that there is a silent final ***e*** in the word. Then have students find the letters to spell ***day*** and add these letters to the word ***some.***

Apply

- Have students brainstorm other compound words from the "some" family. (***somebody***, ***somehow***, ***somewhere***, ***someone***, ***someplace***, ***sometime***, ***something***) Have them use the letter cards to spell the words. As students spell each word, add the words to a word web with the word ***some*** in the inside circle.

Assessment Tip: Note which students correctly make the compound words. Guide students who are having difficulty making the words.

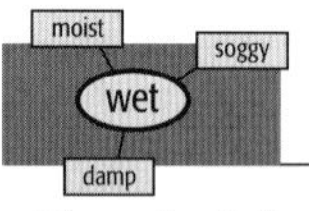

Word Study

- Place the following teacher word cards in a pocket chart in random order: **hands-on**, **hand-feed**, **handshake**, **handmade**, **hand puppet**, **fireworks**, **firefly**, **fire drill**, **fire-eater**, **fire engine**, **play-offs**, **playground**, **playpen**, **playhouse.**
- Ask students to help you sort the words according to the type of compound word. After the words are sorted, ask students to think of another way they could sort the compound words. Have them sort the words according to the compound families: "fire," "hand," and "play."
- Ask students to brainstorm other words for each compound family. Write words they suggest on index cards and add them to the pocket chart.

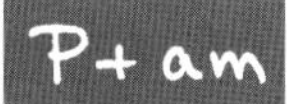

Blend

- Write the word ***doorknob*** on the board. Point out the two compound words and the silent ***k*** at the beginning of the second word. Model blending the sounds to read the word. Then have students blend it with you.
- Give students the word list on blackline master 2 and have them point to and read the first word for Day One.
- Have students independently read the remaining words for Day One. If students need more support, guide them as they read some or all of the words on the list before having them read independently.

Spelling Words: *softball, someone, nighttime*

Model

- Make a three-column spelling chart on chart paper with the following headings: "Closed," "Open," and, "Hyphenated." Tell students that they will be spelling compound words. As you work through the unit, continue to add the spelling words to the chart, and have students use the chart to check their spelling.
- Say the word ***softball*** and model spelling it and writing it on chart paper.
- **Think Aloud: *Softball*** *is a compound word made up of* **soft** *and* **ball.** *I hear a short* **/o/** *sound and a blend:* **/ft/.** *I remember how to spell* **ball**, *so I can write the whole word:* **softball.**

Guide

- Say the word ***someone.*** Have students tell you the two smaller words that make up the compound word. Write them on the chart as students tell you the letters.
- Repeat with the word ***nighttime.*** Point out that there are two ***t***'s in the middle because ***night*** ends with a ***t*** and ***time*** begins with a ***t***.

Apply

- Have students practice writing each of the words in their word study notebooks. Have them write a sentence for each of the words.

Teacher Tips

Tell students that one way they can figure out the meaning of a compound word is to start with the meaning of the second part of the word first and then add the meaning of the first part of the word—for example, a ***bookstore*** is a ***store*** that sells ***books***.

Our Compound Spelling Words

Closed	Open	Hyphenated
softball someone nighttime	cherry pie fire drill high school	good-bye part-time ice-skater

DAY 2

Teacher Tips

Reading Strategies

If students have difficulty applying strategies for challenging words, guide them to use the following strategies:

- look at how the words start and/or end
- look for familiar patterns or parts within the words
- separate the words into syllables and decode each part
- think about what familiar words look like the difficult words
- read forward to check the context
- reread the sentence or paragraph
- mark the words, substitute synonyms, and get on with reading–ask for help later

Comprehension

Use the following questions to ensure that students have understood the passage:

- *What were Vance and his grandma making?*
  (Level 1–facts and details)
- *What made Vance sigh?*
  (Level 2–cause/effect)
- *How would you describe Vance's relationship with his grandma?*
  (Level 3–draw conclusions)

Fluency

Intervene if students are having difficulty reading the passage. Model how to use word and meaning strategies to problem-solve the words. After students have had a chance to read the passage silently, have them read it aloud for fluency. Model fluent reading of the passage. For students who struggle, you may want to read the passage a second time and have them echo-read along with you.

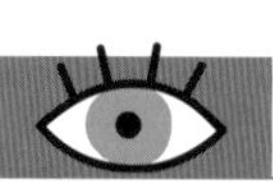

Blend

- Have students blend the words on the word list for Day Two, using the procedure for blending from Day One.

Develop Automaticity in Word Recognition

- Circle the following words on the overhead transparency: ***ask(ed)***, ***face***, ***it's***, ***large***, ***next***, ***saw***, ***watch(ed).***
- Tell students that practicing these words will help them recognize the words automatically so they can read more fluently. Explain that students can sound out some of these words, but they will read more quickly if they don't have to stop and sound out the words each time they see them.
- Read each word. Point out that the ***-ed*** ending on ***asked*** and ***watched*** stands for the **/t/** sound.
- Have students read aloud with you the sentences in the passage that contain the words. Then have them write the words in their word study notebooks.
- Give students a copy of blackline master 7. Point out the words from this lesson as well as other words they have learned previously. Have them cut out the words, store them in an envelope, and use them for practice activities.

Build Fluency with Connected Text

Model

- Begin reading aloud the passage on the overhead transparency, stopping after the first paragraph to point out the compound words.
- **Think Aloud: Bake shop** *is an example of an open compound word. The word* **bake** *tells me what kind of shop Grandma had. I also see an example of a closed compound word. This word looks long but when I separate the compound words, it is easy to read:* **butterscotch**. *I only needed to work out part of* **old-fashioned** *before I recognized it. I read the word* **old**, *and then all I needed to read was the* **/f/ /ash/** *and I knew it said* **old-fashioned.**
- Model making a mistake and correcting it–for example, read **/skent/** instead of ***scent.***
- **Think Aloud:** *That's not right. I'll just read ahead here and see if that helps. Oh, of course. The word is* **scent.** *It's one of those words with a silent letter in it that I need to memorize.*

Guide

- Continue reading and stop at other words in the passage. Guide students as they read the words.

Apply

- Have students take turns reading blackline master 3 to partners or in small groups as you monitor their reading. Use the teacher tips to check comprehension and fluency.

Spelling Words: *cherry pie, fire drill, high school*

- Have students practice writing the spelling words from Day One in their word study notebooks. Have them refer to words on the spelling chart to check their spelling.
- Introduce the Day Two spelling words. Follow the format for Day One as you model spelling the open compound words.
- Have students practice writing each of the words in their word study notebooks. Have them write a sentence for each of the words.

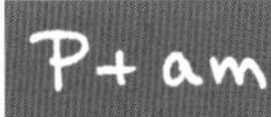

Blend

- Have students blend the words on the word list for Day Three, using the procedure for blending from Day One.

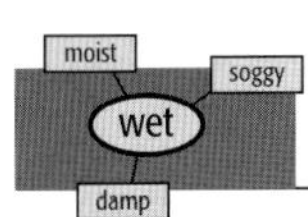

Develop Word Meanings

- Make a chart on the board similar to the one shown below, leaving some blanks for students to fill in. Write the words ***over***, ***back***, ***ball***, ***book***, ***in***, and ***rain*** on the chart.
- Read the words with students. Have them brainstorm compound words that contain the words, either at the beginning or the end of the new compound word. Guide students to complete the first column with compound words from the "ball" family.
- Have students work with a partner to brainstorm words for the other compound word families.
- When they have finished, have them share their words and record them on the chart.
- If someone suggests a word that other students question as being a compound word, have a volunteer look it up in the dictionary.

over	*back*	*ball*	*book*	*in*	*rain*
overcoat	backyard	ballroom	cookbook	inside	raindrop

Spelling Words: *good-bye, part-time, ice-skater*

- Introduce the Day Three spelling words. Follow the format for Day One as you model spelling the hyphenated compound words.
- Point out that ***ice-skater*** is a tricky one to remember because the noun ***ice skate*** is an open compound.
- Have students practice writing each of the words in their word study notebooks. Have them write a sentence for each of the words.

Build Fluency with Connected Text

- Have students read blackline master 4 to partners or in small groups as you monitor their reading. Call attention to the following words in the reading passage before students read it: ***away***, ***even***, ***grow(s)***, ***head***, ***mile(s)***, ***must***, ***start.***

Teacher Tips

More about Compound Words

Explain to students that sometimes it is necessary to add a hyphen between two words that are describing one thing. Write the sentence *The students are taking three week vacations.* Ask students what this sentence means. Then add a hyphen between *three* and *week*. Ask students again what this means. Point out that the hyphen helps clarify that the students are taking one vacation that is three weeks long, not three one-week vacations.

Develop Automaticity in Word Recognition

Have students work in small groups and place the high-frequency word cards from blackline master 7 facedown in the center of a circle. Have students take turns providing clues about a word. The other students race to guess which of the words is in the center circle.

Repeated Reading

Have students practice repeated readings of blackline master 3 to develop fluency.

DAY 4

Teacher Tips

Riddle Me This

Tell the following riddles to students and challenge them to come up with some of their own that they can share with partners:

What horses are the best swimmers? (sea horses)
What kind of dog gets the most ticks? (a watchdog)
What kind of dog likes living where it's sunny and warm? (a hot dog)

Develop Automaticity in Word Recognition

Have students or groups of students sit in a circle and place the high-frequency word cards in a stack. Have a student draw a word, read it, and use it in an oral sentence. Have the student pass the word to the next student in the circle who uses the word in a different oral sentence. Continue around the circle until every student has made up a sentence. Repeat with the remaining words.

Repeated Reading

Have students practice repeated readings of blackline master 3 to develop fluency.

Blend

- Have students blend the words on the word list for Day Four, using the procedure for blending from Day One.

Write

- Tell students that as a group you will write a recount about an imaginary field trip to a snowy mountain. Have students brainstorm words associated with snow and cold weather. Record their ideas on the board. Challenge students to think of as many compound words as they can.
- Model writing a first sentence. Point out that recounts use past tense because the events have already happened.
- Have students tell you what to write. Guide them as needed and record their sentences. Encourage them to use time-order words such as ***first*** and ***next***, and explain that these words help the reader understand the sequence or order of the events in the recount.
- Read the text through aloud, and have students check to see if they need to fix any problems with it.
- Tell students that they can use this text as a model to write their own recount about something they did with their family or friends.

Snow Day

Last winter our class went on a field trip to the mountains. Snowflakes were falling on the windshield of the school bus. A snowplow cleared the road in front of us. First, we had a contest to see who could make the biggest snowman. The best snowman had a corncob pipe and snowshoes. The next thing we did was throw snowballs at each other. Our teacher didn't like that. The last thing we did was drink hot chocolate before getting back on the bus to go home.

Spelling Words

- Provide practice for students in segmenting words and associating sounds with spellings. Dictate the following words to students and have them write the words on their papers: ***nighttime***, ***daytime***, ***thumbnail***, ***bedroom.*** Remind them to think about the spelling of each word that makes up the compound word.
- Write the words on the board and have students self-correct their papers.
- Dictate the following sentence and have students write it on their papers: *Nancy threw a snowball during the high school football game.*
- Write the sentence on the board and have students self-correct their papers.
- Give pairs of students blackline master 6. While one student reads the spelling words, the other student writes them in the "First Try" column. After the student has spelled the words, the partner places a check mark next to words spelled correctly. For the second try, the partner may prompt the student by sounding out the words that were spelled incorrectly the first time. If the second spelling attempt is correct, the partner places a check mark in the "Second Try" column.

Assessment Tip: Use students' completed peer-check blackline masters to note which words gave them difficulty.

Build Fluency with Connected Text

- Have students take turns reading blackline master 5 to partners or in small groups as you monitor their reading. Call attention to the following words in the reading passage before students read it: ***again***, ***always***, ***every***, ***hear***, ***home***, ***should***, ***thought.***

Spelling Assessment

Use the following procedure to assess students' spelling of the Unit Eighteen words.

- Say each spelling word and use it in a sentence.
- Have students write the words on their papers.
- Continue with the next word on the list.
- When students have finished, collect their papers and analyze their spelling of the words.
- Use the assessment to plan small group or individual practice.

Small Group/Independent Activities

The following activities can be used to provide practice for students who need additional support.

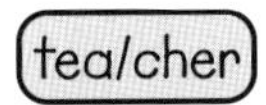

WORD STRATEGIES

Context Puzzles Write the following cloze sentences on the board: *The [butterfly] floats from flower to flower, sipping nectar; Ouch! I was out in the sun too long and got a [sunburn]; When I go camping, I like to sleep on an [air mattress]; There are [step-by-step] instructions to tell me how to put this thing together.* Challenge students to work with a partner to think of compound words that will make sense in the sentences.

Word Hunt Have students hunt through old magazines and newspapers to find compound words. Have them cut out the words and paste them on chart paper. Challenge them to find not just closed but also open and hyphenated compound words.

Make Words Have students use the words on blackline masters 8 and 9 to make as many compound words as they can. Have them make a list of the words in their word study notebooks. Challenge them to find at least one pair for every student word card.

Compound Word Spin Have students sit in a circle with the student word cards (from blackline masters 8 and 9) facedown in a stack in the middle. One student spins a plastic bottle. Whomever the bottle points to selects a word card, reads the word, and identifies the two words that make up the compound word.

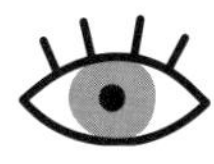

AUTOMATICITY IN WORD RECOGNITION

Read the Word Have students use all of the high-frequency word cards from blackline master 7 and a standard game board. Have them roll dice to find out how many spaces they can move. Then have them draw a card. If they read the word correctly, they can stay on the space on the game board. If not, they must return to where they were before they rolled the dice.

Word Flash Have pairs of students use the set of cards from blackline master 7 to flash words for each other to read.

BUILD FLUENCY WITH CONNECTED TEXT

Repeated Reading Have students practice reading blackline master 3 several times, until they feel they can read it fluently and accurately. Have them work with a partner to time each other as they read the passage aloud. Have them set a goal of reading 90 words per minute.

SPELLING

Make Words Provide a set of letter cards and the week's spelling words on index cards. Have students use the letter cards to spell the words. They should check their spelling by blending the sounds and then looking at the words on the index cards.

Teacher Tips

Home Connection

Have students take blackline master 11 home to complete with a family member. Students can also take the repeated reading passage on blackline master 3 home to share with their family.

Quick-Check

Assess students' mastery of compound words and silent letters using the quick-check for Unit Eighteen in this Teacher Resource System.

ELL Support Tip

During the word meaning activity with compound words described on Day Three, give ELL students words on word cards, which they can use to create compound words to fill in the chart. As the groups brainstorm new compound words, ELL students can use the word cards to form the compound words. For example, if students are creating compound words with *ball*, ELL students will have words such as *room* and *game* on cards to help them form compound words.

UNIT 18 Quick-Check: Compound words and silent letters

Student Name ______________________ Assessment Date __________

Segmenting and Blending

Directions: Explain that these words use sounds the student has been learning. Have the student point to each word on the corresponding student sheet, segment the word parts or syllables, and blend them together. Put a ✓ if the student successfully segments and blends the word or reads it as a complete unit. If the student misses the word, record the error.
Example: rattlesnake

homework		keyboard		
timetable		wastebasket		
doorbell		seaweed		
airline		peppermint		Score **/8**

Sight Words

Directions: Have the student point to the first word on the corresponding student sheet and read across the line, saying each word as quickly as possible. Put a ✓ if the student successfully reads the word and an **X** if the student hesitates more than a few seconds. If the student misses the word, record the error.

ask		about		
it's		made		
face		there		
large		would		
next		one		
saw		be		
watch		with		
after		to		Score **/16**

UNIT 19 Contractions

Unit Objectives

Students will:

- Recognize contractions and the words they stand for
- Review closed-syllable patterns
- Sort contractions into families
- Choose contractions that are in agreement with the subject of a phrase
- Read high-frequency words again, letter, need, never, thought, until, while
- Spell contractions: she's, it's, you're, weren't, won't, didn't, you've, they've, we've
- Write an informal letter that uses contractions

Day 1

Letter Cards: **a, d, e, h, i, n, o, r, s, t, y**

Word Lists (BLM 2)

are

Teacher Word Cards: **are, can't, doesn't, had/would, hasn't, have, he'd, he'll, I'd, is/has, not, that'll, there'd, they're, we're, we've, will, would've, you'll, you're, you've**

Day 2

Word Lists (BLM 2)

Reading Passage 1 (BLM 3)

High-Frequency Word Cards for Unit 19 (BLM 7)

Day 3

Word Lists (BLM 2)

Reading Passages 1 & 2 (BLMs 3 & 4)

High-Frequency Word Cards for Unit 19 (BLM 7)

Day 4

Word Lists (BLM 2)

Reading Passages 1 & 3 (BLMs 3 & 5)

Spelling Peer Check (BLM 6)

High-Frequency Word Cards for Unit 19 (BLM 7)

Day 5

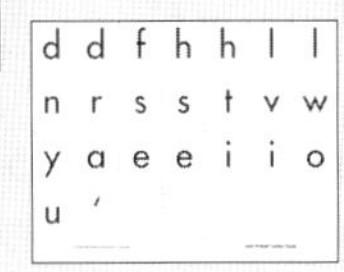

Letter Cards for Unit 19

Reading Passage 1 (BLM 3)

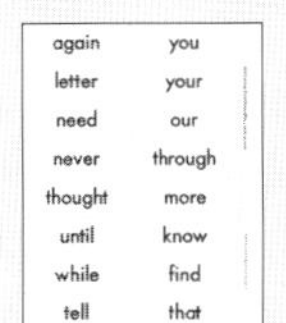

High-Frequency Word Cards for Unit 19 (BLM 7)

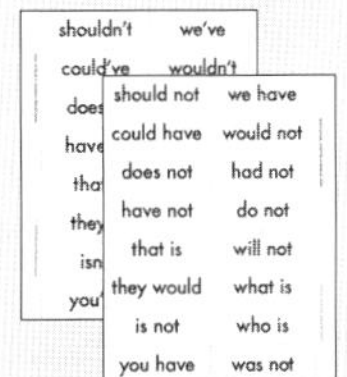

Student Word Cards (BLMs 8 & 9)

Quick-Check Student Sheet

Frieze Card

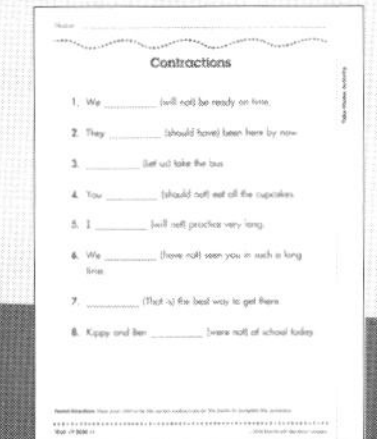

Take-Home Activity

Core Materials

All of these materials can be downloaded from http://phonicsresources.benchmarkeducation.com.

DAY 1

Frieze Card

tea/cher

Review Closed-Syllable Patterns

- Write the words ***frantic***, ***hiccup***, and ***napkin*** on the board. Ask students what they notice about the three words. If necessary, ask them what kind of syllable patterns they see in the words.
- Underline the ***a*** and the ***i*** in ***frantic*** and ask students where you should divide the word. Repeat with the words ***hiccup*** and ***napkin***.
- Write the following words on the board: ***cactus***, ***cannot***, ***insist***, ***kitten***. Have students copy the words in their word study notebooks and divide them into syllables. Then have students explain how they divided the words.

tea/cher

Introduce Contractions

Model

- Explain that a contraction is a short form of two words. One or more letters are replaced by an apostrophe.
- Write the following sentence on the board, underlining the words ***are not*** *Tom and Jane are not going to the party.*
- Tell students that the words ***are not*** can be shortened into one word by replacing the ***o*** with an apostrophe. Write the word ***aren't*** under ***are not***. Read the sentence using the contraction.

Guide

- Show students the contractions frieze card. Discuss the examples of contractions on the card and ask students which letter or letters in each pair of words has been replaced by an apostrophe.
- Guide students as they read each contraction.

Apply

- Give students letter cards **d, d, h, n, o, r, s, t, y, a, e, e, i,** and **o,** plus the apostrophe card. Write the following words on the board: ***has not***, ***did not***, ***he is***, ***they are***, ***here is***. Have students use the letter and apostrophe cards to make contractions for the words, one contraction at a time. As they complete a contraction, write it on the board so students can check their spelling.

Assessment Tip: Note which students make the contractions correctly. Guide students who are having difficulty.

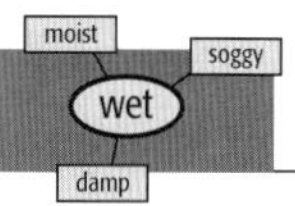

Word Study

- Place the following six teacher word cards in a pocket chart: **is/has, had/would, have, not, will, are.** Explain that you can organize contractions according to their families. Hold up the card **he'd** and ask students what the contraction is short for. Since the contraction for ***he would*** is not as commonly used, you may want to provide oral sentences modeling the contractions for ***he had*** and ***he would***. *He'd better get here soon; He'd have liked to meet you.* Have students tell you under which grouping you should place the card.
- Repeat with the following teacher word cards: **can't, hasn't, doesn't, we've, you've, would've, he'll, that'll, you'll, there'd, I'd, they're, we're, you're.**
- Have students brainstorm other words they could add to each group– for example: ***aren't***, ***don't***, ***I've***, ***they've***, ***it'll I'll who'd***, ***you'd***, etc.

P+am Blend

- Write the word ***can't*** on the board and model blending the sounds to read the word. Then have students blend it with you.
- Give students the word lists on blackline master 2. Have them point to the first word for Day One and read the word.
- Have students independently read the remaining words for Day One. If students need more support, guide them as they read some or all of the words on the list before having them read independently.

Spelling Words: *she's, it's, you're*

Model

- Make a two-column spelling chart on chart paper. Label the first column "Contraction" and the second column "Words Contraction Stands For." Tell students that they will be spelling contractions. As you work through the unit, you can continue to add the spelling words to the chart. Have students use the chart to check their spelling of the words.
- Say the word ***she's*** and model spelling it and writing it on chart paper.
- **Think Aloud: She's** *is a contraction for* **she is.** *I'll write* **she is** *in the second column. I need to replace the letter* **i** *with an apostrophe. I will write the contraction in the first column of the chart.*

Guide

- Say the word ***it's*** Have students tell you the words that the contraction stands for, and write in the second column. Ask what letter is replaced to make Write the contraction in the first column as students tell you the letters.
- Repeat with the word ***you're***.

Apply

- Have students practice writing each of the words in their word study notebooks. Have them write a sentence for each of the words.

Our Spelling Words

Contraction	Words Contraction Stands For
she's	she is
it's	it is
you're	you are
weren't	were not
won't	will not
didn't	did not
you've	you have
they've	they have
we've	we have

DAY 2

Teacher Tips

Reading Strategies

If students have difficulty applying strategies for challenging words, guide them to use the following strategies:

- look at how the words start and/or end
- look for familiar patterns or parts within the words
- separate the words into syllables and decode each part
- think about what familiar words look like the difficult words
- read forward to check the context
- reread the sentence or paragraph
- mark the words, substitute synonyms, and get on with reading–ask for help later

Comprehension

Use the following questions to ensure that students have understood the passage:

- *What was Jake working on?* (Level 1–facts and details)
- *Why couldn't Jake stand the thought of hitting the ball in the woods?* (Level 2–cause/effect)
- *How would you describe Jake and Sam?* (Level 3–analyze character)

Fluency

Intervene if students are having difficulty reading the passage. Model how to use word and meaning strategies to problem-solve the words. After students have had a chance to read the passage silently, have them read it aloud for fluency. Model fluent reading of the passage. For students who struggle, you may want to read the passage a second time and have them echo-read along with you.

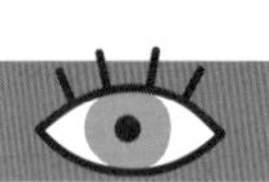

Blend

- Have students blend the words on the word list for Day Two, using the procedure for blending from Day One.

Develop Automaticity in Word Recognition

- Circle the following words on the overhead transparency: ***again***, ***letter***, ***need***, ***never***, ***thought***, ***until***, ***while***.
- Tell students that practicing these words will help them recognize the words automatically so they can read more fluently. Explain that students can sound out some of these words, but they will read more quickly if they don't have to stop and sound out the words each time they see them.
- Read each word. Point out that ***again***, and ***letter*** have two syllables, and highlight the double ***t***'s in ***letter***. Have students read aloud with you the sentences in the passage that contain the words. Then have them write the words in their word study notebooks.
- Give students a copy of blackline master 7. Point out the words from this lesson, as well as other words they have learned previously. Have them cut out the words, store them in an envelope, and use them for practice activities.

Build Fluency with Connected Text

Model

- Read aloud the first sentence from the passage on the overhead. Point out the contraction ***we're***.
- **Think Aloud:** *I know this contraction stands for* **we are.** *It makes sense whether I read the sentence with* **we're** *or with* **we are.**
- Stop at the word ***won't*** and model how the spelling changes in this word.
- **Think Aloud:** *I know the* **n't** *stands for* **not** *but I wonder where the* **wo** *comes from. I think the spelling of this word has been changed when the contraction was formed. Looking at the meaning of the sentence, I think the contraction stands for* **will not** *and the* **i** *has been changed to* **o.** *I must remember that the spelling changes in some contractions.*
- Model making a mistake and correcting it–for example, read ***k-now*** instead of ***know***.
- **Think Aloud:** *That's not right. I'll just read ahead here and see if that helps. Oh, of course. The word is* **know.** *I should have recognized this word when I saw it because it's a high-frequency word that we've practiced before.*

Guide

- Continue reading and stop at other words in the passage. Guide students as they read the words.

Apply

- Have students take turns reading blackline master 3 to partners or in small groups as you monitor their reading. Use the teacher tips to check comprehension and fluency.

Spelling Words: *weren't, won't, didn't*

- Have students practice writing the spelling words from Day One in their word study notebooks. Have them refer to words on the spelling chart to check their spelling.
- Introduce the Day Two spelling words. Follow the format for Day One as you model writing the words the contractions stand for and then writing the contractions.
- Have students practice writing each of the words in their word study notebooks. Have them write a sentence for each of the words.

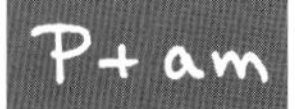

Blend

- Have students blend the words on the word list for Day Three, using the procedure for blending from Day One.

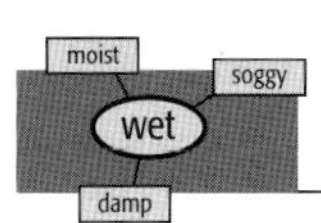

Develop Word Meanings

- Make a chart on the board similar to the one shown below, leaving some blanks for students to fill in. Write the pronouns ***I***, ***you***, ***he***, ***she***, ***it***, ***we***, and ***they*** on the board.
- Read the phrases with students and have them help you fill in the missing words with the pronouns.
- Once the chart is complete, have students draw conclusions about the use of ***is***, ***are***, ***have*** and ***has.*** (When referring to one person or thing, ***is*** and ***has*** are used. When referring to more than one person or thing, ***are*** and ***have*** are used, except in the case of ***I have.***)
- Say the following phrases and have students tell whether the phrase should be written in the is/has columns or the are/have columns: the dog ________; Robert and Sue ______; My two cats ________; Lin, Maria, and Josie _______.
- Have students complete the phrases by saying oral sentences—for example, *The dog is angry; The dog has a red collar.*

is	are	has	have
He is	We are	She has	I have
__________ is	__________ are	__________ has	__________ have
__________ is	__________ are	__________ has	__________ have
			__________ have

Spelling Words: *you've, they've, we've*

- Introduce the Day Three spelling words. Follow the format for Day One as you model writing the words the contractions stand for and then writing the contractions. Point out that all of the words are short for a pronoun plus the word ***have***.
- Have students practice writing each of the words in their word study notebooks. Have them write a sentence for each of the words.

Build Fluency with Connected Text

- Have students read blackline master 4 to partners or in small groups as you monitor their reading. Call attention to the following words in the reading passage before students read it: ***away***, ***grow***, ***important***, ***paper***, ***something***, ***why***, ***world***.

Teacher Tips

More about Contractions

Students need to recognize that sometimes more than one letter is replaced with an apostrophe. Write the words ***he would*** and ***he'd*** on the board and have students tell what letters have been replaced. Repeat with the words ***you would***, ***we would*** and ***should have***. Also point out that the vowel sound can change. Write the words on the board and have students read them with you. Then write the word and read it to illustrate the change in the vowel sound.

Develop Automaticity in Word Recognition

Place the high-frequency word cards on chairs set up facing outward in a circle. Have one less chair than students. Play music and have students march around the chairs. When you stop the music, students pick up the word and sit on a chair. One student will be without a chair and is out of the game. If a student reads a word incorrectly, that student is out as well. Take away a chair and word card for each round, until one student remains.

Repeated Reading

Have students practice repeated readings of blackline master 3 to develop fluency.

DAY 4

Teacher Tips

Contractions and Possessives

Point out that, besides being used for contractions, the apostrophe is used to show possession. Write the following on the board: *This is Fido's dinner*. Point out that the apostrophe in this example shows that the dinner belongs to Fido. Then write this sentence on the board: *My dog ate its dinner.* Explain that this is an exception, and we do not use an apostrophe with the word ***its*** when we want to show possession. Tell students that the way they can tell if the word ***its*** needs an apostrophe or not is to substitute the words ***it*** and ***is*** and see if the sentence makes sense. Read the sentence again, substituting the words ***it is***: *My dog ate it is dinner.*

Develop Automaticity in Word Recognition

Have students work with a partner to find as many of the high-frequency words as they can in a book they are reading in the classroom. Have them write the words they find on self-stick notes and place the notes at the tops of pages where they find the words. After a set time–ten minutes, perhaps–have students count the number of words they found and see which words were most common in the books they read.

Repeated Reading

Have students practice repeated readings of blackline master 3 to develop fluency.

Blend

- Have students blend the words on the word list for Day Four, using the procedure for blending from Day One.

Write

- Tell students that as a group you will write a letter from two children to their aunt. Ask for ideas on what the letter could be about and record the ideas on the board. Then ask students to choose one of the ideas–for example, an invitation to a surprise party.
- Model writing the date and the greeting for the letter on chart paper. Then model writing the first sentence.
- Point out that in an informal letter to someone you know well, you often use lots of contractions. In a more formal letter, you would use fewer contractions, which changes the tone of the letter.
- Have students discuss what you might say next, and then tell you what to write. Guide them as needed and encourage them to use contractions in their suggested sentences. Record their sentences.
- Read the letter aloud, and have students check to see if they need to fix any problems with it. Have them identify the contractions.
- Reread the letter to students, substituting full words for the contractions. Ask them how this changes the tone of the letter.
- Tell students that they can use this letter as a model to write their own letter. (See Day Five activities.)

August 24

Dear Aunt Alice,

We're having a party for Mom on Friday. We'd really like it if you'd be able to come. It's at 6:00 at our house. Mom doesn't know anything about the party, so make sure you don't tell her about it. We want her to be surprised. We're having her favorite food, but you don't have to bring anything. It's all taken care of. Let us know if you'll be able to come.

Love,

Rita and Sammy

Spelling Words

- Provide practice for students in segmenting words and associating sounds with spellings. Dictate the following words to students and have them write the words on their papers:
- Write the words on the board and have students self-correct their papers.
- Dictate the following sentence and have students write it on their papers: ***aren't***, ***isn't***, ***it's***, and ***that's***. *We'd better eat some ice cream before it's gone.*
- Write the sentence on the board and have students self-correct their papers.
- Give pairs of students blackline master 6. While one student reads the spelling words, the other student writes them in the "First Try" column. After the student has spelled the words, the partner places a check mark next to words spelled correctly. For the second try, the partner may prompt the student by sounding out the words that were spelled incorrectly the first time. If the second spelling attempt is correct, the partner places a check mark in the "Second Try" column.

Assessment Tip: Use students' completed peer-check blackline masters to note which words gave students difficulty.

Build Fluency with Connected Text

- Have students take turns reading blackline master 5 to partners or in small groups as you monitor their reading. Call attention to the following words in the reading passage before students read it: ***eat(ing)***, ***last***, ***next***, ***paper***, ***school***.

Spelling Assessment

Use the following procedure to assess students' spelling of the Unit Nineteen words.
- Say each spelling word and use it in a sentence.
- Have students write the word on their papers.
- Continue with the next word on the list.
- When students have finished, collect their papers and analyze their spelling of the words.
- Use the assessment to plan small group or individual practice.

Small Group/Independent Activities

The following activities can be used to provide practice for students who need additional support.

WORD STRATEGIES

Write Have each student write a draft of a letter that uses contractions in their word study notebook. Point out that they can use the letter they wrote as a group as a model. Have students exchange their letters with partners. Have them take turns telling their partners what they like about the writing and what problems they see. Have students revise their drafts in their word study notebooks. Then have them underline all the contractions they used.

Word Play Have students work with a partner and use the student word cards from blackline masters 8 and 9 to play Concentration. Have them spread the cards facedown on a table or the floor and take turns turning over two cards, reading them, and deciding whether they make a pair. If a student's cards are not a pair, the cards are turned facedown again for the other student's turn.

AUTOMATICITY IN WORD RECOGNITION

Read the Word Have students select several high-frequency words and write sentences using the words, leaving blanks in place of the words. Have students exchange sentences with partners and fill in the missing high-frequency words.

Make Sentences Place half the high-frequency word cards in one paper bag, and the other half in another paper bag. Have students select and read a word from each bag, and then use both words in a written sentence.

BUILD FLUENCY WITH CONNECTED TEXT

Repeated Reading Have students practice reading blackline master 3 several times, until they feel they can read it fluently and accurately. Have them work with a partner to time each other as they read the passage aloud. Have them set a goal of reading 90 words per minute.

SPELLING

Make Words Provide a set of letter cards and the week's spelling words on index cards. Have students use the letter cards to spell the words. They should check their spelling by blending the sounds and then looking at the words on the index cards.

Look, Cover, Say, Write Have students who are having difficulty with the spelling words look carefully at one of the words and then say it. Ask them to cover the word and write it without looking. Have them uncover the word and check the spelling. Have them repeat the process with other words on the spelling list.

Teacher Tips

Home Connection

Have students take blackline master 11 home to complete with a family member. Students can also take the repeated reading passage on blackline master 3 home to share with their family.

Quick-Check

Assess students' mastery of contractions using the quick-check for Unit Nineteen in this Teacher Resource System.

ELL Support Tip

Contractions can be very difficult for ELL students to understand since many other languages either do not have contractions or do not have as many as English. A fun way to support the learning process of contractions is to play Bingo with students. Give each student a blank Bingo board to fill with the contractions from the spelling chart. Call out pairs of words that make up the contractions. A student who has a contraction for the pair of words called out places a marker on the word on the board. A student who calls Bingo will need to repeat the pair of words as well as the contraction.

UNIT 19 Quick-Check: Contractions

Student Name ______________________________ Assessment Date ____________

Segmenting and Blending

Directions: Explain that these words use sounds the student has been learning. Have the student point to each word on the corresponding student sheet, segment the word parts or syllables, and blend them together. Put a ✓ if the student successfully segments and blends the word or reads it as a complete unit. If the student misses the word, record the error.
Example: there've

he's		that's		
could've		shouldn't		
she'll		who've		
wasn't		they'll		Score **/8**

Sight Words

Directions: Have the student point to the first word on the corresponding student sheet and read across the line, saying each word as quickly as possible. Put a ✓ if the student successfully reads the word and an **X** if the student hesitates more than a few seconds. If the student misses the word, record the error.

again		you		
letter		your		
need		our		
never		through		
thought		more		
until		know		
while		find		
tell		that		Score **/16**

UNIT 20 Regular plurals

Unit Objectives

Students will:

- Recognize plural words in print and understand they mean more than one
- Understand how to form plurals by adding -s, -es, or -ies
- Review VCe syllable pattern
- Sort words according to their plural endings
- Categorize and label words according to their meanings
- Read high-frequency words children, girl(s), need, should, soon, those
- Spell plural words: spices, acorns, apples, dishes, classes, indexes, watches, ponies, cities
- Write an informational text that uses plurals correctly

Day 1

Letter Cards: **a, b, e, f, h, i, l, n, o, r, s, t, u, x**

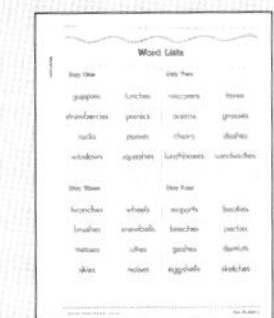

Word Lists (BLM 2)

armies

Teacher Word Cards: **armies, buddies, bushes, crutches, eagles, glasses, horses, latches, losses, masses, passes, riches, sashes, skies, trains**

Day 2

Word Lists (BLM 2)

Reading Passage 1 (BLM 3)

High-Frequency Word Cards (BLM 7)

Day 3

Word Lists (BLM 2)

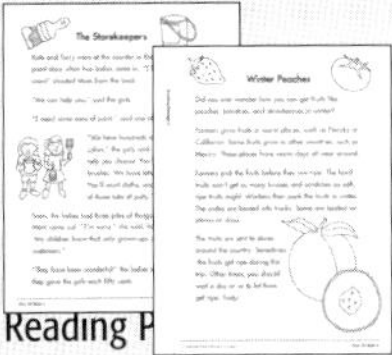

Reading Passages 1 & 2 (BLMs 3 & 4)

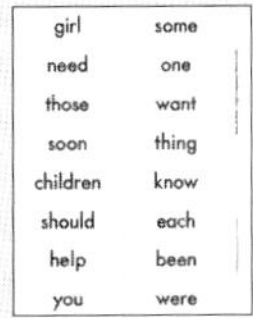

High-Frequency Word Cards (BLM 7)

Day 4

Word Lists (BLM 2)

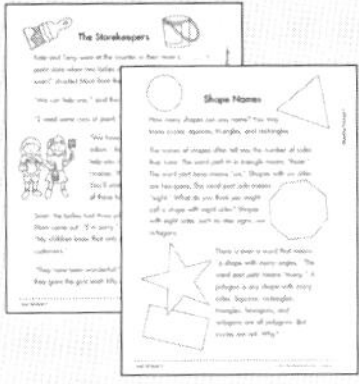

Reading Passages 1 & 3 (BLMs 3 & 5)

High-Frequency Word Cards (BLM 7)

Spelling Peer Check (BLM 6)

Day 5

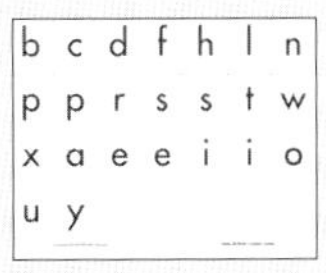

Letter Cards for Unit 20

Reading Passage 1 (BLM 3)

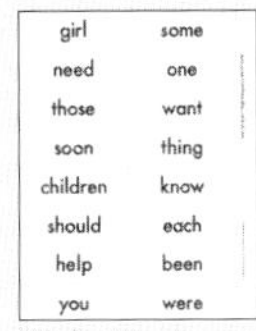

High-Frequency Word Cards (BLM 7)

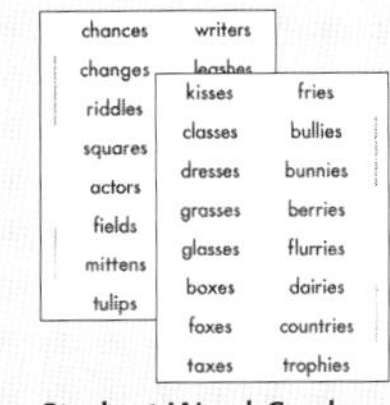

Student Word Cards (BLMs 8 & 9)

Quick-Check Student Sheet

UNIT 20 Regular plurals

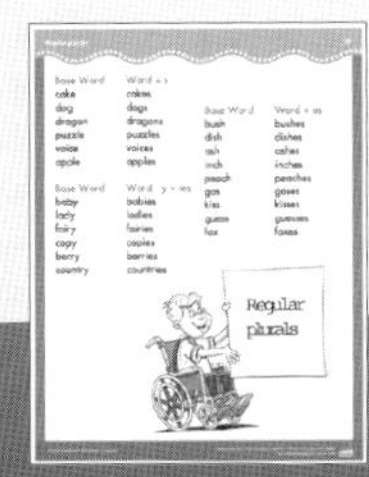

Frieze Card

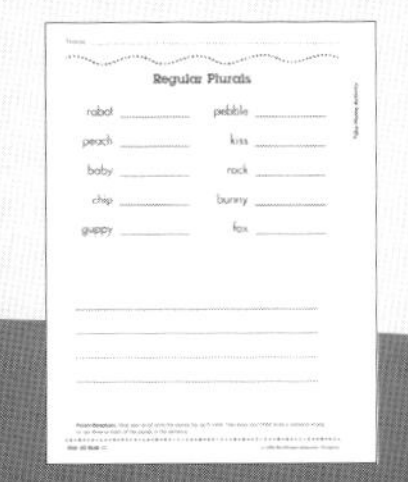

Take-Home Activity

Core Materials

All of these materials can be downloaded from http://phonicsresources.benchmarkeducation.com.

Frieze Card

teacher **Review VCe Syllable Pattern**

- Write the following sentence on the board, underlining the word costume: *I will wear a rabbit costume to the party.* Read aloud the sentence up to the word costume, and model dividing the word into syllables before reading it.
- **Think Aloud:** *I hear two vowel sounds, and I see a final* **e.** *There are two consonants between the vowels* **o** *and* **u,** *so I divide the word between them. The first syllable is a closed syllable with a short /***o***/ sound. The second syllable has a VCe pattern, and I know that the* **e** *is silent and the* **u** *stands for a long sound.*
- Read the word and the rest of the sentence.
- Write the words ***suppose, translate,*** and ***describe*** on the board, and guide students to divide the words into syllables and tell what they know about closed and VCe syllable patterns.

teacher **Introduce Plurals**

Model

- Point out the ***s, es***, or ***ies*** at the ends of words on the regular plurals frieze card, and tell students that the plural words mean *more than one thing.* Point to the word ***cakes*** as an example, and tell students that the ***s*** on ***cakes*** means there is more than one cake.

Guide

- For each grouping on the frieze card, write an example root word on the board and have students compare the way the root word ends with the plural ending that is used on the frieze card: ***cake (cakes), baby (babies), dish (dishes), inch (inches), gas (gases), kiss (kisses), fox (foxes).***
- Guide students as they state in their own words how the ending of the root word affects which plural ending is used.

Apply

- Give students letter cards **b, f, h, l, n, r, s, s, t, x, a, e, i, o,** and **u**. Say the word ***horns.*** Ask students what the root word of ***horns*** is and how the root words ends. Have them look at the frieze card to decide which plural ending is used in ***horns.*** Have students choose the letters they need and spell the word. Write it on the board and have students check their spelling.
- Repeat with the words ***buses, taxes***, and ***flies.***

Assessment Tip: Note which students correctly make the plurals. Guide students who are having difficulty.

Word Study

- Place the following teacher word cards in random order in a pocket chart: **horses, trains, eagles, bushes, sashes, glasses, latches, crutches, riches, losses, passes, masses, skies, buddies, armies.** Have students read each word with you.
- Tell students that you want to organize the words according to their plural endings. Ask students to name different plural endings. As students say an ending, write it on an index card and place it in the chart.
- Hold up one of the word cards and have students tell you what plural ending it has and why. Place the word card under the appropriate index card.
- Repeat with the rest of the word cards.

Blend

- Write the word ***rubies*** on the board and model blending the sounds in the syllables to read the word. Then have students blend it with you.
- Give students the word list on blackline master 2 and have them point to the first word for Day One and read the word.
- Have students independently read the remaining words for Day One. If students need support, guide them as they read some or all of the words on the list before having them read independently.

Spelling Words: *spices, acorns, apples*

Model

- Make a two-column spelling chart on chart paper. Label the first column "Plural" and the second column "Root Word." Tell students that they will be spelling plural words. As you work through the unit, continue to add the spelling words to the chart, and have students use the chart to check their spelling of the words.
- Say the word ***spices*** and model spelling it and writing it on the chart.
- **Think Aloud:** *The root word of* **spices** *is* **spice.** *I hear a VCe pattern, so the word probably has a silent final* **e.** *I'll write the word on the chart. I see that it doesn't end in* **sh, ch, s, ss,** *or* **x,** *so I will just add* **s** *to make it plural.*

Guide

- Say the word ***acorns.*** Have students tell you the root word. Guide them to identify the syllables and the vowel sounds in each. Then have them tell you what letters to use as you write ***acorn*** on the chart. Ask students what letter it ends with and what plural ending to use.
- Repeat with the word ***apples.***

Apply

- Have students practice writing each of the words in their word study notebooks. Have them write a sentence for each of the words. Have them circle the plural ending.

Our Spelling Words

Plural	Root Word
spices	spice
acorns	acorn
apples	apple
dishes	dish
classes	class
taxes	tax
watches	watch
ponies	pony
cities	city

DAY 2

Blend

- Have students blend the words on the word list for Day Two, using the procedure for blending from Day One.

Develop Automaticity in Word Recognition

- Circle the following words on the overhead transparency: ***children, girl(s), need, should, soon.***
- Tell students that practicing these words will help them recognize the words automatically so they can read more fluently. Explain that students can sound out some of these words, but they will read more quickly if they don't have to stop and sound out the words each time they see them.
- Read each word. Point out that the ***ou*** in ***should*** stands for the variant vowel sound **/oo/.**
- Have students read aloud with you the sentences in the passage that contain the words. Then have them write the words in their word study notebooks.
- Give students a copy of blackline master 7. Point out the words from this lesson as well as other words they have learned previously. Have them cut out the words, store them in an envelope, and use them for practice activities.

Build Fluency with Connected Text

Model

- Read aloud the passage on the overhead transparency, stopping at the end of the first paragraph. Point out the use of apostrophes.
- **Think Aloud:** *I saw two apostrophes in this paragraph. The one in the word* **Mom's** *tells me that the shop belongs to Mom. The one in the word* **I'll** *tells me it is a contraction, and I know it stands for the words* **I will.**
- Stop at the word ***hundreds*** and model how to read the word.
- **Think Aloud:** *I can divide this word into syllables to help me read it. I look for the vowels and the consonants between them. I divide the word between the* **n** *and the* **d** *and I get two closed syllables. Easy. Both syllables have short sounds:* **hun/dred.**
- Model making a mistake and correcting it–for example, read ***chose*** instead of ***choose.***
- **Think Aloud: Chose** *doesn't sound right. Let me look at it again. Oh, there are two* **o**'*s in the middle so the sound could be /***o͞o***/ or /***o͝o***/. I will try /***o͞o***/. Yes, that makes sense.*

Guide

- Continue reading and stop at other words in the passage. Guide students as they read the words.

Apply

- Have students take turns reading blackline master 3 to partners or in small groups as you monitor their reading. Use the teacher tips to check comprehension and fluency.

Spelling Words: *dishes, classes, taxes*

- Have students practice writing the spelling words from Day One in their word study notebooks.
- Introduce the Day Two spelling words. Follow the format for Day One, guiding students as they identify the root word and decide on the plural ending.
- Have students practice writing each of the words in their word study notebooks. Have them circle the plural endings and then write a sentence for each of the words.

Teacher Tips

Reading Strategies

If students have difficulty applying strategies for challenging words, guide them to use the following strategies:

- look at how the words start and/or end
- look for familiar patterns or parts within the words
- separate the words into syllables and decode each part
- think about what familiar words look like the difficult words
- read forward to check the context
- reread the sentence or paragraph
- mark the words, substitute synonyms, and get on with reading–ask for help later

Comprehension

Use the following questions to ensure that students have understood the passage:

- *Where was the girls' mom when the ladies came in?*
  (Level 1–facts and details)
- *What was the first thing the girls did to help the ladies?*
  (Level 2–sequence events)
- *How would you describe the girls?*
  (Level 3–analyze character)

Fluency

Intervene if students are having difficulty reading the passage. Model how to use word and meaning strategies to problem-solve the words. After students have had a chance to read the passage silently, have them read it aloud for fluency. Model fluent reading of the passage. For students who struggle, you may want to read the passage a second time and have them echo-read along with you.

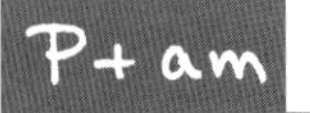 Blend

- Have students blend the words on the word list for Day Three, using the procedure for blending from Day One.

Develop Word Meanings: List/Group/ Label

- Have students brainstorm a list of nouns and record them on the board. To narrow the brainstorming, you could suggest a broad category, such as "things we can see in our house."
- Once students have made their list, have them tell you what endings to add to make the words plural. Record the plurals next to the root words and have students read the words.
- Select several of the words and describe how you could classify them according to their characteristics–for example, *I can put dishes, cups, and pans together because they are all found in a kitchen.* Write the words in a concept web labeled "Things in the Kitchen."
- Place students in small groups or have them work with partners. Give them a blank overhead transparency and a water-soluble pen. Tell them to categorize and label the plural forms of the words on the list, and write the words on the overhead transparency.
- When students have finished, have them share their categories. Discuss how and why the categories created by groups of students differ.

Spelling Words: ***watches, ponies, cities***

- Have students practice writing the spelling words from Day One and Day Two in their word study notebooks.
- Introduce the Day Three spelling words. Follow the format for Day One as you guide students to identify the root words and decide on the plural endings.
- Have students practice writing each of the words in their word study notebooks. Have them circle the plural endings and then write a sentence for each of the words.

 Build Fluency with Connected Text

- Have students read blackline master 4 to partners or in small groups as you monitor their reading. Call attention to the following words in the reading passage before students read it: ***country, grow, hard, let, might, should, sometimes.***

Teacher Tips

Long *i* or Long *e* Sound

Write the words ***fly, sky,*** and ***supply*** on the board. Point out that the ***y*** stands for the long ***i*** sound in the words. Write the plural form next to each word and point out that the plural ending still has the long ***i*** sound. Then write the words ***bunny*** and ***lady*** on the board, and ask what vowel sound the letter ***y*** stands for in these words. Write the plurals next to each word and ask students what vowel sounds they hear at the ends of the words.

Develop Automaticity in Word Recognition

Have students take turns choosing a high-frequency word, saying the word and writing it on the board, using the card as a model. Have the students copy the word in their word study notebooks.

Repeated Reading

Have students practice repeated readings of blackline master 3 to develop fluency.

DAY 4

Teacher Tips

Syllables

Write the word ***cake*** on the board and ask students which plural ending to add to the word. Write the word ***cakes*** and ask how many syllables there are in the word. Write the word ***spice*** on the board and ask students which plural ending to add to the word. Write the word ***spices*** and ask students how many syllables there are. Point out that by adding a consonant to the letter ***s,*** a closed syllable is formed and the letter ***e*** now stands for a short vowel sound. Provide further examples using words such as ***pieces, bases,*** and ***voices.***

Develop Automaticity in Word Recognition

Write some or all of the high-frequency words on the board. Say a word and call on a student to find the word on the board and circle it. Repeat with the remaining words.

Repeated Reading

Have students practice repeated readings of blackline master 3 to develop fluency.

Blend

- Have students blend the words on the word list for Day Four, using the procedure for blending from Day One.

Write

- Tell students that as a group you will write a short informational text about a familiar animal. Have students brainstorm familiar animals they could write about and record their ideas on the board in a word web or in a list. Then ask students to choose one of the animals—for example, cats. Have them brainstorm a list of things they could say about cats.
- Model the first sentence. Point out that the first sentence in an informational text often lets the reader know what the main idea of the text is about.
- Have students discuss what you might say next and then have them tell you what to write. Guide them as needed and record their sentences.
- Read the text through aloud, and have students check to see if they need to fix any problems with it.
- Have students identify the plurals they used in the text and have them say if they are spelled with the correct plural endings.
- Tell students that they can use this text as a model to write their own informational text. (See Day Five activities.)

Cats

Cats are interesting creatures. They have long whiskers and wet noses. Their eyes are closed when they are babies. Cats make good pets. If you have cats, you should give them healthy food and fresh water in clean dishes. Cats like to play. They like hiding in boxes and bags.

Spelling Words

- Provide practice for students in segmenting words and associating sounds with spellings. Dictate the following words to students and have them write the words on their papers: ***riddles, streets, dishes, bunnies.***
- Write the words on the board and have students self-correct their papers.
- Dictate the following sentence and have students write it on their papers: *We made pies from the berries in the boxes.*
- Write the sentence on the board and have students self-correct their papers.
- Give pairs of students blackline master 6. While one student reads the spelling words, the other student writes them in the "First Try" column. After the student has spelled the words, the partner places a check mark next to words spelled correctly. For the second try, the partner may prompt the student by sounding out the words that were spelled incorrectly the first time. If the second spelling attempt is correct, the partner places a check mark in the "Second Try" column.

Assessment Tip: Use students' completed peer-check blackline masters to note which words gave students difficulty.

Build Fluency with Connected Text

- Have students take turns reading blackline master 5 to partners or in small groups as you monitor their reading. Call attention to the following words in the reading passage before students read it: ***even, might, often, sides, stop, such, why.***

DAY 5

Spelling Assessment

Use the following procedure to assess students' spelling of the Unit Twenty words.
- Say each spelling word and use it in a sentence.
- Have students write the words on their papers.
- Continue with the next word on the list.
- When students have finished, collect their papers and analyze their spelling of the words.
- Use the assessment to plan small group or individual practice.

Small Group/Independent Activities

The following activities can be used to provide practice for students who need additional support.

WORD STRATEGIES

Write Have students choose an animal from the brainstormed list, or another animal of their choice. Have them think about what they want to say about the animal and then each write a draft of an informational text in their word study notebooks. Point out the group text on chart paper that they can use as a model. Have them exchange their writing with partners. Have the partners take turns telling each other what they like about the writing and what problems they see. Have them be sure to check for correct endings on plural words. Have students revise their drafts in their word study notebooks. Then have them underline all the plurals they used.

Word Sort Provide bags with the following labels: ***-s, -es, -ies.*** Have students sort their student word cards from blackline masters 8 and 9 into the correct bags.

AUTOMATICITY IN WORD RECOGNITION

Fill in the Grid Draw a grid four boxes by four boxes on the board. Have students take turns drawing one of the high-frequency word cards, reading it, and writing it in the grid. When the grid is full, point to each word and call on a student to come up, read the word, and erase it from the grid.

Make Sentences Place several sets of high-frequency word cards in a bag. Have students draw four words from the bag and place them facedown without looking at them. When everyone has four cards, have students race to see who can write a sentence using all four words first. Have the student read aloud his or her sentence. Place the words back in the bag and repeat the process.

BUILD FLUENCY WITH CONNECTED TEXT

Repeated Reading Have students practice reading blackline master 3 several times, until they feel they can read it fluently and accurately. Have them work with partners to time one another as they read the passage aloud. Have them set a goal of reading 90 words per minute.

SPELLING

Make Words Provide a set of letter cards and the week's spelling words written on index cards. Have students use the letter cards to spell the words. They should check their spelling by blending the sounds and then looking at the words on the index cards.

Missing Vowels Write a spelling word on the board and omit one or more vowels. Say the word and have students write the word in their word study notebooks, filling in the missing vowels. Write the vowels in the word on the board so students can check their spelling. Repeat with other spelling words.

Teacher Tips

Home Connection

Have students take blackline master 11 home to complete with a family member. Students can also take the repeated reading passage on blackline master 3 home to share with their family.

Quick-Check

Assess students' mastery of regular plurals using the quick-check for Unit Twenty in this Teacher Resource System.

ELL Support Tip

Make two sets of word cards, one with plurals and one without. Draw pictures on the cards to show one or more than one. Teach students how to play Fish, and have them create sets by matching one plural word card and one non-plural word card.

Quick-Check: Regular plurals

Student Name ______________________ Assessment Date ____________

Segmenting and Blending

Directions: Explain that these words use sounds the student has been learning. Have the student point to each word on the corresponding student sheet, segment the word parts or syllables, and blend them together. Put a ✓ if the student successfully segments and blends the word or reads it as a complete unit. If the student misses the word, record the error.
Example: scrapbooks

wishes		stories			
daisies		monsters			
pencils		bosses			
waltzes		puppies		Score	**/8**

Sight Words

Directions: Have the student point to the first word on the corresponding student sheet and read across the line, saying each word as quickly as possible. Put a ✓ if the student successfully reads the word and an **X** if the student hesitates more than a few seconds. If the student misses the word, record the error.

girl		some			
need		one			
those		want			
soon		thing			
children		know			
should		each			
help		been			
you		were		Score	**/16**

UNIT 21 Irregular plurals

Unit Objectives

Students will:

- Recognize irregular plural words in print and understand they mean more than one
- Review open-syllable patterns
- Use collective terms for plural words
- Sort words according to their plural endings
- Read high-frequency words almost, animal, every, few, group, might, school
- Spell plural words: sheep, deer, teeth, women, dozen, traffic, moose, geese, oxen
- Write a descriptive text that uses regular and irregular plurals

UNIT 21 Irregular plurals

Day 1

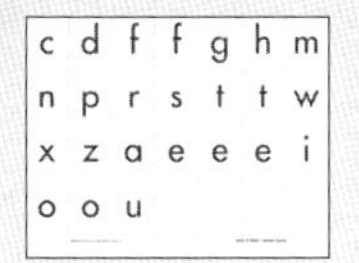

Letter Cards:
a, m, n, o, r, s, t, t, u

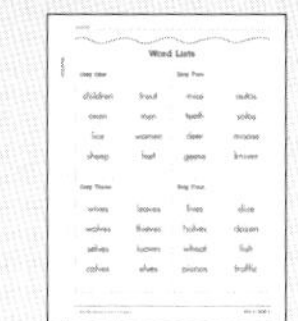

Word Lists
(BLM 2)

Day 2

Word Lists
(BLM 2)

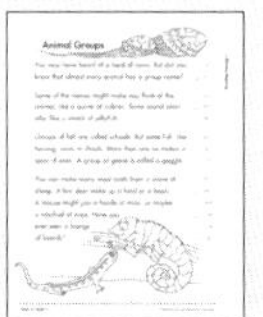

Reading Passage 1
(BLM 3)

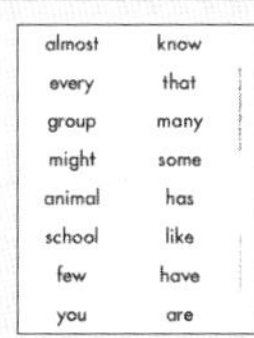

High-Frequency Word Cards for Unit 21 (BLM 7)

Day 3

Word Lists
(BLM 2)

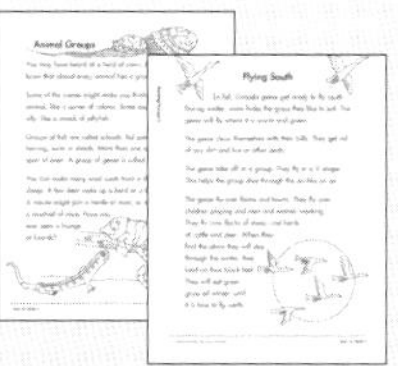

Reading Passages 1 & 2
(BLMs 3 & 4)

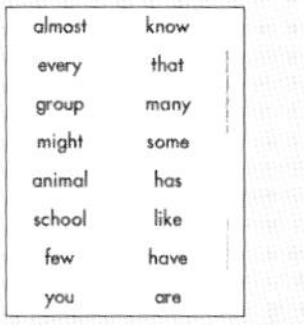

High-Frequency Word Cards for Unit 21
(BLM 7)

auto

Teacher Word Cards: **auto, baby, beach, box, cliff, deer, fish, glass, goat, horse, knife, mouse, ox, penny, potato, sky, solo, tooth, wheat, woman**

Day 4

Word Lists
(BLM 2)

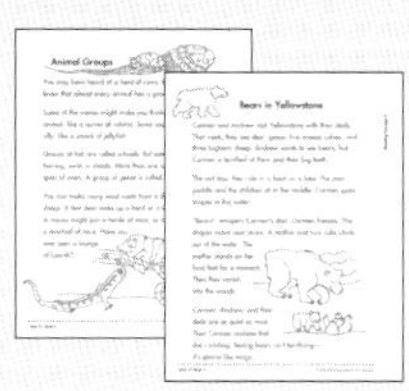

Reading Passages 1 & 3
(BLMs 3 & 5)

cane

Teacher Word Cards: **cane, clop, crane, cube, cute, flute, grape, gripe, hope, plane, ripe, shine, slope, spine, tape**

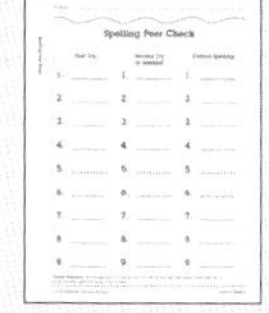

Spelling Peer Check
(BLM 6)

High-Frequency Word Cards for Unit 21
(BLM 7)

Day 5

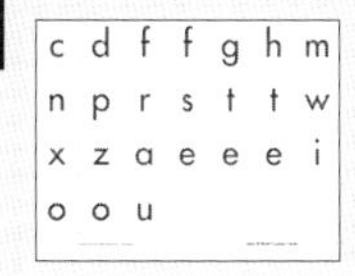

Letter Cards for Unit 21

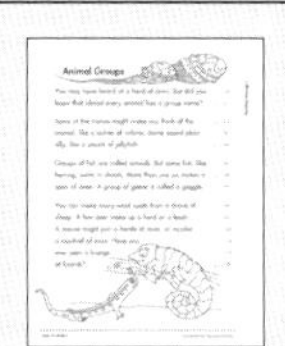

Reading Passage 1
(BLM 3)

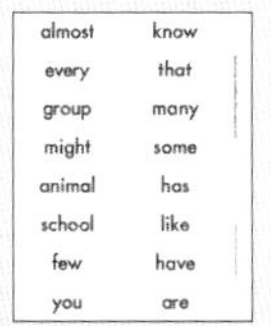

High-Frequency Word Cards for Unit 21 (BLM 7)

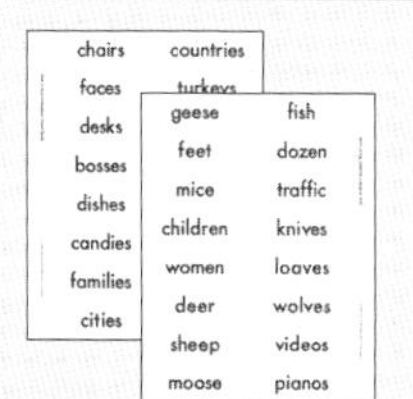

Student Word Cards
(BLMs 8 & 9)

Quick-Check Student Sheet

Frieze Card

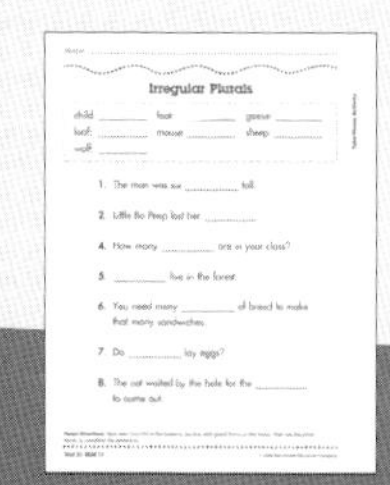

Take-Home Activity

Core Materials

All of these materials can be downloaded from http://phonicsresources.benchmarkeducation.com.

DAY 1

Frieze Card

tea/che Review Open-Syllable Patterns

- Write the following sentence on the board, underlining the word ***chosen:*** *Has the team been chosen?* Read the sentence aloud up to the word ***chosen,*** and model dividing the word into syllables before reading it.
- **Think Aloud:** *If I circle the two vowels, I see one consonant between them, and I divide the word before the letter* **s**. *I have an open syllable, with a long o sound, and a closed syllable.*
- Read the word and repeat the sentence.
- Write the words ***moment, donate,*** and ***gravy*** on the board. Guide students to divide the words into syllables and tell what they know about closed-, VCe, and open-syllable patterns.

tea/ch Introduce Irregular Plurals

Model

- Show students the irregular plurals frieze card and read the first word pair: ***child/ children.*** Explain that some words have irregular plural forms, which means they don't follow the rules for adding ***-s, -ies,*** and ***-es*** endings.
- Read through the list, stopping at the word ***deer.*** Explain that for some words, the singular and plural forms of the words are the same. Read the words ***deer, wheat,*** and ***fish,*** and tell students the spelling of these words is the same for both singular and plural forms.

Guide

- Have students make oral sentences using the singular and plural forms of some of the words on the list.
- Guide students as they state in their own words what an irregular plural is and provide an example of a regular and an irregular plural.

Apply

- Give students letter cards **m, n, r, s, t, t, a, o,** and **u.** Say the word ***man.*** Ask students if the word is singular or plural. Have them use the letters to make the word. Ask students what the plural of ***man*** is. Have them make the word ***men.*** Write ***men*** on the board and have students check their spelling.
- Repeat with the words ***auto/autos*** and ***trout/trout.*** Point out that what makes the spelling of ***autos*** irregular is that usually we add ***-es*** to a word ending with a consonant and the letter ***o.***

Assessment Tip: Note which students correctly make the plurals. Guide students who are having difficulty.

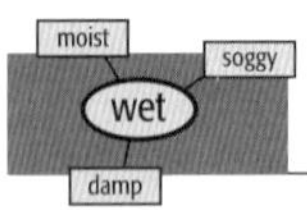

Word Study

- Have students explore some of the interesting collective terms used for groups of animals. Write the following words in one column: ***deer, fish, geese, oxen, sheep.*** Then write these words in a second column: ***herd, school, gaggle, team, flock.***
- Ask students if they recognize any of the words, such as ***herd.*** Have them decide which animal the collective term refers to. (herd of deer)
- Have student pairs try to match the collective nouns with the plural words.
- When students have finished, have them share their lists, discuss whether they think the lists are correct, and then provide the correct pairings of words. ***(herd/deer; school/fish; gaggle/geese; team/oxen; flock/sheep)***
- Have students write sentences in their word study notebooks, using the collective nouns with the plurals.
- Students can research other collective nouns for groups of animals—for example: ***run/fish; yoke/oxen; fold, drove/sheep; hover/trout.***

 Blend

- Write the word ***pianos*** on the board and model blending the sounds in the syllables to read the word. Then have students blend it with you.
- Give students the Day One word list on blackline master 2. Have them point to the first word on the list and read the word.
- Have students independently read the remaining words for Day One. If students need support, guide them as they read some or all of the words on the list before having them read independently.

Spelling Words: *sheep, deer, teeth*

Model

- Make a two-column chart of the singular and plural forms of the week's spelling words. As you work through the unit, continue to add the spelling words to the chart, and have students use it to check their spelling of the words.
- Say the word ***sheep*** and model spelling it and writing it on the chart.
- **Think Aloud: Sheep** *is one of those words that is the same for the singular and the plural. I hear a long* **e** *digraph in the word, and I think it is spelled* **ee.**

Guide

- Say the word ***deer.*** Point out that this word can be spelled in two ways and has different meanings. Have students decide what makes the /ē/ sound in the word if they want to describe a type of woodland animal.
- Have students tell you how to spell the word ***teeth.*** Ask them if they know the singular form of the word ***teeth.***

Apply

- Have students practice writing each of the words in their word study notebooks. Have them write a sentence for each of the words.

Our Spelling Words

Singular	Plural
sheep	sheep
deer	deer
tooth	teeth
woman	women
dozen	dozen
traffic	traffic
moose	moose
goose	geese
ox	oxen

DAY 2

Teacher Tips

Reading Strategies

If students have difficulty applying strategies for challenging words, guide them to use the following strategies:

- look at how the words start and/or end
- look for familiar patterns or parts within the words
- separate the words into syllables and decode each part
- think about what familiar words look like the difficult words
- read forward to check the context
- reread the sentence or paragraph
- mark the words, substitute synonyms, and get on with reading–ask for help later

Comprehension

Use the following questions to ensure that students have understood the passage:

- *What is a group of fish called?* (Level 1–facts and details)
- *What is the main idea of this passage?* (Level 2–main idea)
- *What is a good summary for this passage?* (Level 3–summarize information)

Fluency

Intervene if students are having difficulty reading the passage. Model how to use word and meaning strategies to problem-solve the words. After students have had a chance to read the passage silently, have them read it aloud for fluency. Model fluent reading of the passage. For students who struggle, you may want to read the passage a second time and have them echo-read along with you.

Blend

- Have students blend the words on the word list for Day Two, using the procedure for blending from Day One.

Develop Automaticity in Word Recognition

- Circle the following words on the overhead transparency: ***almost, animal, every, few, group, might, school(s).***
- Tell students that practicing these words will help them recognize the words automatically so they can read more fluently. Explain that students can sound out some of these words, but they will read more quickly if they don't have to stop and sound out the words each time they see them.
- Read each word. Point out that ***school*** and ***group*** have the /o͞o/ sound but are spelled differently. Point out that ***schools*** appears with a plural ***-s*** ending because it follows the plural word ***groups*** (*groups of fish are called schools*).
- Have students read aloud with you the sentences in the passage that contains the words. Then have them write the words in their word study notebooks.
- Give students a copy of blackline master 7. Point out the words from this lesson as well as other words they have learned previously. Have them cut out the words, store them in an envelope, and use them for practice activities.

Build Fluency with Connected Text

Model

- Read aloud the passage on the overhead transparency, stopping at the end of the first paragraph. Point out the spellings of ***heard*** and ***herd.***
- **Think Aloud:** *These two words made me stop just for a second. Both of these words are pronounced the same, but they are spelled differently and have different meanings.*
- Stop at the word ***quiver*** and model how to read the word.
- **Think Aloud:** *I can divide this word into syllables to help me read it. I look for the vowels and the consonant between them. I divide the word before the* **v: qui/ver.** *That doesn't sound like a word, so I try dividing after the* **v** *to make a closed syllable:* **quiver.** *Oh, I know what that means. It means to tremble or shake.*

Guide

- Continue reading and stop at other words in the passage. Guide students as they read the words.

Apply

- Have students take turns reading blackline master 3 to partners or in small groups as you monitor their reading. Use the teacher tips to check comprehension and fluency.

Spelling Words: *women, dozen, traffic*

- Have students practice writing the spelling words from Day One in their word study notebooks.
- Introduce the Day Two spelling words. Follow the format for Day One, guiding students as they identify the singular form and then spell the plural form of each word.
- Have students practice writing each of the words in their word study notebooks. Have them write a sentence for each of the words.

Blend

- Have students blend the words on the word list for Day Three, using the procedure for blending from Day One.

Develop Word Meanings: Plural Forms

- Write the following pluralization options on index cards and place them in a row in a pocket chart: ***-s, -es, -ies,*** same spelling, change ***f*** to ***v,*** different word. Ask students to suggest words that make use of these different pluralization options and word endings.
- Place the following teacher word cards facedown in a stack: **mouse, deer, glass, fish, woman, box, tooth, knife, baby, auto, goat, sky, beach, horse, penny, wheat, solo, ox, cliff, potato.** Have students take turns drawing a card, showing it to the group, and deciding under which pluralization index card to place the word.
- Once students have sorted the word cards, read each word and then have students say the plural form of each word. If they think a word is sorted in the wrong column, write the word on the board using the suggested pluralization method or word ending, and have them decide if the word looks right.

Spelling Words: *moose, geese, oxen*

- Have students practice writing the spelling words from Day One and Day Two in their word study notebooks.
- Introduce the Day Three spelling words. Follow the format for Day One as you guide students to identify the singular forms and then say and spell the plural forms.
- Have students practice writing the plural forms of the Day Three spelling words in their word study notebooks. Have them circle the plural endings and then write a sentence for each of the words.

Build Fluency with Connected Text

- Have students read blackline master 4 to partners or in small groups as you monitor their reading. Call attention to the following words in the reading passage before students read it: ***air, eat, group, land, off, play(ing), until.***

Teacher Tips

Words Ending in /f/

Write the word ***elf*** on the board. Tell students that in order to make some words that end in ***f*** plural, we change the letter ***f*** to ***v,*** as in ***elves.*** Write the words ***loaf*** and ***wolf*** on the board. Have volunteers change the words into plurals. Point out that most plurals for words that end with ***f*** are formed by adding an ***-s*** ending: ***chief/chiefs; reef/reefs.***

Same Spelling

Have students begin making a list of words in their word study notebooks that are the same for both singular and plural–for example: ***cod, moose, traffic, barley, deer, dozen, fish, sheep, wheat, series.***

Develop Automaticity in Word Recognition

Have students spread their set of high-frequency word cards faceup in front of them. Say one of the words and have students race to find the word and hold it up.

Repeated Reading

Have students practice repeated readings of blackline master 3 to develop fluency.

DAY 4

Teacher Tips

Plural Words Chart

Encourage students to begin keeping a chart in their word study notebooks to record different types of plural forms. As they encounter plural words in their reading, they can add the words to the chart. Have them use the chart as a reference for spelling words when they are writing.

Develop Automaticity in Word Recognition

Write some or all of the high-frequency words on the board. Challenge students to create silly sentences that use as many high-frequency words as possible. Have students read their sentences to the group.

Repeated Reading

Have students practice repeated readings of blackline master 3 to develop fluency.

P+ am Blend

- Have students blend the words on the word list for Day Four, using the procedure for blending from Day One.

Write

- Tell students that as a group you will write a short descriptive text about what you might see at the zoo. Have students brainstorm a list of animals they could see and record their ideas on the board, in a word web, or on a list. Have students look at the list/web and note which animal names are regular plurals and which are not.
- Model writing the first sentence. Point out that the first sentence in an informational text often lets the reader know the main idea of the text.
- Have students discuss what you might say next and then have them tell you what to write. Guide them as needed and record their sentences.
- Read the text aloud and have students check to see if they need to fix any problems with it.
- Have students identify the plurals used in the text and whether they are regular or irregular.
- Tell students that they can use this text as a model to write their own informational text. (See Day Five activities.)

Spelling Words

- Provide practice for students in segmenting words and associating sounds with spellings. Dictate the following words to students and have them write the words on their papers: ***goose, geese, leaf/leaves.***
- Write the words on the board and have students self-correct their papers.
- Dictate the following sentence and have students write it on their papers: *The children made loaves of bread from wheat.*
- Write the sentence on the board and have students self-correct their papers.
- Give pairs of students blackline master 6. While one student reads the spelling words, the other student writes them in the "First Try" column. After the student has spelled the words, the partner places a check mark next to words spelled correctly. For the second try, the partner may prompt the student by sounding out the words that were spelled incorrectly the first time. If the second spelling attempt is correct, the partner places a check mark in the "Second Try" column.

Assessment Tip: Use students' completed peer-check blackline masters to note which words gave students difficulty.

Build Fluency with Connected Text

- Have students take turns reading blackline master 5 to partners or in small groups as you monitor their reading. Call attention to the following words in the reading passage before students read it: ***almost, big, last, mother, move, near.***

Spelling Assessment

Use the following procedure to assess students' spelling of the Unit Twenty-One words.

- Say each spelling word and use it in a sentence.
- Have students write the words on their papers.
- Continue with the next word on the list.
- When students have finished, collect their papers and analyze their spelling of the words.
- Use the assessment to plan small group or individual practice.

Small Group/Independent Activities

The following activities can be used to provide practice for students who need additional support.

WORD STRATEGIES

Write Have students write a description of their classroom, bedroom, or another room at home. Have them try to use as many plurals as they can. When they have completed their description, have them circle all the regular plurals in one color and the irregular plurals in another color.

Word Sort Provide bags with the labels "regular plurals" and "irregular plurals." Have students sort their word cards from blackline masters 8 and 9 into the correct bags.

AUTOMATICITY IN WORD RECOGNITION

Find the Words Have students work with partners to reread reading passages from previous units to see how many of the Unit Twenty-One high-frequency words they can find. Have them keep a tally of the number of times they find each word. They could create a graph to show the five most frequently used words. Have them compare their findings with another pair of students.

Time It Have students time themselves to see how many of the high-frequency words from blackline master 7 they can read correctly in twenty seconds. Have them practice to improve their accuracy and time.

BUILD FLUENCY WITH CONNECTED TEXT

Repeated Reading Have students practice reading blackline master 3 several times, until they feel they can read it fluently and accurately. Have them work with partners to time one another as they read the passage aloud. Have them set a goal of reading 90 words per minute.

SPELLING

Make Words Provide a set of letter cards and the week's spelling words on index cards. Have students use the letter cards to spell the words. They should check their spelling by blending the sounds and then looking at the words on the index cards.

Spell On Have students sit in a circle. Say a spelling word and the first letter of the word. Then have the student next to you say the next letter, and so on, until the word is spelled. Have the student who says the last letter write the word on the board. Have the next student say another spelling word and the first letter, and continue around the circle.

Teacher Tips

Home Connection

Have students take blackline master 11 home to complete with a family member. Students can also take the repeated reading passage on blackline master 3 home to share with their family.

Quick-Check

Assess students' mastery of irregular plurals using the quick-check for Unit Twenty-One in this Teacher Resource System.

ELL Support Tip

Use a "preview and review" model with ELL students. A preview of the lesson before the direct instruction of the skill, followed by an immediate review at the end of the lesson, will support students who may have difficulty. Using the model in a small group will help build the confidence ELL students need in order to participate in a whole-group setting.

UNIT 21 Quick-Check: Irregular plurals

Student Name ______________________ Assessment Date ____________

Segmenting and Blending

Directions: Explain that these words use sounds the student has been learning. Have the student point to each word on the corresponding student sheet, segment the word parts or syllables, and blend them together. Put a ✓ if the student successfully segments and blends the word or reads it as a complete unit. If the student misses the word, record the error. **Example:** radii

cod		men		
cacti		lives		
salmon		bass		
feet		thieves		Score **/8**

Sight Words

Directions: Have the student point to the first word on the corresponding student sheet and read across the line, saying each word as quickly as possible. Put a ✓ if the student successfully reads the word and an **X** if the student hesitates more than a few seconds. If the student misses the word, record the error.

almost		you		
every		know		
group		that		
might		many		
animal		some		
such		has		
school		like		
few		have		Score **/16**

UNIT 22 -ed, -ing endings

Unit Objectives

Students will:

- Read words with -ed, -ing and understand that this changes the meaning of the word
- Understand that sometimes consonants need to be doubled before adding -ed or -ing
- Review vowel digraph patterns
- Use synonyms in oral sentences
- Sort words by ending sounds
- Read high-frequency words: another, close, four, high, home, run(s)
- Spell words: helped, helping, printed, printing, sliced, slicing, joked, joking, dropped, dropping, clapped, clapping
- Write a recount

Day 1

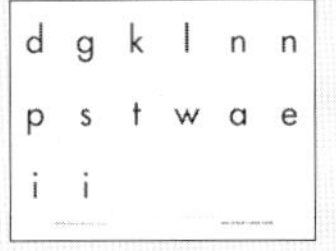

Letter Cards:
a, d, e, g, i, k, l, n, p, s, t, w

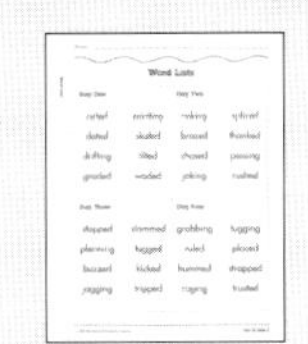
Word Lists (BLM 2)

Day 2

Word Lists (BLM 2)

Reading Passage 1 (BLM 3)

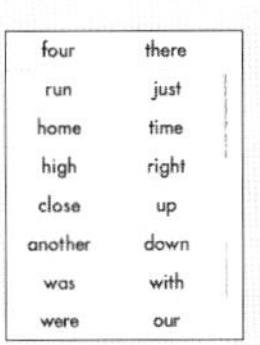

High-Frequency Word Cards (BLM 7)

Day 3

Word Lists (BLM 2)

Reading Passages 1 & 2 (BLMs 3 & 4)

High-Frequency Word Cards (BLM 7)

bake

Teacher Word Cards:
bake, bump, choke, flip, hop, itch, land, pace, rope, skid

Day 4

Word Lists (BLM 2)

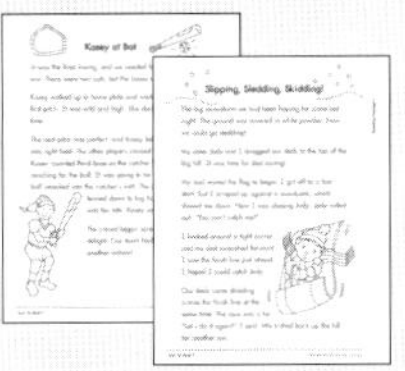
Reading Passages 1 & 3 (BLMs 3 & 5)

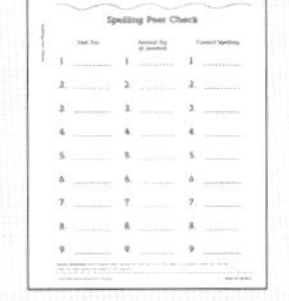
Spelling Peer Check (BLM 6)

High-Frequency Word Cards (BLM 7)

Day 5

Letter Cards for Unit 22

Reading Passage 1 (BLM 3)

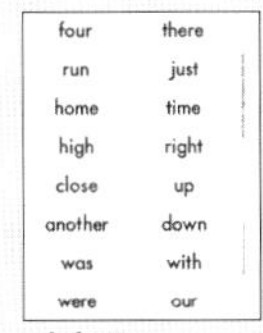

High-Frequency Word Cards (BLM 7)

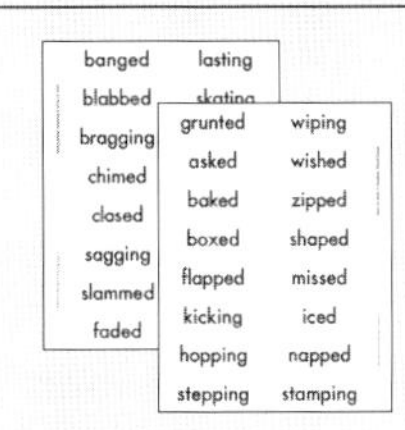

Student Word Cards (BLMs 8 & 9)

Quick-Check Student Sheet

Frieze Card

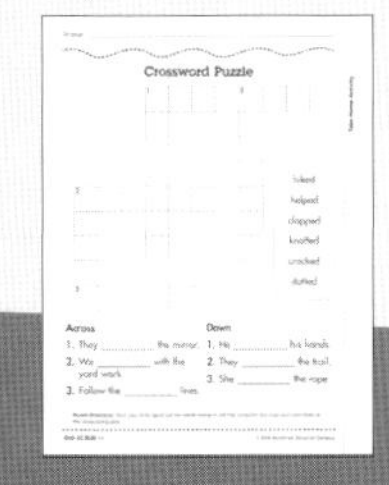

Take-Home Activity

Core Materials

All of these materials can be downloaded from http://phonicsresources.benchmarkeducation.com.

UNIT 22 -ed, -ing endings

Frieze Card

teacher Review Vowel Digraph Syllable Patterns

- Remind students that vowel digraphs are two letters that stand for one vowel sound. Have students think of some vowel digraphs and record them in a list. (***ai, ay, ea, ee, ei, ie, oa, ow***) Remind students that the ***ea*** digraph can stand for the long and the short ***e*** sounds.
- Write the word ***belief*** on the board and have students identify the vowel digraph. Remind them that the digraph stays together in a syllable when dividing the word. Ask students where you should divide the word. If students need support, help them find the two vowels (***e, ie***) and divide the word before the consonant.
- Ask them to tell you which two syllable patterns there are in this word (open, vowel digraph). Then have them blend the word.
- Write the following words on the board: ***canteen, below, decay, explain, foamy, disease.*** Have volunteers circle the digraphs in the words. Then have other students show where they would divide the words.
- Have students blend the words. Time students to see if they can blend each word in three seconds or less.

teacher Introduce *-ed, -ing* Endings

Model

- Write the following sentences on the board: *Is he playing baseball in the park? I played there last Saturday.* Point out that the first sentence talks about a continuing action and the second talks about an action that has already happened.
- Circle the root word in ***playing*** and ***played.*** Explain that by adding the endings ***-ed*** and ***-ing***, we can change the meaning of the root word ***play.***

Guide

- Show students the ***-ed, -ing*** endings frieze card. Have them read the first two words on the list with ***-ed*** and ***-ing*** endings. Point out the **/ed/** sounds at the ends of the words ***added*** and ***lifted.***
- Read the next two sets of words with students. Point out the **/d/** ending on the words ***played*** and ***banged.***
- Read the next two sets of words with students. Ask students to tell how these words are different from the first four sets of words. Point out that the final ***e*** is dropped before adding ***-ed*** or ***-ing.*** (***faded, guided***)
- Have students read the last two sets of words. Point out that the ***-ed*** ending on these words has a **/t/** sound. (***helped, raked***)

Apply

- Give students letter cards **d, g, k, l, n, n, p, s, t, w, a, e, i,** and **i.** Say the word ***skate.*** Ask students to find the letters they need to spell the word. Remind them that the word has a VCe pattern so they will need a final ***e.***
- Say the word ***skated.*** Ask students what ending they need to add to the word. Have them take away the final ***e*** and add ***-ed.***
- Have students change the word back to ***skate*** by taking away the ***-ed*** ending and adding a final ***e.*** Have them change the word ***skate*** to ***skating*** by taking away the final ***e*** and adding ***-ing.***
- Write the words on the board as students check their spelling.
- Repeat with the words ***wipe, wiped, wiping,*** and ***plant, planted, planting.***

Assessment Tip: Note which students correctly make the ***-ed*** and ***-ing*** words. Guide students who are having difficulty.

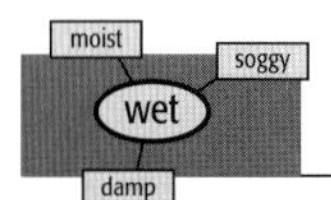

Word Study

- Give students practice using past tense verbs–including verbs with ***-ed*** endings–in context. Have students sit in a circle. Say the following sentence, leaving out the verb: *The girl ________ to school.*
- Go around the circle, having students add different verbs to the sentence. If a student cannot think of a word, allow time for thinking before having the group suggest a word.

Blend

- Write the word ***cleaning*** on the board. Point out that the ***-ing*** ending makes a second syllable. Model blending the sounds in the syllables to read the word. Then have students blend it with you.
- Give students the Day One word list on blackline master 2. Have them point to the first word on the list and read the word.
- Have students independently read the remaining words for Day One or guide them as they read some or all of the words.

Spelling Words: *helped, helping, printed, printing*

Model

- Make a two-column spelling chart on chart paper labeled "-ed Ending" and "-ing Ending." As you work through the unit, continue to add the spelling words to the chart, and have students use the chart to check their spelling of the words.
- Say the word ***helped*** and model spelling it and writing it on the chart.
- **Think Aloud:** *The root word of helped is* **help.** *I hear an* **-ed** *ending on the word.* **Help** *doesn't end with a final* **e,** *so I will just add the ending.*

Guide

- Say the word ***helping.*** Have students tell you the root word. Then have them tell you what letters to use as you write ***helping*** on the chart.
- Repeat with the words ***printed*** and ***printing.***

Apply

- Have students practice writing each of the words in their word study notebooks. Have them write a sentence for each of the words. Have them underline the root word and circle the ***-ed*** and ***-ing*** endings.

Our Spelling Words

-ed Ending	-ing Ending
helped	helping
printed	printing
sliced	slicing
joked	joking
dropped	dropping
clapped	clapping

DAY 2

Teacher Tips

Reading Strategies

If students have difficulty applying strategies for challenging words, guide them to use the following strategies:

- look at how the words start and/or end
- look for familiar patterns or parts within the words
- separate the words into syllables and decode each part
- think about what familiar words look like the difficult words
- read forward to check the context
- reread the sentence or paragraph
- mark the words, substitute synonyms, and get on with reading–ask for help later

Comprehension

Use the following questions to ensure that students have understood the passage:

- *What did the team need to win?* (Level 1–facts and details)
- *Why did Kasey need to duck?* (Level 2–cause/effect)
- *How do you think Kasey felt when she got a home run?* (Level 3–analyze character)

Fluency

Intervene if students are having difficulty reading the passage. Model how to use word and meaning strategies to problem-solve the words. After students have had a chance to read the passage silently, have them read it aloud for fluency. Model fluent reading of the passage. For students who struggle, you may want to read the passage a second time and have them echo-read along with you.

Blend

- Have students blend the words on the word list for Day Two, using the procedure for blending from Day One.

Develop Automaticity in Word Recognition

- Circle the following words on the overhead transparency: ***another, close, four, high, home, run(s).***
- Tell students that practicing these words will help them recognize the words automatically so they can read more fluently. Explain that students can sound out some of these words, but they will read more quickly if they don't have to stop and sound out the words each time they see them.
- Read each word. Point out that ***close*** can be pronounced **/clōz/** or **/clōs/**, and that students need to think about the context to determine which word it is.
- Have students read aloud with you the sentences in the passage that contain the words. Then have them write the words in their word study notebooks.
- Give students a copy of blackline master 7. Point out the words from this lesson as well as other words they have learned previously. Have them cut out the words, store them in an envelope, and use them for practice activities.

Build Fluency with Connected Text

Model

- Read aloud the passage on the overhead transparency, stopping after the first sentence in the second paragraph. Point out the words ***walked*** and ***waited.***
- **Think Aloud:** *Both of these words end with* **-ed** *but* **walked** *ends with a* **/t/** *sound and has one syllable, while* **waited** *ends with the sound* **/ed/** *and has two syllables. These words with* **-ed** *endings tell me that this is written in the past tense and it has already happened.*
- Model making a mistake and correcting it–for example, read ***filed*** instead of ***field.***
- **Think Aloud:** *That doesn't sound right. Let me look at it again. I see a vowel digraph but it's not a long* **i** *digraph. I think it might be a long* **e** *digraph. I'll try that and see if it sounds right.*

Guide

- Continue reading and stop at other words in the passage. Guide students as they read the words.

Apply

- Have students take turns reading blackline master 3 to partners or in small groups as you monitor their reading. Use the teacher tips to check comprehension and fluency.

Spelling Words: *sliced, slicing, joked, joking*

- Have students practice writing the spelling words from Day One in their word study notebooks.
- Introduce the Day Two spelling words. Follow the format for Day One, guiding students as they identify the root words. Point out the VCe patterns in the words, and remind students to drop the ***e*** before adding the endings.
- Have students practice writing each of the words in their word study notebooks. Have them circle the ***-ed*** and ***-ing*** endings and then write a sentence for each of the words.

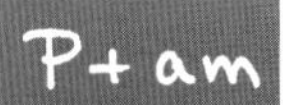

Blend

- Have students blend the words on the word list for Day Three, using the procedure for blending from Day One.

tea/cher Introduce Double Consonants

- Write the words ***stop, stopped,*** and ***stopping*** on the board. Point out that the letter ***p*** was doubled when the endings were added.
- Tell students that the final consonant is usually doubled in words that end with one consonant before adding ***-ed*** or ***-ing.*** Explain that the consonant is doubled in order to create a closed syllable with a short vowel sound. Show students what the word would look like without doubling the consonant: ***stoping.*** Divide the word into syllables ***(sto/ping)*** and point out that the first syllable is an open syllable that should have a long vowel sound. Then divide ***stopping*** into syllables and show students how doubling the letter ***p*** makes a closed syllable with a short vowel sound: ***stop/ping.***
- Write the words ***clip, nap,*** and ***step*** on the board. Have students note the single consonant at the end of the first word and tell you what you need to do to make the word ***clipped.*** Write it on the board.
- Ask volunteers to come up and write the words ***clipping, napped, napping, stepped,*** and ***stepping.***
- Write the following word formulas on index cards: "word - e + ed"; "word + ed"; "word + consonant + ed." Place the index cards in a row in a pocket chart. Model placing the following teacher word cards under the correct index card: **land, bake, hop.**
- **Think Aloud:** *The word* **land** *ends with a consonant blend. I can just add* **-ed** *to this word without doubling the consonant. The word* **bake** *has a final* **e.** *I need to drop the* **e** *before adding* **-ed.** *The word* **hop** *ends with a single consonant. I need to double the* **p** *before adding* **-ed.**
- Write ***landed, baked,*** and ***hopped*** on the board and have students check that the words are correct.
- Have students tell you under which index card you should place the following teacher word cards: **pace, itch, flip, choke, bump, rope, skid.** Once the words are sorted, have students copy the headings from the index cards onto a chart in their word study notebooks. Have them write the base words and then next to each base word have them write each word with both the ***-ed*** and ***-ing*** endings.

Spelling Words: *dropped, dropping, clapped, clapping*

- Have students practice writing the spelling words from Day One and Day Two in their word study notebooks.
- Introduce the Day Three spelling words. Follow the format for Day One to guide students as they decide whether the final consonant needs to be doubled before adding the ending.
- Have students practice writing each of the words in their word study notebooks. Have them write a sentence for each of the words.

Build Fluency with Connected Text

- Have students read blackline master 4 to partners or in small groups as you monitor their reading. Call attention to the following words in the reading passage before students read it: ***group, few, us, off, again, next, those.***

Teacher Tips

Word Hunt

Have students find and circle words with ***-ed*** and ***-ing*** endings in the passages on blackline masters 3 and 4. Have them organize the words into categories according to what happens to the root word when the endings are added.

Develop Automaticity in Word Recognition

Have students choose three of the high-frequency words and write them on self-stick notes. Have them look through familiar books to find the words, marking the pages with the self-stick notes. Let students take turns reading aloud the sentences they found that use the words.

Repeated Reading

Have students practice repeated readings of blackline master 3 to develop fluency.

DAY 4

Teacher Tips

Words Ending with X

Write the word ***flex*** on the board. Point out that although it has one consonant at the end, the letter ***x*** is not doubled when adding ***-ed*** or ***-ing.*** Provide practice in having students add endings to the following words: ***box, fax, fix, mix.***

Develop Automaticity in Word Recognition

Have pairs of students use a set of high-frequency words and place them in alphabetical order. Once the words are in order, have them take turns reading each word on the list.

Repeated Reading

Have students practice repeated readings of blackline master 3 to develop fluency.

Blend

- Have students blend the words on the word list for Day Four, using the procedure for blending from Day One.

Write

- Tell students that as a group you will write a short recount. Explain that a recount tells about something that has already happened, so it uses the past tense. Have students brainstorm ideas for the recount–for example, a school excursion or event. Record their ideas on a list and have the group choose a topic from the list to write about.
- Ask students what the first thing was that happened and write this in the group recount. Continue asking students what happened next to establish the sequence and record their sentences.
- Read the text aloud, and have students check to see if they need to fix any problems with it.
- Have students identify the words with ***-ed*** and ***-ing*** endings and tell if they are spelled correctly.
- Tell students that they can use the finished text as a model to write their own recount. (See Day Five activities.)

A Visit to the Zoo

Last week our class went to the zoo. First we walked to the big cat enclosure, where we saw lions sleeping in the sun. One lion was chasing another lion. Then we hopped on the zoo train for a tour of the zoo. From the zoo train we watched a rhino plodding along beside us. He grunted as we went by. We looked at many different animals, but we
all liked the monkeys the best. They chatted to each other, climbed up ropes, smacked their heads with their fists, and flipped over on a swing. They were very funny.

Spelling Words

- Dictate the following words to students and have them write the words on their papers: ***clapped, clapping, faded, fading.*** Write the words on the board and have students self-correct their papers.
- Dictate the following sentence and have students write it on their papers: *The bird puffed its feathers, flapped its wings, and glided away.*
- Write the sentence on the board and have students self-correct their papers.
- Give pairs of students blackline master 6. While one student reads the spelling words, the other student writes them in the "First Try" column. After the student has spelled the words, the partner places a check mark next to words spelled correctly. For the second try, the partner may prompt the student by sounding out the words that were spelled incorrectly the first time. If the second spelling attempt is correct, the partner places a check mark in the "Second Try" column.

Assessment Tip: Use students' completed peer-check blackline masters to note which words gave students difficulty.

Build Fluency with Connected Text

- Have students take turns reading blackline master 5 to partners or in small groups as you monitor their reading. Call attention to the following words in the reading passage before students read it: ***begin, off, again, saw, another.***

Spelling Assessment

Use the following procedure to assess students' spelling of the Unit 22 words.

- Say each spelling word and use it in a sentence.
- Have students write the words on their papers.
- Continue with the next word on the list.
- When students have finished, collect their papers and analyze their spelling of the words.
- Use the assessment to plan small group or individual practice.

Small Group/Independent Activities

The following activities can be used to provide practice for students who need additional support.

WORD STRATEGIES

Write Have students write a recount about something they did over summer vacation or another vacation period. Remind students that recounts use past tense. Remind them of the group text on chart paper that they can use as a model. Have them exchange their writing with partners. Have the partners take turns telling each other what they like about the writing and what problems they see. Have them be sure to check for correct endings on words. Have students revise their drafts in their word study notebooks. Then have them underline all the words with ***-ed*** or ***-ing*** endings.

Word Sort Have students write the following word equations in their word study notebooks: "word + ed"; "word + consonant + ed"; "word - e + ed." Then have them sort the words on blackline masters 8 and 9 under the appropriate formulas. When students have finished sorting, have them complete another sort using the words, this time sorting according to the ending sounds: **/t/**, **/d/**, or **/ed/**.

AUTOMATICITY IN WORD RECOGNITION

Word Flash Have partners take turns flashing the word cards from blackline master 7 to each other. Then have the partners place the cards facedown in a stack. Have them take turns drawing a word, reading it, and using it in an oral sentence.

Toss and Read Write the high-frequency words randomly on a large sheet of paper and place it on the floor. Have students toss a beanbag onto the paper, read the word closest to the beanbag, and use it in a sentence.

BUILD FLUENCY WITH CONNECTED TEXT

Repeated Reading Have students practice reading blackline master 3 several times, until they feel they can read it fluently and accurately. Have them work with partners to time one another as they read the passage aloud. Have them set a goal of reading 90 words per minute.

SPELLING

Make Words Provide a set of letter cards and the week's spelling words on index cards. Have students use the letter cards to spell the words. They should check their spelling by blending the sounds and then looking at the words on the index cards.

Missing Letters Write the spelling words on the board. Without students seeing, erase one of the letters in one of the words. Have students tell you which letter is missing. Replace the letter and repeat with the other words. To make it more difficult, erase more than one letter and have students tell which letters are missing.

Teacher Tips

Home Connection

Have students take blackline master 11 home to complete with a family member. Students can also take the repeated reading passage on blackline master 3 home to share with their family.

Quick-Check

Assess students' mastery of -ed, -ing endings using the quick-check for Unit 22 in this Teacher Resource System.

ELL Support Tip

Endings such as ***-ed*** can be difficult for ELL students because of the various sounds ***-ed*** stands for. Provide an additional sort for the different sounds of ***-ed.*** For example, write "***ed*** as in ***wanted***," "***t*** as in ***sliced***," and "***d*** as in ***played***" on individual index cards. Read the words on the cards and emphasize the ending sounds. Then have students sort words under the index cards according to the sound of ***-ed.*** This activity will help students distinguish between the sounds they hear.

UNIT 22 Quick-Check: -ed, -ing endings

Student Name ______________________ Assessment Date ____________

Segmenting and Blending

Directions: Explain that these words use sounds the student has been learning. Have the student point to each word on the corresponding student sheet, segment the word parts or syllables, and blend them together. Put a ✓ if the student successfully segments and blends the word or reads it as a complete unit. If the student misses the word, record the error. **Example:** breaking

trotted		chopping		
diving		crawled		
fished		knitted		
smiled		barked		Score **/8**

Sight Words

Directions: Have the student point to the first word on the corresponding student sheet and read across the line, saying each word as quickly as possible. Put a ✓ if the student successfully reads the word and an **X** if the student hesitates more than a few seconds. If the student misses the word, record the error.

four		there		
run		just		
home		time		
high		right		
close		up		
another		down		
was		with		
were		our		Score **/16**

UNIT 23 -er, -or endings

Unit Objectives

Students will:

- Read words with -er and -or endings
- Understand that adding -er or -or to a root word changes the word's meaning
- Review r-controlled syllable patterns
- Use words with -er and -or in meaningful contexts
- Read high-frequency words another, answer, different, later, while
- Spell words with -er and -or endings: painter, writer, farmer, actor, sailor, visitor, swimmer, runner, robber
- Write a comparison using -er and/or -or words

Day 1

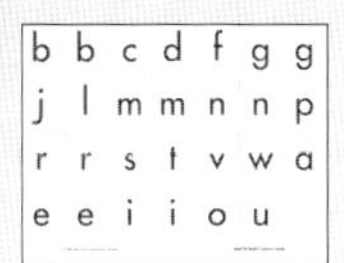

Letter Cards: **a, d, e, g, i, j, n, o, r, s**

Word Lists (BLM 2)

actor

Teacher Word Cards: **actor, cleaner, climber, dreamer, farmer, gardener, jogger, jumper, leader, painter, reader, runner, sailor, singer, speaker, teacher, writer**

Day 2

Word Lists (BLM 2)

Reading Passage 1 (BLM 3)

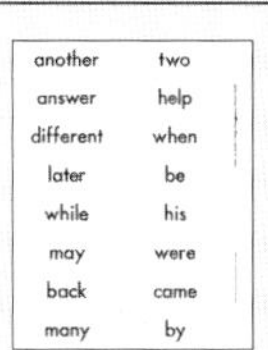

High-Frequency Word Cards for Unit 23 (BLM 7)

Day 3

Word Lists (BLM 2)

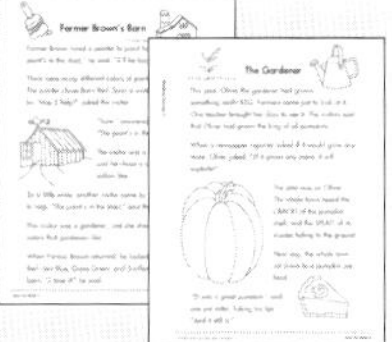

Reading Passages 1 & 2 (BLMs 3 & 4)

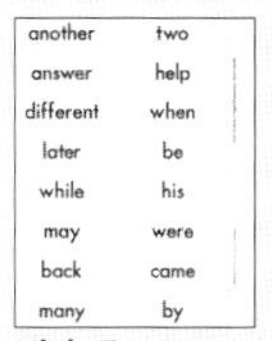

High-Frequency Word Cards for Unit 23 (BLM 7)

Day 4

Word Lists (BLM 2)

Reading Passages 1 & 3 (BLMs 3 & 5)

Spelling Peer Check (BLM 6)

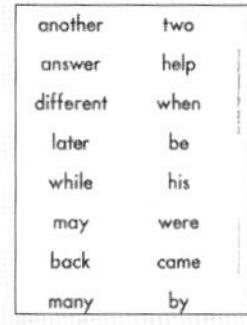

High-Frequency Word Cards for Unit 23 (BLM 7)

Day 5

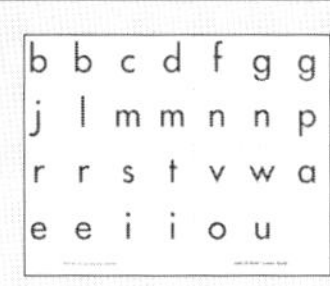

Letter Cards for Unit 23

Reading Passage 1 (BLM 3)

another two
answer help
different when
later be
while his
may were
back came
many by

High-Frequency Word Cards for Unit 23 (BLM 7)

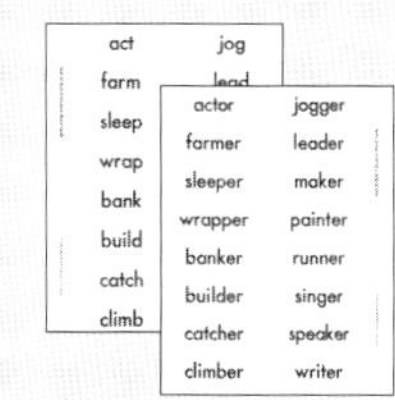

Student Word Cards (BLMs 8 & 9)

Quick-Check Student Sheet

Frieze Card

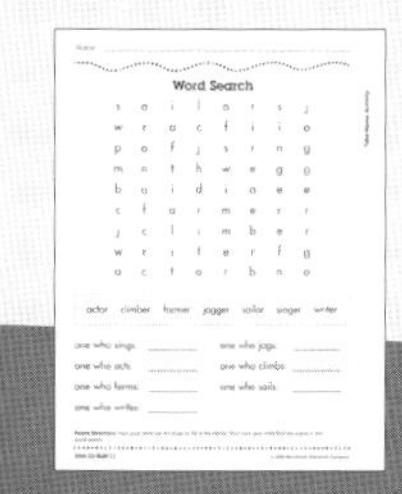

Take-Home Activity

Core Materials

All of these materials can be downloaded from http://phonicsresources.benchmarkeducation.com.

UNIT 23 -er, -or endings

DAY 1

Frieze Card

tea/cher Review r-Controlled Syllable Patterns

- Write the words ***artist, glory***, and ***hermit*** on the board and ask students to circle the r-controlled vowels in the words.
- Ask students where you should divide the word ***artist***. If they have difficulty, remind them to look for the consonants between the two vowels and divide between them (***ar/tist***). Have them tell you what the two syllable patterns are (r-controlled, closed), say what the vowel sounds are, and then blend the word.
- Repeat with the other two words.

tea/cher Introduce *-er, -or* Endings

Model

- Show students the ***-er, -or*** endings frieze card and read the words in the first column with students. Explain that these are action words or verbs.
- Tell students that someone who writes is a writer and point to the word in the second column. Explain that by adding ***-er*** to the word ***write***, we create a noun that means someone who writes. Remind students that they need to drop the final ***e*** before adding the ending.
- Point to the words in the second column of the ***-or*** ending group. Explain that we add ***-or*** instead of ***-er*** to some words. Explain that there is no rule for this and students will need to memorize the spellings of the words.

Guide

- Have students read the rest of the words on the frieze card. Then have them brainstorm other nouns that end with ***-er*** or ***-or*** and describe someone who does something.

Apply

- Give students letter cards **d, g, g, j, n, r, r, s, a, e, e, i,** and **o.** Say the word ***jogger*** and ask students what the root word is. Have them select the letters to spell the word ***jog.*** Then ask them what they remember about adding endings to words that end with one consonant. Have them double the consonant before adding ***-er.***
- Have them make the word ***singer,*** first spelling the root word and then adding the ending. Then have them spell the word ***gardener.*** Have them identify the root word, identify the two r-controlled syllables, and then add the ending.

Assessment Tip: Note which students select the correct letters. Guide students who are having difficulty.

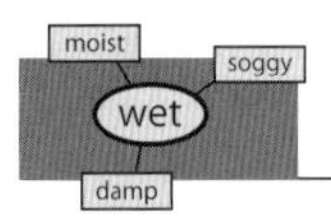

Word Study

- Provide opportunities for students to use the ***-er*** and ***-or*** words in meaningful contexts. Remind students that many words with these endings are nouns that name different things people do, such as ***builder, speaker,*** and ***worker.*** Play the game "Who Am I?" Place the following teacher word cards in a stack: **cleaner, climber, dreamer, farmer, gardener, jogger, leader, jumper, painter, reader, sailor, runner, singer, speaker, teacher, writer, actor.** Have a student draw a card and read it without the rest of the group seeing.

- Have students ask yes/no questions to find clues to the word. Students must try to guess the word before they use up twenty questions. For example, students might ask questions such as these: *Do you work outside?* (no) *Do you work with people?* (yes) *Do you use words in your work?* (yes) *Are you a writer?* (no) *Do you work with children?* (yes) *Are you a teacher?* (yes)

P+ am Blend

- Write the word ***reader*** on the board and model blending the sounds to read the word. Then have students blend it with you.
- Give students the Day One word list from blackline master 2. Have them point to and read the first word on the list.
- Have students independently read the remaining words for Day One. If students need support, guide them as they read some or all of the words on the list before having them read the words independently.

Spelling Words: *painter, writer, farmer*

Model

- Make a two-column spelling chart on chart paper. Label the first column "Root Word" and the second column "Word Plus Ending." Tell students that they will be spelling words with ***-er*** and ***-or*** endings. As you work through the unit, you can continue to add the spelling words to the chart and have students use the chart to check their spelling of the words.
- Say the word ***painter*** and model identifying the root of the word and then adding the ending.
- **Think Aloud:** *The root of* **painter** *is* **paint.** *This word has a long* **a** *vowel digraph and ends with a consonant blend. I can write this word and then add the* **-ed** *ending.*

Guide

- Say the word ***writer.*** Have students tell you how to spell the root word. Remind them of the final ***e*** and ask what you need to do when you add the ending.
- Repeat with the word ***farmer,*** having students first identify the root with the r-controlled vowel.

Apply

- Have students practice writing each of the words in their word study notebooks. Have them write a sentence for each of the words.

Our Spelling Words

Root Word	Word Plus Ending
paint	painter
write	writer
farm	farmer
act	actor
sail	sailor
visit	visitor
swim	swimmer
run	runner
rob	robber

DAY 2

Teacher Tips

Reading Strategies

If students have difficulty applying strategies for challenging words, guide them to use the following strategies:

- look at how the words start and/or end
- look for familiar patterns or parts within the words
- separate the words into syllables and decode each part
- think about what familiar words look like the challenging words
- read forward to check the context
- reread the sentence or paragraph
- mark the words, substitute synonyms, and get on with reading–ask for help later

Comprehension

Use the following questions to ensure that students have understood the passage:

- *Who did the farmer get to paint his barn?* (Level 1–facts and details)
- *What happened after the painter started painting?* (Level 2–sequence)
- *What did the barn look like when Farmer Brown came back?* (Level 3–main idea)

Fluency

Intervene if students are having difficulty reading the passage. Model how to use word and meaning strategies to problem-solve the words. After students have had a chance to read the passage silently, have them read it aloud for fluency. Model fluent reading of the passage. For students who struggle, you may want to read the passage a second time and have them echo-read along with you.

P+am Blend

- Have students blend the words on the word list for Day Two, using the procedure for blending from Day One.

Develop Automaticity in Word Recognition

- Circle the following words on the overhead transparency: ***another, answer(ed), different, later, while.***
- Tell students that practicing these words will help them recognize the words automatically so they can read more fluently. Explain that students can sound out some of these words, but they will read more quickly if they don't have to stop and sound out the words each time they see them.
- Read each word. Point out that ***another*** and ***different*** have three syllables. Point out the silent ***w*** in the word ***answered.*** Have students read aloud with you the sentences in the passage that contain the words. Then have them write the words in their word study notebooks.
- Give students a copy of blackline master 7. Point out the words from this lesson as well as other words they have learned previously. Have them cut out the words, store them in an envelope, and use them for practice activities.

Build Fluency with Connected Text

Model

- Begin reading aloud the passage on the overhead transparency. Stop when you come to the word ***paint's.***
- **Think Aloud:** *This apostrophe is a bit confusing. I know it can show ownership or stand for a missing letter in a contraction. What contraction could it be? Let me read ahead and see if that helps. Oh, now I know. The apostrophe shows it is a contraction and it means that the sentence is* **The paint is in the shed.** *That makes sense.*
- Stop at the word ***visitor*** and model recognizing the root word and the ***-or*** ending.
- **Think Aloud:** *I see an* **-or** *ending on this word. The root of the word is* **visit.** *Because the* **-or** *ending has been added, the word means* someone who visits.

Guide

- Continue reading and stop at other words in the passage. Guide students as they read the words.

Apply

- Have students take turns reading blackline master 3 to partners or in small groups as you monitor their reading. Use the teacher tips to check comprehension and fluency.

Spelling Words: *actor, sailor, visitor*

- Have students practice writing the spelling words from Day One in their word study notebooks. Have them refer to words on the spelling chart to check their spelling.
- Introduce the Day Two spelling words. Follow the format for Day One as you model identifying the root word and then adding the ending. Point out that these words end with the ***-or*** ending.
- Have students practice writing each of the words in their word study notebooks. Have them write a sentence for each of the words.

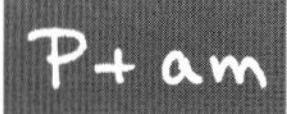

Blend

- Have students blend the words on the word list for Day Three, using the procedure for blending from Day One.

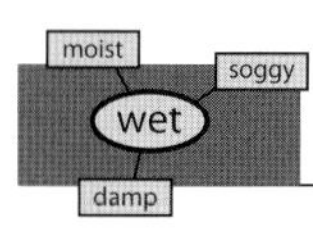

Develop Word Meanings

- Expand students' meaning base for selected root words used in this unit. Create a word web on the board and write one of the root words in the center circle. Model brainstorming other forms of this word and recording them in a web. (See the example word web for the word ***farm*** below.)
- Write a sentence for each form of the word under each word in the web and read it aloud.
- Have students work in small groups or with a partner to create word webs for one or more of the following words: ***play*** (***player, played, playback, play-by-play, playing field, playhouse***), ***sleep*** (***sleeping, sleeper, sleep in, sleepless, sleep out, sleepyhead, sleepwalk***), ***read*** (***reading, reader, read between the lines, readable, reading desk, read out***), ***work*** (***worker, working, worked, workload, work of art, workday, workplace, workshop, workroom, workout***). Encourage students to include idioms when they can.

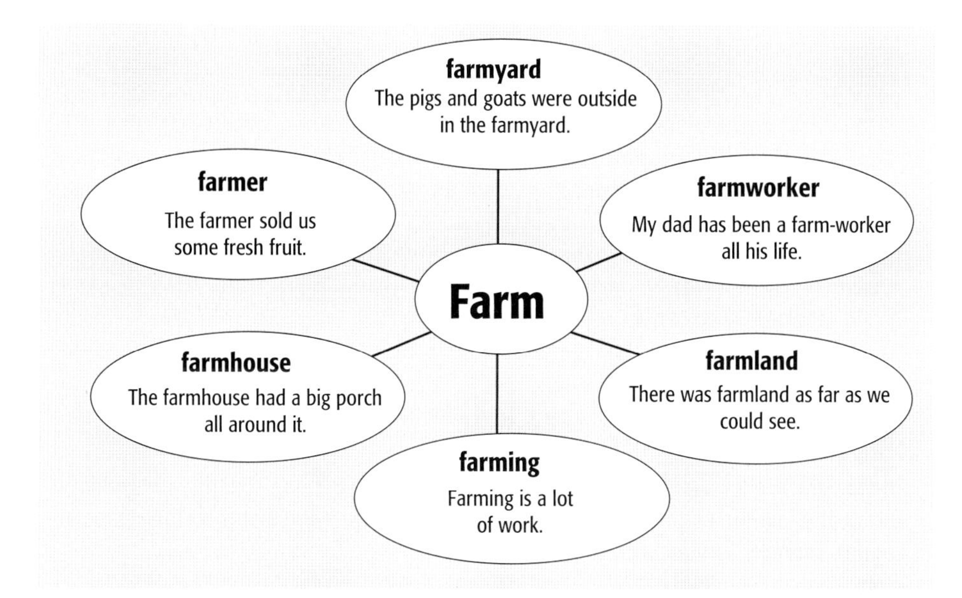

Spelling Words: *swimmer, runner, robber*

- Introduce the Day Three spelling words. Follow the format for Day One as you model writing the root word and then add the ending. Point out that to keep the closed syllable, you need to double the consonant.
- Have students practice writing each of the words in their word study notebooks. Have them write a sentence for each of the words.

Build Fluency with Connected Text

- Have students read blackline master 4 to partners or in small groups as you monitor their reading. Call attention to the following words in the reading passage before students read it: ***asked, big, grow, next, really, something, still.***

Teacher Tips

Develop Automaticity in Word Recognition

Have students practice writing the words ***another, answer, different, later***, and ***while*** in their word study notebooks. Have them use the high-frequency word cards from blackline master 7 as models. Then have them turn over the word cards and try writing the words without looking at the cards. Have them turn the cards back over to check their spelling.

Repeated Reading

Have students practice repeated readings of blackline master 3 to develop fluency.

DAY 4

Teacher Tips

Other -er Words

Tell students that adding an ***-er*** ending to a word doesn't always produce a noun naming someone who does something. Show them the words ***wrap*** and ***close*** and use the words in oral sentences. Then add ***-er*** endings and use the words in oral sentences. Explain that ***wrapper*** is a noun and that ***closer*** is an adverb (a word that tells *how*).

Develop Automaticity in Word Recognition

Have students work in pairs to find as many of the high-frequency words as they can in a book they are reading in the classroom. Have them write the words they find on self-stick notes, and place the notes at the tops of pages. After a set time–ten minutes, perhaps–have students count the number of words they found and see which words were most common in the books they looked at.

Repeated Reading

Have students practice repeated readings of blackline master 3 to develop fluency.

Blend

- Have students blend the words on the word list for Day Four, using the procedure for blending from Day One.

Write

- Tell students that as a group you will write a comparison between two types of jobs. Ask students to brainstorm ideas for the types of jobs and record these in a word web or in a list. Ask students to choose two jobs that use an ***-er*** or an ***-or*** ending in their names.
- Create a Venn diagram on the board and have students brainstorm things the two jobs have in common and things that are different.
- Ask them what the first thing is that they want to say about the jobs. Remind them that the first sentence should let the reader know what the comparison is about. Record the first sentence on chart paper.
- Have students discuss what to say next, and then tell you what to write. Guide them as needed and record their sentences.
- Read the comparison aloud, and have students check to see if they need to fix any problems.
- Have students identify any words with ***-er*** and ***-or*** endings used in the comparison.
- Tell students that they can use this comparison as a model to write their own comparison. (See Day Five activities.)

How Is a Painter Like a Writer?

Painters and writers are alike in some ways. Both are kinds of artists. The writer paints pictures in our minds with words, and the painter paints pictures on canvas with paint. The writer works at a computer, while the painter works in front of a canvas. Both the painter and the writer need to have an idea for a story or a picture before they begin. Both earn a living by selling their ideas and images to people.

Spelling Words

- Provide practice for students in segmenting words and associating sounds with spellings. Dictate the following words to students and have them write the words on their papers: ***reader, worker, builder, actor***.
- Write the words on the board and have students self-correct their papers.
- Dictate the following sentence and have students write it on their papers: *The painter asked the actor if she was a good reader.*
- Write the sentence on the board and have students self-correct their papers.
- Give pairs of students blackline master 6. While one student reads the spelling words, the other student writes them in the "First Try" column. After the student has spelled the words, the partner places a check mark next to words spelled correctly. For the second try, the partner may prompt the student by sounding out the words that were spelled incorrectly the first time. If the second spelling attempt is correct, the partner places a check mark in the "Second Try" column.

Assessment Tip: Use students' completed peer-check blackline masters to note which words gave students difficulty.

Build Fluency with Connected Text

- Have students take turns reading blackline master 5 to partners or in small groups as you monitor their reading. Call attention to the following words in the reading passage before students read it: ***because, house, Miss, never, soon.***

Spelling Assessment

Use the following procedure to assess students' spelling of the Unit Twenty-Three words.
- Say each spelling word and use it in a sentence.
- Have students write the words on their papers.
- Continue with the next word on the list.
- When students have finished, collect their papers and analyze their spelling of the words.
- Use the assessment to plan small group or individual practice.

Small Group/Independent Activities

The following activities can be used to provide practice for students who need additional support.

WORD STRATEGIES

Write Have students write a draft of a paragraph that compares two different jobs that people can do. Make sure they choose a job whose name ends in ***-er*** or ***-or***. When the draft is completed, have them each read the paragraph to a partner and have the partner tell what is good about the piece and what could be changed.

Word Play Have students work in pairs and use the student word cards from blackline masters 8 and 9 to play Concentration. Have them spread the cards facedown on a table or the floor and take turns turning over two cards, reading them, and deciding whether they make a pair. If the first student's cards are not a pair, the cards are turned facedown again and the other student takes a turn.

AUTOMATICITY IN WORD RECOGNITION

Find the Word Give students a newspaper page and one or more of the word cards from blackline master 7. Have them search the page to find and circle the word(s). Have them use a different color crayon for each word if they are looking for more than one word.

Deal the Words Place students in small groups and give each group a set of words from blackline master 7. Choose one student in each group to be the dealer and have him/her give a high-frequency word card to each of the other members of the group. Each student reads his/her high-frequency word and if correct, writes it in his/her word study notebook. After all students have read their words, a new dealer hands out the next round of word cards.

BUILD FLUENCY WITH CONNECTED TEXT

Repeated Reading Have students practice reading blackline master 3 several times, until they feel they can read it fluently and accurately. Have them work with partners to time one another as they read the passage aloud. Have them set a goal of reading 90 words per minute.

SPELLING

Make Words Provide a set of letter cards and the week's spelling words on index cards. Have students use the letter cards to spell the words. They should check their spelling by blending the sounds and then looking at the words on the index cards.

Look, Cover, Say, Write Have students who are having difficulty with the spelling words look carefully at one of the words and then say it. Ask them to cover the word and write it without looking at the model. Have them uncover the word and check the spelling. Have them repeat with other words on the spelling list.

Teacher Tips

Home Connection

Have students take blackline master 11 home to complete with a family member. Students can also take the repeated reading passage on blackline master 3 home to share with their family.

Quick-Check

Assess students' mastery of -er and -or endings using the quick-check for Unit Twenty-Three in this Teacher Resource System.

ELL Support Tip

Monitor your speech when teaching ELL students and make sure you are not speaking too quickly. Do not make dramatic changes, but think about the speed, pronunciation, and how words are run together in English. When saying and writing endings, make sure you are clear so students can hear them correctly.

UNIT 23 Quick-Check: -er, -or endings

Student Name ________________________________ Assessment Date ____________

Segmenting and Blending

Directions: Explain that these words use sounds the student has been learning. Have the student point to each word on the corresponding student sheet, segment the word parts or syllables, and blend them together. Put a ✓ if the student successfully segments and blends the word or reads it as a complete unit. If the student misses the word, record the error.
Example: rancher

author		trimmer		
barber		pastor		
donor		diver		
settler		janitor		Score **/8**

Sight Words

Directions: Have the student point to the first word on the corresponding student sheet and read across the line, saying each word as quickly as possible. Put a ✓ if the student successfully reads the word and an **X** if the student hesitates more than a few seconds. If the student misses the word, record the error.

another		two		
answer		help		
different		when		
later		be		
while		his		
may		were		
back		came		
many		by		Score **/16**

UNIT 24 Comparatives

Unit Objectives

Students will:

- Read and write comparatives
- Add endings to a word to change its meaning
- Change spellings of root words before adding -er or -est
- Review consonant + le, al, and el syllable patterns
- Sort words according to endings
- Read high-frequency words animal, both, talk, those, thought, walk
- Spell comparative words: rounder, smoother, lighter, funniest, earliest, prettiest, bigger, sadder, hottest
- Write a paragraph using comparative language

Day 1

Letter Cards:
a, c, d, d, e, i, l, m, n, o, r, s, t, w

Word Lists
(BLM 2)

bigger

Teacher Word Cards:
bigger, busiest, funnier, hotter, largest, nicest, oldest, prettiest, saddest, safer, thicker, warmest

Day 2

Word Lists
(BLM 2)

Reading Passage 1
(BLM 3)

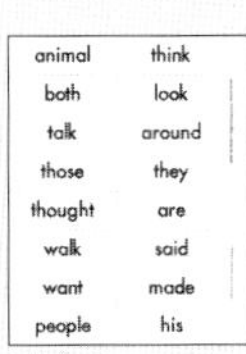

High-Frequency Word Cards for Unit 24 (BLM 7)

Day 3

Word Lists
(BLM 2)

Reading Passages 1 & 2
(BLMs 3 & 4)

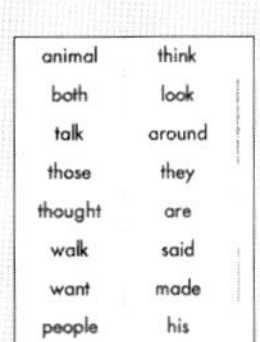

High-Frequency Word Cards for Unit 24 (BLM 7)

Day 4

Word Lists
(BLM 2)

Reading Passages 1 & 3
(BLMs 3 & 5)

Spelling Peer Check
(BLM 6)

High-Frequency Word Cards for Unit 24 (BLM 7)

Day 5

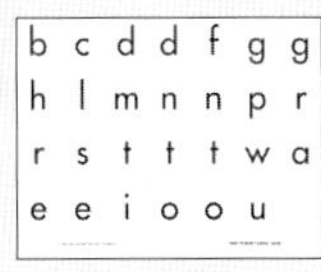

Letter Cards for Unit 24

Reading Passage 1
(BLM 3)

High-Frequency Word Cards for Unit 24 (BLM 7)

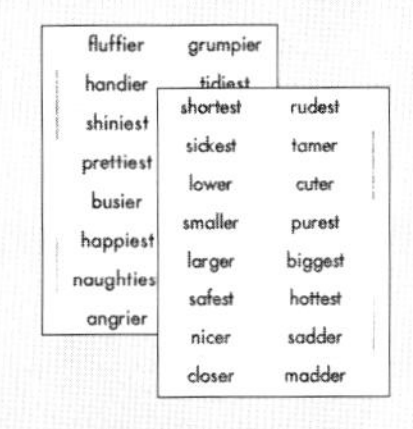

Student Word Cards
(BLMs 8 & 9)

Quick-Check Student Sheet

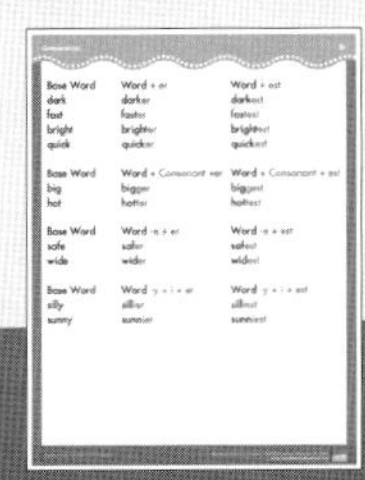

Frieze Card

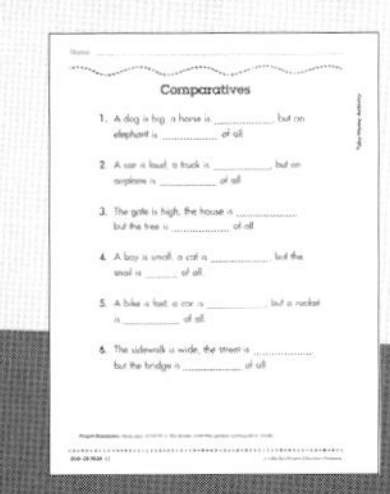

Take-Home Activity

Core Materials

All of these materials can be downloaded from http://phonicsresources.benchmarkeducation.com.

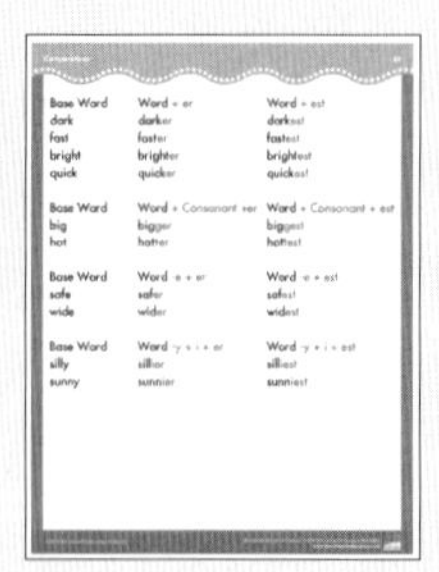
Frieze Card

tea/cher

Review Consonant + *le, al, el* Syllable Patterns

- Say the word ***marble*** and ask students what sound they hear at the end. Ask them what spelling patterns they remember for the **/l/** sound at the end of the word. List ***le, al,*** and ***el*** as students tell you the patterns.
- Ask students to choose the spelling pattern and write the word with the pattern. Ask them if the word looks right.
- Repeat with the words ***needle, squiggle, hospital, pedal,*** and ***nickel.***

tea/cher

Introduce Comparatives

Model

- Show students two pens of different lengths. Ask them which pen is longer and which pen is shorter.
- Add another pen of a different length and ask which pen is now the longest and which one is the shortest.
- Explain that we use an ***-er*** ending when we want to compare two things and an ***-est*** ending when we want to compare three or more things.

Guide

- Show students the comparatives frieze card. Read the words across each row with them. Point out that the ***y*** in words like ***silly*** and ***sunny*** is changed to ***i*** before adding the endings ***-er*** or ***-est***, and that the ***e*** in words like ***safe*** is dropped before adding the endings.
- Point to different words on the frieze card and have students use the words in oral sentences.

Apply

- Give students letter cards **c, d, d, l, m, n, r, s, t, w, a, e, i,** and **o**. Say the word ***nice.*** Ask students to identify the root word and find the letters to spell it. Remind them that they need a final ***e*** for the word's VCe pattern.
- Ask students what they need to do to add the ending ***-er.*** Have them take away the final ***e*** and add the ending ***-er.***
- Have students change the word back to ***nice*** by taking away the ***-er*** ending and adding a final ***e.*** Have them change the word ***nice*** to ***nicest*** by taking away the final ***e*** and adding the ending ***-est.***
- Say the word ***madder*** and ask students to identify the root word and find the letters to spell it. Ask what they need to do before they add the ***-er*** ending. Have them double the consonant and add the ending. Have them explain why they need to double the consonant before adding ***-er*** (to create a closed syllable and keep the short vowel sound). Repeat with the words ***maddest, lower,*** and ***lowest.***

Assessment Tip: Note which students know when to use ***-er*** and when to use ***-est.*** Provide extra practice for students having difficulty.

Word Study

- Place the following teacher word cards in a pocket chart: **largest, nicest, safer, thicker, oldest, warmest, funnier, prettiest, busiest, saddest, hotter, bigger.** Read each word with students.
- Ask students how you could sort the words into groups. One way they might suggest is to sort them by ***-er*** and ***-est*** endings.

- Have students look closely at the root word for each word and decide whether it is changed when the ending is added. Then have students help you group the words according to those that just add the ending to the root word, those that drop the ***e*** before adding the ending, those that change ***y*** to ***i*** before adding the ending, and those that double the consonant before adding the ending.

Blend

- Write the word ***poorest*** on the board. Point out that the ***-est*** ending added to ***poor*** makes a second syllable. Model blending the sounds in the syllables to read the word. Then have students blend them with you.
- Give students the Day One word list from blackline master 2. Have them point to the first word on the list and read the word.
- Have students independently read the remaining words for Day One. If students need support, guide them as they read some or all of the words on the list before having them read independently.

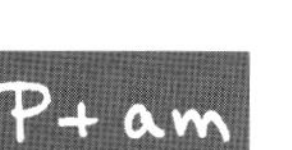

Spelling Words: *rounder, smoother, lighter*

Model

- Make a two-column spelling chart on chart paper labeled "Root Word" and "Word Plus Ending." As you work through the unit, continue to add the spelling words to the chart, and have students use the chart to check their spelling.
- Say the word ***rounder.*** Model spelling it and writing it on the chart.
- **Think Aloud:** *The root word of* **rounder** *is* **round.** *I hear* **/ow/** *in the middle and I remember that this sound in the word* **round** *is spelled* **ou. Round** *ends with a consonant blend so I don't need to double the consonant when I add the ending* **-er.**

Guide

- Say the word ***smoother.*** Have students tell you how to spell the root word and what to do when adding the ending.
- Repeat with the word ***lighter.***

Apply

- Have students practice writing each of the words in their word study notebooks. Have them write a sentence for each of the words. Have them underline the root word and circle the ***-er*** and ***-est*** endings.

Our Spelling Words

Root Word	Word Plus Ending
round	rounder
smooth	smoother
light	lighter
funny	funniest
early	earliest
pretty	prettiest
big	bigger
sad	sadder
hot	hottest

DAY 2

Teacher Tips

Reading Strategies

If students have difficulty applying strategies for challenging words, guide them to use the following strategies:

- look at how the words start and/or end
- look for familiar patterns or parts within the words
- separate the words into syllables and decode each part
- think about what familiar words look like the difficult words
- read forward to check the context
- reread the sentence or paragraph
- mark the words, substitute synonyms, and get on with reading–ask for help later

Comprehension

Use the following questions to ensure that students have understood the passage:

- *How did Squirrel describe his tail?* (Level 1–facts and details)
- *How are Squirrel's, Monkey's, and Peacock's tails different?* (Level 2–compare/contrast)
- *Why didn't the animals want to look at Anaconda's tail?* (Level 3–draw conclusions)

Fluency

Intervene if students are having difficulty reading the passage. Model how to use word and meaning strategies to problem-solve the words. After students have had a chance to read the passage silently, have them read it aloud for fluency. Model fluent reading of the passage. For students who struggle, you may want to read the passage a second time and have them echo-read along with you.

P+am Blend

- Have students blend the words on the word list for Day Two, using the procedure for blending from Day One.

Develop Automaticity in Word Recognition

- Circle the following words on the overhead transparency: ***animal(s), both, talk(ing), those, thought, walk(ed).***
- Tell students that practicing these words will help them recognize the words automatically so they can read more fluently. Explain that students can sound out some of these words, but they will read more quickly if they don't have to stop and sound out the words each time they see them.
- Read each word. Point out that the ***th*** digraph in ***thought*** and ***both*** is pronounced differently from the ***th*** digraph in ***those.***
- Have students read aloud with you the sentences in the passage that contain the words. Then have them write the words in their word study notebooks.
- Give students a copy of blackline master 7. Point out the words from this lesson as well as other words they have learned previously. Have them cut out the words, store them in an envelope, and use them for practice activities.

Build Fluency with Connected Text

Model

- Read aloud the passage on the overhead transparency, stopping at the word ***cleverest.***
- **Think Aloud:** *This word looks hard but I can break it into syllables. I see the ending* **-est.** *I first try to divide the root word before the* **v: /klē/ /vûr/**. *No, that's not right. I'll try dividing after the* **v: /clev/ /ûr/, cleverest.** *Yes, that sounds right.*
- Read on and point out the word ***fluffier.***
- **Think Aloud:** *This word has an* **-er** *ending because it's comparing two things. The writer is comparing the squirrel's tail after he fluffed it up to his tail before he fluffed it up.*

Guide

- Continue reading and stop at other words in the passage. Guide students as they read the words. Use the teacher tips to check comprehension and fluency.

Apply

- Have students take turns reading blackline master 3 to partners or in small groups as you monitor their reading.

Spelling Words: *funniest, earliest, prettiest*

- Have students practice writing the spelling words from Day One in their word study notebooks.
- Introduce the Day Two spelling words. Follow the format for Day One, guiding students as they identify the root words. Point out that each root word ends with a ***y*** that needs to be changed to ***i*** before adding an ending.
- Have students practice writing each of the words in their word study notebooks. Have them circle the endings and then write a sentence for each of the words.

Blend

- Have students blend the words on the word list for Day Three, using the procedure for blending from Day One.

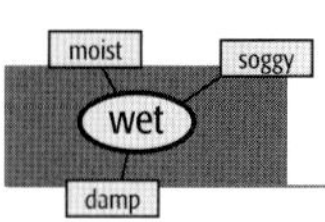

Develop Word Meanings

- Write the following phrase on the board: *slower than a snail.* Ask students what they picture in their heads when they think of how a snail moves. Explain that the phrase describes how something moves by comparing it to how a snail moves. The writer wants the reader to picture something moving very slowly.
- Write this sentence on the board: *The old, battered truck was slower than a snail as it inched up the steep hill.* Read the sentence with students and have them describe how they picture the truck in their minds.
- Write the following phrase on the board: *busier than an ant.* Pair students and have them think of a sentence that uses the comparison. Call the pairs together and have them share their sentences. As each pair reads its sentence, have the rest of the group try to picture what the sentence is describing. Have students tell which comparisons they liked best and why.
- Repeat with these phrases: *softer than a cloud; brighter than the sun; darker than the night.*

Spelling Words: *bigger, sadder, hottest*

- Have students practice writing the spelling words from Day One and Day Two in their word study notebooks.
- Introduce the Day Three spelling words. Follow the format for Day One as you guide students to identify the root word and then decide if the final consonant needs to be doubled before adding the ending.
- Have students practice writing each of the words in their word study notebooks. Have them write a sentence for each of the words.

Build Fluency with Connected Text

- Have students read blackline master 4 to partners or in small groups as you monitor their reading. Call attention to the following words in the reading passage before students read it: ***animal(s), earth, leave(s), night, often, plant(s).***

Teacher Tips

More with Comparative Phrases

Extend the activity by having students think of words that could complete the following phrases:
taller than ________;
faster than ________;
wider than ________;
lighter than ________;
deeper than ________;
fresher than ________;
meaner than ________;
prettier than ________.

Develop Automaticity in Word Recognition

Write the high-frequency words ***animal, both, talk, those, thought,*** and ***walk*** on the board. Focus on one word at a time and have students spell the word as you point to each letter. Then erase the word, say it, and have students write it in their word study notebooks. Rewrite the word on the board and have students check their spelling.

Repeated Reading

Have students practice repeated readings of blackline master 3 to develop fluency.

DAY 4

Teacher Tips

Develop Automaticity in Word Recognition

Have students create a 3 X 3 grid on a sheet of paper. Have them write high-frequency words from blackline master 7 in the squares. Using one set of word cards, draw a word and read it. If a student has the word on his/her paper, he/she can cover it with a marker. The first student to cover all the squares on his or her grid wins.

Repeated Reading

Have students practice repeated readings of blackline master 3 to develop fluency.

Blend

- Have students blend the words on the word list for Day Four, using the procedure for blending from Day One.

Write

- Tell students that as a group you will write a descriptive paragraph that tells how a tiger is different from a cat. Have students brainstorm ways that the two animals are different. Record their ideas on a list.
- Model writing an opening sentence and explain that this tells the reader what the paragraph is about.
- Ask students what they want to say first and record it on the board. Continue asking students for their ideas and record their sentences.
- Read the text aloud, and have students check to see if they need to fix any problems with it.
- Have students identify the words with the ending ***-er***. Have them tell you if the words are spelled correctly.
- Tell students that they can use the finished text as a model to write their own paragraphs. (See Day Five activities.)

A Tiger and a House Cat

How is a tiger different from a house cat? One difference is that a tiger is bigger and taller than a cat. It also has longer legs and a longer tail. A tiger makes a louder noise than a cat does. Both cats and tigers have sharp teeth, but a tiger's teeth are sharper. A tiger's hair is rougher, while a cat's hair is fluffier and smoother. The tiger and the house cat may be different in many ways, but they are both part of the cat family.

Spelling Words

- Provide practice for students in segmenting words and associating sounds with spellings. Dictate the following words to students and have them write the words on their papers: ***shiny, shinier, shiniest; tall, taller, tallest.***
- Write the words on the board and have students self-correct their papers.
- Dictate the following sentence and have students write it on their papers: *Ron is the tallest and quickest of the boys, while Steve is the oldest.*
- Write the sentence on the board and have students self-correct their papers.
- Give pairs of students blackline master 6. While one student reads the spelling words, the other student writes them in the "First Try" column. After the student has spelled the words, the partner places a check mark next to words spelled correctly. For the second try, the partner may prompt the student by sounding out the words that were spelled incorrectly the first time. If the second spelling attempt is correct, the partner places a check mark in the "Second Try" column.

Assessment Tip: Use students' completed peer-check blackline masters to note which words gave students difficulty.

Build Fluency with Connected Text

- Have students take turns reading blackline master 5 to partners or in small groups as you monitor their reading. Call attention to the following words in the reading passage before students read it: ***even, found, house, keep, life, open(ed), world.***

Spelling Assessment

Use the following procedure to assess students' spelling of the Unit Twenty-Four words.

- Say each spelling word and use it in a sentence.
- Have students write the words on their papers.
- Continue with the next word on the list.
- When students have finished, collect their papers and analyze their spelling of the words.
- Use the assessment to plan small group or individual practice.

Small Group/Independent Activities

The following activities can be used to provide practice for students who need additional support.

WORD STRATEGIES

Write Have students select two objects, people, or animals and write a paragraph telling how one is different from the other. Have them write a draft in their word study notebooks. After they have written the paragraph, have them check it for spelling and grammar. Have them circle any comparative words they used.

Word Sort Write the following word equations on small paper bags: "word + er/est"; "word + consonant + er/est"; "word - e + er/est". Have students sort the words from blackline masters 8 and 9 into the correct bags. When students have finished sorting, have them copy the words from their groups into their word study notebooks.

AUTOMATICITY IN WORD RECOGNITION

Write Sentences Have partners choose several words from the high-frequency words on blackline master 7 and also from blackline masters 8 and 9 to use in a sentence. Have them exchange sentences with another pair of students and have them see if they can find the words from the blackline masters.

Roll the Ball Have groups of students sit in circles with a word card from blackline master 7 faceup in front of each student. Have one student roll a ball to another student. That student must then read the word in front of the student who rolled the ball. The student who reads the word then takes a turn rolling the ball to another student.

BUILD FLUENCY WITH CONNECTED TEXT

Repeated Reading Have students practice reading blackline master 3 several times, until they feel they can read it fluently and accurately. Have them work with partners to time one another as they read the passage aloud. Have them set a goal of reading 90 words per minute.

SPELLING

Make Words Provide a set of letter cards and the week's spelling words on index cards. Have students use the letter cards to spell the words. They should check their spelling by blending the sounds and then looking at the words on the index cards.

Scrambled Words Write the following spelling words with scrambled letters on the board: ***nufniest (funniest), gergib (bigger), thoosmer (smoother), gihtler (lighter), realeist (earliest).*** Have students unscramble the words and write them in their word study notebooks.

Teacher Tips

Home Connection

Have students take blackline master 11 home to complete with a family member. Students can also take the repeated reading passage on blackline master 3 home to share with their family.

Quick-Check

Assess students' mastery of comparatives using the quick-check for Unit Twenty-Four in this Teacher Resource System.

ELL Support Tip

The passages for reading are a key component to the understanding of the skill in each lesson. These passages help build the context for your students as they learn the new skills. Point out the words you want students to listen for prior to reading the passage. As you read the passage, have them hold up their hand when they hear one of the words. On a second reading of the passage, give students a highlighter to highlight the words.

UNIT 24 Quick-Check: Comparatives

Student Name ______________________ Assessment Date ____________

Segmenting and Blending

Directions: Explain that these words use sounds the student has been learning. Have the student point to each word on the corresponding student sheet, segment the word parts or syllables, and blend them together. Put a ✓ if the student successfully segments and blends the word or reads it as a complete unit. If the student misses the word, record the error. **Example:** shrewder

fluffiest		nobler			
cuddlier		crispest			
wisest		jollier			
brighter		heaviest		Score	**/8**

Sight Words

Directions: Have the student point to the first word on the corresponding student sheet and read across the line, saying each word as quickly as possible. Put a ✓ if the student successfully reads the word and an **X** if the student hesitates more than a few seconds. If the student misses the word, record the error.

animal		think			
both		look			
talk		around			
those		they			
thought		are			
walk		said			
want		made			
people		his		Score	**/16**

UNIT 25 -y endings

Unit Objectives

Students will:

- Read words with -y endings
- Understand that adding a -y ending to a root word changes the word's meaning
- Review contractions
- Use adjectives to describe objects
- Sort words according to their meanings
- Read high-frequency words air, don't, near, thought, took, went
- Spell words with -y endings: easy, squeaky, needy, gloomy, snoopy, goofy, jerky, thirsty, wormy
- Write a descriptive passage

Day 1

Letter Cards: **a, i, l, m, o, r, s, t, t, y**

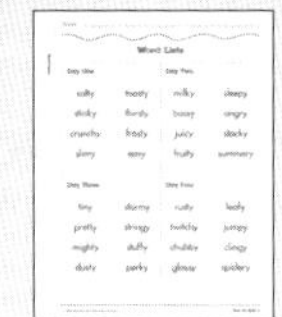

Word Lists (BLM 2)

Day 2

Word Lists (BLM 2)

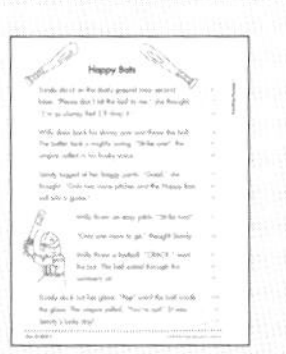

Reading Passage 1 (BLM 3)

High-Frequency Word Cards for Unit 25 (BLM 7)

Day 3

Word Lists (BLM 2)

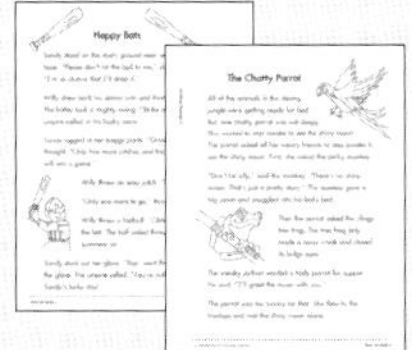

Reading Passages 1 & 2 (BLMs 3 & 4)

High-Frequency Word Cards for Unit 25 (BLM 7)

bossy

Teacher Word Cards: **bossy, chewy, crispy, crunchy, easy, frosty, fruity, funny, gloomy, gooey, goofy, hairy, messy, oily, patchy, slimy, snoopy, squeaky, stinky, tricky**

Day 4

Word Lists (BLM 2)

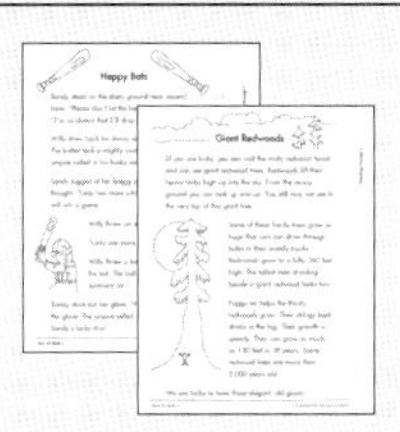

Reading Passages 1 & 3 (BLMs 3 & 5)

High-Frequency Word Cards for Unit 25 (BLM 7)

Spelling Peer Check (BLM 6)

Day 5

Letter Cards for Unit 25

Reading Passage 1 (BLM 3)

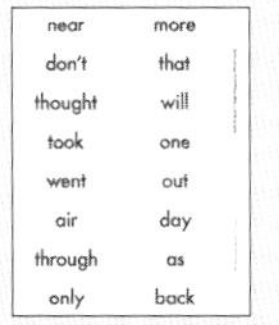

High-Frequency Word Cards for Unit 25 (BLM 7)

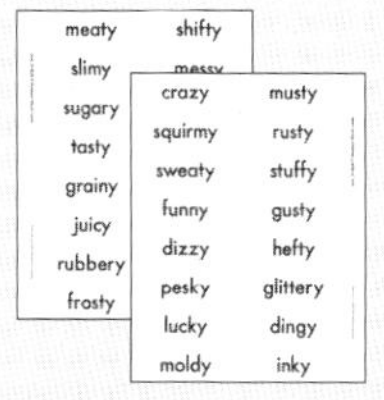

Student Word Cards (BLMs 8 & 9)

Quick-Check Student Sheet

Frieze Card

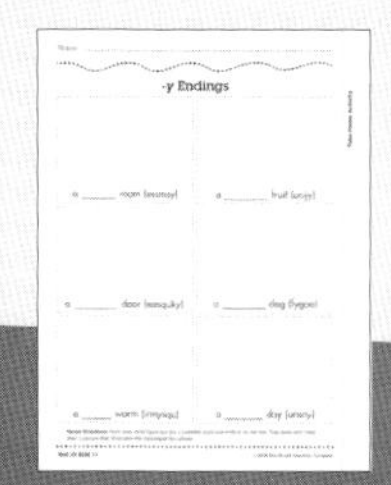

Take-Home Activity

Core Materials

All of these materials can be downloaded from http://phonicsresources.benchmarkeducation.com.

DAY 1

Review Contractions

- Write the word ***aren't*** on the board and ask students to read it. Circle the apostrophe and ask students what it stands for. If necessary, model writing ***are not*** on the board and replacing the letter ***o*** with an apostrophe.
- Ask students to name other contractions with ***not*** and record them on the board under ***aren't*** (***can't, couldn't, didn't, don't hadn't, isn't, doesn't,*** etc.).
- Point to a contraction and ask a student to read it and use it in an oral sentence.
- Repeat with contractions for ***have*** (***I've, we've, they've, you've,*** etc.), ***will*** (***I'll, she'll, he'll, they'll, that'll,*** etc.), and ***is*** (***here's, it's, he's, what's, who's,*** etc.).

Frieze Card

Introduce *-y* Endings

Model

- Show students the ***-y*** endings frieze card and point to the first word in the second column: ***grassy.*** Explain that the root of ***grassy*** is ***grass,*** which is a noun that names something. Tell students that when we add ***y*** to the word ***grass,*** we make a describing word. Provide example phrases that show how the word ***grassy*** can be used to describe something: ***a grassy field, a grassy hilltop,*** etc.

Guide

- Have students read the rest of the words on the frieze card. Point to several of the words and have students use them in oral descriptive phrases or sentences.

Apply

- Give students letter cards **l, m, r, s, t, t, a, i, o**, and **y.** Say the word ***stormy*** and ask students what the root word is. Have them select the letters to spell the word ***storm,*** reminding them that the vowel sound is r-controlled. Have them add the ***y*** to make the word ***stormy.***
- Have them make the word ***slimy***, first spelling the root word and then adding the ending. Remind them that the root word has a VCe pattern. Ask what they need to do before they add the ***y.*** Then have them spell the word ***toasty.*** Have them identify the root word with vowel digraph ***oa*** and then add the ending.

Assessment Tip: Note which students select the correct letters. Guide students who are having difficulty.

Word Study

- Ask students to think of words to describe a rabbit and record their suggestions in a word web. Ask a volunteer to circle all the describing words that end with ***-y.***
- Pair students and tell them you are going to give them one minute to list describing words for an object. Encourage them to be creative in selecting words, and explain that as long as they can tell why the adjective fits, they can keep the word on their lists.
- Say the phrase ***French fry*** and have the pairs begin listing words.

- After a minute, have the pairs count the number of adjectives they listed and the number of those adjectives that have ***-y*** endings. Have the pairs share their words. Pairs are allowed to challenge another pair's adjective. That pair must explain their choice.
- Have students describe other words and phrases—for example, a mosquito, a summer day, an elephant, and broccoli.

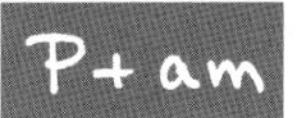

Blend

- Write the word ***stinky*** on the board and model blending the sounds to read the word. Then have students blend it with you.
- Give students the Day One word list from blackline master 2. Have them point to the first word on the list and read the word.
- Have students independently read the remaining words for Day One. If students need support, guide them as they read some or all of the words on the list before having them read them independently.

Spelling Words: *easy, squeaky, needy*

Model

- Make a two-column spelling chart on chart paper labeled "Root Word" and "Word Plus Ending." As you work through the unit, continue to add the spelling words to the chart, and have students use the chart to check their spelling.
- Say the word ***easy*** and model identifying the root of the word and then adding the ending.
- **Think Aloud:** *The root of* **easy** *is* **ease.** *This word has a long* **e** *vowel digraph and I remember that it ends with a silent* **e.** *I know that* **ee** *and* **ea** *are both long* **e** *digraphs. I will try* **ea** *and see if it looks right. Then I will add the* **-y** *ending.*

Guide

- Say the word ***squeaky.*** Have students tell you how to spell the root word. Remind them to listen for the blend at the beginning and decide which long ***e*** digraph they will use.
- Repeat with the word ***needy***, having students first identify the root word and decide on which long ***e*** digraph to use.

Apply

- Have students practice writing each of the words in their word study notebooks. Have them write a sentence for each of the words.

Our Spelling Words

Root Word	Word Plus Ending
ease	easy
squeak	squeaky
need	needy
gloom	gloomy
snoop	snoopy
goof	goofy
jerk	jerky
thirst	thirsty
worm	wormy

DAY 2

Blend

- Have students blend the words on the word list for Day Two, using the procedure for blending from Day One.

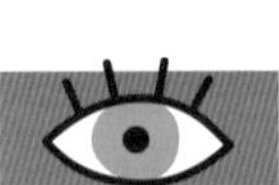

Develop Automaticity in Word Recognition

- Circle the following words on the overhead transparency: ***air, don't, near, thought, took,*** and ***went.***
- Tell students that practicing these words will help them recognize the words automatically so they can read more fluently. Explain that students can sound out some of these words, but they will read more quickly if they don't have to stop and sound out the words each time they see them.
- Read each word. Point out that ***don't*** is a contraction, and emphasize the ***ought*** pattern in the word ***thought.*** Have students read aloud with you the sentences in the passage that contain the words. Then have them write the words in their word study notebooks.
- Give students a copy of blackline master 7. Point out the words from this lesson as well as other words they have learned previously. Have them cut out the words, store them in an envelope, and use them for practice activities.

Build Fluency with Connected Text

Model

- Begin reading aloud the passage on the overhead transparency. Stop after the first paragraph and point out the words with ***-y*** endings.
- **Think Aloud:** *The word* **dusty** *is a describing word that helps me picture the playing field. The word* **clumsy** *also ends with* **-y,** *and it's how Sandy describes herself. That explains why she doesn't want the batter to hit the ball to her.*
- Model making a mistake and correcting it—for example, read **/skīny/** instead of ***skinny.***
- **Think Aloud:** *That's not right. I'll just read ahead here and see if that helps. The word ends with* **y** *and describes his arm. Oh, I see. There are two consonants, which means the word has a closed syllable with a short* **i** *sound.* **Skinny.** *Yes, that makes sense.*

Guide

- Continue reading and stop at other words in the passage. Guide students as they read the words.

Apply

- Have students take turns reading blackline master 3 to partners or in small groups as you monitor their reading. Use the teacher tips to check comprehension and fluency.

Spelling Words: *gloomy, snoopy, goofy*

- Have students practice writing the spelling words from Day One in their word study notebooks. Have them refer to words on the spelling chart to check their spelling.
- Introduce the Day Two spelling words. Say the words and ask students what vowel sound they hear and what two letters stand for the sound. Have them identify the root word in each word, and then tell you how to spell the words on the chart.
- Have students practice writing each of the words in their word study notebooks. Have them write a sentence for each of the words.

Teacher Tips

Reading Strategies

If students have difficulty applying strategies for challenging words, guide them to use the following strategies:

- look at how the words start and/or end
- look for familiar patterns or parts within the words
- separate the words into syllables and decode each part
- think about what familiar words look like the difficult words
- read forward to check the context
- reread the sentence or paragraph
- mark the words, substitute synonyms, and get on with reading—ask for help later

Comprehension

Use the following questions to ensure that students have understood the passage:

- *Why didn't Sandy want the batter to hit the ball?*
  (Level 1—facts and details)
- *What happened after the third pitch?*
  (Level 2—sequence)
- *How do you think Sandy feels about herself now?*
  (Level 3—analyze character)

Fluency

Intervene if students are having difficulty reading the passage. Model how to use word and meaning strategies to problem-solve the words. After students have had a chance to read the passage silently, have them read it aloud for fluency. Model fluent reading of the passage. For students who struggle, you may want to read the passage a second time and have them echo-read along with you.

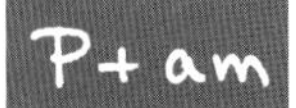

Blend

- Have students blend the words on the word list for Day Three, using the procedure for blending from Day One.

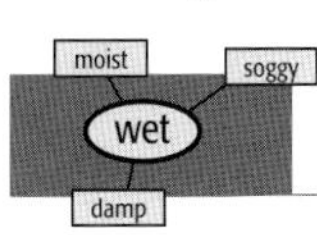

Develop Word Meanings

- Place the following teacher word cards in a pocket chart: **tricky, bossy, fruity, gooey, chewy, stinky, crispy, crunchy, funny, gloomy, goofy, messy, snoopy, squeaky, frosty, slimy, oily, patchy, hairy, easy.** Read each word with students and ensure that they know the meanings of all the words.
- Place students in small groups and have them talk about ways they could group the words.
- Call the groups together and have them arrange the words in the pocket chart. Have the other groups tell how the words were sorted.

Spelling Words: *jerky, thirsty, wormy*

- Introduce the Day Three spelling words. Follow the format for Day One as you guide students to identify the root words and the r-controlled vowel and then add the ***-y*** ending.
- Have students practice writing each of the words in their word study notebooks. Have them write a sentence for each of the words.

Build Fluency with Connected Text

- Have students read blackline master 4 to partners or in small groups as you monitor their reading. Call attention to the following words in the reading passage before students read it: ***animals, asked, don't, eyes, story, tree.***

Teacher Tips

Other Words with -y endings

Point out that not all words that end with ***y*** are formed by adding the ***-y*** ending to a root word. Write the words ***happy, pretty***, and ***tiny*** on the board. Explain that these words are also adjectives, but they don't have a root word. Have students read the words and use them in oral sentences.

Develop Automaticity in Word Recognition

Have students practice reading the words from blackline master 7 with a partner. Have them see how many words they can read correctly in twenty seconds. Have them spend extra time practicing the words they read incorrectly.

Repeated Reading

Have students practice repeated readings of blackline master 3 to develop fluency.

DAY 4

Teacher Tips

Nouns with -*y* Endings

Make sure that students understand that simply because a word ends in ***y*** does not mean it is an adjective. Write the words ***baby, lady,*** and ***story*** on the board. Have students read the words and use the words in oral sentences. Point out that the words are not adjectives but are nouns.

Develop Automaticity in Word Recognition

Have students work with a partner to find as many of the high-frequency words as they can in a book they are reading in the classroom. Have them write the words they find on self-stick notes and place the notes at the tops of pages. After a set time–for example, ten minutes–have students count the number of words they found and see which words were most common in the books they looked at.

Repeated Reading

Have students practice repeated readings of blackline master 3 to develop fluency.

P+ am Blend

- Have students blend the words on the word list for Day Four, using the procedure for blending from Day One.

Write

- Tell students that as a group you will write a description that uses adjectives, including those that have **-*y*** endings.
- Ask students for suggestions for a topic and create a list. As a group, select a topic and then brainstorm a list of descriptive words.
- Ask students how they want to start the description, reminding them that the first sentence gives the reader an idea of what the description is about.
- Have students discuss what you might say next, and then have them tell you what to write. Guide them as needed and encourage them to use adjectives when they can. Have them refer to the list the group made before writing. Record their sentences.
- Read the description aloud, and have students check to see if they need to fix any problems with it.
- Have students identify the adjectives used.
- Tell students that they can use this description as a model to write their own descriptions. (See Day Five activities.)

Picnic Lunch

For a good picnic, you need tasty but simple foods that are easy to prepare. Juicy watermelon is a good choice, although it can be a bit messy. Strawberries are less tricky to eat and not as messy to eat. You can't go wrong with a meaty sandwich piled high with crunchy lettuce, tomatoes, and pickles—just forget the stinky cheese, please! If you're thirsty, you need a frosty glass of lemonade. A few tangy, salty potato chips complete a happy, healthy summer picnic lunch.

Spelling Words

- Dictate the following words to students and have them write the words on their papers: ***bouncy, bubbly, jumpy, thirsty.*** Write the words on the board and have students self-correct their papers.
- Dictate the following sentence and have students write it on their papers: *I'm lucky that my pesky sister didn't leave her sweaty socks on my bed.*
- Write the sentence on the board and have students self-correct their papers.
- Give pairs of students blackline master 6. While one student reads the spelling words, the other student writes them in the "First Try" column. After the student has spelled the words, the partner places a check mark next to words spelled correctly. For the second try, the partner may prompt the student by sounding out the words that were spelled incorrectly the first time. If the second spelling attempt is correct, the partner places a check mark in the "Second Try" column.

Assessment Tip: Use students' completed peer-check blackline masters to note which words gave students difficulty.

Build Fluency with Connected Text

- Have students take turns reading blackline master 5 to partners or in small groups as you monitor their reading. Call attention to the following words in the reading passage before students read it: ***air, car(s), feet, grow, high, still, tree(s).***

Spelling Assessment

Use the following procedure to assess students' spelling of the Unit Twenty-Five words.
- Say each spelling word and use it in a sentence.
- Have students write the words on their papers.
- Continue with the next word on the list.
- When students have finished, collect their papers and analyze their spelling of the words.
- Use the assessment to plan small group or individual practice.

Small Group/Independent Activities

The following activities can be used to provide practice for students who need additional support.

WORD STRATEGIES

Write Have students write a description using a good selection of adjectives, including ones with ***-y*** endings. Before they begin, have them think of something they want to describe and then make a list of words that describe the topic. After they finish writing, have them underline all the adjectives they used, and circle the adjectives that end with ***y***.

Word Sorts Have students work with a partner and sort the words on blackline masters 8 and 9 any way they can. Encourage them to use the meanings of the words as they sort. One way they could sort the words is: words that are good for describing people, words that are good for describing animals, words for describing food, etc. When students have finished their sorts, have them copy the words in their word study notebooks and write why they sorted the words the way they did.

AUTOMATICITY IN WORD RECOGNITION

Climb the Steps Draw a series of steps on the board and write high-frequency words on the steps. Have students take turns seeing how high they can climb by correctly reading the words. Change the words after every few students.

In Order Have pairs of students place the word cards from blackline master 7 in alphabetical order. Remind them to look at the second and third letters of words that start with the same letter, such as ***thought*** and ***through***. Once the words are in order, have the partners alternate reading the words.

BUILD FLUENCY WITH CONNECTED TEXT

Repeated Reading Have students practice reading blackline master 3 several times, until they feel they can read it fluently and accurately. Have them work with a partner and time each other as they read the passage aloud. Have them set a goal of reading 90 words per minute.

SPELLING

Make Words Provide a set of letter cards and the week's spelling words on index cards. Have students use the letter cards to spell the words. They should check their spelling by blending the sounds and then looking at the words on the index cards.

Look, Cover, Say, Write Have students who are having difficulty with the spelling words look carefully at one of the words and then say it. Ask them to cover the word and write it without looking at the model. Have them uncover the word and check the spelling. Have them repeat with other words on the spelling list.

Teacher Tips

Home Connection

Have students take blackline master 11 home to complete with a family member. Students can also take the repeated reading passage on blackline master 3 home to share with their family.

Quick-Check

Assess students' mastery of -y endings using the quick-check for Unit Twenty-Five in this Teacher Resource System.

ELL Support Tip

During the introduction of words, the reading of the passage, or the writing portion of the lesson, ask students to raise one hand as in a cheer every time they hear ***y*** as **/ē/**. This will actively involve ELL students as they process the skill.

UNIT 25 Quick-Check: -y endings

Student Name ____________________ Assessment Date __________

Segmenting and Blending

Directions: Explain that these words use sounds the student has been learning. Have the student point to each word on the corresponding student sheet, segment the word parts or syllables, and blend them together. Put a ✓ if the student successfully segments and blends the word or reads it as a complete unit. If the student misses the word, record the error. **Example:** curly

beefy		witty		
glossy		scary		
worthy		noisy		
spicy		queasy		Score **/8**

Sight Words

Directions: Have the student point to the first word on the corresponding student sheet and read across the line, saying each word as quickly as possible. Put a ✓ if the student successfully reads the word and an **X** if the student hesitates more than a few seconds. If the student misses the word, record the error.

near		more		
don't		that		
thought		will		
took		one		
went		out		
air		day		
through		as		
only		back		Score **/16**

UNIT 26 -ly ending

Unit Objectives

Students will:

- Read words with -ly ending
- Understand that adding -ly to a base word changes the word's meaning
- Review plurals
- Use -ly adverbs to describe how something is done
- Sort words according to their meanings
- Read high-frequency words change, every, off, saw, side, start
- Spell words with -ly endings: closely, friendly, directly, gloomily, happily, angrily, quietly, safely, luckily
- Write a procedural passage

Day 1

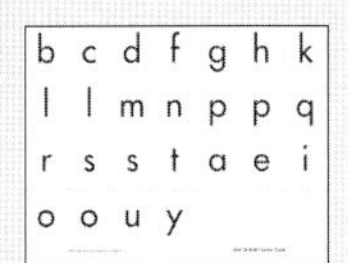

Letter Cards: **a, b, c, e, h, i, l, o, p, s, u, y**

Word Lists (BLM 2)

Day 2

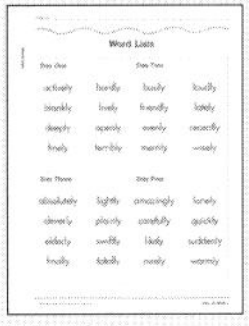

Word Lists (BLM 2)

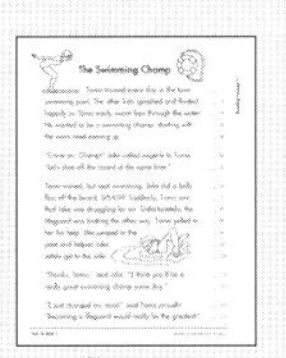

Reading Passage 1 (BLM 3)

High-Frequency Word Cards for Unit 26 (BLM 7)

Day 3

Word Lists (BLM 2)

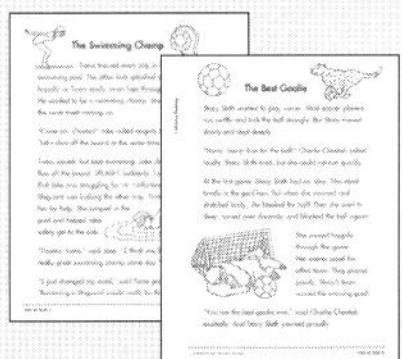

Reading Passages 1 & 2 (BLMs 3 & 4)

every help
start through
off water
saw great
side some
change would
just other
come get

High-Frequency Word Cards for Unit 26 (BLM 7)

chilly

Teacher Word Cards: **chilly, closely, easy, finally, friendly, frosty, gladly, grassy, greasy, happily, jumpy, lazily, likely, merrily, messy, nicely, stormy, thirsty**

Day 4

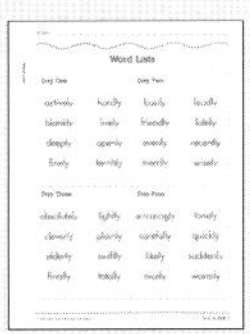

Word Lists (BLM 2)

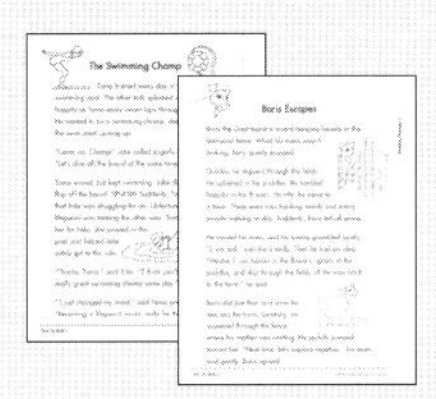

Reading Passages 1 & 3 (BLMs 3 & 5)

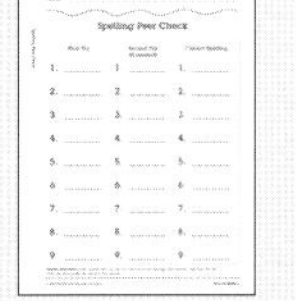

Spelling Peer Check (BLM 6)

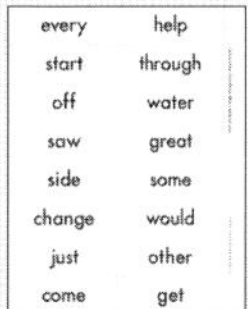

High-Frequency Word Cards for Unit 26 (BLM 7)

Day 5

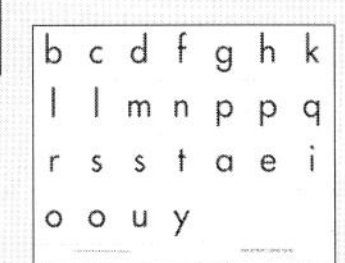

Letter Cards for Unit 26

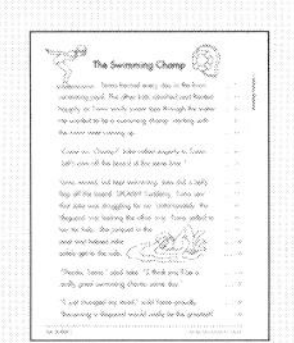

Reading Passage 1 (BLM 3)

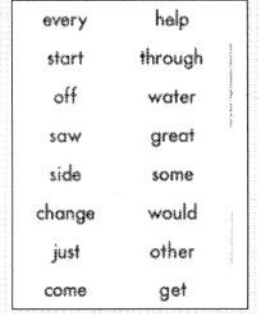

High-Frequency Word Cards for Unit 26 (BLM 7)

Student Word Cards (BLMs 8 & 9)

Quick-Check Student Sheet

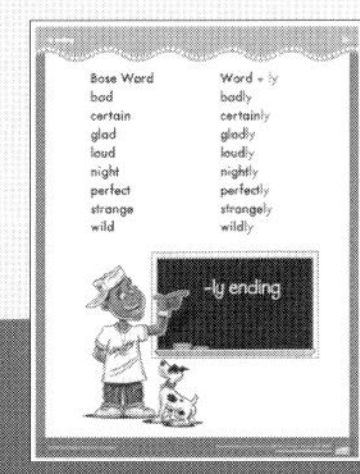

Frieze Card

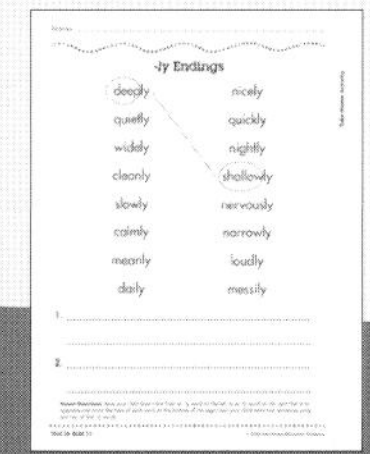

Take-Home Activity

Core Materials

All of these materials can be downloaded from http://phonicsresources.benchmarkeducation.com.

DAY 1

Frieze Card

tea/cher

Review Plurals

- Say the word ***baby*** and ask students what the rule is for pluralizing nouns that end in ***y.*** Write ***babies*** on the board.
- Ask students to name other words that change the ***y*** to ***i*** before adding ***es*** for the plural. Write the words on the board. (***puppies***, ***cherries***, ***daisies***, etc.)
- Repeat with irregular plurals (***children***, ***mice***, ***women***, ***feet***, etc.)
- Ask for volunteers to use both the singular and plural forms of nouns in oral sentences.

tea/cher

Introduce *-ly* ending

Model

- Show students the ***-ly*** ending frieze card and point to the first word in the second column, ***badly.*** Explain that the base of ***badly*** is ***bad***, which is an adjective that describes something. Tell students that when we add ***-ly*** to the word ***bad***, we make an adverb, which is a word that tells how something is done. Explain that adverbs describe verbs, adjectives, and other adverbs.
- Provide examples of phrases that show how the word ***badly*** can be used to describe something–for example, ***he behaved badly***.

Guide

- Have students read the rest of the words on the frieze card. Point to several of the words and have students use them in oral descriptive phrases or sentences.

Apply

- Give students letter cards **b**, **c**, **h**, **l**, **p**, **s**, **s**, **a**, **e**, **i**, **o**, **u**, and **y.** Say the word ***cheaply*** and ask students what the base word is. Have them select the letters to spell the word ***cheap***, reminding them that the vowel sound is a long ***e*** digraph. Have them add the ***-ly*** ending to make the word ***cheaply.***
- Have them make the word ***busily***, first spelling the base word and then adding the ending. Before adding the ***-ly*** ending, ask students what they think should be done with the ***y*** at the end of ***busy.*** Then have them spell the word ***possibly.*** Have them identify the base word, and tell them they need to drop the ***le*** before adding ***ly.***

Assessment Tip: Note which students select the correct letters. Guide students who are having difficulty making the words.

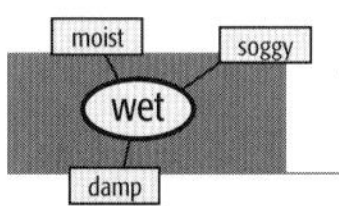

Word Study

- Give students practice using ***-ly*** adverbs in context. Have students sit in a circle with you. Say the following sentence, leaving out the verb: *The child walked ________ to school.* Ask the student next to you to repeat the sentence, supplying an adverb with an ***-ly*** ending.
- Continue around the circle, having students add different adverbs to the sentence. If a student cannot think of a word, allow time for thinking before having the group suggest a word. Then have the student repeat the sentence using the suggested word. Possible words to use in this sentence are: ***happily***, ***sadly***, ***slowly***, ***quickly***, ***proudly***, ***quietly***, ***bravely***, etc.

Blend

- Write the word ***instantly*** on the board and model blending the sounds to read the word. Then have students blend it with you.
- Give students the Day One word list from blackline master 2 and have them point to and read the first word on the list.
- Have students independently read the remaining words for Day One. If students need support, guide them to use what they know about syllable patterns as they read some or all of the words on the list before having them read them independently.

Spelling Words: *closely, friendly, really*

Model

- Make a two-column spelling chart on chart paper. Label the first column "Base Word" and the second column "Word Plus Ending." Tell students that they will be spelling words with ***-ly*** endings. As you work through the unit, continue to add the spelling words to the chart, and have students use the chart to check their spelling of the words.
- Say the word ***closely*** and model identifying the base of the word and then adding the ending.
- **Think Aloud:** *The base of* **closely** *is* **close.** *I think this word has a VCe syllable pattern. I will try* **close** *and see if it looks right. Then I will add the* **-ly** *ending.*

Guide

- Say the word ***friendly.*** Have students tell you the how to spell the base word. Remind them that the base word ***friend*** has an unusual spelling for short vowel sound **e**, so this is a good word to memorize. Then add the ***-ly*** ending. Repeat with the word ***really***, having students first identify the base word and decide on which vowel digraph to use. Point out to students that ***friendly***, like ***ugly***, is one of the few ***-ly*** words that is an adjective, not an adverb.

Apply

- Have students practice writing each of the words in their word study notebooks. Have them write a sentence for each of the words.

Our Spelling Words

Base Word	Word Plus Ending
close	closely
friend	friendly
real	really
gloomy	gloomily
happy	happily
angry	angrily
quiet	quietly
safe	safely
luck	luckily

DAY 2

Teacher Tips

Reading Strategies

If students have difficulty applying strategies for challenging words, guide them to use the following strategies:

- look at how the words start and/or end
- look for familiar patterns or parts within the words
- separate the words into syllables and decode each part
- think about what familiar words look like the difficult words
- read forward to check the context
- reread the sentence or paragraph
- mark the words, substitute synonyms, and get on with reading–ask for help later

Comprehension

Use the following questions to ensure that students have understood the passage:

- *What was Tomo training for?*
  (Level 1–facts and details)
- *What happened after Jake dove off the board?*
  (Level 2–sequence events)
- *Why did Tomo change his mind about being a swimming champ?*
  (Level 3–inference)

Fluency

Intervene if students are having difficulty reading the passage. Model how to use word and meaning strategies to problem-solve the words. After students have had a chance to read the passage silently, have them read it aloud for fluency. Model fluent reading of the passage. For students who struggle, you may want to read the passage a second time and have them echo-read along with you.

Blend

- Have students blend the words on the word list for Day Two, using the procedure for blending from Day One.

Develop Automaticity in Word Recognition

- Circle the following words on the overhead transparency: ***off***, ***saw***, ***side***, ***change(d).***
- Tell students that practicing these words will help them recognize the words automatically so they can read more fluently. Explain that students can sound out most of these words, but they will read more quickly if they don't have to stop and sound out the words each time they see them.
- Read each word. Point out that ***changed*** is the past tense of ***change*** and is made by dropping the ***e*** before adding ***ed.*** Have students read aloud with you the sentences in the passage that contain the words. Then have them write the words in their word study notebooks.
- Give students a copy of blackline master 7. Point out the words from this lesson as well as other words they have learned previously. Have them cut out the words, store them in an envelope, and use them for practice activities.

Build Fluency with Connected Text

Model

- Begin reading aloud the passage on the overhead transparency. Stop after the first paragraph and point out the words with ***-ly*** endings.
- **Think Aloud:** *The word* **happily** *is a describing word that helps me picture the way the kids were playing in the pool. The word* **easily** *also ends with* **ly**, *and it tells us how Tomo swam laps. I can see that Tomo takes his swimming seriously.*
- Model making a mistake and correcting it–for example, read ***eagle*** instead of ***eagerly.***
- **Think Aloud:** *That's not right. I'll just read ahead here and see if that helps. The word ends with* **ly** *and describes how he calls out to Tomo. Oh, I see. There's an r-controlled vowel after the long* **e** *digraph, but before the* **-ly** *ending.* **Eagerly.** *Yes, that makes sense.*

Guide

- Continue reading and stop at other words in the passage. Guide students as they read the words.

Apply

- Have students take turns reading blackline master 3 to partners or in small groups as you monitor their reading. Use the teacher tips to check comprehension and fluency.

Spelling Words: ***gloomily***, ***happily***, ***angrily***

- Have students practice writing the spelling words from Day One in their word study notebooks. Have them refer to words on the spelling chart to check their spelling.
- Introduce the Day Two spelling words. Say the words and ask students to identify the base word. Point out that the ***y*** changes to ***i*** before adding ***-ly.*** Have students tell you how to spell the words as you add them to the chart.
- Have students practice writing each of the words in their word study notebooks. Have them write a sentence for each of the words.

Blend

- Have students blend the words on the word list for Day Three, using the procedure for blending from Day One.

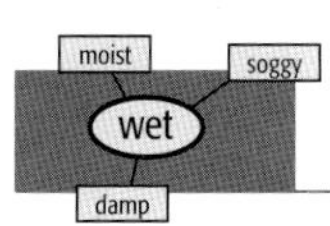

Develop Word Meanings

- Place the following teacher word cards in a pocket chart: **grassy**, **easy**, **frosty**, **chilly**, **jumpy**, **messy**, **stormy**, **thirsty**, **greasy**, **closely**, **finally**, **gladly**, **friendly**, **likely**, **nicely**, **happily**, **lazily**, **merrily**.
- Read each word with students and ensure that they know the meanings of all the words
- Place the word cards **grassy** and **gladly** next to each other in the pocket chart and ask students what is different about the way the two words end. Once students identify that one ends with ***y*** and the other with ***ly***, have students tell you which of the words you should place under ***grassy*** and which you should place under ***gladly.*** Make sure they realize that the word ***chill*** ends with two ***l***'s, and that the ending added to it to make the word ***chilly*** is ***-y*** and not ***-ly.***
- Ask students to help you sort the words in other ways. They may suggest you sort the words according to number of syllables, words whose base words end in ***e***, words that begin with digraphs or blends, those that begin with single consonants, etc.
- After sorting the word cards, give small groups of students two word cards that are adverbs and two word cards that are adjectives. Have them write group sentences and underline the words in the sentences. As a group, have them write a generalization about how the adverbs and adjectives end.

Spelling Words: *quietly, safely, luckily*

- Introduce the Day Three spelling words. Follow the format for Day One as you guide students to identify the base words and then add the ***-ly*** endings.
- Have students practice writing each of the words in their word study notebooks. Have them write a sentence for each of the words.

Build Fluency with Connected Text

- Have students read blackline master 4 to partners or in small groups as you monitor their reading. Call attention to the following high-frequency words in the reading passage before students read it: ***again***, ***idea***, ***mov(ed)***, ***play***, ***run***, ***turn(ed).***

Teacher Tips

Word Hunt

Have students find and circle words with -ly endings in the passages on blackline masters 3 and 4. Have them organize the words into categories according to what happens to the base word when the endings are added.

Develop Automaticity in Word Recognition

Draw a set of steps on the board and write the high-frequency words from blackline master 7 on the steps. Have students take turns seeing how high they can climb by reading the high-frequency words correctly. Change the high-frequency words often.

Repeated Reading

Have students practice repeated readings of blackline master 3 to develop fluency.

DAY 4

Blend

- Have students blend the words on the word list for Day Four, using the procedure for blending from Day One.

Write

- Tell students that as a group you will write a procedure that uses several adverbs, including those with ***-ly*** endings. Explain that using adverbs and adjectives in a procedural text helps make directions clearer.
- Ask students for suggestions for a topic and create a list. As a group, select a topic and then brainstorm a list of words that describes how something is done.
- Ask students how they want to start the directions. Remind them that directions are written in the order that they are to be carried out.
- Have students discuss the next step, and then tell you what to write. Guide them as needed and encourage them to use adverbs when they can. Have them refer to the list the group made before writing. Record their sentences.
- Read the set of directions aloud, and have students check to see if they need to fix any problems with them.
- Have students identify the adverbs used.
- Tell students that they can use these directions as a model to write their own directions. (See Day Five activities.)

Chocolate-Covered Marshmallows

Follow these steps to make a tasty treat:

1. Turn the heat on the stove to medium.
2. Slowly pour a bag of chocolate chips into a large pan and set it on the stove.
3. Stir the melting chocolate frequently.
4. Stab a marshmallow with a fork and carefully dip it in the melted chocolate.
5. Be sure the marshmallow is covered entirely in chocolate!
6. Place the marshmallows on a plate to cool.
7. Eat the treats when they are finally cool!

Spelling Words

- Dictate the following words to students and have them write the words on their papers: ***lightly***, ***knowingly***, ***cleverly***, ***humanly.*** Write the words on the board and have students self-correct their papers.
- Dictate the following sentence and have students write it on their papers: ***I'm finally ready to make my lunch entirely by myself.***
- Write the sentence on the board and have students self-correct their papers.
- Give pairs of students blackline master 6. While one student reads the spelling words, the other student writes them in the "First Try" column. After the student has spelled the words, the partner places a check mark next to words spelled correctly. For the second try, the partner may prompt the student by sounding out the words that were spelled incorrectly the first time. If the second spelling attempt is correct, the partner places a check mark in the "Second Try" column.

Assessment Tip: Use students' completed peer-check blackline masters to note which words gave students difficulty.

Build Fluency with Connected Text

- Have students take turns reading blackline master 5 to partners or in small groups as you monitor their reading. Call attention to the following words in the reading passage before students read it: ***car(s)***, ***found***, ***idea***, ***miss(ed)***, ***next***, ***together***, ***walk(ing).***

Teacher Tips

Nouns and Adjectives with -ly Endings

Make sure students understand that simply because a word ends in ***-ly*** does not mean it is an adverb. Write the words ***bully***, ***belly***, and ***jolly*** on the board. Have students read the words and use the words in oral sentences. Point out that the words are not adverbs but are nouns and an adjective.

Develop Automaticity in Word Recognition

Have partners flash a set of high-frequency word cards for each other to read. Words that are read incorrectly are placed in a pile and read again. Once students feel confident, have them time themselves while the partner flashes the words. Have them try to beat their own times as they read the words again.

Repeated Reading

Have students practice repeated readings of blackline master 3 to develop fluency.

Spelling Assessment

Use the following procedure to assess students' spelling of the Unit Twenty-Six words.
- Say each spelling word and use it in a sentence.
- Have students write the words on their papers.
- Continue with the next word on the list.
- When students have finished, collect their papers and analyze their spelling of the words.
- Use the assessment to plan small group or individual practice.

Small Group/Independent Activities

The following activities can be used to provide practice for students who need additional support.

WORD STRATEGIES

Write Have students write a procedural text that tells how to do or make something. Have them select something familiar such as how to make their favorite sandwich or how to play a familiar game. Encourage students to use adverbs and adjectives to make the directions more clear about things such as how long, how much, etc. Remind them that the steps in a procedural text must follow in sequential order.

Bingo Have each student divide a sheet of paper by drawing a three-row by three-column grid. Have them select words from blackline masters 8 and 9 to write in the grid. Have a student draw a student word card and read the word aloud. If students have the word on their papers, they can place a counter over the word. Continue with the next word. The first student to cover all of his or her words wins.

AUTOMATICITY IN WORD RECOGNITION

High-Frequency Word Toss Place the high-frequency word cards in cups, one per cup. Have students toss a button into a cup, take the card out of the cup and read it, and then use the word in an oral sentence.

Word Spin Have students sit in a circle with the high-frequency word cards from blackline master 7 facedown in a stack in the middle. One student spins a plastic bottle. Whomever the bottle points to selects a word card, reads the word, and uses it in an oral sentence.

BUILD FLUENCY WITH CONNECTED TEXT

Repeated Reading Have students practice reading blackline master 3 several times, until they feel they can read it fluently and accurately. Have them work with a partner to time each other as they read the passage aloud. Have them set a goal of reading 90 words per minute.

SPELLING

Make Words Provide a set of letter cards and the week's spelling words on index cards. Have students use the letter cards to spell the words. They should check their spelling by blending the sounds and then looking at the words on the index cards.

Around the Circle Have students sit in a circle. Say a spelling word and have a student say the first letter in the word. Have the next student say the next letter, and so on, until the word is spelled. Have the student who says the last letter write the word on the board.

Teacher Tips

Home Connection

Have students take blackline master 11 home to complete with a family member. Students can also take the repeated reading passage on blackline master 3 home to share with their family.

Quick-Check

Assess students' mastery of the -ly ending using the quick-check for Unit Twenty-Six in the *Teacher Resource System.*

ELL Support Tip

Use cloze activities to support ELL students' reading and language acquisition. Cloze activities will promote and support active involvement in learning oral language and help create an anxiety-free environment. There are four types of cloze activities: leave out words randomly, leave out structure words, leave out content words, or leave out letters.

UNIT 26 Quick-Check: -ly ending

Student Name ______________________ Assessment Date ____________

Segmenting and Blending

Directions: Explain that these words use sounds the student has been learning. Have the student point to each word on the corresponding student sheet, segment the word parts or syllables, and blend them together. Put a ✓ if the student successfully segments and blends the word or reads it as a complete unit. If the student misses the word, record the error.
Example: keenly

lovely		helpfully			
quaintly		idly			
bumpily		massively			
early		regally		Score	**/8**

Sight Words

Directions: Have the student point to the first word on the corresponding student sheet and read across the line, saying each word as quickly as possible. Put a ✓ if the student successfully reads the word and an **X** if the student hesitates more than a few seconds. If the student misses the word, record the error.

every		help			
start		through			
off		water			
saw		great			
side		some			
change		would			
just		other			
come		get		Score	**/16**

UNIT 27 Prefix un-

Unit Objectives

Students will:

- Read words with the prefix un-
- Understand that adding the prefix un- to a base word changes the word's meaning
- Review -er, -or, -ed, -ing endings
- Use adjectives to describe objects
- Sort words according to their meanings
- Read high-frequency words feet, mother, own, really, saw, stop, try
- Spell words with prefix un-: unfair, unhappy, unload, unfold, unafraid, unlikely
- Write a descriptive passage

Day 1

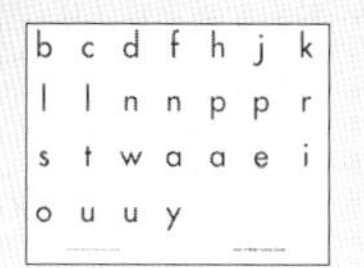

Letter Cards:
c, e, i, j, l, n, p, s, t, w, u, u

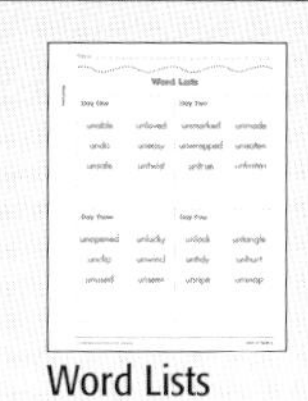

Word Lists (BLM 2)

unbalanced

Teacher Word Cards:
unbalanced, unbend, unclip, undress, unfriendly, unglue, unhealthy, unhelpful, unhinge, unready, unscrew, unsorted

Day 2

Word Lists (BLM 2)

Reading Passage 1 (BLM 3)

High-Frequency Word Cards for Unit 27 (BLM 7)

Day 3

Word Lists (BLM 2)

Reading Passages 1 & 2 (BLMs 3 & 4)

High-Frequency Word Cards for Unit 27 (BLM 7)

Day 4

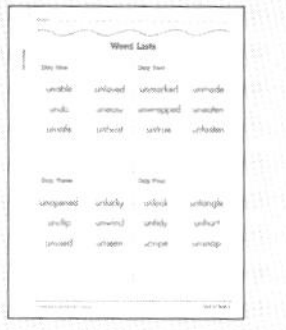

Word Lists (BLM 2)

Reading Passages 1 & 3 (BLMs 3 & 5)

High-Frequency Word Cards for Unit 27 (BLM 7)

Spelling Peer Check (BLM 6)

Day 5

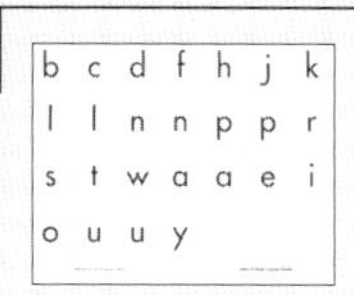

Letter Cards for Unit 27

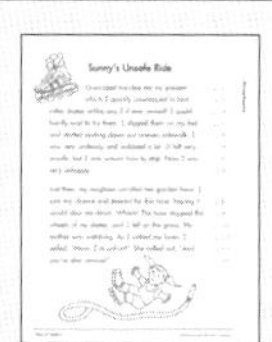

Reading Passage 1 (BLM 3)

High-Frequency Word Cards for Unit 27 (BLM 7)

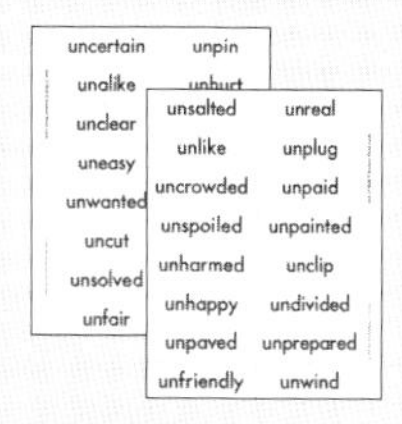

Student Word Cards (BLMs 8 & 9)

Quick-Check Student Sheet

Frieze Card

Take-Home Activity

Core Materials

All of these materials can be downloaded from http://phonicsresources.benchmarkeducation.com.

UNIT 27 Prefix un-

Frieze Card

tea/cher

Review Inflectional Endings *-er, -or, -ed, -ing*

- Write the following sentence on the board and read it: *The painter told the actor that singing helped him work harder*. Underline the words ***painter*** and ***actor*** and ask students what parts of speech these words are and what endings they have.
- Underline the word ***helped*** and ask a volunteer to circle the ending on the word. Ask students why the word has an ***-ed*** ending.
- Point out the ***-ing*** ending on ***singing*** and remind students that adding ***ing*** can change the verb ***sing*** to a noun.
- Write the following sets of words on the board and have students use the different parts of speech in oral sentences: ***work, worked, worker, working; dance, danced, dancer, dancing; visit, visited, visitor, visiting.***

tea/cher

Introduce prefix *un-*

Model

- Point to the word ***unpack*** on the frieze card. Explain that ***un-*** is a prefix, which is a group of letters that appears at the front of a word. Tell students that when we add ***un-*** to the base word ***pack,*** we make a new word that means to do the opposite of ***packing***. Provide examples to show that the word ***unpack*** is a verb that means to do the opposite of pack: *unpack my suitcase, unpack the groceries,* etc.
- Demonstrate how the prefix ***un-*** is one that can mean more than one thing. Write the word ***unkind*** on the board and explain that in this word ***un-*** means ***not,*** as in *not kind.*

Guide

- Have students read the rest of the words on the frieze card. Point to several of the words and have students use them in oral phrases or sentences.

Apply

- Give students letter cards **c, j, l, n, p, s, t, w, e, i, u,** and **u**. Say the word ***unwise*** and ask students to identify the base word. Have them select the letters to spell the word ***wise,*** reminding them that the */z/* sound is spelled with an ***s.*** Have them add the ***un-*** to make the word ***unwise.***
- Have them make the word ***unjustly,*** first spelling the base word, then adding the prefix ***un-,*** and then adding the suffix ***-ly.***
- Have them spell the word ***unclip.*** Have them identify the base word and then add the prefix.

Assessment Tip: Note which students select the correct letters. Guide students who are having difficulty.

Word Study

- Place the following teacher word cards in random order in a pocket chart: **unready, unscrew, unfriendly, undress, unhealthy, unclip, unbalanced, unhinge, unsorted, unglue, unhelpful, unbend.** Have students read each word with you.

- Tell students that you want to organize the words according to those in which ***un-*** means "not" and those that mean "do the opposite of." Hold up the cards one at a time and have students tell you which meaning ***un-*** has in the word.
- When the words are sorted, point out that those where ***un-*** means "not" are describing words and those that mean "do the opposite of" are verbs.

P+am Blend

- Write the word ***unbroken*** on the board and model using the syllable patterns to blend the sounds and read the word. Then have students read it with you.
- Give students the Day One word list from blackline master 2. Have them point to the first word on the list and read the word.
- Have students independently read the remaining words for Day One. Remind them to use what they know about syllable patterns to decode the words. If students need support, guide them as they read some or all of the words on the list before having them read them independently.

Spelling Words: *unfair, unhappy*

Model

- Make a three-column spelling chart on chart paper labeled "Base Word," "Word Plus Prefix," and "Meaning of Prefix." As you work through the unit, continue to add the spelling words to the chart, and have students use the chart to check their spelling of the words.
- Say the word **unfair** and model identifying the base of the word and then adding the prefix.
- **Think Aloud:** *The base of* **unfair** *is* **fair**. *This word ends in an r-controlled vowel pattern. I know that* **ear** *and* **air** *are both r-controlled vowel patterns. I will try* **air** *and see if it looks right. Then I will add the prefix* **un-**.

Base Word	Word Plus Prefix	Meaning of Prefix
fair	unfair	not
happy	unhappy	not
load	unload	do the opposite
fold	unfold	do the opposite
afraid	unafraid	not
likely	unlikely	not

Guide

- Say the word ***unhappy***. Have students tell you how to spell the base word. Remind them to think about what vowel patterns are in the word and how they would separate the syllables.

Apply

- Have students practice writing each of the words in their word study notebooks. Have them write a sentence for each of the words.

DAY 2

Blend

- Have students blend the words on the word list for Day Two, using the procedure for blending from Day One.

Develop Automaticity in Word Recognition

- Circle the following words on the overhead transparency: ***feet, mother, own(ed), really, saw, stop, try.***
- Tell students that practicing these words will help them recognize the words automatically so they can read more fluently. Explain that students can sound out some of these words, but they will read more quickly if they don't have to stop and sound out the words each time they see them.
- Read each word. Point out that ***own(ed)*** and ***saw*** are both past tense verbs and point out that the suffix ***-ly*** added to the word ***real*** makes an adverb. Have students read aloud with you the sentences in the passage that contain the words. Then have them write the words in their word study notebooks.
- Give students a copy of blackline master 7. Point out the words from this lesson as well as other words they have learned previously. Have them cut out the words, store them in an envelope, and use them for practice activities.

Build Fluency with Connected Text

Model

- Begin reading aloud the passage on the overhead transparency. Stop after the first paragraph and point out the words with the prefix ***un-.***
- **Think Aloud:** *The word* **unload** *is an action word that tells me Granddad is doing the opposite of loading his truck. The word* **unpack** *is similar–Granddad is taking things out of the truck and then out of his suitcase or pack. I think Granddad must have just arrived.*
- Model making a mistake and correcting it–for example, read ***unroping*** instead of ***unwrapping.***
- **Think Aloud:** *That's not right. I'll just read ahead here and see if that helps. I know the* **w** *is silent, and the word describes how she got her skates. Oh, I see. There are two consonants, which means the word has a closed syllable with a short* **a** *sound.* **Unwrapping.** *Yes, that makes sense.*

Guide

- Continue reading and stop at other words in the passage. Guide students as they read the words.

Apply

- Have students take turns reading blackline master 3 to partners or in small groups as you monitor their reading. Use the teacher tips to check comprehension and fluency.

Spelling Words: *unload, unfold*

- Have students practice writing the spelling words from Day One in their word study notebooks. Have them refer to words on the spelling chart to check their spelling.
- Introduce the Day Two spelling words. Say the words and have students identify the base word in each word. Then have them tell you how to spell the words as you write them on the chart. Point out the different spellings for long ***o*** sound in the words.
- Have students practice writing each of the words in their word study notebooks. Have them write a sentence for each of the words.

Teacher Tips

Reading Strategies

If students have difficulty applying strategies for challenging words, guide them to use the following strategies:

- look at how the words start and/or end
- look for familiar patterns or parts within the words
- separate the words into syllables and decode each part
- think about what familiar words look like the difficult words
- read forward to check the context
- reread the sentence or paragraph
- mark the words, substitute synonyms, and get on with reading–ask for help later

Comprehension

Use the following questions to ensure that students have understood the passage:

- *Whom did Sunny get the roller skates from?* (Level 1–facts and details)
- *What made Sunny wobble?* (Level 2–cause/effect)
- *How did Sunny feel by the end of her ride?* (Level 3–analyze character)

Fluency

Intervene if students are having difficulty reading the passage. Model how to use word and meaning strategies to problem-solve the words. After students have had a chance to read the passage silently, have them read it aloud for fluency. Model fluent reading of the passage. For students who struggle, you may want to read the passage a second time and have them echo-read along with you.

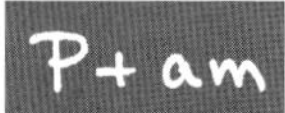

Blend

- Have students blend the words on the word list for Day Three, using the procedure for blending from Day One.

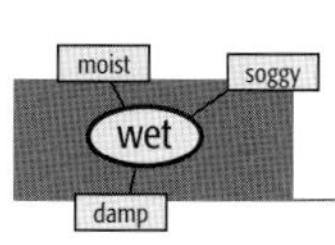

Develop Word Meanings

- Explain that an antonym is a word that means the opposite. Write the following example on the board: ***happy/unhappy.*** Have volunteers use the words in oral sentences.
- Write the following base words on the board: ***pack, clear, clean, fair, kind, plug, sure.*** Ask a volunteer to choose one of the words and use it in an oral sentence. When the student says the sentence, say a sentence back that says the opposite. For example, the student might say, "I will pack my suitcase to go on the trip." Your response might be, "I will unpack my suitcase when I come home."
- Have volunteers select a word, say a sentence, and call on someone to say the opposite of the sentence. Continue until the words have been used in several sentences.

Spelling Words: ***unafraid, unlikely***

- Introduce the Day Three spelling words. Follow the format for Day One as you guide students to identify the base words, the prefix ***un-***, and the different word endings.
- Have students practice writing each of the words in their word study notebooks. Have them write a sentence for each of the words.

Build Fluency with Connected Text

- Have students read blackline master 4 to partners or in small groups as you monitor their reading. Call attention to the following words in the reading passage before students read it: ***even, hand, next, took.***

Teacher Tips

Other Words with un-

Point out that the letters ***un*** at the beginning of a word don't always stand for the prefix ***un-***. Write the words ***under, unique,*** and ***uncle*** on the board. Explain that none of these words has a base word. Have students read the words and use them in oral sentences.

Develop Automaticity in Word Recognition

Have students choose three of the high-frequency words from blackline master 7 and write them on self-stick notes. Have them look through familiar books to find the words, marking the pages with the self-stick notes. Let students take turns reading aloud the sentences they found that use the words.

Repeated Reading

Have students practice repeated readings of blackline master 3 to develop fluency.

DAY 4

Teacher Tips

Develop Automaticity in Word Recognition

Place the high-frequency word cards on chairs set up facing outward in a circle. Have one less chair than students. Play music and have students march around the chairs. When you stop the music, students pick up the word and sit on a chair. One student will be without a chair and is out of the game. If a student reads a word incorrectly, that student is out as well. Take away a chair and word card for each round, until one student remains.

Repeated Reading

Have students practice repeated readings of blackline master 3 to develop fluency.

Blend

- Have students blend the words on the word list for Day Four, using the procedure for blending from Day One.

Write

- Tell students that as a group you will write a journal entry about a bad day, where everything turned out the opposite of how you had hoped. Have students brainstorm ways that a day can go bad, using as many ***un-*** words as they can. Record their ideas on a list.
- Model writing an opening sentence and explain that this tells the reader what the paragraph is about.
- Ask students what they want to say first and record it on the board. Continue asking students for their ideas and record their sentences.
- Read the text aloud, and have students check to see if they need to fix any problems with it.
- Have students identify the words with the prefix ***un-***. Have them tell you if the words are spelled correctly.
- Tell students that they can use the finished text as a model to write their own journal entries. (See Day Five activities.)

A Very Bad Day

Today was a very bad day. First, I was unable to wake up when my alarm went off, so I was late to school. At school, I couldn't unzip my coat, so I had to wear it all day long. That was uncomfortable! The pear I brought for lunch was unripe. I was unprepared for the surprise test in math—my parents will be unhappy with me! And an unfriendly dog chased me on the way home. Now all I want to do is relax and unwind!

Spelling Words

- Provide practice for students in segmenting words and associating sounds with spellings. Dictate the following words to students and have them write the words on their papers: ***unplug, untie, unanswered, uncommon.***
- Write the words on the board and have students self-correct their papers.
- Dictate the following sentence and have students write it on their papers: *Unless you unlock the door, you will be unable to see your unusual surprise.*
- Write the sentence on the board and have students self-correct their papers.
- Give pairs of students blackline master 6. While one student reads the spelling words, the other student writes them in the "First Try" column. After the student has spelled the words, the partner places a check mark next to words spelled correctly. For the second try, the partner may prompt the student by sounding out the words that were spelled incorrectly the first time. If the second spelling attempt is correct, the partner places a check mark in the "Second Try" column.

Assessment Tip: Use students' completed peer-check blackline masters to note which words gave students difficulty.

Build Fluency with Connected Text

- Have students take turns reading blackline master 5 to partners or in small groups as you monitor their reading. Call attention to the following words in the reading passage before students read it: ***always, don't, head, let.***

DAY 5

Spelling Assessment

Use the following procedure to assess students' spelling of the Unit Twenty-Seven words.

- Say each spelling word and use it in a sentence.
- Have students write the words on their papers.
- Continue with the next word on the list.
- When students have finished, collect their papers and analyze their spelling of the words.
- Use the assessment to plan small group or individual practice.

Small Group/Independent Activities

The following activities can be used to provide practice for students who need additional support.

WORD STRATEGIES

Have students write a journal entry about an imaginary trip they went on that didn't go so well. Before they begin, have them make a list of things that happened on the trip, using a good selection of adverbs, adjectives, and verbs beginning with the prefix ***un-***. After they finish writing, have them underline all the describing words they used, and circle the ones that begin with the prefix ***un-***.

Write Sentences Have partners choose several words from blackline masters 8 and 9. Have them write a sentence for each word they choose, and then use the base word, or the antonym, in another sentence.

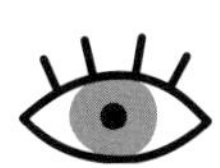

AUTOMATICITY IN WORD RECOGNITION

Read the Word Have students select several high-frequency words from blackline master 7 and write sentences using the words, leaving blanks in place of the words. Have students exchange sentences with partners and fill in the missing high-frequency words.

Toss and Read Write the high-frequency words randomly on a large sheet of paper and place it on the floor. Have students toss a small beanbag onto the paper, read the word closest to the beanbag, and use it in a sentence.

BUILD FLUENCY WITH CONNECTED TEXT

Repeated Reading Have students practice reading blackline master 3 several times, until they feel they can read it fluently and accurately. Have them work with a partner and time each other as they read the passage aloud. Have them set a goal of reading ninety words per minute.

SPELLING

Make Words Provide a set of letter cards and the week's spelling words on index cards. Have students use the letter cards to spell the words. They should check their spelling by blending the sounds and then looking at the words on the index cards.

Spell On Have students sit in a circle. Say a spelling word and the first letter of the word. Then have the student next to you say the next letter, and so on, until the word is spelled. Have the student who says the last letter write the word on the board. Have the next student say another spelling word and the first letter, and continue around the circle.

Teacher Tips

Home Connection

Have students take blackline master 11 home to complete with a family member. Students can also take the repeated reading passage on blackline master 3 home to share with their family.

Quick-Check

Assess students' mastery of the prefix ***un-*** using the quick-check for Unit Twenty-Seven in this Teacher Resource System.

ELL Support Tip

Have pairs of students stand in front of the board to demonstrate the use of the prefix ***un-***. For example, one student could have shoes that are tied and the other student could have shoes untied; one student could have a buttoned shirt and the other an unbuttoned shirt; one student could have a happy face and the other student an unhappy face, etc. Model using the prefixes, for example, "Natasha has a happy face; Linh has an unhappy face." Have students use the same language pattern to describe the other student pairs. Write the words that describe each student above them on the board; for example, ***happy, unhappy***. Highlight the prefix.

UNIT 27 Quick-Check: Prefix un-

Student Name ______________________ Assessment Date ____________

Segmenting and Blending

Directions: Explain that these words use sounds the student has been learning. Have the student point to each word on the corresponding student sheet, segment the word parts or syllables, and blend them together. Put a ✓ if the student successfully segments and blends the word or reads it as a complete unit. If the student misses the word, record the error.
Example: unpack

uncaught		uncap		
unzip		unedited		
unsalted		unnamed		
unneeded		unstack		Score **/8**

Sight Words

Directions: Have the student point to the first word on the corresponding student sheet and read across the line, saying each word as quickly as possible. Put a ✓ if the student successfully reads the word and an **X** if the student hesitates more than a few seconds. If the student misses the word, record the error.

own		saw		
mother		try		
which		any		
but		just		
feet		stop		
really		your		
could		very		
how		would		Score **/16**

UNIT 28 Prefix re-

Unit Objectives

Students will:

- Read words with the prefix re-
- Understand that adding the prefix re- to a base word changes the word's meaning
- Review comparatives
- Make new words from selected base words by adding the prefixes re- and un-
- Use words with the prefix re- correctly in oral sentences
- Read high-frequency words again, car, earth, food, important, let, something
- Spell words with the prefix re-: repaint, repay, regroup, renew, return, recheck
- Write a passage that uses words with the prefix re-

Day 1

Letter Cards: **a, c, e, e, i, l, p, r, r, s, t, u, w**

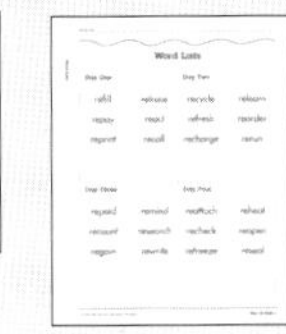
Word Lists (BLM 2)

build

Teacher Word Cards: **build, cover, equal, even, fair, fill, happy, kind, learn, new, pack, pay, print, ripe, run, safe, take, tie**

Day 2

Word Lists (BLM 2)

Reading Passage 1 (BLM 3)

High-Frequency Word Cards for Unit 28 (BLM 7)

Day 3

Word Lists (BLM 2)

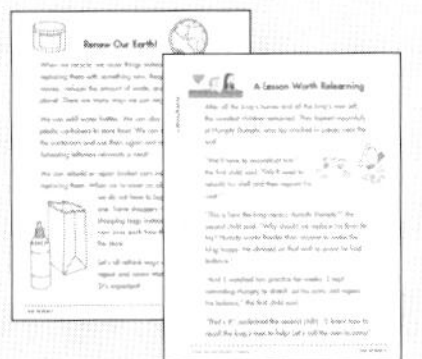
Reading Passages 1 & 2 (BLMs 3 & 4)

High-Frequency Word Cards for Unit 28 (BLM 7)

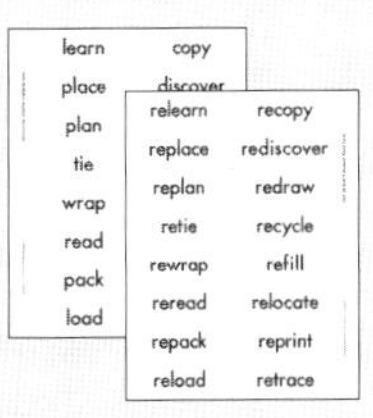

Student Word Cards (BLMs 8 & 9)

Day 4

Word Lists (BLM 2)

Reading Passages 1 & 3 (BLMs 3 & 5)

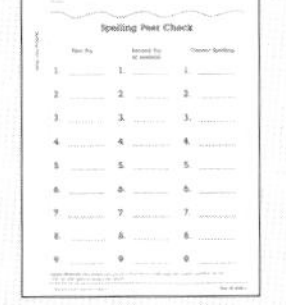
Spelling Peer Check (BLM 6)

High-Frequency Word Cards for Unit 28 (BLM 7)

Day 5

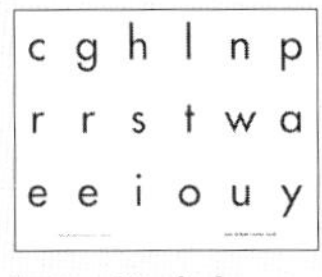
Letter Cards for Unit 28

Reading Passage 1 (BLM 3)

High-Frequency Word Cards for Unit 28 (BLM 7)

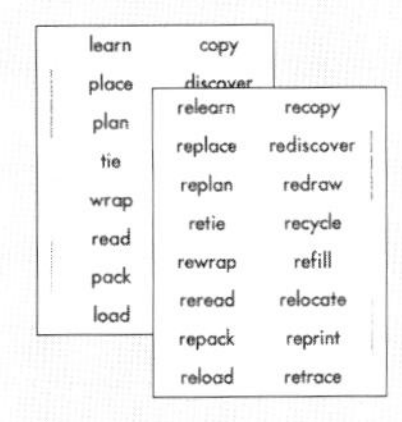
Student Word Cards (BLMs 8 & 9)

Quick-Check Student Sheet

Frieze Card

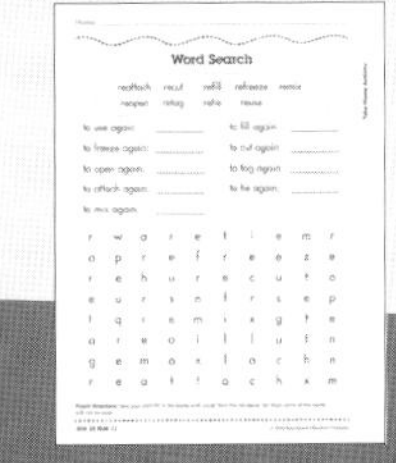
Take-Home Activity

Core Materials

All of these materials can be downloaded from http://phonicsresources.benchmarkeducation.com.

UNIT 28 Prefix re-

DAY 1

Frieze Card

tea/cher Review Comparatives

- Draw a line on the board and under it write the following sentence: *This line is short.* Draw another line next to it that is shorter. Ask students for a sentence that compares the length of the second line to the first line: (*This line is shorter*). Highlight the ***-er*** ending.
- Draw a third line that is shorter than the other two. Ask students for a sentence that compares this line with the other lines (*This line is the shortest*). Highlight the ***-est*** ending.
- Ask students to tell you in their own words when to use ***-er*** and ***-est*** endings for comparing things.
- Have students create oral sentences that compare things they see in the room, for example: *This book is thicker than that one; This book is the thickest*, etc.

tea/cher Introduce the Prefix *re-*

Model

- Show students the prefix ***re-*** frieze card and point to the first word in the second column: ***reread.*** Use the word in an oral sentence: *I want you to* **reread** *the book.* Tell students that when you reread something, you read it again. Point out the prefix ***re-*** and explain that when we add ***re*** to a word, we make a new word that means to do something again.

Guide

- Have students read the rest of the words on the frieze card. Point to several of the words and have students use them in oral phrases or sentences.

Apply

- Give students letter cards **c**, **l**, **p**, **r**, **r**, **s**, **t**, **w**, **a**, **e**, **e**, **i**, and **u.** Say the word ***replace*** and ask students what the base word is. Have them select the letters to spell the word ***place***, having them decide what letters they need for the VCe pattern in this word. Once students have made the word, have a volunteer use it in an oral sentence. Have them add the prefix ***re-*** to make the word ***replace.***
- Have them make the word ***rewrite***, first spelling the base word and deciding what letters stand for the /ī/, then adding the prefix ***re-.***
- Have students spell the word ***reuse.*** Have them identify the base word and the letter that stands for the **/ū/** sound and then add the ending.

Assessment Tip: Note which students select the correct letters. Guide students who are having difficulty.

Word Study

- Remind students that the prefix ***un-*** means not, and when added to words, creates an opposite.
- Place the following teacher word cards in a pocket chart: **safe**, **kind**, **build**, **run**, **pack**, **new**, **fair**, **even**, **learn**, **tie**, **equal**, **fill**, **pay**, **ripe**, **cover**, **print**, **take**, **happy.**
- Have students work with partners and make a two-column chart on a piece of paper, labeled "re-" and "un-". Tell them they are to use the base words in the pocket chart and make new words by adding the prefix ***re-*** or ***un-*** to the words. Tell them that some of the words can have either prefix, and have them circle these words on their chart.
- Have the pairs share the words they made.

Blend

- Write the word ***reenter*** on the board and model segmenting the syllables and blending the sounds to read the word. Then have students blend it with you.
- Give students the Day One word list from blackline master 2. Have them point to the first word on the list and read the word.

- Have students independently read the remaining words for Day One. Remind them to use what they know about syllable patterns to read the words. If students need support, guide them as they read some or all of the words on the list before having them read them independently.

Spelling Words: *repaint, repay*

Model

- Make a two-column spelling chart on chart paper. Label the first column "Base Word" and the second column "Word Plus Prefix." Tell students that they will be spelling words that begin with the prefix ***re-***. As you work through the unit, add the spelling words to the chart, and have students use the chart to check their spelling of the words.
- Say the word ***repaint*** and model identifying the base of the word and adding the prefix.
- **Think Aloud:** *The base of* **repaint** *is* **paint.** *I hear a long* **a** *sound and I know this sound can be spelled in different ways. I think in this word it is spelled with the long* **a** *digraph* **ai.** *I will write the word and see if it looks right.*

Guide

- Say the word ***repay.*** Have students identify the base word and the letters that stand for the long ***a*** in this word. Have them tell you how to spell the word on the chart.

Apply

- Have students practice writing each of the words in their word study notebooks. Have them write a sentence for each of the words.

Our Spelling Words

Base Word	Word Plus Prefix
paint	repaint
pay	repay
group	regroup
new	renew
turn	return
check	recheck

DAY 2

Teacher Tips

Reading Strategies

If students have difficulty applying strategies for challenging words, guide them to use the following strategies:

- look at how the words start and/or end
- look for familiar patterns or parts within the words
- separate the words into syllables and decode each part
- think about what familiar words look like the difficult words
- read forward to check the context
- reread the sentence or paragraph
- mark the words, substitute synonyms, and get on with reading–ask for help later

Comprehension

Use the following questions to ensure that students have understood the passage:

- *What does it mean to recycle?* (Level 1–facts and details)
- *What happens when we re-cover an old couch?* (Level 2–cause/effect)
- *How does recycling help the earth?* (Level 3–draw conclusions)

Fluency

Intervene if students are having difficulty reading the passage. Model how to use word and meaning strategies to problem-solve the words. After students have had a chance to read the passage silently, have them read it aloud for fluency. Model fluent reading of the passage. For students who struggle, you may want to read the passage a second time and have them echo-read along with you.

Blend

- Have students blend the words on the word list for Day Two, using the procedure for blending from Day One.

Develop Automaticity in Word Recognition

- Circle the following words on the overhead transparency: ***again***, ***car(s)***, ***earth***, ***food***, ***important***, ***let('s)***, ***something.***
- Tell students that practicing these words will help them recognize the words automatically so they can read more fluently. Explain that students can sound out some of these words, but they will read more quickly if they don't have to stop and sound out the words each time they see them.
- Read each word. Point out that ***something*** is a compound word. Have students read aloud with you the sentences in the passage that contain the words. Then have them write the words in their word study notebooks.
- Give students a copy of blackline master 7. Point out the words from this lesson as well as other words they have learned previously. Have them cut out the words, store them in an envelope, and use them for practice activities.

Build Fluency with Connected Text

Model

- Begin reading aloud the passage on the overhead transparency. Stop after the first sentences and point out the words with the prefix ***re-.***
- **Think Aloud** *There are three words in this sentence that have the prefix* **re-: recycle, reuse, and replacing.** *It helps me understand the meanings of these words if I remember that the prefix* **re-** *means* **again.**
- Model making a mistake and correcting it–for example, read ***reducks*** instead of ***reduces.***
- **Think Aloud:** *That's doesn't make sense, so I need to look at the letters and sounds in this word again. Oh, I see where I went wrong. This word has a VCe syllable pattern, so the vowel sound is /o͞o/ not /ŭ/:* **reduces.** *That makes sense.*

Guide

- Continue reading and stop at other words in the passage. Guide students as they read the words.

Apply

- Have students take turns reading blackline master 3 to partners or in small groups as you monitor their reading. Use the teacher tips to check comprehension and fluency.

Spelling Words: *regroup, renew*

- Have students practice writing the spelling words from Day One in their word study notebooks. Have them refer to words on the spelling chart to check their spelling.
- Introduce the Day Two spelling words. Say the words and have students identify the base word in each word, and the vowel sound in each. Remind them that the /o͞o/ sound can be spelled in different ways and have them select the spelling and see if the word looks right.
- Have students practice writing each of the words in their word study notebooks. Have them write a sentence for each of the words.

Blend

- Have students blend the words on the word list for Day Three, using the procedure for blending from Day One.

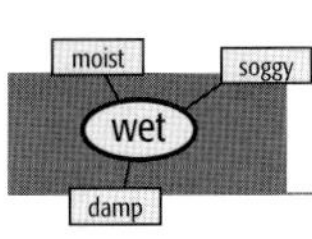

Develop Word Meanings

- Have each student work with a partner. One partner has a set of word cards from blackline master 8 with the base words. The other partner has a set of word cards from blackline master 9 with the word-and-prefix combinations. Have the student with the base words place them facedown in a stack. Have the other student spread his/her cards out faceup.
- The student with the base words draws a card and uses the word in an oral sentence, for example: *I need to pay him for his work.* The other student must find the word card with the prefix and use it in a sentence: *I need to repay him for his work.* As students use the words, have them place the words to the side.
- After students have used all the words, have them mix up the words and then spread them facedown on the floor or desk. Have them take turns turning over the cards two at a time to try to make pairs.

Spelling Words: ***return, recheck***

- Introduce the Day Three spelling words. Follow the format for Day One as you guide students to identify the base words and the vowel sound. Have them tell which letters stand for the /**k**/ sound at the end of the word, spell the word, and then see if it looks right. Then have students add the prefix.
- Have students practice writing each of the words in their word study notebooks. Have them write a sentence for each of the words.

Build Fluency with Connected Text

- Have students read blackline master 4 to partners or in small groups as you monitor their reading. Call attention to the following high-frequency words before students read them: ***add(ing)***, ***house***, ***left***, ***should***, ***us***, ***why***.

Teacher Tips

Double *e*

Point out to students that when the base word begins with the letter ***e***, the prefix is added to make a double ***e***, each in its own syllable. Write the words ***elect***, ***enact***, and ***enter*** on the board. Model dividing the words into syllables and reading them: ***e/lect***, ***en/act***, ***en/ter***. Then add the prefix ***re-*** and show students how this creates an extra syllable: ***re/e/lect***, ***re/en/act***, ***re/en/ter***.

Develop Automaticity in Word Recognition

Have students take turns reading the high-frequency word cards from blackline master 7 to a partner. Have them put any cards they have trouble reading to one side and read those again.

Repeated Reading

Have students practice repeated readings of blackline master 3 to develop fluency.

DAY 4

Teacher Tips

Parts of Speech

Show students how adding the prefix ***re-*** to words does not change the way the words are used in sentences. Write the following sentence on the board: *I will use my pencil.* Ask students what part of speech the word ***use*** is. (verb) Then write the following sentence under the first sentence: *I will reuse my pencil.* Ask students what part of speech ***reuse*** is (verb). Point out that ***use*** and ***reuse*** are both verbs. Have students use the following words in oral sentences with and without the prefix ***re-*** to see if all of the words are used as verbs: ***stack***, ***wash***, ***heat***, ***build.***

Develop Automaticity in Word Recognition

Have students spread their sets of high-frequency words facedown in front of them. Read one of the words and have students race to see who can find the word in his or her set of cards first.

Repeated Reading

Have students practice repeated readings of blackline master 3 to develop fluency.

Blend

- Have students blend the words on the word list for Day Four, using the procedure for blending from Day One.

Write

- Tell students that as a group you will write a story about something the group would like to do again. Have students brainstorm a list of things they would like to do again and record their ideas on a list. Have them select a topic from the list.
- Have students suggest an opening sentence and remind them that this is important because it tells the reader what the paragraph is about.
- Ask students what they want to say next and record it on the board. Continue asking students for their ideas and record their sentences.
- Read the text aloud, and have students check to see if they need to fix any problems with it.
- Have students identify the words with the prefix ***re-.*** Have them tell you if the words are spelled correctly.
- Tell students that they can use the finished text as a model to write their own stories. (See Day Five activities.)

> Let's Do It Again
>
> If we had the chance, our class would like to retake last week's spelling test. We could recheck the words and revise our mistakes. Then we could rewrite the words and spell them correctly this time. We can request that we be able to redo the test, but we think our teacher will most likely refuse.

Spelling Words

- Provide practice for students in segmenting words and associating sounds with spellings. Dictate the following words to students and have them write the words on their papers: ***reship***, ***redraw***, ***regain***, ***retie.***
- Write the words on the board and have students self-correct their papers.
- Dictate the following sentence and have students write it on their papers: *Reseal the container before you return the food to the microwave to be reheated.*
- Write the sentence on the board and have students self-correct their papers.
- Give pairs of students blackline master 6. While one student reads the spelling words, the other student writes them in the "First Try" column. After the student has spelled the words, the partner places a check mark next to words spelled correctly. For the second try, the partner may prompt the student by sounding out the words that were spelled incorrectly the first time. If the second spelling attempt is correct, the partner places a check mark in the "Second Try" column.

Assessment Tip: Use students' completed peer-check blackline masters to note which words gave students difficulty.

Build Fluency with Connected Text

- Have students take turns reading blackline master 5 to partners or in small groups as you monitor their reading. Call attention to these high-frequency words before students read the BLM: ***always***, ***girl***, ***life***, ***miss***, ***sometimes***, ***story***, ***try(ing).***

Spelling Assessment

Use the following procedure to assess students' spelling of the Unit Twenty-Eight words.
- Say each spelling word and use it in a sentence.
- Have students write the words on their papers.
- Continue with the next word on the list.
- When students have finished, collect their papers and analyze their spelling of the words.
- Use the assessment to plan small group or individual practice.

Small Group/Independent Activities

The following activities can be used to provide practice for students who need additional support.

WORD STRATEGIES

Write Have students write about something they would like to do again. Have them look at the list of topics created during the group writing activity if they need ideas. Challenge them to use as many words with the prefix ***re-*** as they can.

Word Hunt Give students pages from old newspapers and have them hunt for words that start with the prefix ***re-***. As they find a word, they should circle it. Have students see how many of the words they find they can sound out, using what they know about syllables and syllable patterns.

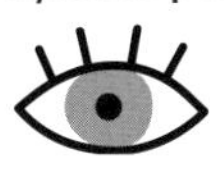

AUTOMATICITY IN WORD RECOGNITION

Spell the Word Have students place their set of high-frequency word cards in a stack. Have them draw a word, read it, and then turn the card over and spell the word in their word study notebooks. Have them turn the card back over to check their spelling.

Toss and Read Write the high-frequency words randomly on a large sheet of paper and place it on the floor. Have students toss a beanbag onto the paper, read the word closest to the beanbag, and use it in a sentence.

BUILD FLUENCY WITH CONNECTED TEXT

Repeated Reading Have students practice reading blackline master 3 several times, until they feel they can read it fluently and accurately. Have them work with partners and time one another as they read the passage aloud. Have them set a goal of reading 90 words per minute.

SPELLING

Make Words Provide a set of letter cards and the week's spelling words on index cards. Have students use the letter cards to spell the words. They should check their spelling by blending the sounds and then looking at the words on the index cards.

Beat the Teacher Select a spelling word and make a blank for each letter in the word. Have students guess the letters. If they correctly guess a letter, write it on the blank where it fits in the word. If they do not guess a letter correctly, begin drawing a stick figure. Each time they guess incorrectly, add another body part. Have students try to figure out the spelling word before you complete the drawing.

Teacher Tips

Home Connection

Have students take blackline master 11 home to complete with a family member. Students can also take the repeated reading passage on blackline master 3 home to share with their family.

Quick-Check

Assess students' mastery of the prefix ***re-*** using the quick-check for Unit Twenty-Eight in the *Teacher Resource System.*

ELL Support Tip

Use shared writing with the class, using the words with prefix ***re-*** taught during this lesson. Negotiate the text with students to produce a class story. As you are creating the text, have students continuously reread to gain fluency. Once the story is complete, return to it on the next day to underline the prefix and root words, using two different colors.

UNIT 28 Quick-Check: Prefix re-

Student Name ______________________ Assessment Date __________

Segmenting and Blending

Directions: Explain that these words use sounds the student has been learning. Have the student point to each word on the corresponding student sheet, segment the word parts or syllables, and blend them together. Put a ✓ if the student successfully segments and blends the word or reads it as a complete unit. If the student misses the word, record the error.
Example: rewind

respect		remove		
rejoin		reclaim		
reshuffle		refocus		
replace		relax		Score **/8**

Sight Words

Directions: Have the student point to the first word on the corresponding student sheet and read across the line, saying each word as quickly as possible. Put a ✓ if the student successfully reads the word and an **X** if the student hesitates more than a few seconds. If the student misses the word, record the error.

something		our		
earth		water		
food		also		
again		time		
important		their		
let		them		
car		use		
thing		new		Score **/16**

UNIT 29 Prefix dis-

Unit Objectives

Students will:

- Read words with the prefix dis-
- Understand that adding the prefix dis- to a base word changes the word's meaning
- Review -y, -ly endings
- Use adjectives to describe objects
- Sort words according to their prefixes
- Read high-frequency words: being, family, miss, off, plant, until, well
- Spell words with prefix dis-: disorder, disagree, distrust, dishonest, disgrace, disappear
- Write an advertisement

UNIT 29 Prefix dis-

Day 1

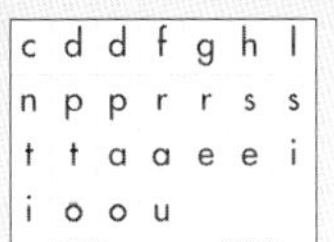

Letter Cards:
a, c, d, e, f, i, l, n, o, p, r, s, t

Word Lists
(BLM 2)

able

Teacher Word Cards:
able, clear, count, color, cover, friendly, glue, happy, heat, kind, learn, locate, mind, obey, pack, play, pleased, turn, write

Day 2

Word Lists
(BLM 2)

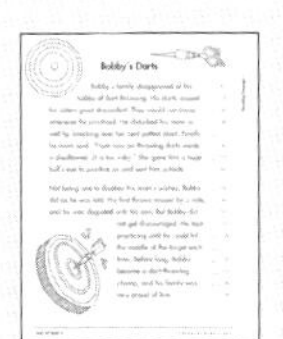

Reading Passage 1
(BLM 3)

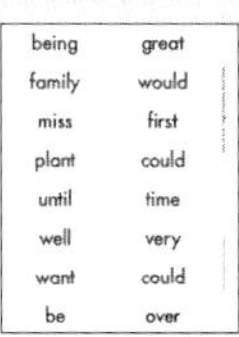

High-Frequency Word Cards for Unit 29 (BLM 7)

Day 3

Word Lists
(BLM 2)

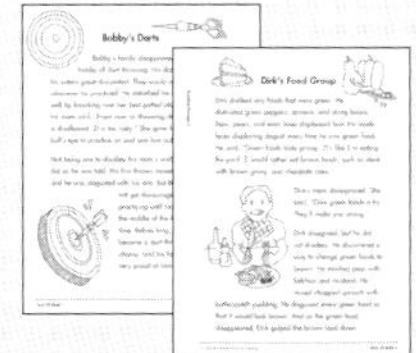

Reading Passages 1 & 2
(BLMs 3 & 4)

Day 4

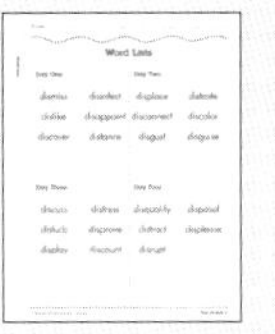

Word Lists (BLM 2)

Reading Passages 1 & 3
(BLMs 3 & 5)

being great
family would
miss first
plant could
until time
well very
want could
be over

High-Frequency Word Cards for Unit 29
(BLM 7)

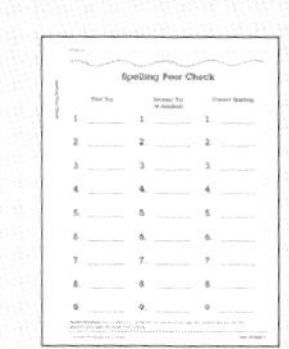

Spelling Peer Check
(BLM 6)

Day 5

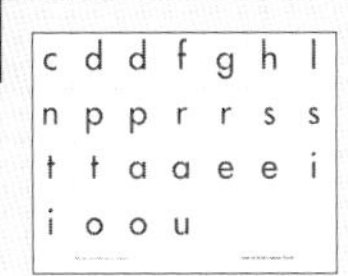

Letter Cards for Unit 29

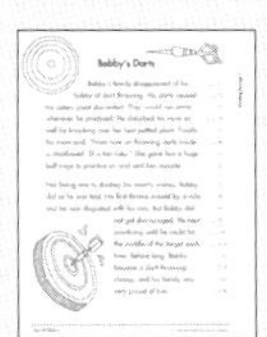

Reading Passage 1
(BLM 3)

High-Frequency Word Cards for Unit 29 (BLM 7)

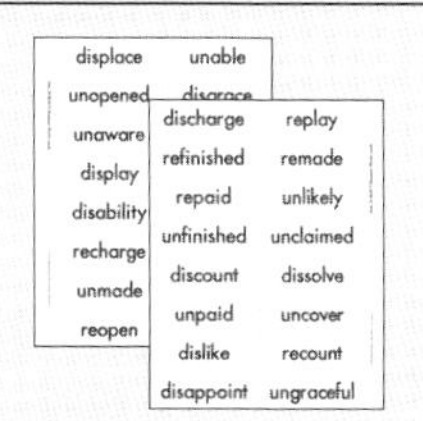

Student Word Cards
(BLMs 8 & 9)

Quick-Check Student Sheet

Frieze Card

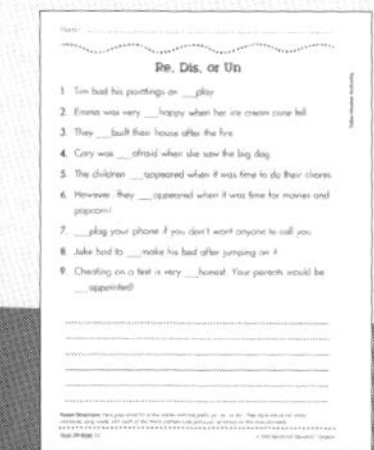

Take-Home Activity

Core Materials

All of these materials can be downloaded from http://phonicsresources.benchmarkeducation.com.

DAY 1

tea/c

Review *-y, -ly* Endings

Frieze Card

- Write the word ***rain*** on the board and point out that it's a noun that names something. Then add a ***-y*** ending and ask students to read the new word and use it in a sentence. Point out that ***rainy*** is an adjective that describes something. Repeat with ***leak/leaky***, ***rust/rusty***, and ***storm/stormy***.
- Write the word ***gentle*** on the board and point out that it describes something. Have a student use it in an oral sentence. Then add the suffix ***-ly***, pointing out that you drop the ***-le*** ending before you do this. Explain that ***gently*** is an adverb that tells how. Have a student use it in an oral sentence.
- Repeat with the words ***smooth***, ***quiet***, and ***slow***, adding an ***-ly*** ending to each.

tea/c

Introduce Prefix *dis-*

Model

- Show students the prefix ***dis-*** frieze card and point to the first word in the second column: ***disbelieve.*** Point out the prefix ***dis-*** and remind students that a prefix is a group of letters that appears at the front of a word. Tell students that when we add ***dis-*** to the word ***believe***, we make a new word that means the opposite of ***believe.***

Guide

- Have students read the rest of the words on the frieze card. Point to several of the words and have students use them in oral phrases or sentences.

Apply

- Give students letter cards **c**, **d**, **f**, **l**, **n**, **p**, **r**, **s**, **s**, **t**, **a**, **e**, **e**, **i**, **i**, **o**, and **o.** Say the word ***discolor*** and ask students to identify the base word. Have them select the letters to spell the word ***color.*** Have them add the ***dis-*** to make the word ***discolor.***
- Have them make the word ***disinfect***, spelling the base word first and then adding the prefix ***dis-.***
- Repeat with the word ***displease.***

Assessment Tip: Note which students select the correct letters. Guide students who are having difficulty.

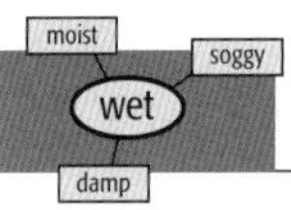

Word Study

- Place the following teacher word cards in a pocket chart: **cover**, **pack**, **glue**, **learn**, **able**, **locate**, **count**, **obey**, **color**, **play**, **mind**, **write**, **turn**, **heat**, **happy**, **clear**, **kind**, **friendly**, **pleased.**
- Have each student work with a partner to make a three-column chart on a sheet of paper labeled "re-," "un-," and "dis-." Tell students they are to use the base words in the pocket chart and make new words by adding the prefix ***re-***, ***dis-***, or ***un-*** to them. Tell students that some of the base words can be used with more than one of the prefixes, and have them circle these base words on their chart.
- Have the student pairs share the words they made with other pairs. Encourage students to look up any words they are unsure of in a dictionary.

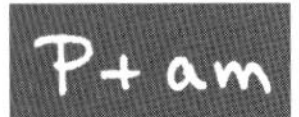

Blend

- Write the word ***discomfort*** on the board and model segmenting the word into syllables to blend the sounds and read the word. Then have students blend it with you.
- Give students the Day One word list from blackline master 2. Have them point to the first word on the list and read the word.
- Have students independently read the remaining words for Day One. Remind them to use what they know about syllable patterns to read the words. If students need support, guide them as they read some or all of the words on the list before having them read them independently.

Spelling Words: *disorder, disobey, disagree*

Model

- Make a two-column spelling chart on chart paper. Label the first column "Base Word," the second column "Word Plus Prefix." Tell students that they will be spelling words that begin with ***dis-***. As you work through the unit, continue to add the spelling words to the chart, and have students use the chart to check their spelling of the words.
- Say the word ***disorder*** and model identifying the base of the word and then adding the prefix.
- **Think Aloud:** *The base of* **disorder** *is* **order.** *The first syllable of* **order** *has an r-controlled vowel sound:* **/ôr/.** *I know that this sound can be spelled* **oar** *or* **or.** *I will try* **or** *and see if it looks right. Then I will add the prefix* **dis-.**

Guide

- Say the word ***disagree***. Have students identify the base word and tell you how to spell it. Then have them add the prefix.

Apply

- Have students practice writing each of the words in their word study notebooks. Have them circle each prefix and then write a sentence for each of the words.

Our Spelling Words

Base Word	Word Plus Prefix
order	disorder
agree	disagree
obey	disobey
trust	distrust
honest	dishonest
grace	disgrace
appear	disappear

DAY 2

Teacher Tips

Reading Strategies

If students have difficulty applying strategies for challenging words, guide them to use the following strategies:

- look at how the words start and/or end
- look for familiar patterns or parts within the words
- separate the words into syllables and decode each part
- think about what familiar words look like the difficult words
- read forward to check the context
- reread the sentence or paragraph
- mark the words, substitute synonyms, and get on with reading–ask for help later

Comprehension

Use the following questions to ensure that students have understood the passage:

- *What hobby did Bobby have that was so disruptive?*
  (Level 1–facts and details)
- *Why did his mom send him outside?*
  (Level 2–cause/effect)
- *How do you think Bobby felt after winning the championship?*
  (Level 3–analyze character)

Fluency

Intervene if students are having difficulty reading the passage. Model how to use word and meaning strategies to problem-solve the words. After students have had a chance to read the passage silently, have them read it aloud for fluency. Model fluent reading of the passage. For students who struggle, you may want to read the passage a second time and have them echo-read along with you.

Blend

- Have students blend the words on the word list for Day Two, using the procedure for blending from Day One.

Develop Automaticity in Word Recognition

- Circle the following words on the overhead transparency: ***being***, ***family***, ***miss(ed)***, ***plant***, ***until***, ***well.***
- Tell students that practicing these words will help them recognize the words automatically so they can read more fluently. Explain that students can sound out some of these words, but they will read more quickly if they don't have to stop and sound out the words each time they see them.
- Read each word. Point out that ***missed*** is a past tense verb. Have students read aloud with you the sentences in the passage that contain the words. Then have them write the words in their word study notebooks.
- Give students a copy of blackline master 7. Point out the words from this lesson as well as other words they have learned previously. Have them cut out the words, store them in an envelope, and use them for practice activities.

Build Fluency with Connected Text

Model

- Begin reading aloud the passage on the overhead transparency. Stop after the second sentence and model how to use the context to figure out the meaning of the word ***discomfort.***
- **Think Aloud:** *I can read this word by dividing it into syllables. I recognize the prefix* **dis-**. *The next syllable is a closed syllable, and the third syllable has an r-controlled* **o** *sound:* **discomfort.** *But I need to make sure I know what the word means. His sisters ran away from him, so they must have been afraid of or annoyed by his darts. I think that's what it means to be discomforted by something: annoyed or distressed.*
- Stop after the word ***disfigured*** and model using its context to figure out its meaning.
- **Think Aloud:** *I recognize the base,* **figure**, *and the prefix,* **dis: disfigured.** *From the context, I get the idea that Bobby's darts hit the doll, probably in the face, and spoiled the way the doll looked.*

Guide

- Continue reading and stop at other words in the passage. Guide students as they read the words.

Apply

- Have students take turns reading blackline master 3 to partners or in small groups as you monitor their reading. Use the teacher tips to check comprehension and fluency.

Spelling Words: *distrust, dishonest*

- Have students practice writing the spelling words from Day One in their word study notebooks. Have them refer to words on the spelling chart to check their spelling.
- Introduce the Day Two spelling words. Say the words. Have students identify the base word in each spelling word and then tell you how to spell the words as you write them on the chart.
- Have students practice writing each of the words in their word study notebooks. Have them write a sentence for each of the words.

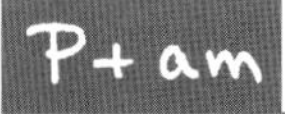

Blend

- Have students blend the words on the word list for Day Three, using the procedure for blending from Day One.

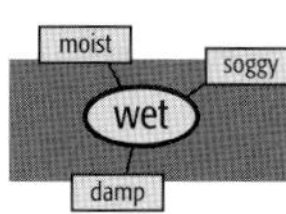

Develop Word Meanings

- Have students copy the chart below in their word study notebooks. Write the following words on the board and have students copy them in the "Word" column of the chart: ***disobey***, ***dishonestly***, ***replay***, ***reviewing***, ***unlock***, ***unfriendly.***
- Place students in small groups and have them discuss each word as a group. Have them begin by finding the base word and talking about what they know about its meaning. Then have students discuss the meaning of the word with the prefix and/or suffix if either has been added.
- Have each group collaborate to write a sentence that uses each word.
- Call the groups together and have them share their understandings of the words and also their sentences.

Word	Prefix	Base Word	Suffix	Meaning	Sentence
disobey	dis	obey	-		
dishonestly	dis	honest	ly		
replay	re	play	-		
reviewing	re	view	ing		
unlock	un	lock	-		
unfriendly	un	friend	ly		

Spelling Words: *disgrace, disappear*

- Introduce the Day Three spelling words. Follow the format for Day One as you guide students to identify the base words and the vowel sounds in each root. Then have students tell you what letters to write on the spelling words chart.
- Have students practice writing each of the words in their word study notebooks. Have them write a sentence for each of the words.

Build Fluency with Connected Text

- Have students read blackline master 4 to partners or in small groups as you monitor their reading. Call attention to the following words in the reading passage before students read it: ***eat(ing), even, every, food, it's, saw, try.***

Teacher Tips

Other Words with the Prefix dis-

Point out that the prefix ***dis-*** won't always be in front of a recognizable base word. For example, the word ***disaster*** comes from Latin words meaning without stars, and got its meaning from the belief that if the stars were in an unfavorable position in the sky, then something bad was going to happen. Write the words ***discussion***, ***dispute***, and ***distant*** on the board. Explain that these are also examples of words that have the prefix ***dis-*** in front of non-English base words.

Develop Automaticity in Word Recognition

Have students cut out letters from newspaper headlines to spell the high-frequency words ***being***, ***family***, ***miss***, ***plant***, ***run***, and ***until***. Have them paste the letters on a sheet of paper or in their word study notebooks. Challenge them to make as many of the words as they can.

Repeated Reading

Have students practice repeated readings of blackline master 3 to develop fluency.

DAY 4

Teacher Tips

Words with Prefixes and Suffixes

Write the word ***dishonest*** on the board and have students identify the prefix and the base word. Then add the suffix ***-ly*** and ask students how the meaning of the word changes. Have volunteers use the words ***dishonest*** and ***dishonestly*** in oral sentences that demonstrate the difference in meaning. Repeat with the words ***discover/discovered*** and ***disgust/disgusted.***

Develop Automaticity in Word Recognition

Write some or all of the high-frequency words on the board. Say a word and call on a student to find the word on the board and circle it. Repeat with the remaining words.

Repeated Reading

Have students practice repeated readings of blackline master 3 to develop fluency.

Blend

- Have students blend the words on the word list for Day Four, using the procedure for blending from Day One.

Write

- As a group, write a newspaper advertisement selling tickets to a newly discovered planet where anything is possible. Have students brainstorm a wish list for this planet and record their ideas.
- Model writing an opening sentence and explain that this tells the reader what the advertisement is about.
- Ask students what they want to say next and record it on the board. Continue asking students for their ideas, and record their sentences.
- Read the text aloud, and have students check to see if they need to fix any problems with it.
- Have students identify the words with the prefixes ***dis-***, ***un-***, and ***re-.*** Underline the words on the board. Have them tell you if the words are spelled correctly.
- Tell students that they can use the finished text as a model to write their own word study notebook entries. (See Day Five activities.)

Fantasy Planet

Today a fantasy planet was discovered. It's unbelievable—anything you could wish for is possible! Are you unhappy that cookies don't grow on trees? They do here! Are you displeased that your mom reminds you to remake your bed every day? Not here! Your bed is made of clouds! Are you unsure about what homework is due the next day? Don't worry—there is no homework here! (Unless you want some, of course!) Discounted spaceship tickets to the fantasy planet will be available tomorrow. Buy yours right away, before they disappear!

Spelling Words

- Provide practice for students in segmenting words and associating sounds with spellings. Dictate the following words to students and have them write the words on their papers: ***disagree, dislike, displeased.***
- Write the words on the board and have students self-correct their papers.
- Dictate the following sentence and have students write it on their papers: *The boys disliked being dismissed so late.*
- Write the sentence on the board and have students self-correct their papers.
- Give pairs of students blackline master 6. While one student reads the spelling words, the other student writes them in the "First Try" column. After the student has spelled the words, the partner places a check mark next to words spelled correctly. For the second try, the partner may prompt the student by sounding out the words that were spelled incorrectly the first time. If the second spelling attempt is correct, the partner places a check mark in the "Second Try" column.

Assessment Tip: Use students' completed peer-check blackline masters to note which words gave students difficulty.

Build Fluency with Connected Text

- Have students take turns reading blackline master 5 to partners or in small groups as you monitor their reading. Call attention to the following words in the reading passage before students read it: ***even, hear, might, something, try, change(d).***

Spelling Assessment

Use the following procedure to assess students' spelling of the Unit Twenty-Nine words.

- Say each spelling word and use it in a sentence.
- Have students write the words on their papers.
- Continue with the next word on the list.
- When students have finished, collect their papers and analyze their spelling of the words.
- Use the assessment to plan small group or individual practice.

Small Group/Independent Activities

The following activities can be used to provide practice for students who need additional support.

WORD STRATEGIES

Write Have students write an advertisement about an imaginary island they discovered. Before they begin, have them make a list of things to do on the island, using a good selection of adverbs, adjectives, and verbs beginning with the prefixes ***dis-***, ***un-***, and ***re-***. After they finish writing, have them circle all the words that begin with the prefixes.

Word Sorts Have partners sort the student word cards from blackline masters 8 and 9. Point out that there is more than one way to sort them. For example, they could sort the words according to their prefixes, number of syllables, base words, parts of speech, etc.

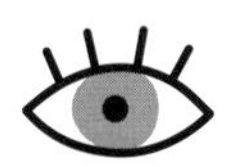

AUTOMATICITY IN WORD RECOGNITION

Find the Word Give students a newspaper page and one or more of the high-frequency word cards from blackline master 7. Have them search the page to find and circle the word(s). Have them use a different color crayon for each word if they are looking for more than one word.

Make Sentences Place several sets of high-frequency word cards in a bag. Have students draw four cards from the bag and place them facedown without looking at them. When everyone has four cards, have students race to see who can be the first to write a sentence using all four words. Have the winning student read aloud his or her sentence. Place the words back in the bag and repeat the process.

BUILD FLUENCY WITH CONNECTED TEXT

Repeated Reading Have students practice reading blackline master 3 several times, until they feel they can read it fluently and accurately. Have them work with a partner and time each other as they read the passage aloud. Have them set a goal of reading 90 words per minute.

SPELLING

Make Words Provide a set of letter cards and the week's spelling words on index cards. Have students use the letter cards to spell the words. They should check their spelling by blending the sounds and then looking at the words on the index cards.

Missing Vowels Write the spelling words on the board. Without students seeing, erase one of the letters in one of the words. Have students tell you which letter is missing. Replace the letter and repeat with the other words. To make it more difficult, erase more than one letter and have students tell which letters are missing.

Teacher Tips

Home Connection

Have students take blackline master 11 home to complete with a family member. Students can also take the repeated reading passage on blackline master 3 home to share with their family.

Quick-Check

Assess students' mastery of the prefix ***dis-*** using the quick-check for Unit Twenty-Nine in the *Teacher Resource System.*

ELL Support Tip

Create word cards with opposite words and pictures on them, for example ***happy***, ***unhappy*** or ***like***, ***dislike.*** Have students play a matching game such as Concentration, where they have to match the opposite pairs and read the words. Once you have played the game as a group, put the game in a word study center. When students have completed the game with a partner, they can sort the words according to their prefixes.

UNIT 29 Quick-Check: Prefix dis-

Student Name ______________________________ Assessment Date ______________

Segmenting and Blending

Directions: Explain that these words use sounds the student has been learning. Have the student point to each word on the corresponding student sheet, segment the word parts or syllables, and blend them together. Put a ✓ if the student successfully segments and blends the word or reads it as a complete unit. If the student misses the word, record the error.
Example: dislike

disagree		disloyal		
disrupted		disown		
disband		distrusted		
disposed		disappear		Score **/8**

Sight Words

Directions: Have the student point to the first word on the corresponding student sheet and read across the line, saying each word as quickly as possible. Put a ✓ if the student successfully reads the word and an **X** if the student hesitates more than a few seconds. If the student misses the word, record the error.

being		be		
family		great		
miss		would		
off		first		
plant		could		
run		time		
until		very		
want		could		Score **/16**

Unit Objectives

Students will:

- Read words with the suffix -less
- Understand that adding a suffix to a base word changes the word's meaning
- Review prefixes un-, re-, dis-
- Sort words according to their prefixes and suffixes
- Read high-frequency words does, keep, let, off, paper, those, white
- Spell words with suffix -less: priceless, useless, powerless, cloudless, breathless, fearless
- Write a quatrain using words with suffix -less

Day 1

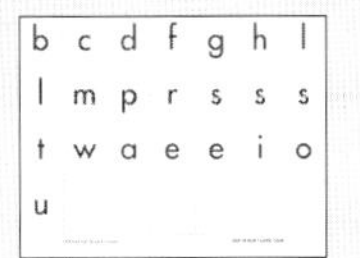

Letter Cards:
a, c, e, g, h, l, m, r, s

Word Lists
(BLM 2)

coverless

Teacher Word Cards:
coverless, discover, dislike, disorder, disorderly, friendless, friendly, happily, needless, needlessly, needy, recover, reorder, uncover, unfriendly, unhappily, unhappy, unlike, unlikely

Day 2

Word Lists
(BLM 2)

Reading Passage 1
(BLM 3)

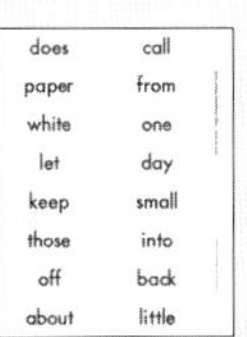

High-Frequency Word Cards for Unit 30 (BLM 7)

Day 3

Word Lists
(BLM 2)

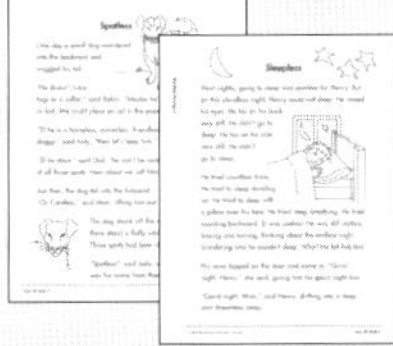

Reading Passages 1 & 2
(BLMs 3 & 4)

High-Frequency Word Cards for Unit 30 (BLM 7)

Day 4

Word Lists (BLM 2)

Reading Passages 1 & 3
(BLMs 3 & 5)

Spelling Peer Check
(BLM 6)

High-Frequency Word Cards for Unit 30

Day 5

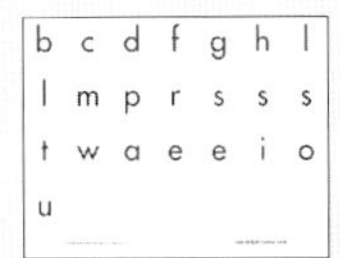

Letter Cards for Unit 30

Reading Passage 1
(BLM 3)

does call
paper from
white one
let day
keep small
those into
off back
about little

High-Frequency Word Cards for Unit 30 (BLM 7)

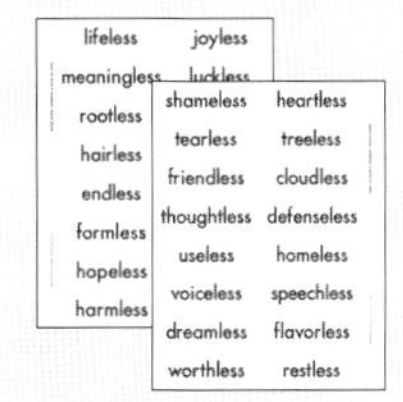

Student Word Cards
(BLMs 8 & 9)

Quick-Check Student Sheet

Frieze Card

Take-Home Activity

Core Materials

All of these materials can be downloaded from http://phonicsresources.benchmarkeducation.com.

UNIT 30 Suffix -less

DAY 1

Frieze Card

tea/cher

Review Prefixes *un-, re-, dis-*

- Ask students if they can tell you what a prefix is. If necessary, remind them that a prefix is a group of letters added to the beginning of a word that changes its meaning.
- Write the prefixes ***un-, re-,*** and ***dis-*** in a row on the board. Have students brainstorm words that begin with each prefix. Write them on the board under the appropriate prefix.
- Have volunteers circle the base word in each of the words on the board. Have them tell how the prefix changes the meaning of the base word.
- Select several words from the lists and call on students to use them in oral sentences.

tea/cher

Introduce Suffix *-less*

Model

- Point out the highlighted suffix in the first word in the second column of the frieze card and remind students that a group of letters that is added to the end of a word is called a suffix. Remind them that they have learned other suffixes in previous lessons (***-er, -or, -ed, -ing, -y, -ly***), and that adding suffixes to a base word changes the meaning of the word.
- Point out how you would divide the first word on the list into syllables to read it: ***spot/less***. Explain that the suffix ***-less*** means "without," and so the word ***spotless*** literally means "without spots" or, in other words, something that is really clean without any dirt or marks on it.

Guide

- Have students read the next base word ***weight*** with you, pointing out the digraph ***ei.*** Then have them read the word plus the suffix. Discuss the word's meaning and have them use it in an oral sentence.
- Have them read the remaining words on the frieze card, pointing out the different syllable patterns in the words and discussing the meanings.

Apply

- Give students letter cards **c, g, h, l, m, r, s, s, a, e,** and **e.** Say the word ***ageless*** and ask students what the base of the word is. Ask them what letters they will need to spell ***age,*** and remind them of the silent final ***e.*** Then have them find the letters to add the suffix ***-less.***
- Repeat with the words ***harm/harmless,*** pointing out the r-controlled vowel. Repeat with the words ***care/careless,*** pointing out the **/âr/** vowel sound.

Assessment Tip: Note which students select the correct letters. Guide students who are having difficulty.

Word Study

- Place the following teacher word cards in a pocket chart: **uncover, coverless, discover, recover, friendless, friendly, unfriendly, needy, needless, needlessly, unhappily, happily, unhappy, disorderly, disorder, reorder, dislike, unlike, unlikely.** Read each word with students and ensure that they know the meanings of all the words.
- Place students in small groups to talk about how they would group the words. Groups might sort the words according to their prefixes and suffixes, base words, numbers of syllables, numbers of letters, etc.
- Call students together and have them share ideas for sorting. As they suggest different ways, move the words into groups and have the whole class discuss whether the sort works. Point out that some of the words have both a prefix and a suffix, or even two suffixes.

 Blend

- Write the word ***meaningless*** on the board and model dividing the word into syllables and blending the sounds to read the word. Then have students blend it with you.
- Give students the Day One word list from blackline master 2. Have them point to and read the first word on the list.
- Have students independently read the remaining words for Day One. If students need support, guide them as they read some or all of the words on the list before having them read them independently.

Spelling Words: *priceless, useless*

Model

- Make a two-column spelling chart on chart paper labeled "Base Word" and "Word Plus Suffix." As you work through the unit, continue to add the spelling words to the chart and have students use the chart to check their spelling of the words.
- Say the word ***priceless*** and model identifying the base word and then adding the ending.
- **Think Aloud:** *The base of* **priceless** *is* **price.** *I know that* **price** *has a VCe pattern. Then I just add the suffix* **-less** *to spell the word* **priceless.** *If* **less** *means without, then this helps me understand that the word describes something that is so valuable that you can't name a price for it.*

Guide

- Repeat with the word ***useless,*** having students first tell you the base word and its syllable pattern, and then tell the meaning of the word with the suffix added.

Apply

- Have students practice writing the words in their word study notebooks and write a sentence for each. Have students circle the base words and underline the suffix.

Our Spelling Words

Base Word	Word Plus Suffix
price	priceless
use	useless
power	powerless
cloud	cloudless
breath	breathless
fear	fearless

DAY 2

Teacher Tips

Reading Strategies

If students have difficulty applying strategies for challenging words, guide them to use the following strategies:

- look at how the words start and/or end
- look for familiar patterns or parts within the words
- separate the words into syllables and decode each part
- think about what familiar words look like the challenging words
- read forward to check the context
- reread the sentence or paragraph
- mark the words, substitute synonyms, and get on with reading–ask for help later

Comprehension

Use the following questions to ensure that students have understood the passage:

- *What were the spots on the dog?* (Level 1–facts and details)
- *What led Robin to believe the dog was lost?* (Level 2–cause/effect)
- *Did the family ever find the dog's owner? How can you tell?* (Level 3–make inferences)

Fluency

Intervene if students are having difficulty reading the passage. Model how to use word and meaning strategies to problem-solve the words. After students have had a chance to read the passage silently, have them read it aloud for fluency. Model fluent reading of the passage. For students who struggle, you may want to read the passage a second time and have them echo-read along with you.

Blend

- Have students blend the words on the word list for Day Two, using the procedure for blending from Day One.

Develop Automaticity in Word Recognition

- Circle the following words on the overhead: ***does(n't), keep, let('s), off, paper, those, white.***
- Tell students that practicing these words will help them recognize the words automatically so they can read more fluently. Explain that students can sound out some of these words, but they will read more quickly if they don't have to stop and sound out the words each time they see them.
- Read each word. Point out that ***doesn't*** and ***let's*** are contractions.
- Have students read aloud with you the sentences in the passage that contain the words. Then have them write the words in their word study notebooks.
- Give students a copy of blackline master 7. Point out the words from this lesson as well as other words they have learned previously. Have them cut out the words, store them in an envelope, and use them for practice activities.

Build Fluency with Connected Text

Model

- Begin reading aloud the passage on the overhead and model making a mistake, reading ***wondered*** for ***wandered.***
- **Think Aloud:** *This doesn't make sense. Let me look again at that word. I see a part I recognize:* **wand.** *Then I add* **-er** *and* **-ed: wandered.** *I think this word tells how the dog came into the yard. He didn't just walk in purposely, but kind of ambled along.*
- Continue reading and point out words with the suffix ***-less***.
- **Think Aloud:** *I read three words with the suffix* **-less: homeless, friendless,** *and* **ownerless.** *This means the dog didn't have a home or people to care for him.*

Guide

- Continue reading and stop at other words in the passage. Guide students as they read the words.

Apply

- Have students take turns reading blackline master 3 to partners or in small groups as you monitor their reading. Use the teacher tips to check comprehension and fluency.

Spelling Words: *powerless, cloudless*

- Have students practice writing the spelling words from Day One in their word study notebooks. Have them refer to words on the spelling chart to check their spelling.
- Introduce the Day Two spelling words. Follow the format for Day One as you guide students to first identify the base word and the spellings for the ***/ou/*** sound. Then have them add the suffix.
- Have students practice writing each of the words in their word study notebooks. Have them write a sentence for each of the words.

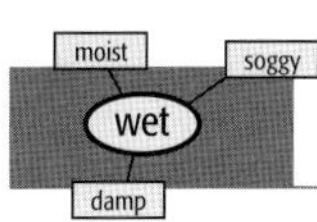

Blend

- Have students blend the words on the word list for Day Three, using the procedure for blending from Day One.

Develop Word Meanings

- Expand students' meaning base for selected base words used in this and other units covering prefixes and suffixes. Create a word web on the board and write one of the base words in the center circle. Model brainstorming other forms of this word using the suffixes and prefixes students have learned. Model recording the words in a web. (See the example word web for the word ***color*** below.)
- Write a sentence for each form of the word under each word in the web and read it aloud.
- Have students work in small groups or with partners to create word webs for one or more of the following words: ***play (display, replay, playfully), grace (disgrace, graceless, gracefully), ease (disease, easy, uneasy, easily), cover (discover, coverless, uncover, recover), count (uncounted, recount, discount, countless).***

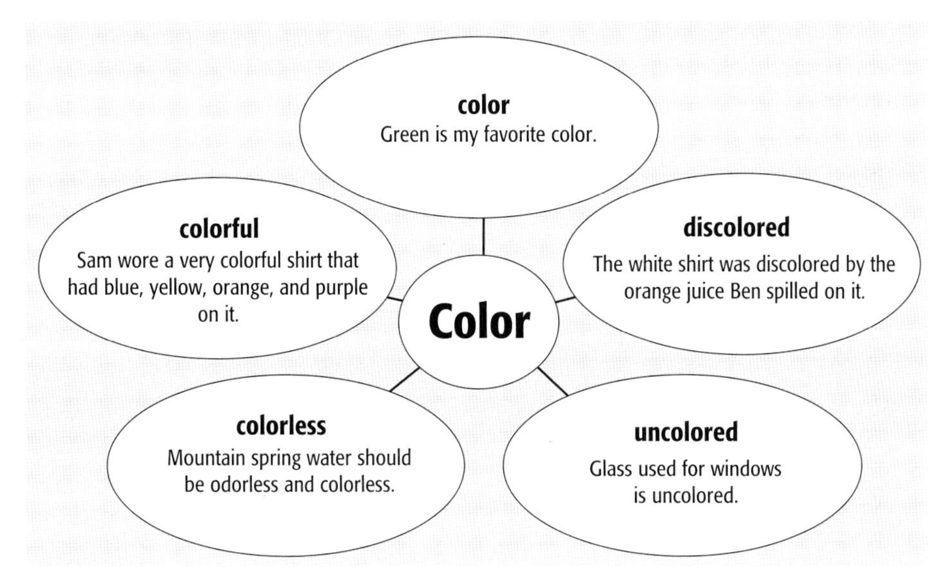

Spelling Words: *breathless, fearless*

- Introduce the Day Three spelling words. Follow the format for Day One as you guide students first to identify the roots, then to identify the syllable patterns and vowel sounds, and finally to add the suffix ***-less.*** Point out the short and r-controlled ***ea*** digraphs in the words.
- Have students practice writing each of the words in their word study notebooks. Have them write a sentence for each of the words.

Build Fluency with Connected Text

- Have students read blackline master 4 to partners or in small groups as you monitor their reading. Call attention to the following words in the reading passage before students read it: ***close(d), eye(s), night, side, still, turn(ing), why.***

Teacher Tips

Opposites

Write the following sentences on the board, underlining the word with the suffix ***-less***: *The teacher had the power to stop the fight. The boy was <u>powerless</u> to stop the fight.* Point out that adding the suffix changes the meaning of the base word to create its opposite. Have students create oral sentences for the following words and discuss how the meanings change: ***hope/hopeless; meat/meatless; color/colorless.***

Develop Automaticity in Word Recognition

Give partners the high-frequency word cards from blackline master 7. As one student reads the passage from blackline master 3 aloud, another student holds up the appropriate high-frequency word card when that word is read in the story.

Repeated Reading

Have students practice repeated readings of blackline master 3 to develop fluency.

DAY 4

Teacher Tips

Making Adverbs

Write the following words on the board: ***endless, fearless, careless, thoughtless.*** Have students use the words in oral sentences and tell how the words are used in the sentences (as adjectives). Add the suffix ***-ly*** to the words and have students use these in oral sentences. Ask how these words are used in the sentences (as adverbs). Have students copy the following words in their word study notebooks, change them into adverbs, and write a sentence for each adverb: ***breathless, spotless, harmless.***

Develop Automaticity in Word Recognition

Make a simple jigsaw puzzle by drawing shapes on cardboard, writing a high-frequency word inside the shape, and then cutting up the shape. Place the cut-up pieces in envelopes. Have students put together the puzzles and then read the words. Students could also make their own jigsaw puzzles using the high-frequency words.

Repeated Reading

Have students practice repeated readings of blackline master 3 to develop fluency.

Blend

- Have students blend the words on the word list for Day Four, using the procedure for blending from Day One.

Write

- Read several rhyming quatrains to students to familiarize them with this poetry form. You may want to copy one on the board and use it to point out its features. Point out that the only hard and fast rule about quatrains is that they are made up of four lines. Quatrain poems don't have to have a set number of syllables, nor does there need to be a matching rhythm from one line to the next.
- Explain that rhyming quatrains have two lines that rhyme with the other two lines.
- Tell students that as a group you are going to try to write a rhyming quatrain that uses words with the suffix ***-less.*** Have students brainstorm a list of words with ***-less*** and a list of words that rhyme with ***less***. Record students' suggestions on the board.
- Have students look at the words and see if they can come up with an idea for using them in a quatrain and which words might work together. As a group, write the quatrain.
- Read the quatrain and have students suggest ways to perfect the rhyme and rhythm.
- Tell students that they can use this quatrain as a model to write their own. (See Day Five activities.)

When Mom and I Paint

When Mom paints a picture of our dog Bo, she makes it look so effortless.

When I paint a picture of our dog Bo, I make a super gooey mess.

I want my picture to be wonderful.

But for now, Bo looks like a one-legged bull.

Spelling Words

- Dictate the following words to students and have them write the words on their papers: ***careless, painless, shoeless, helpless.*** Write the words on the board and have students self-correct their papers.
- Dictate the following sentence and have students write it on their papers: *It was thoughtless of Maria to talk endlessly about herself.*
- Write the sentence on the board and have students self-correct their papers.
- Give pairs of students blackline master 6. While one student reads the spelling words, the other student writes them in the "First Try" column. After the student has spelled the words, the partner places a check mark next to words spelled correctly. For the second try, the partner may prompt the student by sounding out the words that were spelled incorrectly the first time. If the second spelling attempt is correct, the partner places a check mark in the "Second Try" column.

Assessment Tip: Use students' completed peer-check blackline masters to note which words gave students difficulty.

Build Fluency with Connected Text

- Have students take turns reading blackline master 5 to partners or in small groups as you monitor their reading. Call attention to the following words in the reading passage before students read it: ***always, away, eye, here, need(ed), thought, watch(ed).***

Spelling Assessment

Use the following procedure to assess students' spelling of the Unit 30 words.

- Say each spelling word and use it in a sentence.
- Have students write the words on their papers.
- Continue with the next word on the list.
- When students have finished, collect their papers and analyze their spelling of the words.
- Use the assessment to plan small group or individual practice.

Small Group/Independent Activities

The following activities can be used to provide practice for students who need additional support.

WORD STRATEGIES

Write Have students work in small groups or with a partner to write a quatrain. You may want them first to try writing a quatrain with no restrictions on the words they should use. Then challenge them to write a quatrain using words with the suffix ***-less.***

Word Play Have students work with partners and practice reading the words from blackline masters 8 and 9. Then have them combine their sets of word cards to play concentration. Have them spread the cards facedown on a table or the floor and take turns turning over two cards, reading them, and deciding whether they make a pair. If a student's cards are not a pair, the cards are turned facedown again for the other student's turn.

AUTOMATICITY IN WORD RECOGNITION

What's the Word? Have students work in small groups and place the high-frequency words from blackline master 7 facedown in the center of the circle. Have students take turns providing clues about a word. The other students race to guess the word.

Develop Automaticity in Word Recognition Have students place all sixteen high-frequency word cards from blackline master 7 in alphabetical order. Have a partner check the order. Then have partners alternate reading the word cards one at a time.

BUILD FLUENCY WITH CONNECTED TEXT

Repeated Reading Have students practice reading blackline master 3 several times, until they feel they can read it fluently and accurately. Have them work with partners to time one another as they read the passage aloud. Have them set a goal of reading 90 words per minute.

SPELLING

Make Words Provide a set of letter cards and the week's spelling words on index cards. Have students use the letter cards to spell the words. They should check their spelling by blending the sounds and then looking at the words on the index cards.

Unscramble Write the following spelling words on the board, by scrambling the letters: ***slecripes, teabrslehs, lsucodlse, ralsefes, eslrpwoes,*** and ***suesles.*** Have students unscramble the letters and write the words in their word study notebooks.

Teacher Tips

Home Connection

Have students take blackline master 11 home to complete with a family member. Students can also take the repeated reading passage on blackline master 3 home to share with their family.

Quick-Check

Assess students' mastery of the suffix -less using the quick-check for Unit Thirty in this Teacher Resource System.

ELL Support Tip

After modeling how to write rhyming quatrains, pull some of your ELL students into a small group for interactive writing, in which you and the students share the pen to compose the text. Decide as a group which words from their spelling list they would like to use in the poem. Then model the first line of the quatrain to get the group started.

UNIT 30 Quick-Check: Suffix -less

Student Name ______________________ Assessment Date __________

Segmenting and Blending

Directions: Explain that these words use sounds the student has been learning. Have the student point to each word on the corresponding student sheet, segment the word parts or syllables, and blend them together. Put a ✓ if the student successfully segments and blends the word or reads it as a complete unit. If the student misses the word, record the error. **Example:** backless

penniless		toothless		
joyless		boundless		
fearless		flawless		
paperless		thoughtless		Score **/8**

Sight Words

Directions: Have the student point to the first word on the corresponding student sheet and read across the line, saying each word as quickly as possible. Put a ✓ if the student successfully reads the word and an **X** if the student hesitates more than a few seconds. If the student misses the word, record the error.

does		call		
paper		from		
white		one		
let		day		
keep		small		
those		into		
off		back		
about		little		Score **/16**

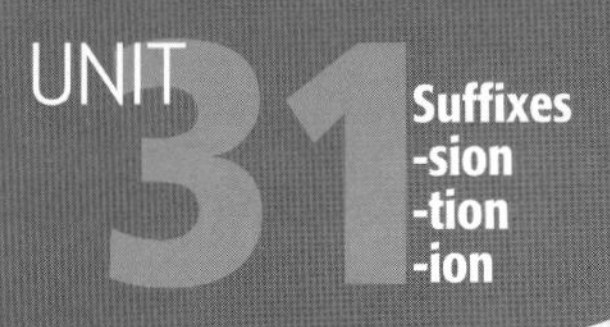

UNIT 31 Suffixes -sion -tion -ion

Unit Objectives

Students will:

- Read words with suffixes -sion, -tion, -ion
- Understand suffixes change a word's meaning
- Review suffix -less
- Expand understanding of selected words with suffixes
- Read high-frequency words ask, does, eat, family, here, while
- Spell words with -ion and -tion endings: rejection, suggestion, direction, decoration, celebration, hesitation, competition, addition, definition
- Write a limerick using words with suffixes -sion, -tion

Day 1

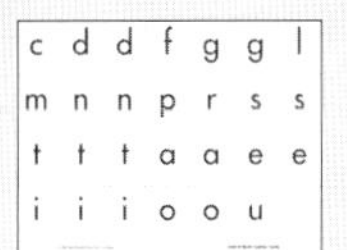

Letter Cards:
a, a, c, e, e, i, l, m, n, o, o, p, r, t, t, t, u

Word Lists (BLM 2)

admission

Teacher Word Cards:
admission, ambition, appreciation, audition, celebration, collision, companion, completion, depression, exhibition, investigation, reaction, suggestion

Day 2

Word Lists (BLM 2)

Reading Passage 1 (BLM 3)

High-Frequency Word Cards for Unit 31 (BLM 7)

Day 3

Word Lists (BLM 2)

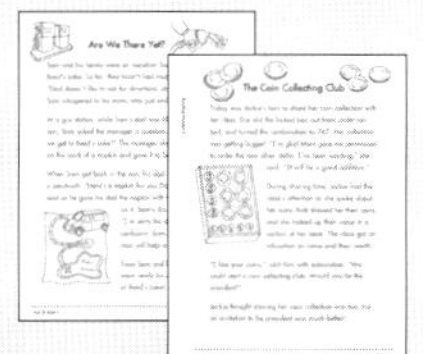

Reading Passages 1 & 2 (BLMs 3 & 4)

High-Frequency Word Cards for Unit 31 (BLM 7)

Day 4

Word Lists (BLM 2)

Reading Passages 1 & 3 (BLMs 3 & 5)

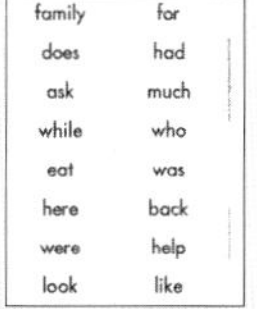

High-Frequency Word Cards for Unit 31 (BLM 7)

Spelling Peer Check (BLM 6)

Day 5

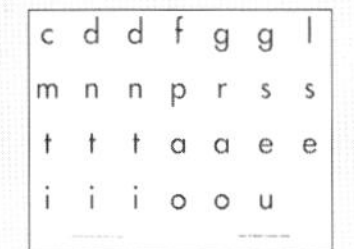

Letter Cards for Unit 31

Reading Passage 1 (BLM 3)

High-Frequency Word Cards for Unit 31 (BLM 7)

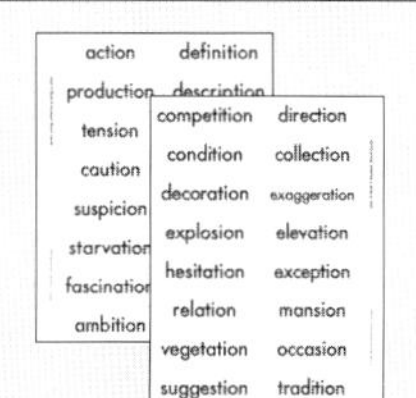

Student Word Cards (BLMs 8 & 9)

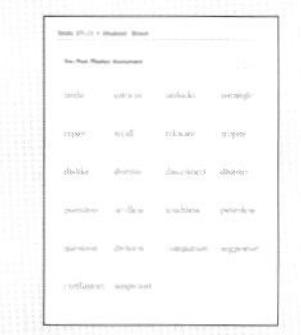

Quick-Check Student Sheet

Frieze Card

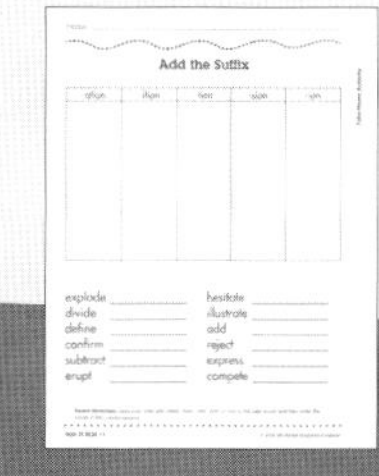

Take-Home Activity

Core Materials

All of these materials can be downloaded from http://phonicsresources.benchmarkeducation.com.

DAY 1

tea/cher Review

- Write the word ***homeless*** on the board and circle the suffix. Ask students what the suffix means and how it helps them understand the meaning of the word.
- Provide students with word clues and have them write the word in their word study notebook. Use the following clues: without pain (***painless***); without fear (***fearless***); without hair (***hairless***); without any dirt (***spotless***); without end (***endless***). After each word, write the word on the board so that students can check their words.

Frieze Card

tea/cher Introduce Suffixes *-sion, -tion, -ion*

Model

- Show students the suffixes ***-sion, -tion, -ion*** frieze card and point out that the highlighted parts of the words in the second column are called suffixes. Remind them that they have already learned other suffixes in previous lessons: ***-er, -or, -ed, -ing, -y,*** and ***-ly.*** Remind them that adding suffixes to a base word changes the meaning of the word and changes the part of speech.
- Point out how you would divide the first word on the list into syllables to read it: ***ex/plo/sion.***

Guide

- Have students read the next base word with you and help them divide the word with the suffix into syllables. Read the word: ***ex/pres/sion***.
- Continue guiding them to first read the base word, and then divide the word plus the suffix into syllables before reading it.
- Have them tell what they notice about how the spelling of the word changes as the suffix is added. For example, for the word ***add, -ition*** is added to the base word; for ***explode, -sion*** is added; and for ***explain, -ation*** is added to the base word.

Apply

- Give students letter cards **c, l, m, n, p, r, t, t, t, a, a, e, e, i, o, o**, and **u.** Say the word ***complete*** and ask students how many syllables they hear. Ask them what vowel sound they hear in the first syllable and to find the letters to spell it: ***com.*** Then have them find the letters to spell the next syllable: ***plete.*** If necessary, remind them of the silent final ***e.*** Ask what they need to do with the final ***e*** when they add the suffix to make ***completion.*** Have them find the letters, make the word, and read it. Having them physically move the letters to make space between the syllables will help them see the closed syllable, the open syllable, and the ending.
- Repeat with the words ***erupt/eruption*** and ***attract/attraction.***

Assessment Tip: Note which students select the correct letters. Guide students who are having difficulty.

Word Study

- Place the following teacher word cards in a pocket chart in random order: **appreciation, celebration, investigation, depression, admission, collision, exhibition, ambition, audition, suggestion, reaction, completion, companion.** Read each word and have students repeat it.
- Have students tell a partner how they would sort the words. After several minutes, ask the groups for their ideas. If students do not consider sorting the words according to their suffixes, show them how you can group the words this way.

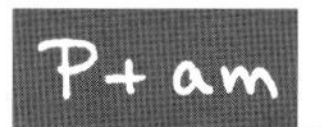

Blend

- Write the word ***illustration*** on the board and model dividing the word into syllables and blending the sounds to read the word. Then have students blend it with you.
- Give students the Day One word list from blackline master 2. Have them point to and read the first word on the list.
- Have students independently read the remaining words for Day One. If students need support, guide them as they read some or all of the words on the list before having them read them independently.

Spelling Words: suggestion, direction

Model

- Make a two-column spelling chart on chart paper labeled "Base Word" and "Word Plus Suffix." As you work through the unit, continue to add the spelling words to the chart.
- Say the word ***suggestion*** and model identifying the base of the word and then adding the ending.
- **Think Aloud:** *The base of* **suggestion** *is* **suggest.** *I hear short vowel sounds in the first and second syllables, so they are closed syllables. To add the suffix, I drop the final* **t** *and add* **-tion.**

Guide

- Repeat with the word ***direction***, having students first identify the base, then identify the syllable patterns and vowel sound, and finally add the suffix.

Apply

- Have students practice writing each of the words in their word study notebooks. Have them write a sentence for each of the words.

Our Spelling Words

Base Word	Word Plus Suffix
suggest	suggestion
direct	direction
decorate	decoration
celebrate	celebration
add	addition
define	definition

DAY 2

Teacher Tips

Reading Strategies

If students have difficulty applying strategies for challenging words, guide them to use the following strategies:

- look at how the words start and/or end
- look for familiar patterns or parts within the words
- separate the words into syllables and decode each part
- think about what familiar words look like the challenging words
- read forward to check the context
- reread the sentence or paragraph
- mark the words, substitute synonyms, and get on with reading–ask for help later

Comprehension

Use the following questions to ensure that students have understood the passage:

- *Where was the family going?* (Level 1–facts and details)
- *Why did Sam ask the manager at the gas station for directions?* (Level 2–cause/effect)
- *Why did Sam's dad laugh when Sam gave him the napkin?* (Level 3–make inferences)

Fluency

Intervene if students are having difficulty reading the passage. Model how to use word and meaning strategies to problem-solve the words. After students have had a chance to read the passage silently, have them read it aloud for fluency. Model fluent reading of the passage. For students who struggle, you may want to read the passage a second time and have them echo-read along with you.

Blend

- Have students blend the words on the word list for Day Two, using the procedure for blending from Day One.

Develop Automaticity in Word Recognition

- Circle the following words on the overhead transparency: ***ask, does, eat(ing), family, here('s), while.***
- Tell students that practicing these words will help them recognize the words automatically so they can read more fluently. Explain that students can sound out some of these words, but they will read more quickly if they don't have to stop and sound out the words each time they see them.
- Read each word. Point out that ***does*** doesn't sound the way it looks. Have students read aloud with you the sentences in the passage that contain the words. Then have them write the words in their word study notebooks.
- Give students a copy of blackline master 7. Point out the words from this lesson as well as other words they have learned previously. Have them cut out the words, store them in an envelope, and use them for practice activities.

Build Fluency with Connected Text

Model

- Begin reading aloud the passage on the overhead transparency. Stop when you come to the word ***vacation.***
- **Think Aloud:** *To help me read this word, one thing I can do is divide it into syllables and sound out each part:* **/vā/ /cā/ /shun/**. *I see other words in this passage that end with the same suffix. If I have trouble reading them, I'll just break them into syllables and read each part.*
- Model making a mistake and self-correcting. For example, read **filing** instead of ***filling.***
- **Think Aloud:** *I read "while Sam's Dad was filing up the van," but that can't be right. It must be "filling up the van." It can't be a long* **i** *sound because when I divide the word into syllables, there are two closed syllables with short vowel sounds.*

Guide

- Continue reading and stop at other words in the passage. Guide students as they read the words.

Apply

- Have students take turns reading blackline master 3 to a partner or in small groups as you monitor the reading. Use the teacher tips to check comprehension and fluency.

Spelling Words: decoration, celebration

- Have students practice writing the spelling words from Day One in their word study notebooks. Have them refer to words on the spelling chart to check their spelling.
- Introduce the Day Two spelling words. Follow the format for Day One as you guide students to first identify the base word, then to identify the syllable patterns and vowel sounds, and finally to add the suffix. Point out that each base word ends with a final ***e***, which is dropped when the suffix is added.
- Have students practice writing each of the words in their word study notebooks. Have them write a sentence for each of the words.

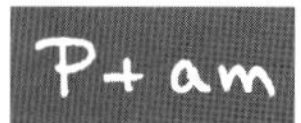

Blend

- Have students blend the words on the word list for Day Three, using the procedure for blending from Day One.

Develop Word Meanings

- Have students copy the chart below in their word study notebooks. Write the following words on the board and have students copy them in the "Word" section of the chart: ***appreciation, identification, location, concentration.***
- Have students put check marks in the columns that show how much they know about each word.
- Place students in small groups and have them discuss each word as a group. Have them begin by finding the base word and talking about what they know about its meaning. Then have them discuss the meaning of the word with the suffix added.
- Have each group collaborate to write a sentence that uses the word.
- Call the groups together and have them share their understandings of the words and share their sentences.
- Have students use a pen with a different color from their first check marks to make new check marks showing their understanding of the word after the group discussion.

Word	Don't know it	I've seen it	I've heard it	I know it	Base word	Suffix
appreciation	✓				appreciate	ion
identification		✓			identify	tion
location				✓	locate	ion
concentration			✓		concentrate	ion

Spelling Words: *addition, definition*

- Introduce the Day Three spelling words. Follow the format for Day One as you guide students to first identify the base words and their syllable patterns and vowel sounds before adding the suffix. Point out that each word adds ***i*** before adding ***-tion.*** Point out that the base word ***define*** ends with a final ***e,*** which is dropped before adding the ***i*** and ***-tion.***
- Have students practice writing each of the words in their word study notebooks. Have them write a sentence for each of the words.

Build Fluency with Connected Text

- Have students read blackline master 4 to partners or in small groups as you monitor their reading. Call attention to the following words in the reading passage before students read it: ***big(ger), book, got, start, thought, turn, under***.

Teacher Tips

Develop Automaticity in Word Recognition

Place students in small groups and give each group a set of the high-frequency word cards from blackline master 7. Have them put the words into a bowl or bag. Have the first student draw a word from the bowl, read the word, and start a story using the word. Have the next student draw a card, read it, and continue the story, using the word. Continue until all the words have been used.

Repeated Reading

Have students practice repeated readings of blackline master 3 to develop fluency.

DAY 4

Teacher Tips

Develop Automaticity in Word Recognition

Have students select six high-frequency words from blackline master 7. Have them read the words, and then turn the cards over while they spell the words. Have them check their spelling by looking at the cards. Then have them write a paragraph that uses all of the words they have selected.

Repeated Reading

Have students practice repeated readings of blackline master 3 to develop fluency.

Other words with -tion

Point out that the letters ***-tion***, ***-sion***, and ***-ion*** at the end of a word do not always represent a suffix. For example, the words ***fashion, champion***, and ***nation*** have no base words. However, students can learn to recognize the ending, which will help them pronounce the word.

Blend

- Have students blend the words on the word list for Day Four, using the procedure for blending from Day One.

Write

- Read several limericks to students to familiarize them with the genre. You may want to copy one on the board and use it to point out its features. Explain that limericks have five lines–the first, second, and fifth lines rhyme, and the third and fourth lines rhyme. Tell students that limericks are meant to be funny and often contain made-up words.
- Tell students that as a group you are going to try to write a limerick that uses ***-sion*** or ***-tion*** suffix words. Have students brainstorm a list of words with these suffixes and record them on the board.
- Circle words with ***-ation*** in one color, words with ***-ition*** in another, and so on. Tell students that they need to pick words from one of the groups so the words will rhyme.
- Have students look at the words and see if they can come up with an idea for using them in a limerick. Have them think about which words might work together. As a group, write the limerick.
- Read the limerick and have students suggest ways to perfect the rhyme and rhythm.
- Tell students that they can use this limerick as a model to write their own. (See Day Five activities.)

A Young Man on Vacation

There was a young man on vacation
Who was looking for some recreation.
He came to a stream,
Which looked so serene
That he jumped in without hesitation.

Spelling Words

- Provide practice for students in segmenting words and associating sounds with spellings. Dictate the following words to students and have them write the words on their papers: ***division, expression, attention, operation.***
- Write the words on the board and have students self-correct their papers.
- Dictate the following sentence and have students write it on their papers: *The conversation was all about the collision of the two buses.*
- Write the sentence on the board and have students self-correct their papers.
- Give pairs of students blackline master 6. While one student reads the spelling words, the other student writes them in the "First Try" column. After the student has spelled the words, the partner places a check mark next to words spelled correctly. For the second try, the partner may prompt the student by sounding out the words that were spelled incorrectly the first time. If the second spelling attempt is correct, the partner places a check mark in the "Second Try" column.

Assessment Tip: Use students' completed peer-check blackline masters to note which words gave students difficulty.

Build Fluency with Connected Text

- Have students take turns reading blackline master 5 to partners or in small groups as you monitor their reading. Call attention to the following words in the reading passage before students read it: ***began, big, family, near, need.***

Spelling Assessment

Use the following procedure to assess students' spelling of the Unit Thirty-One words.
- Say each spelling word and use it in a sentence.
- Have students write the words on their papers.
- Continue with the next word on the list.
- When students have finished, collect their papers and analyze their spelling of the words.
- Use the assessment to plan small group or individual practice.

Small Group/Independent Activities

The following activities can be used to provide practice for students who need additional support.

WORD STRATEGIES

Write Have students work in small groups or with a partner to write a limerick. You may want them to first try writing a limerick with no restrictions on the words they should use. Then challenge them to write a limerick using words with suffixes ***-sion*** or ***-tion.***

Word Sort Have students work in pairs. Have them think of creative ways they can sort the words on blackline masters 8 and 9. When they have grouped the words, have them ask another pair if they can figure out how the words are grouped.

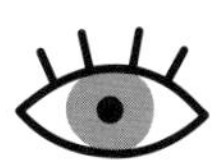

AUTOMATICITY IN WORD RECOGNITION

Find the Word Give students a newspaper page and one or more of the word cards from blackline master 7. Have them search the page to find and circle the word(s). Have them use a different color crayon for each word if they are looking for more than one word.

Game Have students work with a partner or in a small group, using a basic game board like Snakes and Ladders and a dice. Have them take turns throwing the dice, drawing a high-frequency word, and reading it. If they read the word correctly, they can move along the game board the number of spaces indicated on the dice. If they read the word incorrectly, they can either stay where they are or go back the number of spaces on the dice.

BUILD FLUENCY WITH CONNECTED TEXT

Repeated Reading Have students practice reading blackline master 3 several times, until they feel they can read it fluently and accurately. Have them work with partners to time one another as they read the passage aloud. Have them set a goal of reading ninety words per minute.

SPELLING

Make Words Provide a set of letter cards and the week's spelling words on index cards. Have students use the letter cards to spell the words. They should check their spelling by blending the sounds and then looking at the words on the index cards.

Riddles Place students in small groups and give each group several self-stick notes. Give a clue to one of the spelling words. Have the groups race to figure out the spelling word, spell it correctly, and bring it to you. The team that gets the word to you spelled correctly gets a point. Continue with the next word. Example clues are: *something that can slow you down (**hesitation**); a refusal (**rejection**); a proposal (**suggestion**); opposite of subtraction (**addition**); the way to go (**direction**); a meaning (**definition**); something that beautifies (**decoration**); an enjoyable occasion (**celebration**); where athletes perform (**competition**).*

Teacher Tips

Home Connection

Have students take blackline master 11 home to complete with a family member. Students can also take the repeated reading passage on blackline master 3 home to share with their family.

Quick-Check

Assess students' mastery of suffixes ***-sion***, ***-tion***, and ***-ion*** using the quick-check for Unit Thirty-One in this Teacher Resource System.

ELL Support Tip

Depending on language proficiency of the students, the sounds of suffixes ***-sion*** and ***-tion*** can be difficult. For lower language proficiency students, have pairs of students use two different color highlighter pens and examples of simple text to highlight words with the suffixes as they find them in the text. This will give students the opportunity to see and say the sound. For higher level language proficiency students, have them sort words according to the suffixes.

UNIT 31 Quick-Check: Suffixes -sion, -tion, -ion

Student Name ______________________ Assessment Date __________

Segmenting and Blending

Directions: Explain that these words use sounds the student has been learning. Have the student point to each word on the corresponding student sheet, segment the word parts or syllables, and blend them together. Put a ✓ if the student successfully segments and blends the word or reads it as a complete unit. If the student misses the word, record the error.
Example: motion

vision		donation		
edition		erosion		
illusion		solution		
suspicion		invasion		Score **/8**

Sight Words

Directions: Have the student point to the first word on the corresponding student sheet and read across the line, saying each word as quickly as possible. Put a ✓ if the student successfully reads the word and an X if the student hesitates more than a few seconds. If the student misses the word, record the error.

family		ask		
eat		were		
for		much		
was		help		
does		while		
here		look		
had		who		
back		like		Score **/16**

UNIT 32 Greek roots

Unit Objectives

Students will:

- Recognize Greek roots in words and understand that they give clues to the meanings of words
- Review suffixes -sion, -tion
- Understand how words grow from root words
- Analyze words according to their roots and affixes
- Read high-frequency words book, does, got, idea, let, start, watch
- Spell words with Greek roots: biography, geography, biology, geology, telegraph, television
- Write an explanatory paragraph about one of the Greek roots

Day 1

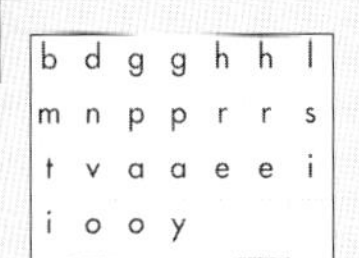

Letter Cards:
a, a, d, e, g, h, h, i, m, p, p, o, o, r, r, t

Word Lists (BLM 2)

Day 2

Word Lists (BLM 2)

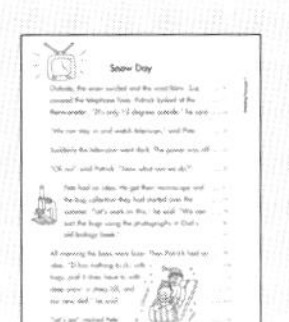
Reading Passage 1 (BLM 3)

High-Frequency Word Cards for Unit 32 (BLM 7)

Day 3

Word Lists (BLM 2)

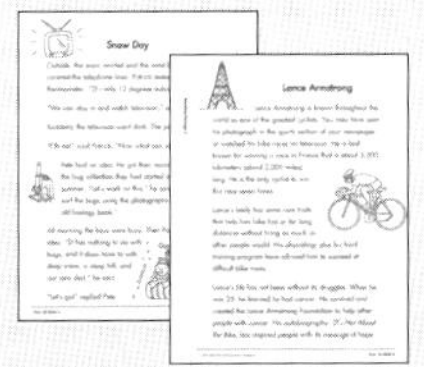
Reading Passages 1 & 2 (BLMs 3 & 4)

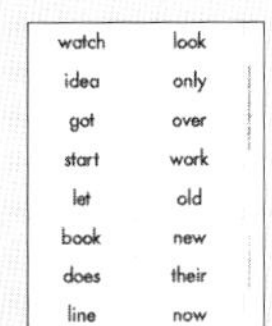

High-Frequency Word Cards for Unit 32 (BLM 7)

Day 4

Word Lists (BLM 2)

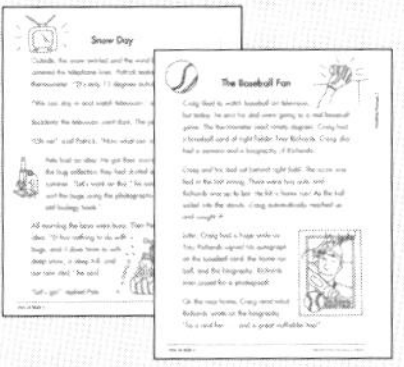
Reading Passages 1 & 3 (BLMs 3 & 5)

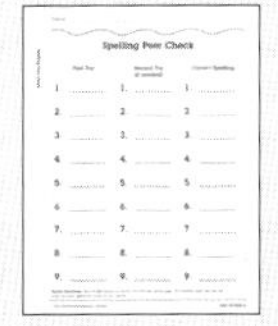
Spelling Peer Check (BLM 6)

Day 5

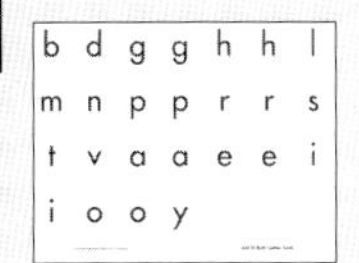

Letter Cards for Unit 32

Reading Passage 1 (BLM 3)

High-Frequency Word Cards for Unit 32 (BLM 7)

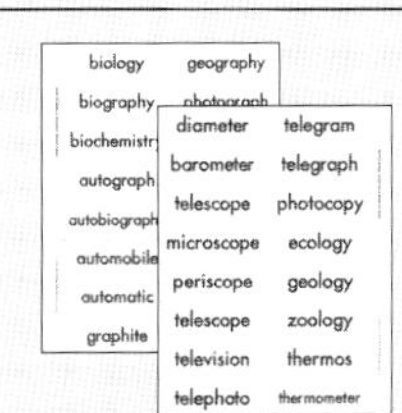

Student Word Cards (BLMs 8 & 9)

Quick-Check Student Sheet

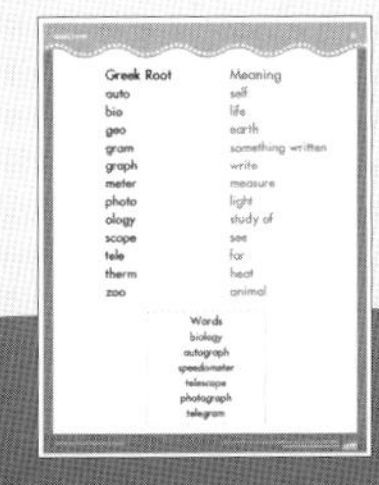

Frieze Card

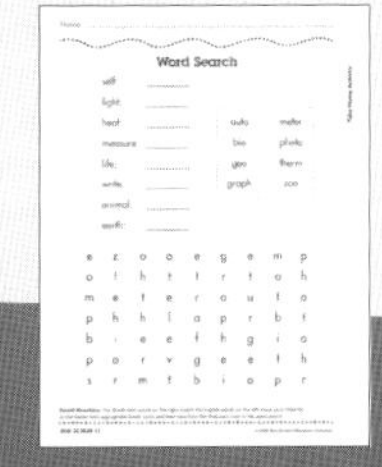

Take-Home Activity

Core Materials

All of these materials can be downloaded from http://phonicsresources.benchmarkeducation.com.

DAY 1

Greek Root	Meaning
auto	self
bio	life
geo	earth
gram	something written
graph	write
meter	measure
photo	light
ology	study of
scope	see
tele	far
therm	heat
zoo	animal

Words
biology
autograph
speedometer
telescope
photograph
telegram

Frieze Card

tea/cher Review Suffixes *-tion, -sion*

- Write the word ***addition*** on the board. Model how you would divide the word into syllables in order to read it: ***ad/di/tion.*** Point out that the open syllable in this case has a short sound. Circle the suffix ***-ition*** and explain that students could also work out the word by first recognizing the suffix and then reading the root: ***add/ition.*** Explain that both ways will work to help them read unfamiliar words.
- Write the following words on the board and guide students to read them by dividing the words into syllables or by recognizing the root and the suffix: ***ab/bre/vi/a/tion (abbreviate, ation); des/crip/tion (describe, tion); con/clu/sion (conclude, sion).***

tea/cher Introduce Greek Roots

Model

- Explain that many words in our language have their beginnings in other languages. Use the Greek roots frieze card to model the root words and their meanings.
- Tell students that it will help them read unfamiliar words, especially in their content-area reading, if they can recognize the root of a word and remember its meaning. Point to the word ***biology*** and model how you can use the meanings of ***bio*** and ***ology*** to understand that the word means the study of living things.

Guide

- Have students look at each word on the list and use the information about the roots and their meanings to tell the meaning of each word.
- Have students use what they know about syllable patterns to help them sound out the words.

Apply

- Give students letter cards **d, g, h, h, m, p, p, r, r, t, a, a, e, i, o,** and **o.** Have students find the letters to spell the root ***gram.*** Then say the word ***diagram*** and ask what letters they need to add to ***gram*** to make the word. Repeat with ***gram*** and the word ***program*** and the root ***graph*** and the word ***photograph.***

Assessment Tip: Note which students correctly make the words and guide students who are having difficulty.

Word Study

- On chart paper, draw the outline of a tree with several branches. Write the root ***ology*** at the base of the tree. Have students brainstorm as many words that use the root as possible and record the words on the tree branches.
- Talk about the meanings of the words and have students use their dictionaries to locate the words, check their meanings, and find their origins.
- Post the tree in the room and have students be on the lookout for other ***ology*** words that can be added to the tree.
- Have students choose one of the Greek roots from the frieze card and make a tree in their word study notebooks. Have them continue to add to their tree as they discover other words in their reading.

P+ am Blend

- Write the word ***geometry*** on the board and model dividing it into syllables to pronounce the word: *ge/om/et/ry*. Then circle the root and model using it to figure out the meaning of the word.
- Give students the word list on blackline master 2 and have them point to the first word for Day One and read the word. Have them circle the root and use it to tell the meaning of the word.
- Have students independently read the remaining words for Day One. Guide students who need support to read some or all of the words on the list before having them read them independently.

Spelling Words: *biography, geography*

Model

- Make a two-column spelling chart on chart paper labeled "Greek Roots" and "Spelling Word." Add the spelling words to the chart each day.
- Say the word ***biography*** and model spelling it and writing it on chart paper.
- **Think Aloud:** *It helps to spell this word if I divide it into syllables:* **bi/og/raph/y.** *Then I can use what I know about vowel sounds in open and closed syllables to spell the word. To figure out its meaning, I use what I know about Greek roots.* **Bio** *means life and* **graph** *means writing, so from that I know the word means something written about a person's life.*

Guide

- Guide students as they say ***geography*** with you, dividing the word into syllables. Have them use what they know about syllable patterns to tell you what letters to write on the spelling chart. Point out that it is easier to spell the words if they know how to spell ***graph***. Then all they have to do is add ***bio, geo,*** or ***-y.*** Have students use the roots to make sure they understand the meanings of the words.

Apply

- Have students practice writing each of the words in their word study notebooks. Have them circle the root in the words and then write a sentence for each of the words.

Our Spelling Words

Greek Roots	Spelling Word
bio, graph	biography
geo, graph	geography
bio, ology	biology
geo, ology	geology
tele, graph	telegraph
tele	television

DAY 2

Teacher Tips

Reading Strategies

If students have difficulty applying strategies for challenging words, guide them to use the following strategies:

- look at how the words start and/or end
- look for familiar patterns or parts within the words
- separate the words into syllables and decode each part
- think about what familiar words look like the difficult words
- read forward to check the context
- reread the sentence or paragraph
- mark the words, substitute synonyms, and get on with reading–ask for help later

Comprehension

Use the following questions to ensure that students have understood the passage:

- *What was it like outside?*
  (Level 1–facts and details)
- *Why did the boys decide to sort the bugs instead of watching television?*
  (Level 2–cause/effect)
- *How would you describe Pete and Patrick?*
  (Level 3–analyze character)

Fluency

Intervene if students are having difficulty reading the passage. Model how to use word and meaning strategies to problem-solve the words. After students have had a chance to read the passage silently, have them read it aloud for fluency. Model fluent reading of the passage. For students who struggle, you may want to read the passage a second time and have them echo-read along with you.

Blend

- Have students blend the words on the word list for Day Two, using the procedure for blending from Day One.

Develop Automaticity in Word Recognition

- Circle the following words on the overhead transparency: ***book, does, got, idea, let('s), start(ed), watch.***
- Tell students that practicing these words will help them recognize the words automatically so they can read more fluently. Explain that students can sound out some of these words, but they will read more quickly if they don't have to stop and sound out the words each time they see them.
- Read each word. Point out that the ***t*** in ***watch*** is silent and that the ***s*** in ***does*** stands for the **/z/** sound. Have students read aloud with you the sentences in the passage that contain the words. Then have them write the words in their word study notebooks.
- Give students a copy of blackline master 7. Point out the words from this lesson as well as other words they have learned previously. Have them cut out the words, store them in an envelope, and use them for practice activities.

Build Fluency with Connected Text

Model

- Begin reading aloud the passage on the overhead transparency. Stop when you come to the word ***thermometer.*** Model sounding out and reading the word.
- **Think Aloud:** *I can divide this word into syllables and sound out each part. The first syllable has an r-controlled sound:* **/ûr/**. *The second syllable is a closed syllable:* **/mom/**. *I know that the end of the word is the Greek root* **meter,** *which means measure. The word is* **thermometer** *and it means something we use to measure temperature.*
- Model making a mistake and correcting it–for example, read ***po/wer*** instead of ***pow/er.***
- **Think Aloud:** *That's not right. I divided the word before the* **w** *and got an open syllable, but the long vowel sound doesn't sound right. If I divide the word after the* **w,** *I have a syllable with the letters* **ow.** *I know this can stand for the long sound, but that didn't work. The letters can also stand for the* **/ou/** *sound. The word is* **power.** *In this sentence, it means that the electricity went off. That makes sense because the television didn't work.*

Guide

- Continue reading and stop at other words in the passage. Guide students as they read the words.

Apply

- Have students take turns reading blackline master 3 to partners or in small groups as you monitor their reading. Use the teacher tips to check comprehension and fluency.

Spelling Words: *biology, geology*

- Have students practice writing the spelling words from Day One in their word study notebooks. Have them refer to words on the spelling chart to check their spelling.
- Introduce the Day Two spelling words. Follow the format for Day One as you guide students to say each word, identify the syllables and their vowel sounds, and then tell you what letters to write on the spelling chart. Point out the words are from the ***ology*** family.
- Have students practice writing each of the words in their word study notebooks. Have them write a sentence for each of the words.

DAY 3

Blend

- Have students blend the words on the word list for Day Three, using the procedure for blending from Day One.

Develop Word Meanings

- Create a semantic feature analysis chart similar to the one shown below. Write the features of the words across the top. Write the first word in the column on the left. Model how you identify the features of the word and record them in the appropriate spaces.
- **Think Aloud:** *This word* **(biography)** *has two Greek roots,* **bio** *and* **graph.** *I will write these in the column labeled "Greek Roots." It also has the suffix* **-y** *which I will record in the "Suffix" column.*
- Write the next word in the column on the left. Guide students as they identify its features.
- You may want to continue guiding students as they analyze each word. Alternatively, students could make a copy of the chart in their word study notebooks and analyze the words independently or in pairs.

	Prefix	Suffix	Greek Roots	Base Words
biography		y	bio, graph	
untied	un	ed		tie
hesitation		tion		hesitate
discovered	dis	ed		cover
carelessly		less, ly		care
telegraph	tele		tele, graph	
dishonest	dis			honest
refreshed	re	ed		fresh
geology		y	geo, ology	
telescope			tele, scope	
timeless		less		time
television		ion	tele	

Spelling Words: *telegraph, television*

- Introduce the Day Three spelling words. Say each word and have students identify the Greek root(s). Have them tell you what letters to use to write the words on the spelling chart. Point out that all the words use the Greek root ***tele***. Ask students what the Greek root ***vis*** means and how it helps them understand the meaning of ***television.***
- Have students practice writing each of the words in their word study notebooks. Have them write a sentence for each of the words. Have them circle the Greek roots.

Build Fluency with Connected Text

- Have students read blackline master 4 to partners or in small groups as you monitor their reading. Call attention to the following words in the reading passage before students read it: ***hard, its, life, mile(s), watch(ed), without, world.***

Teacher Tips

Using Greek Roots

After students have completed the chart, either working with you or independently, have them select several words from the chart and use them in written sentences. Have students share their sentences.

Glossary

Divide students into groups and assign each group a Greek root. Have the group find words that use the root, write definitions for the words, and draw a picture that illustrates the meaning of the root. Compile the pages the groups create into a class glossary.

Develop Automaticity in Word Recognition

Have students work with a partner to flash the words on blackline master 7 for each other. Have them put any words they have difficulty with in a pile and read these a second time.

Repeated Reading

Have students practice repeated readings of blackline master 3 to develop fluency.

DAY 4

Teacher Tips

Greek Roots in Science

Reinforce that understanding the meanings of Greek roots will help students read content-area texts, particularly science. Give students a selection of science books from the library and from their reading and have them work with a partner to search for words using the Greek roots they have learned in this unit. Have students share their findings and discuss how knowing the meaning of the roots can help them work out the meanings of the words.

Develop Automaticity in Word Recognition

Write the following high-frequency words on the board: ***book, does, got, idea, let, start, watch.*** Randomly point to the words and have students read them. Vary the pace and repeat several times. Then ask volunteers to create oral sentences using one of the words. Instead of saying the word, they are to say the word ***blank.*** Have the volunteers call on someone to point to the words on the board that were used in the sentences.

Repeated Reading

Have students practice repeated readings of blackline master 3 to develop fluency.

Blend

- Have students blend the words on the word list for Day Four, using the procedure for blending from Day One.

Write

- Tell students that, as a group, they will write a paragraph about one of the Greek roots. Have them brainstorm words for the root ***therm*** and record their suggestions.
- Have students suggest an opening for the paragraph. Then have them tell you what to write next. Guide them as needed and encourage them to use words from the brainstormed list.
- Ask students how the paragraph should end and, if necessary, model writing the ending sentence.
- Read the paragraph aloud, and have students check to see if they need to fix any problems with it. Ask them if the paragraph describes the root clearly so that someone who is unfamiliar with it will know what it means and how to use it.
- Tell students that they can use this paragraph as a model to write their own descriptions of a Greek root of their choice. (See Day Five activities.)

The root "therm" comes from Greek and means "heat." Knowing this root word can help you understand many other words. If you read that someone is wearing thermal clothing, knowing that "therm" means "heat" will help you understand that the person is wearing clothing to keep warm. If you read that this person has put hot chocolate in a thermos, you understand that this is a container that keeps things warm. The person then looks at a thermometer. Not only do you recognize the root "therm," but you also recognize the Greek root, "meter," which means "to measure." Now you know that the person is looking at something that measures how warm it is.

Spelling Words

- Dictate the following words to students and have them write the words on their papers: ***digraph, photograph, zoology, automatic.***
- Write the words on the board and have students self-correct their papers.
- Dictate the following sentence and have students write it on their papers: *The special telescope could take photographs.*
- Write the sentence on the board and have students self-correct their papers.
- Give pairs of students blackline master 6. While one student reads the spelling words, the other student writes them in the "First Try" column. After the student has spelled the words, the partner places a check mark next to words spelled correctly. For the second try, the partner may prompt the student by sounding out the words that were spelled incorrectly the first time. If the second spelling attempt is correct, the partner places a check mark in the "Second Try" column.

Assessment Tip: Use students' completed peer-check blackline masters to note which words gave students difficulty.

Build Fluency with Connected Text

- Have students take turns reading blackline master 5 to partners or in small groups as you monitor their reading. Call attention to the following words in the reading passage before students read it: ***even, home, last, later, read, watch.***

Spelling Assessment

Use the following procedure to assess students' spelling of the Unit Thirty-Two words.
- Say each spelling word and use it in a sentence.
- Have students write the words on their papers.
- Continue with the next word on the list.
- When students have finished, collect their papers and analyze their spelling of the words.
- Use the assessment to plan small group or individual practice.

Small Group/Independent Activities

The following activities can be used to provide practice for students who need additional support.

WORD STRATEGIES

Write Have students select Greek roots and write paragraphs about them, similar to the group paragraph. When they have finished, have them reread their paragraphs to check whether they have clearly explained the meaning of a root so that someone who didn't know what it meant could understand it by reading the paragraph.

Word Sort Have students use the student word cards from blackline masters 8 and 9 and sort the words into categories of their choice.

Guess the Word Have students work with a partner. The partner draws one of the student word cards from blackline masters 8 or 9 and provides clues about the word–for example, "The root means self and the word can describe a washing machine."

AUTOMATICITY IN WORD RECOGNITION

Read the Word Have students work with a partner to combine their sets of high-frequency word cards from blackline master 7 to play a game of concentration. Have them spread out the words facedown on the floor or desk. Have them take turns turning over two cards, reading them, and seeing whether they match.

Spin the Bottle Have a group of students sit in a circle with one of the high-frequency word cards in front of them facing out. Have them take turns spinning the bottle. When the bottle stops, have them read the word it is pointing to. To make it more of a challenge, have students place two or more words in front of them. When the bottle stops, they must read all the words the bottle is pointing at.

BUILD FLUENCY WITH CONNECTED TEXT

Repeated Reading Have students practice reading blackline master 3 several times, until they feel they can read it fluently and accurately. Have them work with a partner to time each other as they read the passage aloud. Have them set a goal of reading 90 words per minute.

SPELLING

Make Words Provide a set of letter cards and the week's spelling words on index cards. Have students use the letter cards to spell the words. They should check their spelling by blending the sounds and then looking at the words on the index cards.

Look, Cover, Say, Write Have students who are having difficulty with the spelling words look carefully at one of the words and then say it. Ask them to cover the word and write it without looking at the model. Have them uncover the word and check the spelling. Have them repeat with other words on the spelling list.

Teacher Tips

Home Connection

Have students take blackline master 11 home to complete with a family member. Students can also take the repeated reading passage on blackline master 3 home to share with their family.

Quick-Check

Assess students' mastery of greek roots using the quick-check for Unit Thirty-Two in this Teacher Resource System.

ELL Support Tip

Greek roots can be difficult for any student, but even more difficult for ELL students. Make clear connections to what they already know when introducing the Greek roots. For example, use ***tele*** or ***zoo*** first, since these roots will be the easiest to find realia to use to activate students' background. Once students begin to gain understanding of the concept of Greek roots, move to the more difficult or less common Greek roots.

Quick-Check: Greek roots

Student Name ______________________________ Assessment Date ____________

Segmenting and Blending

Directions: Explain that these words use sounds the student has been learning. Have the student point to each word on the corresponding student sheet, segment the word parts or syllables, and blend them together. Put a ✓ if the student successfully segments and blends the word or reads it as a complete unit. If the student misses the word, record the error. **Example:** thermosphere

stethoscope		biopsy		
pathology		holograph		
visible		photon		
diagram		altimeter		Score **/8**

Sight Words

Directions: Have the student point to the first word on the corresponding student sheet and read across the line, saying each word as quickly as possible. Put a ✓ if the student successfully reads the word and an **X** if the student hesitates more than a few seconds. If the student misses the word, record the error.

watch		look		
idea		only		
got		over		
start		work		
let		old		
book		new		
does		their		
line		now		Score **/16**

Pre/Post Phonics Assessment Instructions

1. Make a copy of the student sheet. Laminate if desired.
2. Make a copy of the teacher record form for each student.
3. Administer the assessment one-on-one.
4. Count a response correct if the student successfully segments and blends the word by word parts or syllables or reads it as a complete unit. Document any errors.
5. Stop the testing in any unit in which the student misses ONE item. Begin instruction in this unit for explicit systematic instruction.
6. For intervention purposes, you may administer the whole pretest and analyze the results to determine if the student has mastered the unit skills or needs further instruction, reinforcement, or practice.

Quick-Check Assessment Instructions

1. Make a copy of the student sheet. Laminate if desired.
2. Make a copy of the teacher record form for each student.
3. Administer the Quick-Check one-on-one.
4. For segmenting and blending, use the example word provided with the directions to ensure the student understands what to do. Count a response correct if the student successfully segments and blends the word by word parts or syllables or reads it as a complete unit. Document any errors.
5. For sight words, have the student read each word as quickly as possible, documenting hesitations or misses.
6. Analyze the results to determine if the student has mastered the unit skills or needs further instruction, reinforcement, or practice.

Reading Rate Assessment Instructions

Reading fluency, phrasing, and rate may be assessed whenever a student reads aloud. Use the procedure below to measure oral reading fluency.

1. Make two copies of BLM 3 from the Reproducible Tools and Activities Booklet. One is for the teacher and one is for the student.
2. Give the student a brief introduction to the passage. Set a timer for one minute. Ask the student to read the passage using his or her best voice.
3. As the student reads, mark any errors with a / (slash) through the words. Use the assessment guidelines below.
4. At the end of one minute, mark the point in the text where the student was reading by circling the last word read. Allow the student to finish reading the passage.
5. Count the number of words read correctly. Use the chart on page xxxix to compare the student's performance to the national norm for the grade level and time of year. Document this on the My Fluency Practice Graph.
6. Use the Oral Fluency and Phrasing Rating Rubric to rate the student's fluency and phrasing while reading.

Guidelines

Words read correctly include words that are self-corrected within three seconds of an error. (Mark each self-correction with SC above the word.) Correctly read words that are repeated are not counted as errors. Words read incorrectly should be marked with a / (slash). The following errors are counted as incorrect:

- Mispronounced words—words that are misread.
- Word substitutions—one word read for another word. For example, *boat* for *ship*.
- Omissions or skipped words—words that are not read.
- Hesitations—If the student hesitates for three seconds or longer, say the word and have the student continue reading.

Pre/Post Phonics Assessment

clam	kept	limp	sock
brush	cactus	hiccup	consent
made	smile	quote	tune
mistake	inside	tadpole	excuse
be	so	pry	lady
silent	doughnut		

Pre/Post Phonics Assessment

mail	sway	they	weigh
detail	playmate	obey	eighty
throat	flown	foe	below
foamy	rowboat	treat	sneeze
grief	easy	between	relief
people	hockey	thigh	pie
brighten	design	untie	twilight

Pre/Post Phonics Assessment

charm	star	artist	racecar
storm	wore	pour	forest
explore	yourself	learn	serve
twirl	surf	early	perfect
thirsty	turnip	share	fair
wear	berry	prepare	stairway
bearskin			

Pre/Post Phonics Assessment

moist	joy	poison	employ
growl	pouch	towel	aloud
crew	youth	glue	broom
chewy	regroup	pursue	cartoon
shook	bush	pull	would
crooked	pushpin	bully	lawn
small	floss	walk	vault
sought	jigsaw	recall	bossy
salty	faultless	thoughtful	wiggle
twinkle	fable	shuffle	

Pre/Post Phonics Assessment

wildlife	playpen	fingerprint	understand
I'm	she'll	he'd	didn't
you've	we're	let's	that's
stones	papers	lunches	ponies
mice	geese	knives	children
women	oxen		

Pre/Post Phonics Assessment

played	stacked	graded	trusting
planning	joking	farmer	actor
jogger	sailor	faster	wider
funnier	longest	safest	prettiest
crunchy	juicy	fluffy	stringy
deeply	lively	busily	finally

Pre/Post Phonics Assessment

undo	untwist	unlucky	untangle
repay	recall	relocate	reopen
dislike	dismiss	disconnect	disaster
pointless	seedless	toothless	penniless
question	division	companion	suggestion
confusion	suspicion		

Pre/Post Phonics Assessment

biology	diagram	microscope
thermometer	photography	geometry
telephone	digraph	program
grammar	zoology	graphic

Student Name: ______________________________________

Pre/Post Phonics Assessment

Directions: Have the student point to each word on the corresponding student sheet, segment the word parts or syllables, and blend them together. Put a ✔ if the student successfully segments and blends the word or reads it as a complete unit. If the student misses the word, record the error.

	Pretest Date:	**Posttest Date:**
Unit 1: Closed-syllable patterns		
clam		
kept		
limp		
sock		
brush		
cactus		
hiccup		
consent		
Unit 2: CVCe syllable patterns		
made		
smile		
quote		
tune		
mistake		
inside		
tadpole		
excuse		
Unit 3: Open-syllable patterns		
be		
so		
pry		
lady		
silent		
doughnut		
	Score /22	**Score** /22

Teacher Record Form ▪ Units 4–7

Student Name: ____

Pre/Post Phonics Assessment

Directions: Have the student point to each word on the corresponding student sheet, segment the word parts or syllables, and blend them together. Put a ✔ if the student successfully segments and blends the word or reads it as a complete unit. If the student misses the word, record the error.

	Pretest Date:	**Posttest Date:**
Unit 4: Long a digraph syllable patterns		
mail		
sway		
they		
weigh		
detail		
playmate		
obey		
eighty		
Unit 5: Long o digraph syllable patterns		
throat		
flown		
foe		
below		
foamy		
rowboat		
Unit 6: Long e digraph syllable patterns		
treat		
sneeze		
grief		
easy		
between		
relief		
people		
hockey		
Unit 7: Long i digraph syllable patterns		
thigh		
pie		
brighten		
design		
untie		
twilight		
	Score /28	**Score /28**

Student Name: ______________________________

Pre/Post Phonics Assessment

Directions: Have the student point to each word on the corresponding student sheet, segment the word parts or syllables, and blend them together. Put a ✔ if the student successfully segments and blends the word or reads it as a complete unit. If the student misses the word, record the error.

	Pretest Date:	**Posttest Date:**
Unit 8: r-controlled a syllable patterns		
charm		
star		
artist		
racecar		
Unit 9: r-controlled o syllable patterns		
storm		
wore		
pour		
forest		
explore		
yourself		
Unit 10: r-controlled e, i, u syllable patterns		
learn		
serve		
twirl		
surf		
early		
perfect		
thirsty		
turnip		
Unit 11: r-controlled /âr/ syllable patterns		
share		
fair		
wear		
berry		
prepare		
stairway		
bearskin		
	Score /25	**Score /25**

Teacher Record Form ▪ Units 12–17

Student Name: ____

Pre/Post Phonics Assessment

Directions: Have the student point to each word on the corresponding student sheet, segment the word parts or syllables, and blend them together. Put a ✔ if the student successfully segments and blends the word or reads it as a complete unit. If the student misses the word, record the error.

	Pretest Date:	**Posttest Date:**		**Pretest Date:**	**Posttest Date:**
Unit 12: Vowel diphthong /oi/ syllable patterns			**Unit 16: Variant vowel /ô/ syllable patterns**		
moist			lawn		
joy			small		
poison			floss		
employ			walk		
Unit 13: Vowel diphthong /ou/ syllable patterns			vault		
growl			sought		
pouch			jigsaw		
towel			recall		
aloud			bossy		
Unit 14: Variant vowel /o͞o/ syllable patterns			salty		
crew			faultless		
youth			thoughtful		
glue					
broom					
chewy					
regroup					
pursue					
cartoon					
Unit 15: Variant vowel /o͝o/ syllable patterns			**Unit 17: Consonant +le syllable patterns**		
shook			wiggle		
bush			twinkle		
pull			fable		
would			shuffle		
crooked					
pushpin					
bully					
				Score	/39 Score

Student Name: ____________________

Pre/Post Phonics Assessment

Directions: Have the student point to each word on the corresponding student sheet, segment the word parts or syllables, and blend them together. Put a ✔ if the student successfully segments and blends the word or reads it as a complete unit. If the student misses the word, record the error.

	Pretest Date:	Posttest Date:
Unit 18: Compound words and silent letters		
wildlife		
playpen		
fingerprint		
understand		
Unit 19: Contractions		
I'm		
she'll		
he'd		
didn't		
you've		
we're		
let's		
that's		
Unit 20: Regular plurals		
stones		
papers		
lunches		
ponies		
Unit 21: Irregular plurals		
mice		
geese		
knives		
children		
women		
oxen		
	Score /22	**Score /22**

Teacher Record Form ▪ Units 22–26

Student Name: ______________________________

Pre/Post Phonics Assessment

Directions: Have the student point to each word on the corresponding student sheet, segment the word parts or syllables, and blend them together. Put a ✔ if the student successfully segments and blends the word or reads it as a complete unit. If the student misses the word, record the error.

	Pretest Date:	Posttest Date:
Unit 22: -ed, -ing endings		
played		
stacked		
graded		
trusting		
planning		
joking		
Unit 23: -er, -or endings		
farmer		
actor		
jogger		
sailor		
Unit 24: Comparatives		
faster		
wider		
funnier		
longest		
safest		
prettiest		
Unit 25: -y endings		
crunchy		
juicy		
fluffy		
stringy		
Unit 26: -ly ending		
deeply		
lively		
busily		
finally		
	Score /24	**Score /24**

Student Name: ______________________________

Pre/Post Phonics Assessment

Directions: Have the student point to each word on the corresponding student sheet, segment the word parts or syllables, and blend them together. Put a ✔ if the student successfully segments and blends the word or reads it as a complete unit. If the student misses the word, record the error.

	Pretest Date:	Posttest Date:
Unit 27: Prefix un-		
undo		
untwist		
unlucky		
untangle		
Unit 28: Prefix re-		
repay		
recall		
relocate		
reopen		
Unit 29: Prefix dis-		
dislike		
dismiss		
disconnect		
disaster		
Unit 30: Suffix -less		
pointless		
seedless		
toothless		
penniless		
Unit 31: Suffixes -sion, -tion, -ion		
question		
division		
companion		
suggestion		
confusion		
suspicion		
	Score /22	**Score /22**

Student Name: ____

Pre/Post Phonics Assessment

Directions: Have the student point to each word on the corresponding student sheet, segment the word parts or syllables, and blend them together. Put a ✔ if the student successfully segments and blends the word or reads it as a complete unit. If the student misses the word, record the error.

	Pretest Date:	Posttest Date:
Unit 32: Greek roots		
biology		
diagram		
microscope		
thermometer		
photography		
geometry		
telephone		
digraph		
program		
grammar		
zoology		
graphic		
	Score /12	Score /12

Words Correct Per Minute
Norms for Oral Reading Fluency Grades 1–5*

Figure 1

Grade Level	Fall	Winter	Spring
1			60
2	53	78	94
3	79	93	114
4	99	112	118
5	105	118	128

* Adapted from Hasbrouck, J.E., & Pindal, G. (1992). Curriculum-based oral reading fluency norms for students in Grades 2–5. *Teaching Exceptional Children*, 24, 41–44.

Oral Fluency and Phrasing Rating Rubric

Figure 2

Rubric Score	Phrasing and Fluency
1	Reads word by word. Does not attend to the author's syntax or sentence structures.
2	Reads slowly and in a choppy manner, usually in two-word phrases. Some attention is given to the author's syntax and sentence structures.
3	Reads in phrases of three or four words. Appropriate syntax is used.
4	Reads in longer, more meaningful phrases. Regularly uses pitch, stress, and author's syntax to reflect comprehension.
Rubric Score	**Intonation**
1	Reads with a monotone voice.
2	Reads with some intonation and some attention to punctuation. At times reads in a monotone voice.
3	Reads by adjusting intonation appropriately. Consistently attends to punctuation.
4	Reads with intonation that reflects feeling, anticipation, tension, character development, and mood.

Rubric Score Key: 1 and 2: Student has not achieved an appropriate level of fluency at the level of the passage.
3: Fluent reading is being refined at the level of the passage.
4: Fluent reading has been achieved for the level at which the passage is written.

My Fluency Practice Graph

Name:______________________________ Level:______________

Card:______________________________ Reading Rate Goal:_____

Color in the graph to show how many words you read in one minute.

60 59 58 57 56 55 54 53 52 51 50 49 48 47 46 45 44 43 42 41 40 39 38 37 36 35 34 33 32 31 30 29 28 27 26 25 24 23 22 21 20 19 18 17 16 15 14 13 12 11 10 9 8 7 6 5 4 3 2 1 0

1st Reading	**2nd Reading**	**3rd Reading**
Date ______	Date ______	Date ______

120 119 118 117 116 115 114 113 112 111 110 109 108 107 106 105 104 103 102 101 100 99 98 97 96 95 94 93 92 91 90 89 88 87 86 85 84 83 82 81 80 79 78 77 76 75 74 73 72 71 70 69 68 67 66 65 64 63 62 61 60

1st Reading	**2nd Reading**	**3rd Reading**
Date ______	Date ______	Date ______

Dear Parent/Guardian,

This year your child will learn all about sounds, letters, and words. There are many ways you can help your child learn to read. In class we will read many passages. I will send copies of these passages home. Please listen to and help your child read the passages to you. I will also send home some fun activities and games for your family to enjoy together.

I look forward to an exciting year of learning. Thank you in advance for the important part you play in helping your child learn to read.

Sincerely,

Estimado padre de familia:

En el curso de este año escolar, su hijo aprenderá sobre sonidos, letras y palabras. Hay muchas maneras en que usted puede ayudar a su hijo a aprender a leer. En el aula leeremos muchos pasajes de texto. Enviaré copias de los pasajes a su casa. Tenga la amabilidad de escuchar y ayudar a su hijo a leer los pasajes. También enviaré algunos juegos y actividades divertidas a su casa para que los disfruten juntos.

Será un año de aprendizaje emocionante. Le agradezco de antemano el apoyo que aportará al ayudar a su hijo a aprender a leer. Sin más por el momento, me despido cordialmente.

Atentamente,

Glossary

Closed Syllable — a syllable or morpheme that precedes one or more consonants, as in /a/ in hat

Diphthong — a vowel sound produced when the tongue moves or glides from one vowel sound to another vowel or semivowel sound in the same syllable. Example: bee, bay, boo, boy, and bough

Formal Assessment — an assessment that is both an instructional tool that a teacher and student use while learning is occurring and an accountability tool to determine if learning has occurred. Note: Benchmark Literacy Formal Assessments include Comprehension Strategy Assessment Handbooks for grades K-6.

Formal Assessments — the collection of data using standardized tests or procedures under controlled conditions

Grapheme — a written or printed representation of a phoneme, as b for /b/ and oy for /oi/ in boy

High-frequency Word — a word that appears many more times than most other words in spoken or written language

Homograph — a word with the same spelling as another word whether or not pronounced alike, as pen (a writing instrument) vs. pen (enclosure).

Homonym — a word with different origin and meaning but the same oral or written form as one or more other words, as bear (an animal) vs. bear (to support) vs. bare (exposed)

Homophone — a word with different origin and meaning, but the same pronunciation as another word, whether or not spelled alike, as hare and hair

Informal Assessments — evaluations by casual observation or by other nonstandardized procedures. Note: Benchmark Literacy Informal Assessments include Informal Assessment Handbooks for reading comprehension, writing, spelling, fluency, vocabulary and English Language development, and provide teacher observation checklists, forms, and rubrics for ongoing assessment.

Initial Blend — the joining of two or more consonant sounds, represented by letters that begin a word without losing the identity of the sounds, as /bl/ in black, /skr/ in scramble.

Listening Center — a place where a student can use a headset to listen to recorded instructional material

Miscue — a term used to describe a deviation from text during oral reading or a shift in comprehension of a passage

Modeling	teacher's use of clear demonstrations and explicit language
Open Syllable	a syllable ending in a vowel sound rather than a consonant
Oral Reading	the process of reading aloud to communicate to another or to an audience
Phonological Awareness	awareness of the constituent sounds of words in learning to read and spell (by syllables, onsets and rimes, and phonemes)
Print Awareness	a learner's growing recognition of conventions and characteristics of a written language, including directionality, spaces between words, etc.
Sight Word	a word that is immediately recognized as a whole and does not require word analysis for identification
Teacher Resource System	the analysis of the structural characteristics of the text, coherence, organization, concept load, etc.
Teacher Resource Web Site	a free Benchmark Education Web site that provides a searchable database of titles, levels, subject areas, themes, and comprehension strategies; the site contains downloadable resources including literacy texts and teacher's guides, comprehension question cards, oral reading records, take-home books, and assessment resources

Bibliography

Baumann, J. F., E. C. Edwards, G. Font, C. A. Tereshinksi, E. J. Kame'enui, and S. Olejnik. "Teaching Morphemic and Contextual Analysis to Fifth-Grade Students." *Reading Research Quarterly*: 37 (2), pp. 150–176. 2002.

Bear, D. R., M. Invernizzi,, S. Templeton, and F. Johnston. *Words Their Way: Word Study for Phonics, Vocabulary, and Spelling Instruction*. Columbus, OH: Merrill Publishing Company, 1995.

Blevins, W. *Teaching Phonics & Word Study in the Intermediate Grades*. New York: Scholastic, 2001.

Cunningham, Patricia M. *Phonics They Use: Words for Reading and Writing*. Boston: Allyn & Bacon. 2005.

Cunningham, Patricia M., and Dorothy P. Hall. *Making Words*. Torrance, CA: Good Apple, 1994.

Ganske, K. *Mindful of Words: Spelling and Vocabulary Explorations 4-8*. New York: Guilford Press, 2008.

Ganske, K. *Word Journeys: Assessment-guided Phonics, Spelling, and Vocabulary Instruction*. New York: Guilford Press, 2000.

Ganske, K. *Word Sorts and More: Sound, Pattern, and Meaning Explorations K–3*. New York: Guilford Press, 2006.

Gill, S. "Teaching Rimes with Shared Reading." *The Reading Teacher* 60, pp. 191–193. 2006.

Moats, L. "How Spelling Supports Reading–And Why It Is More Regular and Predictable than You May Think." *American Educator*, pp. 12-16, 20-22, 42-43. Winter 2005/2006.

Moats, L. C. "Teaching Decoding." *American Educator*, pp. 42–49. Spring/Summer 1998.

Schreiber, P. A., and C. Read. "Children's Use of Phonetic Cues in Spelling, Parsing, and–Maybe–Reading." *Bulletin of the Orton Society*, 30, pp. 209–224. 1980.

Tunmer, W. E. and Nesdale, A. R. "Phonemic Segmentation Skill and Beginning Reading." *Journal of Educational Psychology*, 77, pp. 417–427. 1985.

Zutell, J. "Word Sorting: A Developmental Spelling Approach to Word Study for Delayed Readers." *Reading & Writing Quarterly*, 14, pp. 219–238. 1998.